EVISCERATE

DANIELLE RENINO

ISBN: 979-8-9865241-4-6 (paperback);

979-8-9865241-3-9 (ebook)

For Melissa,
Thanks for loving "the escape room book" more than most people love... well, literally anything. Your enthusiasm is contagious and this book wouldn't exist without you.

CONTENT WARNING

Eviscerate contains material that might be upsetting to some readers including self-harm, domestic violence, blood, gore, mentions of suicide attempts, and mentions of sexual assault.

CONTENTS

10:45PM

They have six minutes to decide who dies.

A steak knife, a bone saw, and a scalpel lay at their feet. A treasure trove of ways to butcher a body, peel back the skin and get to the soft meat beneath. The instruments glint, a row of sharp teeth lined up in the center of what used to be a bowling lane, the floor scuffed and spotted with mold. The scalpel and bone saw are already stained red.

Nausea roils Mallory's stomach even though she should be used to the sight of blood by now. It's matted through her hair, gooey and disturbingly warm. It's dried to a crust down the front of her shirt, cracking and flaking every time she moves. She's painted in it.

Still, a strangled cry leaves her throat, swallowed by the cacophony of noises inside the arcade.

Bursts of maniacal laughter escape the game machines, puncture wounds of sound without any recognizable cadence, and carnival music blares in a constant loop as the room screams itself raw.

"Step right up!"

"Try your luck!"

"Win, win, win!"

"It's up to you," Rowan grits out from between clenched teeth. His face is cast in streaks of purple and blue from the neon sign which barely clings to the peeling wall above the pins. The word STRIKE flickers with deadly precision and in the glow, he looks like a character torn directly from the pages of a splatterpunk novel. Lip split, shirt ripped, and so completely drenched in blood that the whites of his eyes shine with unearthly brightness.

Mallory stares at him blankly from across the lane, pulse pounding in her ears.

"It's up to you," he repeats, holding up the cell phone to show off the instructions on the screen. Its plastic case is the same red as a rare steak, a fresh cut, a crime scene.

"I know," Mallory hisses, her heart rate spiking at the sight of the phone. "Give me time to think."

"We don't have time."

Mallory curls her arms around her middle. She wishes she could collapse in on herself, squeeze her eyes shut and disappear, but there's no pretending this away. Not with the discordant screeches of the machines, not with the blood gloving her hands, or the wet, horrible squish of it beneath her boots.

Far off, beyond the locked doors of the arcade, emo music thumps in as if through the walls of an apartment building—an indistinct pulsing, keeping time to the pounding in Mallory's chest. She feels the rhythm everywhere, the deep bass snaking up through the ground and causing the arcade's foundation to rumble.

Rowan slips the phone back into his pocket and bends to pick up the knife, tossing it between his hands, testing the weight. "I can't get over how heavy this thing is. The handle is so solid."

"Not the bone saw? Wouldn't that make things quicker?"

He shakes his head. "The knife is the only option."

"But don't we need to—"

"I know what we need to do! And I'll use the knife. I'll make it work—but *you* need to make the decision."

"Five minutes left," Olivia calls from across the room, her voice high-pitched, panicked. She's crouched next to a row of pinball machines, her hair damp with sweat and plastered against her forehead. Like Mallory and Rowan, she's saturated in red. It butterflies out over her torso. There's an artful smear on her cheek, and a fine spray tracing the line of her jaw down to her neck. The blood looks more like ink in the neon glow of the machines, and Olivia, with her delicate features and wide eyes looks like an avant-garde painting, just as unearthly as Rowan.

Then there's the fourth player in this sick game.

They lay sprawled at Olivia's feet, a dark shape in an even darker pool, a series of low moans the only indication that the soul inside still clings to life.

"Has the bleeding stopped?" Mallory asks, not sure if she wants to know the answer.

Olivia shakes her head, her face flashing yellow, orange, red in the glow of the pinball machines. "You need to make a decision. Now."

"How are we supposed to do this in six minutes?"

"Four," Olivia says after a quick glance at the screen fastened to the wall above her head. It counts down the minutes and seconds in bright, bleeding color. "We're running out of time."

"Fine, I'll decide for you." Rowan grips the knife and turns to cross the arcade, but Mallory rushes forward, grabbing him by the arm. He spins as the neon sign, STRIKE, flickers again. Blue. Purple. His face is bruised in the light as he pulls away. "Don't try to stop me. Remember what happened the last time."

Mallory's insides curdle.

"Three minutes!" Olivia warns.

Above them, a thin slice of crescent moon stares down through a hole the size of a grave. Flat black sky. Starless dark.

Mallory's heartbeat reaches a crescendo, and the music shaking the walls keeps getting louder, and louder until she can make out the lyrics— "Sulking Seething," of course it's "Sulking Seething." Bile scorches the back of her throat, and she clamps a hand down over her mouth.

I won't puke, she thinks desperately. *I won't puke.*

"Sulking Seething" blasts even louder, and the machines all laugh, and scream, and cry until she's drowning in sound.

Then, the intercom system crackles.

White noise devoured by the panicked din of the room.

A warning that there are only—

"Two minutes!"

—left before someone needs to die.

Mallory wishes she could feel horrified. She wishes she could free anything, but her nausea swells, and all she can do is wonder why the human body is so fragile.

Isn't the purpose of the rib cage to protect all the organs inside?

What the hell is the point of the spaces between, the parts where a knife can get in?

FOUR HOURS EARLIER

1

MALLORY

Mallory hasn't seen the building in almost a year. It looks the same as it did last summer: deceptively squat, bricks painted a queasy shade of pink. Beyond the No Trespassing signs and abandoned construction equipment, it cowers like a stray dog: neglected, afraid.

Mallory isn't fooled. The building is a predator and she's intimately familiar with its insides; the miniature golf course stuck like a clot in its stomach, the swirl of waterslides knotted through it in meaty, unsettling colors. It's where she learned that fear smells bitter and blood tastes like copper.

Starling Indoor Water Park and Resort, closed indefinitely after Jared bit the dust nearly a year ago. May he rest in pieces.

His picture stares up at her from the makeshift memorial tacked along the outer wall. He's laughing, his dark hair pushed back from his face, the tattoos on his neck adding a punch of color to his pale skin. She imagines tracing the fangs inked across his jugular, his pulse racing beneath her fingertips. She imagines squeezing until she feels a crunch.

Most animals resort to violence when provoked, but Mallory has never quite known how to externalize the cocktail of pain and rage that churns her insides daily. Instead, she does what she has since she was a child. She pretends. She stains her daydreams red to avoid the constant strobe of images inside her head.

Office chair.

Silver flask.

Blood splatter.

Memories that fester in the heat.

Coming back here was a mistake.

Lip curled, she nudges Jared's photo over with the toe of her boot, and it lands face down with a dusty smack.

A hand latches onto her shoulder and she jolts as her friend Erika comes up behind her, the delicate, floral scent of her perfume soft against her viselike grip.

"What the hell, Mal? It's got to be bad luck to mess with a murder victim's memorial."

"We don't know if he was murdered," Mallory says as Erika releases her, crouching to pull the photo from the dirt. "They never found his body."

"Yeah, but didn't they find a hand?"

"It was a foot." More like a few of his toes laying unceremoniously at the end of a blood trail that snaked all the way through the arcade into the resort's lobby. A fitting end as far as Mallory is concerned.

"Hand, foot, whatever. It's not like he did that to himself." Erika frowns as she straightens up, tucking the photo under her arm. Her strawberry blonde hair is pulled back into a loose bun, and she's dressed in a pastel workout set, her sneakers shockingly white against the cracked concrete in front of the memorial.

Mallory's chest aches. During their teen years, they were practically twins—raccoon tail streaks in their hair, studded belts, smudged eyeliner. Mallory never grew out of it. At twenty-seven, she still wears fishnet shirts over her tank tops and rocks an eyebrow ring. She's been dying her hair black for almost three years, and it would be purple if unnatural colors didn't go against her job's dress code.

Meanwhile, Erika's acrylic nails are painted the softest shade of rose gold, every aspect of her appearance carefully curated, like a blanket of frosting on a cake. Sometimes Mallory worries that if she touches Erika the wrong way, the façade will smear, and she'll crumble.

Back in elementary school, Erika was dangerous, unpredictable. Spending time with her was synonymous with breaking the rules: swimming in the creek they weren't supposed to go near, wandering along the stretch of train tracks they weren't supposed to play on. Now, their conversations are confined to coffee shops and yoga studios. Or they used to be, before last spring.

"Can you please put the photo back?" Mallory asks, eyes fixed on the dimple in Jared's left cheek, peeking out from under Erika's arm. Her mind clicks through a slideshow of his smile (doesn't reach his eyes), his nose (broken, bloody), the tattoo on the back of his hand (a black star). She shifts uncomfortably.

"Why, so you can kick it again and saddle us with even more bad luck? No way." Erika's tone is light and teasing, but her mouth is set in a serious line as she shuffles Jared to her other arm. She pulls his image tight against her side and Mallory frowns.

Erika wasn't always superstitious. Beyond using a Ouija board as a cheap gimmick at parties, she didn't buy into anything that carried even a whiff of the occult. But since last spring, she's been obsessed with karma, and crystals, and astrological charts. Mallory figures that it's her way of coping, of finding meaning in chaos.

Mallory's scheduled enough euthanizations at the animal shelter where she works to know that there is no meaning in chaos. An otherwise friendly dog can snap one day, damn near rip the arm off a child, and suddenly it's lights out forever. An otherwise loyal best friend can make one mistake, let jealousy get the better of her one time, and suddenly it's twenty years of friendship down the garbage disposal.

"How much longer until your online friends get here?" Erika asks, and Mallory bristles at the thinly masked contempt in her voice. The more time they spend together, the more obvious it is that Erika still isn't over what happened between them last spring.

Not that Mallory can blame her. How's a wound supposed to heal when it never even got the chance to scab?

"Well?" Erika asks when Mallory fails to answer.

"They'll be here soon." She twists away, squinting against the sun.

The sky is a vicious blue against the tall grass which surrounds them on all sides. Standing watch over the grass and the abandoned resort sits an amphitheater, and tomorrow, dozens of bands will play on a series of makeshift stages for this year's iteration of HyveFest—a festival headlined by Mallory's favorite band, HyveMind. She can practically smell weed and the sour tinge of beer wafting down from the hill. Nostalgia sweetens the ache in her chest. She'll always love HyveFest. Always. Even if the memories are tainted now.

Mallory turns back to find Erika cradling the photo so that Jared stares up at her.

"Come on Mal, I blew off work for this thing," she says, tracing a line down the curve of Jared's cheek, the tip of her nail scraping viciously against the glass. "If you're getting catfished, I'll literally die."

Erika's finger moves back and forth across Jared's neck in leisurely sawing motions. Her nail continues to rake against the glass, and the sound sends ripples of unease up Mallory's spine.

"Stop doing that," she says, her voice a thick clot in her throat.

Erika grins in response. "What, finally ready to admit that it was a bad idea to mess with the photo?"

"I just... I don't like the sound." She breathes a sigh of relief when Erika's hand stills, though her finger continues to lay flat against Jared's cheek, and his photo is still nestled in the crook of her arm.

"My bad. I'm just so over this, Mal. Where are these people? Are we even in the right place?"

"We're supposed to meet by the memorial." Mallory picks at a hangnail as she struggles to remember what Rowan told her last night over voice chat, a quiet panic stirring as she fails. Even when she was little she liked to know exactly what to do and exactly how to do it. Vague instructions are agents of chaos. She rips the hangnail away leaving a gash, red as a notification bell, in its place. The possibility that she might have messed up the meeting spot or time, fills her with dread. Everything needs to go perfectly tonight. "I'm pretty sure that's what Rowan said, anyway."

"Oh, Rowan," Erika says knowingly, and heat rises to Mallory's cheeks.

Rowan has been a conversation staple since their slumber party days.

When Mallory first told Erika about him, she had to bury her face in her pillow to hide how violently she was blushing. "He understands me, he understands *everything*. He writes me these poems that are, like, so heartfelt and—"

"What kind of boy our age writes poetry?" Erika scoffed, and Mallory lifted her head to find her best friend sitting cross-legged on the carpet, coating her nails in bright, neon polish.

"You better not spill that." Mallory eyed the pink stain from the last time Erika decided to paint her nails on the bedroom floor.

"Don't worry. I never make the same mistake twice." Erika capped the bottle, shaking it for emphasis. "Now, don't tell me you're falling head over heels for some rando because he writes you *poetry*." She spits the last word out like it tastes bad.

"It's not just the poetry. I *like* him, and I think he likes me. I think he's going to ask me out."

Erika made a noncommittal noise as she fanned her fingers out, gloss glinting viciously against the stark white of the carpet.

Rowan did ask Mallory out, and they dated, briefly, the bulk of their relationship taking place over AIM chat, with Neopets and RuneScape filling the gaps until the distance, and Rowan's refusal to show his face on Skype, got to be too much.

Mallory still lives for the times when he's single and flirts with her, even though she knows it would never work. They're too different.

Rowan's Instagram feed is gritty and sharp. Pictures of him shirtless, throwing up the middle finger, and slumping his shoulders on rocky beaches. Green mohawk and chipped black nail polish. Lots of cigarette smoke, and even more tattoos. He's a rough, unpolished kind of handsome but it's more than that. Well-read and in tune with his emotions, he's sensitive to a fault. His messages are so much softer than his pictures. He's an accomplished travel writer, weeks away from finishing his first book: a memoir about how he was able to pick up the pieces after leaving his abusive ex.

As much as Mallory admires his drive, she can't help the jealousy that claws at her when she thinks of everything he's accomplished. She hasn't felt like she could accomplish anything in a long time and blames her feelings of inadequacy on the fact that she was practically force-fed participation ribbons as a child, a testament to the fact that life is a game, and the rules are clear. Try your best, and you will succeed. No matter what. Except Mallory never cared about praise or payment, she wanted to run, to write, to play. Everything she ever did was evaluated and rewarded, and it sucked the motivation right out of her. She got ribbons for nothing and the same people who forced them on her then are now saying that she has no work ethic. Because in the real world, trying your best but coming up short isn't an achievement at all. In the real world there's no such thing as a participation ribbon.

"I'm dying to see what it'll be like when you guys get together," Erika says, pulling her out of her thoughts.

"We're not getting together."

"Come on, you shouldn't let your fear of commitment hold you back."

"I'm not afraid of commitment." Mallory is afraid of the mess. Between Rowan's abusive ex, and the *office chair, silver flask, blood splatter* on a constant, sickening loop inside her head, it would be less a relationship and more of a trauma dump if they ever did get together. She traces the gash in her finger, shivers of pain traveling up her hand. "Besides, we're here for Jared."

"Because you knew him so well?" Erika finally places the picture back in its nest of tea lights and matted stuffed animals with a bit too much reverence for Mallory's taste. "Following someone on Instagram and occasionally catching a glimpse of them at a music festival isn't the same thing as actually knowing them. And you don't know these people you're meeting at all."

"I know them. We've been talking for months now."

"Yeah, in a Discord channel that was only created because some HyveMind super fan got butchered during the festival last year." She shakes her head. "You're gonna get yourself killed one of these days; you're way too reckless on social media."

Mallory's insides cramp. The comment seems innocent enough, but the spark in Erika's eye says she's aware that she just ripped open a wound that stings worse than Mallory's hangnail.

Erika has always been an expert at a softly perfumed, distinctly feminine brand of warfare. Behind her cotton candy exterior is a forked tongue and a talent for staying in someone's good graces just long enough to strike them down. Cross her and she's powdered sugar laced with arsenic.

"Is that why you wanted to come along today, so you can throw what happened back in my face?"

Erika's eyes widen, as if she truly didn't realize what she was saying. "You know that I didn't mean it like that."

Except Mallory knows Erika, she knows her so well it hurts. She swallows, and it's as if there's a fist jammed down her throat crushing her windpipe, making it impossible to breathe. "Really? Because this is what you do. You pretend to stay friends with people, pepper them with passive aggressive comments, and—"

"When I was sixteen, maybe. Psychological warfare is so not my thing anymore."

"But you—"

Erika's phone pings, and it's like a pin stuck in a balloon. The tension that's been building pops and Mallory's left with a hollow feeling in her chest.

Erika frowns down at the screen.

"Is that Kimber?" Mallory asks, even though judging by the scowl on Erika's face there's no one else it can be.

"What do you think?" She slips the phone back into her pocket without opening the message. "She's driving me insane. I keep thinking she's gonna *Single White Female* me."

"Isn't she already? I mean, based on the pictures..."

Kimber and Erika look so much alike that they could be sisters, a fact that Kimber tries to play up every chance she gets —styling her hair the same way, wearing similar clothes. She even orders the same cocktails when they go out together.

Cosmos in thin stemmed glasses. Dirty martinis with blue cheese stuffed olives. The kind of drinks that are served at restaurants with velvet furniture and lighting so low all the photos come out blurred. It would seem innocuous, except prior to latching onto Erika, Kimber hated alcohol. She also hated athletic wear and silver jewelry, both of which are now wardrobe staples. Scrolling through Kimber's posts, it's like a stop motion horror show of her slowly morphing into a knock-off version of Erika.

"I'm surprised she hasn't blocked you," Erika says, her frown deepening. "But yeah, it's sketchy as hell. She wanted me to sleep over her apartment three times last week—*three times*. I think she's taken the whole 'never blame the other woman' thing to this freaky extreme where she feels the need to become my best friend... or become me."

The back of Mallory's neck prickles.

"I don't get why she's obsessed with me but hates you," Erika continues. "You didn't even do anything."

"I posted the pictures." Mallory braces for the fallout—they haven't spoken about what happened since their pseudo-reconciliation a few weeks ago, and the pictures are only the first in a long line of increasingly fucked up dominos that came crashing down last spring—but instead, Erika shakes her head.

"I know you think that I'll never forgive you, but I don't think you want me to. This is the same shit you used to pull when we were kids. Any time you feel guilty about something you practically force other people to punish you for it. It's sick, Mal. You need therapy."

Mallory's shoulders tense and she traces patterns across the gash in her finger until there's so much burning pain that she goes numb to it. She's been picking at her skin more since last year, and her upper arms are dotted with pin-point sized scabs in various stages of healing. She can't help it. When everything inside her head gets to be too much, she can drown the images out with a scratch, a tear, a satisfying bubble of blood. Only then does she finally relax. No shit, she needs therapy.

"This is supposed to be a fresh start for us, so you need to get over whatever mental block has you convinced that I'm still pissed. I'm over it, really. I think you can't forgive yourself and that's the real issue here," Erika adds, and they fall into an uneasy silence.

The grass sways, blades scraping together in a dry scream. The sound wraps around them like a plastic sleeve and it's almost enough to make Mallory believe in ghosts. Beyond the chorus of greenery, she can almost make out footsteps, heavy breaths.

Jared, she thinks, sinking a nail into her wound as the grass continues to scrape. She tugs at the flesh around the corners, drilling a hole deeper into herself, a bright red tunnel under the skin. But the pain doesn't help, her heart pounds against her ribs, and it's only a matter of time before Jared's ghost reaches out and pulls her, screaming, into the sea of green.

Then two strong hands collide with her back.

2

MALLORY

Panic bleeds through Mallory's forehead and the slideshow inside her mind flashes *red, red, red* as she's jolted forward.

She bites back a scream, struggling to regain her footing, and her heartbeat thumps in her ears as she turns stiffly, dreading what comes next. But instead of Jared's ghost come back to butcher her, she finds a green mohawk and a lopsided grin. Rowan.

"Sorry," he says, his eyes sparkling mischievously. "I couldn't resist."

Heart still hammering in her chest, she straightens up as Rowan closes the gap between them. He looks exactly like his pictures, dressed in black skinny jeans and a leather jacket, his nails painted with chipping polish. Taller than she expected, his strong jaw peppered with a hint of stubble, he's exactly the punk-rock kind of handsome that she's come to know from his Instagram profile. She dives at him, pulling him close. He smells like sandalwood and vanilla, and she's about to lose herself in the scent, when he pulls back abruptly, throwing his hands up. "Woah, I'm not a hugger."

She steps back, frowning. It's not like she expected some

huge romantic gesture or anything, they put the nail in that coffin a long time ago. But she was hoping for at least a scrap of affection—*something* to validate the closeness she thought they built through their messages. His dismissal sends a burning through her that lingers somewhere between embarrassment and devastation, and her fingers graze the scabs that line her upper arm.

"No worries," she says, swallowing down her disappointment. "I'm just excited to meet you in person. It's been a long time coming."

Before he has a chance to respond, Mallory's attention is pulled back to the grass as a short girl with a bleach blonde pixie cut steps out to join them. Britt. Her features are small and sharp, her eyes rimmed with messily applied smoky eyeshadow. She wears ripped fishnet stockings and a baggy HyveMind sweatshirt, so long that it comes down below her knees. Mallory wonders how she can stand something so bulky in this heat.

Britt stares at the building for a moment before shaking her head. "It's Baker-Miller pink. That's a bad sign."

"Britt," Mallory says a little too brightly, still attempting to shake off Rowan's rejection.

"Found her out by the parking lot," Rowan says, cocking his thumb over his shoulder toward the patch of concrete just beyond the tall grass.

"What am I, a stray cat?" There isn't a drop of humor in her voice, which is typical of Britt. She's been monotone and slightly removed since she first joined the Discord, never once sharing anything personal about herself. The only things Mallory knows for sure are that Britt's favorite band is Hyve-Mind and she loves them almost as much as she loves to drink. She'll occasionally interrupt their voice chats to run to the liquor store. Mallory has no clue what she does for work or how she fills her free time. She hates to admit it, but Erika has every right to be concerned, at least when it comes to Britt. Even after months of talking, she's a stranger.

Rowan laughs lightly, then turns back to the grass. "Liv? Quit hiding behind the car and get over here, there's nothing to be nervous about."

"Liv?" Mallory asks, tension returning to her shoulders. He didn't mention bringing anyone, and she wonders for a horrible second if it might be a girlfriend that he was keeping secret from them. That would explain his standoffishness. Or worse, he got back with his ex. He's never mentioned them by name, so it's a possibility, and the thought of him going back to someone who hurt him like that makes her sick to her stomach.

"My twin sister, Olivia," Rowan explains, and Mallory relaxes slightly, though his response only raises more questions.

"I didn't know you had a sister... yet alone a twin."

He shrugs, flashing another mischievous grin. "There are a lot of things you don't know about me."

The grass rustles, and after some more gentle prodding, a whisper of a young woman steps out to join them. Olivia wears a cream-colored, button-down dress. Her tiny frame drowns in the fabric, and the straps keep slipping down her shoulders. She looks like a child who went rooting around in her mother's closet to play dress up. Her makeup seems to wear her rather than the other way around, and bright red lipstick makes her teeth appear brutally white as she offers a shy smile.

Mallory can sort of see the resemblance to Rowan—same dark eyes and bone structure—but Rowan has such a presence about him while Olivia seems to blend into her surroundings. It's something that Erika would explain through their astrological charts or the lines in their palms, but Mallory chalks it up to luck of the draw. Rowan is clearly the more attractive and confident sibling. Olivia's bizarre choice of dress and makeup seems like a desperate bid to keep up with her brother.

Olivia slips wordlessly into step behind Rowan, completely eclipsed by him. Mallory can't help but think that it's fitting.

"She's not great around new people." Rowan rolls his eyes before he focuses in on Erika. "It looks like you brought someone too."

Erika offers what appears at face value to be a genuine smile, but her eyes are narrowed, and she angles herself away from the group, reminding Mallory of a cat with its ears back. It's body language Mallory has seen from her only twice before. Once on the train tracks behind their houses when they were sixteen, and once last year, right after Mallory posted the pictures. The memories intertwine, sticking to her ribs like clotted blood until she's afraid she'll be sick. "Oh, yeah. This is Erika. She's my... She didn't want me to come here by myself."

"Were we supposed to bring plus ones?" Britt asks.

"Who would you have brought?" Rowan quips. "I thought we were your only friends."

If the comment bothers her, Britt doesn't show it. She's too focused on the outer wall of the building, leaning over Jared's memorial to run her fingers along the bricks as if there's a message hidden in the paint. She repeats the motion a few times before stepping back, and the group forms a tight semi-circle around the memorial.

Rowan checks his phone and curses under his breath. "No service. I should have known; this place is notorious for being a dead zone. Hopefully Peyton didn't get lost on her way here."

Peyton, channel founder and the sugar-crusted center of it all.

None of the others would have pegged her for the type of person who would know anything about Jared or HyveMind, and Mallory figured it was a joke when she first reached out about the Discord, but she has the kind of online presence that can't be ignored. When Peyton knocks, you answer.

Peyton with her expertly filtered photos—everything

slightly bleached out, as if you've been staring into the sun for too long. Peyton, the quintessential Cali-girl, all sharp angles, and beauty. Peyton with her hundreds of thousands of followers, her bright life, her McMansion. Marble floors, and marble countertops, and décor that looks as if it's been ripped directly from Pinterest. It was her decision to meet in person, practically on the anniversary of Jared's death no less. There's always a level of calculated finesse to what she does.

"I don't think she'd get lost; she's been here before. And I wouldn't have expected her to be late either," Mallory says, thinking of how meticulous Peyton can be. "Didn't she fly in yesterday?"

"It's another one of her games." Rowan fumbles around in his jacket pocket. "Trust me, she'll come jumping out at any minute to scare the shit out of us."

"You mean like you did?" Erika crosses her arms. She's still standing back from the group, her body angled toward the parking lot as if she can't decide whether or not to run. "And what do you mean her 'games'?"

"Peyton loves puzzles and practical jokes. She has a sick sense of humor."

Mallory wouldn't call Peyton's humor sick, but it's definitely off-color, like every aspect of her personality, from her fascination with unsolved murders, to her strange hobbies—like writing letters to convicted killers and collecting crime scene photos. She's hard to get a read on. It's part of what makes Peyton so fascinating. She's sun kissed and bubblegum sweet on the surface, but once you begin to peel back the layers, she's morbid enough to be put on a watchlist.

Rowan finally finds what he's been searching for and pulls a slim silver flask from his pocket. Sticky heat pools in the back of Mallory's head. It looks exactly like the flask Jared had with him last year. Roughly the size of a fist with a black cap, there's even a dent in the side—just like Jared's. She searches Rowan's face for any indication that he's screwing with her, but he stares straight ahead, grinning. Either he has an excellent poker face or she's being paranoid. No one knows what happened that night, least of all Rowan. Though that does little to stop the memory, raw and bloody that strobes through her head.

Star tattoo.

Silver flask.

Red. Red. Red.

She swallows hard, gulping back the images. They stick in her throat, tasting gummy and congealed.

"While we wait for Peyton, what do you say we get this party started?" Rowan raises the flask and steps in front of the memorial, turning to face the group. "We're here because of Jared, so we should take a shot in his honor, don't you think?"

Before anyone has a chance to answer, he uncaps the flask and takes a swig, a dribble of amber liquid dripping over his chin.

"Any excuse to get drunk," Britt shrugs, accepting the flask and tipping it back. Instead of a quick swig, she begins to chug it and shows no sign of stopping.

"I'm not talking about getting drunk, I'm talking about a shot." Rowan rips it away from her, passing it to Erika, who takes a dainty sip before passing it on to Olivia.

Olivia raises it to her lips, but Rowan shakes his head. "No way, Liv. You know how you get when you drink."

Olivia lets out a huff but doesn't argue as she passes the flask to Mallory, who immediately hands it back to Rowan. "Alcohol isn't my thing."

Erika raises an eyebrow. "Since when?"

It's a fair question. Back when they shared an apartment, Mallory had an entire bar cart—matte black cocktail shaker, jalapeño infused vodka, lemon wedges in a decorative bowl. Every Friday, without fail she'd test a different cocktail recipe—lemon drops, cosmopolitans, martinis with a twist. Erika used to teasingly call her the cocktail queen, and anytime they had company over, Mallory would be the one to play bartender. Now her collection of recipe books sits in a pile at the back of her closet, and her bar cart is a glorified coat rack.

Mallory frowns. "Last year."

Erika turns to Rowan, motioning for the flask with a flick of her wrist. Once she has it, she shoves it into Mallory's hands.

"Last year is over." She taps the side with the sharp tip of her stiletto nail. "Fresh start, come on."

"I don't drink anymore."

"Bullshit. Drinking is like, one of your core personality traits."

"Not anymore."

"Come on, Mal." Erika drags her teeth along her lower lip and her eyes burn into Mallory's until she crumbles under the pressure, tilting the flask back and taking a long sip. She flinches as the alcohol burns down her throat. She drops the flask to the ground, coughing.

There's a strange, almost chalky aftertaste and Mallory struggles to pin down what she drank. It's not vodka, since the liquid is dark, but it doesn't taste familiar at all. Beyond the burn and the powdery tinge, she can't place it.

"What's in there, whiskey?" she sputters.

Rowan opens his mouth to answer but stops suddenly, slapping his palm against his forehead, the movement jerky and borderline cartoonish. "You know what I just remembered? Peyton told me she was going to set something up for us by the loading docks around the back of the building. That's probably where she is."

Britt scoops up the flask, lifts it to her ear, and gives it a shake. Seemingly satisfied, she recaps it and stuffs it into the front pocket of her sweatshirt. Mallory frowns. She knows Britt loves alcohol, but nothing in the world could make her take another sip of whatever was in that flask.

"You know that's mine, right?" Rowan snaps at Britt, but she ignores him. He runs a hand over the top of his mohawk before stepping away from the memorial and motioning to the others with a nod of his head. "All right then, let's go see what Peyton has waiting for us."

The group swoops around to the back of the building which consists of a slab of concrete and two long ramps that lead to matching garage-style doors, one of which is propped open with a stack of cinderblocks. It's like the slit of an eye. Darkness stares through the opening with a watchfulness that sends chills up Mallory's spine.

Next to the open loading dock door is a small table with a wicker basket set on top of it, an oversized red ribbon pinned to the side.

"See," Rowan grins. "This is classic Peyton. She's probably inside putting finishing touches on the scavenger hunt."

Erika's brow furrows. "The what?"

"You didn't tell her?" Rowan asks Mallory and she shakes her head. She's about to defend her decision—there's no way Erika would have agreed to this, Erika doesn't know the whole story and it's too overwhelming to explain, this is her last chance to fix what she broke—when Rowan turns to Erika. "How much do you know about what happened to Jared?"

"That he was probably murdered?"

"Probably is the key word. They never found his body, only pieces."

"A foot, right?"

"Like I said, pieces. But there are all these theories about what really happened. Some say that the rest of his body was scattered around the property, some say it was poured into the foundation, and some say that he's still alive in there and the murder never happened—it was faked."

Erika scoffs. "That's the dumbest thing I've ever heard."

"Is it? His family owns the development company that was

building this place. Would it really be that hard for them to hide him? They're loaded. They have money dating back to the fucking Mayflower, and you're telling me they wouldn't be able to pay off the cops or whatever they had to do to keep this thing under wraps?"

"You're saying he faked his death?"

"I'm not saying that *he* faked his death—I'm saying that *someone* faked his death. Look, he was a popular HyveMind influencer, right? Well, you don't get that big without some notoriety."

"Meaning what exactly?"

"He was into some dark shit. Drugs, domestic abuse, at least four assault allegations—a real son of a bitch. He had a reputation and no one in his family wanted him to take over the business because of it, so how convenient would it be to incapacitate him and get him out of the way? And if not them, there were plenty of other people who would jump at the chance to fuck him up, believe me."

"And he's what? Been being held against his will inside a half-constructed resort for the last year? It's a conspiracy theory," Erika says with a wave of her hand. "And a weak one at that. The whole thing sounds like the kind of bullshit I'd scare Mallory with when we were kids."

Britt pulls the flask from her pocket, tilts it to her lips, and drains it.

"Peyton thinks it's real," she mumbles, wiping her mouth with the sleeve of her hoodie. "That's why she wanted us to meet here. Based on the blood trails, and where the investigators found what little of him that they could find, she's figured out where he is."

Erika turns to Mallory, her mouth set in a thin line. "What are you guys really doing here, Mal?" Rowan starts to answer, but Erika holds up a finger. "No, I want to hear it from her."

Mallory picks at a scab on the back of her arm. There are so many ways to respond, and none of them come even close to the truth. She considers all the hours spent staring at her ceiling, wishing she could decompose into the sheets as she replayed the events of last year's festival. She considers all the ways that she's tried to bury what happened, all the ways she's failed to keep it down. Mallory digs her fingers into her arm and presses until she sees spots. Through the spots, there's a flash of red, of soft glow, the back of Jared's head caved in. Goosebumps break out along her skin.

She takes a deep breath before answering. "We're going to find Jared and make sure that he's really dead."

Erika raises an eyebrow. "And if he isn't?"

"Then we're going to kill him."

3

MALLORY

The first time Peyton DMed her, Mallory had been scrolling Reddit for almost an hour. She sat cross-legged on her living room floor, the cheap carpet scratching the backs of her legs. Lights off, curtains drawn, only a small slice of the world outside her screen was visible through a gap in the fabric. What little brightness trickled in was gray and bloated, signaling an oncoming storm and the notification cut across her screen like a synthetic lightning strike.

Hey, my name is Peyton. I've been reading your posts for a few days now and figured it's a safe bet to share my theory with you. I think Jared may still be in the resort somewhere. Dead or alive, I'm not sure... but he's still there, and I'm pretty sure I can prove it.

Mallory had been posting on Reddit for about a week, finally getting up the courage after lurking the threads for close to a month. Her posts were messy and raw, the kind of stuff she'd usually reserve for her diary. But watching so many strangers sensationalize Jared's disappearance caused the scabs over her heart to flake and bleed fresh. He wasn't a victim. He wasn't a villain. She wasn't sure what he was exactly, but watching strangers spin him into fiction was too much to take.

It turned him into a celebrity in a way that he didn't deserve. She bit back the messy, unnamable emotions for as long as she could, until it all spilled out in a jumbled of half-baked, half-true musings that were mostly swallowed into the cold vacuum of the internet.

She knew it wasn't healthy to obsess over Jared, but she couldn't help herself.

She spent hours scrolling, combing through theories. Hardly anyone believed that Jared really was dead, and even fewer suspected foul play. The most popular theory was that he faked his death and fled the state. He was staring down the latest in a long line of assault charges, only this time it looked like his sordid history was finally going to catch up with him. His body was never found, and neither was his phone, so it would make sense that he had booked it, leaving pieces of himself behind to throw authorities off his trail.

Jared was the kind of guy who would gladly sacrifice a few toes if it meant avoiding the consequences of his own actions, and if Mallory didn't know the truth about what happened that night, she would have bought into it without hesitation.

In the threads, most of Mallory's posts were downvoted or deleted by moderators, so she was shocked that Peyton not only saw them but chose to reach out to her of all people. They exchanged dozens of messages before Peyton invited her to the Discord, and she was surprised to find that Rowan—who Peyton apparently found posting on a Facebook page dedicated to the case—had been invited as well. Peyton insisted on keeping the group small, limited to the select few people who not only believed there was a chance that Jared may still be inside the resort somewhere, but who agreed that if he was, they needed to find him.

Personally, I hope we find him in pieces. He's a public safety hazard, Peyton wrote at one point. *I think we all can agree that the assault allegations are only the tip of the iceberg.*

Earning her money through affiliate links on social media, Peyton made her own schedule and could travel as much as she wanted. If Mallory had that kind of freedom, she'd be traveling the country, attending a different music festival every week, but Peyton couldn't care less about that stuff. She poured all of her resources into visiting the resort as often as possible, and posted her findings to the Discord.

Most of the time it seemed like she was trying to construct a mystery where there wasn't one, but her sincerity kept Mallory hanging onto every word.

This door was locked from the inside... a clue?

Followed what remains of the blood trails again... nothing new, but I get the feeling that this isn't the actual path he took...

More certain than ever that someone was with him that night.

The others, Mallory included, never understood why Peyton didn't invite them out on her expeditions. Not that Mallory was exactly chomping at the bit to get inside the resort again, but Peyton had the kind of magnetic energy that made you want her to like you, include you, choose you. It burned to know that she had flown out to Massachusetts so many times without even telling them she'd been there until she was already back in California.

We'll meet soon enough, I promise, Peyton assured them. *But not until I'm sure that I've found what I'm looking for.*

Last week, Mallory received the message she had been dreading since Peyton first invited her to join the Discord: *I think I found Jared, when can you meet?*

Mallory wasn't prepared for how deeply it would cut into her. Like a knife plunged up to the hilt in her side. She blinked rapidly, typing and deleting her response half a dozen times before she finally settled on what to say. *Found him? Dead or alive?*

Meet up and find out.

Can't you just tell me?

I could, but where's the fun in that?

Peyton's idea of fun is a scavenger hunt that would lead them through the resort to wherever Jared is hidden. Even though Mallory knows that Peyton's insistence on turning it into a game means that the chances of finding Jared alive are low, the possibility remains, and it sickens her.

"You still with us?" Erika claps her hands in front of Mallory's face, and she jumps.

"Sorry," Mallory mutters. "I zoned out for a minute there. What did you say?"

"I said that it's pretty fucked up that you came out here to find a missing person and murder him." Erika glances around the group, her eyebrow still raised.

"Mallory's being dramatic," Rowan waves his hand dismissively. "On the off chance that we do find him alive, we'll call the police."

"And if we find his body, that won't be a problem," Mallory adds, her stomach in knots. If Erika was on the fence about staying before, she's probably dead set on leaving now. But to Mallory's surprise, Erika stays where she is, her expression unreadable.

"You'd still have to call the police if you found a body though, right?"

Mallory doesn't have the heart to tell her that no, she wouldn't call anyone. She'd leave what's left of Jared there in pieces.

Britt gives up on the empty flask and passes it back to Rowan, who glares at her as he pockets it.

"I know that he's probably dead. It would be stupid to believe he could still be alive after all this time," Britt says, her words blurring into one another. The alcohol seems to have loosened her tongue and there's slightly more inflection to her voice, her signature monotone chipped away by the liquor.

"Peyton's probably messing with us, but if there's even a chance that he's alive, I need to be there for him. I owe Jared that."

"Owe him for what?" Olivia asks, and Mallory jumps at the sound of her voice—soft and cautious, like leaves rustling. She's been quiet for so long that Mallory almost forgot she was there at all. "It sounds like he was a terrible person and deserved whatever happened to him."

"Oh, he definitely deserved it," Britt agrees but doesn't elaborate.

Erika finally lets out a sharp laugh and turns to Mallory. "Mal, think about this for a minute. You're crazy to believe that a man is being held inside some half-built resort against his will. You're even crazier for wanting to find the *butchered remains* of his body."

Mallory opens her mouth, but Erika continues before she gets a chance to cut her off. "However, as completely unhinged as all this sounds, I'm kind of into it. I mean, this sounds like something I would do. I would never have imagined you as the type to buy into conspiracy theories—like, that's the most surprising part of this."

Mallory's not sure how to respond so she twists to face the table, focusing on the contents of the basket. A bright red burner phone sits cradled at the bottom; a note stuck to the back. *Take me with you and leave yours behind* it reads in swirling cursive. Rowan lets out a soft chuckle as he drops his cell into the basket, exchanging it for the red phone.

"It's one of Peyton's games, might as well play along." He turns to Britt and Mallory. "She'll give us hell if we don't, you know that."

"What's the point of leaving us the phone?" Britt asks. "This place has no service."

Rowan shrugs before clicking it on, soft blue light exploding through the screen. Mallory immediately reaches out and grabs it, feeling like an insect pulled in by the sticky brightness.

"What the fuck," Rowan hisses, but she's too focused on the phone to care.

The wallpaper image is from HyveFest. It's a photo taken from the pit in front of the stage, angled up so that the lead singer looks like a giant, his jaw unhinged around the microphone as if to swallow it whole. Behind him, purple lights, a hand painted banner, and a massive Styrofoam skull. Mallory wasn't there when the HyveMind took the stage last year—she would have been inside the arcade by then—but the image isn't from last year, and she recognizes it immediately. Posted to the band's website the week before the festival, it's the last photo Jared uploaded to Instagram before he disappeared.

Throwback to last year's set. Can't wait to see what they have in store for us this year.

Except by the time HyveMind started playing, Jared was already... Mallory's hand shakes and it takes all of her effort not to let the phone slip from her grasp.

Erika catches her by the wrist and points to the top right corner of the screen. "Looks like it's connected to Wi-Fi. You should check the network name so we can connect our phones."

Rowan scowls. "Peyton said to leave our phones out here."

"And I'm saying that's a shitty idea." She releases Mallory's wrist and gestures for her to check. Mallory clicks through to settings, and her stomach clenches. The network it's connected to is called "Sulking Seething," HyveMind's most popular song... and Jared's favorite.

The blood leaks from his nose, dripping down his upper lip. "I'm always embarrassed to admit that it's my favorite song because it's so popular." He squeezes her thigh, his hand warm through the fabric of her jeans. "Usually, I prefer things that are overlooked by other people."

The phone slips from her hand and Rowan dives to grab it.

"Can you people stop dropping everything?" he barks.

"Sorry." The tips of Mallory's fingers and toes go fuzzy, and she peels a scab from her shoulder, the rip of skin helping to bring things back into perspective. Of course, Peyton would choose "Sulking Seething" as the network name. Jared was a popular influencer, his opinions were posted online for everyone to see, especially when it came to HyveMind. He's why they're here after all. Peyton has a morbid sense of humor; she probably meant it as a joke.

Erika fumbles with her own phone, attempting to connect to Wi-Fi for a few seconds before tilting the screen towards Mallory and pouting. "The network is password protected. Any ideas?"

They try Jared's name, Peyton's name, HyveMind, and "Sulking Seething" again before giving up and choosing to deposit their phones in the basket. It feels wrong to leave them, but Rowan sells them on how phones would be useless anyway since the resort is a dead zone.

Mallory is about to drop hers in as a notification pops up on Rowan's screen. It's not the message preview that twists her insides, it's the wallpaper. In it, Rowan crouches in front of a row of sunflowers, his hands gripping a toddler beneath his armpits, helping him stand. The child is mid laugh, his head tilted back, and Rowan grins down at him. The shallow depth of field gives the image a dreamlike quality, the sunflowers hardly more than blurs, softening Rowan and the child around the edges. It's clearly a professional photograph and even though he's still sporting a mohawk, Rowan is dressed in a collared shirt and khaki pants. He looks like a stranger.

"Who's this?" She points to the child and does her best to suppress the sick feeling in her gut. In all their time talking, Rowan's never once mentioned having a kid... same as he never mentioned having a twin.

"My nephew, Gabriel," he says without missing a beat, quickly reaching over her to shut the phone off.

Mallory glances at Olivia. It's impossible to imagine her as a mother, she's too childlike herself. Maybe Rowan has another sibling that he hasn't told her about. The thought sends pinpricks of heat up her neck and she's still fixating on the photo as the others drop their phones into the basket.

Even Erika eventually relents and adds hers to the pile. "If someone comes by and swipes them, or if it rains, you're gonna owe me a new phone." She shakes her head before leading the group up the ramp attached to the loading dock. "Now come on. Let's get this thing started."

Mallory cocks her head to the side and Erika laughs. "What?"

"You're just so eager all of a sudden."

"I told you, this may be completely unhinged, but I'm kind of into it."

They stop in front of the entrance, and the air leaking from the gap between the garage-style door and the cinder blocks wedged beneath is cold and breathy.

Erika gives Mallory's hand a squeeze before crouching down and slipping inside, the building swallowing her greedily.

She makes it look so easy to disappear.

There's a gentleness to how Erika folds into the dark that sets Mallory's teeth on edge. The resort, after all, is a predator, and Mallory knows too well what predators are willing to do to the weak. She stands back, letting her friends filter in ahead of her, looking too much like they're entering the jaws of a monster.

Her pulse thrums in her ears, and for a moment, she's struck by the urge to turn and run.

"It's not the arcade," she reminds herself, her chest tight and hands trembling. "It's not the arcade and I'm here with friends. Everything's okay." Except, a small, panicked voice in the back of her head howls that it isn't, that she's in danger. But as it pleads for her to run, she reasons that the others are already inside. No one's screaming. No one's yelling for her to go get help. Everything's okay. She sucks in a breath and enters the building.

The dark hits her like a slap to the face. At first, it's a wall of black so solid that she hesitates to move. But as she stands in the cool wash of darkness, her eyes slowly adjust.

The rest of the group is already fanning out, soft at the edges, folding into their surroundings as Mallory continues to muse over the lack of light and the prickle in the back of her head, still warning that this is a mistake.

The loading dock empties into a stock room with metal shelves and a concrete floor. The air, stagnant and sour, causes Mallory to wrinkle her nose. It's like curdled milk in a flooded basement.

Cuts of light struggle in through windows that dot the walls like acne: small, and square, and painted over with thick, haphazard strokes of black paint. The room is wide and rectangular, with rows of metal shelves creating makeshift walkways in the otherwise empty space. Each shelf is packed to the brim with jars of pickled pig's feet, fermented pears, and sticky jams and jellies.

"This is weird, right?" Britt picks up one of the jars, a squat thing with a red and white checkered lid, what looks like peaches or apricots floating through the cloudy liquid inside.

"I mean, this place was supposed to be a resort. I imagine they'd have all kinds of stuff for like breakfasts and lunches and shit," Rowan says.

"Does this look like lunch to you?" Britt grabs the pig's feet off the shelf and turns it to the rest of the group. "I wouldn't be caught dead eating this."

Rowan smirks. "Give me twenty bucks and I'll do it."

"You're disgusting." Britt places it back on the shelf and the two continue to argue back and forth.

Mallory can't help but feel a pang of jealousy. She always thought it would be her and Rowan who'd click immediately. Instead, the spark simply isn't there. It's worse than rejection, he's completely indifferent to her. She wanders along the walls of the room, putting as much distance between the others and herself as possible.

Mallory's never been inside this part of the building before. The horrors of Jared's final night were confined to the arcade, bathed in a pool of pink and blue neon. She never bothered to explore the rest of the place except through the pictures that were posted online once the project was abandoned. She has a folder on her laptop dedicated to the images with subfolders for each room: water park, food court, miniature golf course, escape room. Night after night, she lays back, stares at her ceiling, and tries to map it out. She walks the hallways, enters the rooms, scans the corners for pieces of Jared. His blood. His breath. Whatever's left.

As she wanders the stockroom, she keeps glancing over her shoulder, waiting for him to pop out from behind one of the shelves and slide a knife across her throat. The thought sends waves of cold through her.

Past the final shelf of fermented jams and pickled vegetables, Mallory finds a door with a brass knob, and a giant red arrow painted in the center like a bullseye.

"Hey, everyone?" she calls. "I think I know where we're supposed to go."

Footsteps sound across the concrete floor as the others join her, but Mallory can't take her eyes off the door. Harsh ribbons of light bisect the arrow, and the shadows cast across the wood seeming to split it until it bleeds. Icy fear creeps up Mallory's spine.

Rowan and Britt rib each other, speaking in low, hushed

voices about how Peyton really went all out with whatever she has planned for them. Olivia stands back from the group clutching at the collar of her dress. She looks like a housewife who was just told that her husband isn't coming home from war; she's the only other one who seems to sense how wrong this is.

Even Erika nods approvingly.

"You look impressed," Mallory says tentatively, wondering how Erika doesn't see this as a bad omen, how she isn't fishing for the crystals she keeps in her pocket and running her fingers over them as if to ward away the bad vibes.

"I am impressed. Like, yeah, it's a little over the top, a little unsettling, but you know what it reminds me of?" she asks, adjusting her bun.

Mallory shakes her head.

"That haunted house we used to go to all the time in high school."

Mallory smiles despite the lump in her throat. Neither of them are horror fans, but when they were teenagers, they loved running through the massive corn maze in the back of the attraction and screaming until their throats were raw. The only horror film Mallory's ever seen from beginning to end is *Hellraiser*, which the girls watched while waiting in line outside the haunted house one particularly busy Halloween night. For weeks afterward, Erika would reach out, pinch the back of her arm, and whisper "Jesus wept" in her ear. Mallory used to collapse into a fit of laughter every time, but thinking back on it now, she shudders.

Rowan opens the door, ushering Britt and Olivia through. Erika hurries after the group, and Mallory sucks in another breath before following into a narrow hallway. It's pitch-black inside, and Mallory flattens her hand against the wall, the coolness, the bumps in the paint keeping her steady as she inches forward. Then, Rowan turns on the flashlight app on the red phone, and the light cuts a path for them, particles of dust floating lazily through the beam.

"Ugh, it stinks," Erika mutters, and Mallory nods though the motion is lost to the darkness.

The air has a rotten quality to it, like it's been percolating since they halted construction on the place, and Mallory pulls the front of her shirt up over her nose, though it does little to block the smell.

"Seriously, what is this," Erika continues. "It's like someone died in here."

"Someone did die in here," Rowan says, his deep baritone drifting back from the front of the group.

"Not here, the arcade." Mallory's voice is muffled by the fabric of her shirt. "Jared died in the arcade."

"Unless he didn't die at all," Erika says.

Rowan shrugs. "We'll find out soon, won't we?"

Mallory's shoulders tense and the others laugh nervously as they continue to walk. The hall opens up ahead of them, the ceiling peeling away to reveal a network of rusted pipes that drip over the tile floors. The drops of water are so thick, so much like saliva that Mallory can't help but feel like the building is a second away from clamping down its jaw.

Rowan flicks off the light on the phone as the hallway spills into the main lobby of the resort, and Mallory lets her shirt drop, gulping in the air. There's still a musty tinge to it, but it's not nearly as bad as the hall. Thin windows line the top of the walls and light cuts in with surgical precision, casting long, thin shadows across the tile floor. The room appears alien, wrong, somehow with the way the light cuts through it, and Mallory can't seem to release the tension from her shoulders.

There's a reception desk with a black landline still tacked in place and a massive neon sign above it, which is turned off but clearly some shade of blue. *Starling Indoor Water Park and Resort* is written in elaborate cursive. The floors are tiled and shiny.

The walls the same shade of pink as the outside of the building. The place looks like it's a few weeks shy of being Instagram goals, clearly targeting a younger Millennial and Gen Z crowd even though most water parks cater to families with children. It's an interesting choice to say the least, and Mallory wonders what the resort might have become if not for Jared's death. Whether the halls would be packed with influencers, phones held out, lips pursed, with a whole library of filters at the ready.

A soft buzzing fills the room and Mallory steps up to the neon sign, attempting to pinpoint its origins. But it's not coming from the sign. It seems to run through the very bones of the space despite there being no obvious source—nothing's plugged in, nothing's turned on.

Mallory's always been sensitive to sound. The static whine of the refrigerator, the hiss and snap of current moving through her walls—everything so loud that it feels like a claw hooked into her eardrum. One time she asked Erika if she was as bothered by the appliances in their old apartment, but she shook her head, insisting even as a high-pitched whistle pierced Mallory's ear, that they weren't making any noise at all. But here, in the lobby, the sound is overpowering.

"Do you hear that?" she asks.

"What?" Rowan stands directly in the center of the lobby, scanning the room for some sign of Peyton.

"Buzzing. It's like the electricity is on in here or something."

"No way, they would have shut all that down when they halted construction. If they even got that far before Jared was dismembered."

"I hear it though." Mallory walks around the space, trying desperately to hunt down the source of the whine. She paces like the dogs at the shelter do right before it rains. The air inside the lobby is thick with last year's trauma and Mallory wonders if the hum is a warning that another storm is about to hit.

Erika grabs her by the arm. "Chill, Mal. You're putting me on edge."

"Maybe we should be on edge. Something is very wrong here."

"You're telling me," Britt says, shaking her head. She's standing directly in front of the wall behind the reception desk. "It's Baker-Miller pink again."

"What's that supposed to mean?"

"It increases anxiety and aggression."

Mallory stares at the wall, the shade reminding her of chewed bubblegum—bringing back memories of playgrounds and happy meals, childhood comforts that she didn't think to miss until they were gone. While it's not enough to distract from the electric whine, it does help her to feel more settled in her skin. "I think it's actually calming me down."

"Give it time," Britt says. "The initial effects of the color are calming. They actually started painting drunk tanks and hospitals this particular shade of pink because it's supposed to mellow you out, but after a few minutes it increases aggression. Studies have shown that there's more violent crime in prisons with Baker-Miller pink in the color palette. I'm starting to understand how Jared could be killed in this place."

"You're saying that Jared was murdered because someone painted the walls pink? A *color* got him killed?" Rowan scoffs.

"Colors have been killing people for hundreds of years." Britt runs her fingers along the wall, tracing patterns into the plaster as she stares intently at the color. "There was a shade of green back in Victorian times, Scheele's green, that was made with arsenic. Women kept dying because their dresses were dyed with it. People in green rooms kept getting sick because it was in the wallpaper. You can't underestimate the importance of color palette when building a home, or an office, or an indoor water park and resort—it could mean the difference between a lucrative opening day and a grisly murder."

"Wow, Britt," Rowan says, his voice dripping with sarcasm. "Thank you for that incredibly useful and relevant information."

"Of course," Britt says sincerely, and Rowan frowns, turning away from her.

"Peyton?" he calls, his voice echoing off the walls. One of the lobby's skylights is missing and lazy shafts of light drip down over the tile floor, breaking up the otherwise uniform cuts of shadow.

The back of Mallory's neck prickles and she turns to find Olivia staring intently at her. The moment she locks eyes with her, Olivia looks away and a curious dread takes root in the pit of Mallory's stomach. She can't understand why she's here. Rowan hardly seems like the type who would need to bring someone along for moral support, and Olivia hasn't said more than a few words to the group since arriving. Britt, who Mallory would have pegged for the antisocial one, has been more engaged with the others than she is. Even Erika, who looked like she was ready to bolt the moment Mallory's friends showed up, is making more of an effort.

"Aha! Peyton's been through here." Rowan stands at the neck of a hallway and points down to the tile. "See?"

There's another bright red arrow painted on the floor.

Mallory turns from Olivia and hurries to Erika's side.

"Should we?" Mallory asks her best friend, secretly hoping that she'll say no. The static whine is starting to burrow under her skin, and the discomfort is like an itch she can't scratch away.

Erika shrugs. "We've come this far, might as well see it through."

Cautiously, they step into the hall.

There's something wrong here. The thought is as sudden as it is unwanted, and Mallory shivers as she takes stock of the narrow corridor. A random hodgepodge of windows, set high up, dot the walls like freckles. They're practically ceiling height with thick panes of glass, reminding her of coke bottle lenses: warped, *wrong*. The light seeps through them, crisscrossing the walls—shadows coloring the spaces between. It's jarringly organic for such a sterile, carefully constructed space.

The top half of the walls are painted a shade of blue so light that it borders on white, while the bottom half are covered in dark lacquered wooden paneling. It's an odd choice considering the otherwise modern design of the place. Mallory wonders if they were updating a preexisting structure before construction stopped and how many haunted layers exist within this space, how many ghosts are fused through the foundation.

Another dimmed neon sign sits mounted at the far end over the doorway. Written in the same swooping penmanship as the sign in the lobby, it announces the indoor water park, as if the tangle of half-finished waterslides visible through the doorway isn't enough of an indication.

The farther they squeeze down the hall, the louder the electric hum. Mallory's mind wanders to bug zappers and the curled bodies of flies, and she wants nothing more than to run. Even without the high-pitched noise, there's too much of Jared laced through the resort, and if her increasing paranoia is any indication, it can't be healthy for her to be here.

Erika's hand settles on her shoulder. "Not to freak you out more than you already are, but there are cameras in here." She points to where the wall meets the ceiling and sure enough, Mallory cranes her neck to see two cameras and what looks like a speaker fastened to the place where the wall meets the ceiling.

"They're probably not on." The cameras make her nervous but the weight of Erika's hand drains some of the panic, and she reasons that the resort would need cameras for security reasons. Even the speaker system seems reasonable. If this place were to be open, they'd be playing music, wouldn't they? She convinces herself to stick it out, if only long enough to meet up with Peyton. She can leave if things still feel uncomfortable after that.

They approach the end of the hall, and the waterslides slip into focus. They're deep shades of red and pink: shiny, and plastic, and so much livelier than the photos Mallory found online. The colors are aggressively saturated, and the sheen reflecting off the plastic pieces gives them the impression of being tightly wrapped in sausage casings. While unnerving, it helps Mallory relax. It's proof that the entirety of the resort is distorted in one way or another and the panic she's been teetering at the edge of since entering has nothing to do with Jared's death. The building feels wrong. It's wrong now, and it would have been wrong before last year.

Erika jerks her arm, and Mallory stumbles, turning.

"You okay?" Erika asks. "You looked like you were spacing out again."

She steps back and Mallory steps forward, eager to share her realization when there's a click and her foot sinks into the floor. She lifts her boot as there's a terrible grinding noise and the electric buzzing reaches a fever pitch. The floor vibrates beneath her feet, and she looks back right as a large metal panel slams down where the door used to be, effectively sealing them off from the lobby.

Tension ricochets up Mallory's spine, and she freezes in place feeling trapped in a way that she hasn't felt since the night Jared died. The others pause as well, their eyes wide, and silence bloats the space around them. It's as if the hallway is holding its breath, and Mallory scans the ceiling, weary of whatever additional surprises lurk in the tight space.

But nothing happens, there's only silence and the metal sheet glinting wickedly from down the hall in a humorless wink.

Mallory curls her fingers into the flesh of her upper arms, the tart sting enough to unlock her muscles, and she takes off running back down the length of the hallway. Her heart hammers in her chest, and the only sound is the slap of her boots against the tile floor—pounding in time to her pulse. The hurried, frantic cry of a snare drum.

The door seems so far away, the hallway impossibly long, and Mallory's reminded of nightmares where no matter how hard she pumps her legs or tries to run, her body remains heavy and sluggish. Like running through mud. Like drowning in slow motion.

It takes her far too long to make it back to where they entered and when she skids to a stop in front of the metal panel, she flings herself against it. She pounds at the barrier, her fists making hollow cries as they connect with it. The others swarm around the door—kicking, clawing, hitting. They attack it as a pack, as if they're all part of the same animal, but it doesn't make any difference. The panel won't budge. Rowan is the only one who doesn't join in. Instead, he stands back from the group, watching calmly. He pulls a lighter and pack of cigarettes out of his front pocket and sticks one into his mouth.

"Relax," he says, lighting up the cigarette and inhaling deeply. "It's just one of Peyton's games."

"This isn't a game," Erika snaps. "She locked us in here."

"We're not locked in; the water park is right there." He gestures to the knot of water slides.

Britt tugs the sleeves of her hoodie down over her hands. She holds them up to her face, inhaling deeply.

Rowan cocks an eyebrow. "What are you doing?"

"Lavender." She peeks out over the sleeves. "My detergent smells like lavender... It helps calm me down when I get stressed."

"You're a freak, Britt," he says between drags of his cigarette.

Erika glares at him. "Oh, so you're fine with us getting locked in here, but she's the freak?"

"We're not locked in—the water park is right there, you stupid bitch."

"What did you call me?" Erika slaps the cigarette out of his mouth, and he barely catches it in the palm of his hand, his jaw twitching. Mallory steps forward to separate them when piercing feedback screeches into the hall and everyone clamps their hands over their ears. Mallory leans against the wall and squeezes her eyes shut as the feedback continues to blare.

"Hello darlings," Peyton's voice leaks in over the speaker that's fastened to the wall. It's the same as when she would enter voice chat in the Discord, except there's a cold edge to it. The bubblegum sweetness is gone, replaced with something darker, more predatory.

Mallory's throat goes dry. All the static in the air has come to a head. The storm is finally hitting.

"You don't know how long I've been waiting for this," Peyton says. "In the words of one of my favorite horror villains, I want to play a game. And you fuckers are gonna bleed."

4

ERIKA

For months after Mallory screwed her over, Erika would close her eyes and imagine knives. Big ones. Butcher knives, and bread knives, and cleaving knives. Digging into Mal's shoulders, slipping between her ribs, shucking her jaw like an oyster. She doesn't consider herself a violent person, but something about Mallory always brings out the worst in her—a fact that she used to relish in, but now finds tedious. Everyone wants to be a bad bitch until they realize how tiring it is. Then it's easy to drown yourself in questions. Like, when do I finally get to peel off my mask? Who the hell am I underneath all the glitter and grit? Erika doesn't have time for the questions. Existential crises are only cute when you're in college.

Erika's key to success? Changing her mindset, repeating her affirmations, and getting the fuck over what happened last spring. But she directed so much energy towards healing that when she actually healed, it left her more hollowed out than the pain.

Plus, there's Kimber, always following her around like a puppy that's been kicked one too many times. Always up for martinis, or hot yoga, or bottomless fucking brunches. Kimber's enthusiasm exhausted her, depleted her, beat her down within an inch of her life.

The horror unfolding now though, breathes new life into her. She feels wide awake for the first time in nearly a year. Her pulse thrums in her ears, a trickle of sweat slipping down from her hairline across her cheek. Once the sheet of metal falls, once Peyton's voice slides in over the intercom, it's chaos. The others scramble for the water park, crowding the doorway, clawing at each other. They trip, they flail. Erika stifles a giggle as she follows them. She has a bad habit of laughing anytime she feels intense emotion—fear, anger, sadness. She's feeling a hell of a lot of things as she steps into the water park, and she can't contain her laughter anymore. It's frenzied, sharp as a razor blade. She feels like the fucking Joker.

This time Erika feels the tile sink beneath her designer shoes before she hears the terrible grinding noise, and she doesn't even need to turn around to know that another metal panel has fallen, sealing them deeper inside. Erika takes a deep breath and strokes the carnelian stone that she carries in her pocket. It's a reminder that she will make it through this. Everything will happen exactly as it's meant to. It has to... right? The universe wouldn't knock her down last year just to kick her in the jaw right when she began to find her footing again... Would it?

Erika used to work for a tech start up selling SaaS software to real estate developers. She still has a ton of company merch in her closet, folded neatly in a corner: t-shirts, sweatshirts, Patagonia vests. She showed Mallory before they drove over, making a point to pull back the sliding door revealing the clothes, and around them, a loose circle of other company branded items. Yetis, and mousepads, and mugs strewn across the floor like confetti. Her own private memorial to a dead career.

Not dead, Erika reminds herself, *murdered.*

And the blood is on Mallory's hands.

Her once best friend is the reason why she bartends three nights a week, supplementing her meager income with tip money and monthly deposits from her mother.

Static crackles in through the speaker system, pulling Erika from her thoughts. She listens as Peyton's voice echoes through the water park. Mocking them. Bragging about how she catfished them with fake photos and bought followers to make herself seem like a legitimate influencer. She rambles on and on as Mallory and her friends scatter like ants. They crawl over every inch of the water park, trying without success to find a crack in Peyton's perfect trap. But the only exposed windows are massive glass panels built into the ceiling. The few thin panes that line the very tops of the walls are sealed—a combination of plywood, metal bars, screws and nails. The two emergency exit doors have been welded over with sheets of metal and there's a third door at the far end that won't budge.

"Because we need to clear this round before moving on," Erika murmurs, her eyes wide. This isn't a game, it's a maze, and Peyton is herding them through it.

Erika isn't surprised that Mallory trails after her online friends. She's always been a follower, a people pleaser, so afraid of hurting others that she doesn't even notice when she's hurting herself. Erika figures if she hadn't been there, Mallory wouldn't have entered the water park at all; she would have sunken against the wall and cowered.

She should be grateful to Rowan and the others for forcing Mallory out. She doesn't know what she would have done if Mal had been sealed away from her, but she can't help but feel abandoned as she navigates Peyton's trap alone.

Even though the air is thick with panic and a vaguely chemical smell, like chlorine left to ferment, Erika marvels at the curation of the trap.

Sections of the water park have been roped off, and the parts that are highlighted by bright lights, signs, cuts of light—an empty wave pool, and trio of half-completed water slides—are served to them as if on a platter. There's a table set up next to the slides, and Peyton doesn't even need to tell the group to go there, they gather at its base as if on instinct.

Erika steps up to the table first, and although her heart pounds against her ribs, she refuses to let her nerves show.

Olivia inches up next to her, inhaling sharply when she notices what's on the table. Erika braces herself in case she faints, which she wouldn't put past the wallflower and some sick part of her is actually proud when Olivia manages to stay standing.

Britt suddenly tenses, her spine shooting ramrod straight.

"Yellow," she barely breathes, wringing at the sleeves of her hoodie. Agitation radiates off her in waves.

Finally, Rowan saunters over, a freshly lit cigarette perched between his lips, Mallory tight on his heels. He blows smoke through his nostrils as he takes stock of what they're up against. "Oh, that is so fucked up."

Erika agrees, it is fucked up, and it's all she can do to contain the frenzied laugh bubbling up in her throat.

A neon sign sits fastened above the table, electric blue and flickering in a sharp staccato that's like an exclamation point at the end of a scream.

A steak knife, a bone saw, and a scalpel sit directly beneath it. Three sharp instruments illuminated in the haze of sunlight that tumbles in through the windowed ceiling. They seem to wink, to twist, to beg for flesh.

Yellow button, the neon sign declares, and above the trio of weapons, there's a panel lined with buttons. Three are small and red; one is fat and yellow.

"Do you still think she's playing a trick on us?" Olivia asks, seeming to curl in on herself, drowning in the fabric of her fifties-style dress. The effect is ridiculous, and Erika stifles another laugh. Olivia reminds her of a kitten that keeps being left out in the rain but doesn't have the good sense to recognize that it's being abused. She's anxious in a way that makes Erika itch to slap her. Usually, she would find Olivia's brand of hopelessness endearing—it's what initially drew her to Mallory after all—but in her post-personal transformation era, becoming the best version of herself and all that, it's just sad. And Erika doesn't have the time or patience for sad.

"It's pretty elaborate for a trick." Britt steps in line with her. She's been throwing sideways glances at Erika since they were out in front of the memorial and it's enough to make her skin crawl. Britt is the weirdest one out of the bunch. She seems like she's operating on a different frequency, and Erika figures she's either an Aquarius or has a few screws loose. Maybe both.

There's a pang of disappointment when she realizes that Mallory is standing back next to Rowan.

He's been a shadow looming over their friendship since the eighth grade. Erika doesn't consider herself possessive, and in fact, would be the first person to condemn others for being too clingy, but she doesn't like sharing Mallory. She never has.

Looking in from the outside, Erika and Mal were an odd pairing, even when they were younger and their interests aligned. Mallory was so broody, Erika so rowdy. She used to love the way Mallory followed her lead, always a step behind but down for whatever. And she listened. Oh my god, she actually listened. Where other girls would pretend they were listening when they were really just waiting for their turn to speak, Mallory absorbed everything that was thrown her way. She heard Erika, and Erika could trust her with anything. They were coiled together, twin snakes against the world. Until they weren't. Until it all unraveled.

Thinking about the way they used to be makes the back of Erika's throat ache.

"I'm doing this for you," she wants to scream. "I'm here for you and this is what I get... ignored in favor of *him*? Ungrateful doesn't even begin to cover it."

Not that Rowan's paying Mallory any mind. He's busy making short work of his second cigarette, the slight shake in his hand the only indication that any of this is getting to him. Mallory hovers by his side like a dog begging for scraps. All she gets is a face full of smoke.

"Why are you so calm all of a sudden?" Erika asks Rowan. "You were just running around like a chicken with its head cut off."

"Nicotine," he says flatly. He pulls what remains of the cigarette from his mouth and flicks it at her.

She steps back from the smoldering butt and scrunches her nose. "That stuff will give you cancer, you know."

"Hardly," he says, reaching in his pocket for another. "This is the most I've smoked in years. I can't do it at home anymore because of Gabriel."

Mallory doesn't seem to like this answer one bit.

"Your nephew?" She asks, her brow knotted. "Does he live with you?"

"He visits a lot." Rowan answers quickly, but Erika notices how he shoots a glance at Olivia before responding. She's sure that she's the only one who catches it, and it's all she can do to contain her smirk. She's always been good at catching things that other people overlook.

"What now?" Olivia asks.

Britt gestures toward the neon sign, her voice trembling as she answers. "Yellow button."

The group stares at the sign, moths to the flame, the rapid blink of the neon as hypnotizing as it is maddening. Everyone speaks at once, the panicked din of their voices hooking into the sides of Erika's head. It's like she's gripped in a vice that keeps getting squeezed tighter and tighter.

"Who's gonna press it?"

"What's the worst that could happen?"

"Not me. I'm fucking done with this shi—"

"There's no way she's serious, this is just part of—"

"You heard what Peyton said, she wants to—"

"Does this seem fake to you?"

"Then who is going to press the button?!"

"This is a nightmare!"

"Oh my god, will you all shut up?" Erika slams her palm down on the yellow button before she even realizes what she's doing. It's an impulsiveness she hasn't fallen prey to in almost a year, and something inside of her stirs. Something dark, something purely hedonistic in its self-destruction, and she shudders as it wakes. She shouldn't be here; it's undoing all her progress.

Erika repeats her affirmations, attempting to cage the monstrous thing that's clawed to the surface. *Everything I want, I already have. I am abundant. I am in control.*

There's a distinct click, and the button lights up as white noise trickles in over the intercom, an echo through the empty water park.

Everything I want, I already have, she thinks desperately. *I am abundant. I am in control.*

I am in control, I am in control, I am in control.

Peyton's voice fills the space around them, sticky sweet, piercing Erika's eardrums like an ice pick.

I am in control.

"Hello darlings," Peyton coos. "You've made it to the first round of our game. So exciting!"

A cartoonishly loud round of applause filters in through the speaker and Erika cringes at how cheesy it sounds.

"I cannot wait for us to play. But before we get started, I'm sure you're wondering about all the sharp objects on the table. Don't worry, you won't need them for this round, but I thought I'd be nice and give you a way to defend yourselves, you know, in case things get a little 'every man for himself' in there. I want you all to feel safe and have fun during our game after all. So go ahead and pick a weapon. One per person. I'll give you a few moments to decide who gets what."

No one moves at first and static hums through the water park.

Blood rushes to Erika's forehead, her palms slick with sweat. She surveys the weapons, but like the others, makes no attempt to grab them.

Would they even allow her to? They aren't meant for her.

She swallows back a lump in her throat.

Finally, Rowan gathers the blades as if they're a bouquet. They fan out at the top, their sharp tips glinting and Erika watches as he parses them out—bone saw for Britt, scalpel for Mallory, and steak knife for himself.

"Why do you get to be the one to divvy them out?" Britt asks, her knuckles white as she grips the bone saw.

"Someone had to, and I didn't see any of you taking initiative."

Olivia shoots him a concerned look. "Erika and I don't get anything?"

Rowan hooks the knife through his belt so that the thick handle pokes over the leather and the blade rests against his hip. "What do you expect me to do, split the weapons in half?"

"No but—"

"But what? You don't think I'm gonna protect you if it comes to that, Liv?"

"I-I think we should all get the opportunity to protect ourselves."

"There are only three weapons."

"I know but—"

"It's only fair that they go to the people who are actually supposed to be here, don't you think?" He stares at her, his expression hardened.

Olivia opens her mouth as if to say something but quickly closes it again, nodding meekly.

Erika watches with fascination. It would be amusing if it wasn't so sad… There's a lot to unpack between the twins, and she's so laser focused on them that she doesn't notice Mallory until her hand settles on her shoulder. The faint scent of her coconut shampoo soaks the space between them, and something inside Erika cracks open and bleeds. Mallory's always smelled like the beach, and the scent brings her back to their slumber party days. It's that hit of coconut that makes her realize how much she truly lost in the last year. The mild aroma is a welcome change from Kimber, whose cheap perfume practically strangles everyone around her—not to mention lingers in the worst possible way on clothes, bedding, couch cushions. Erika knows that Mallory is jealous of how easily she was replaced. Once she vacated her position, the coveted role of Erika's best friend was filled within a week. It hardly mattered that Kimber had a few screws loose, or that Erika was just looking for a rebound.

No one ever talks about how similar friendships are to dating. If anything, they're worse. If someone rejects romantic advances it can be chalked up to any number of things: lack of physical attraction, or compatibility—the spark just not being there or not burning bright enough. If someone doesn't want to be your friend, it cuts deeper. It cuts to the bone.

Not that Erika ever had that issue with Kimber. If anything, she was too enthusiastic. Constant calls and texts. If Erika went more than a few days without seeing Kimber, she'd pitch a fit.

Why didn't you invite me?

Why didn't you call me?

When am I seeing you next?

Erika chalked it up to Kimber's birth chart at first—a Pisces sun, Gemini moon—and her trying to find stability after a tumultuous breakup. Not to mention, Kimber's former bestie moved out of state a few months before everything went down. The best friend was navigating a particularly traumatic set of circumstances that trumped anything Kimber needed to process, especially something as mundane as a failed relationship. She was alone and hurting. It's natural for someone with such unhinged, mutable sign energy to cling. And go full on psychotic. Most serial killers are mutable signs after all.

It's gotten bad recently though, worse than Erika's willing to admit. It was difficult enough to tell Mallory that she needs financial help from her mother. She can't stand owning up to the depth of her mistakes with Kimber.

Erika turns to find Mallory wide-eyed and skin drained of color. Her grip on the scalpel loosens, and after nearly dropping the instrument, she shoves it into Erika's hands. "You take it. I don't want it."

Erika passes it back immediately. "Neither do I."

"Please, take it."

"I can't."

"Take it!" Mallory shrieks.

"Okay, okay." The last thing Erika wants to do is nick an artery while playing hot potato with the thing. Gingerly, she plucks it from Mallory's hand and slips it into the pocket of her leggings, terrified that it'll cut through the fabric even with the plastic cap over the blade. The weight of it against her leg makes her realize how wrong all this is.

Mallory is the reason she's not home watching re-runs of *The Bachelor*, or sipping white wine, or doing literally anything other than getting locked in a water park with a bunch of strangers and sharp knives.

I am in control, she repeats inside her mind, not that the affirmation does anything other than spike her panic. Because how can she truly be in control in a situation like this? There are too many variables… too many blades.

The group stands awkwardly for a few more seconds before Peyton's voice slices back in over the speaker system. "Everyone have a weapon? Good. Now, about the first game you're going to play. I need two volunteers. One of you will go up to the trio of waterslides and stand on the platform, and one of you will be in charge of the buttons that you see in front of you. The red ones, of course, not the yellow. But you guys are so dense, I figure it won't hurt to be *extra clear* about things. So yeah, red buttons.

"There are a series of trapdoors in front of each slide, and a series of buttons on the top of each trapdoor that correspond to the buttons downstairs—following me so far? Well, whoever goes up there needs to choose a trapdoor and stand on its button so that it lights up green—otherwise the buttons downstairs won't work. The game is easy. A kind of Russian roulette. One of the trapdoors is rigged to swing open when the corresponding button downstairs is pressed. You need to press two of the buttons downstairs to complete the round, so in the first round there's a one in three chance that you'll fall to your death, then it's fifty-fifty but if you survive, then the door at the edge of the room will open and you'll get to move on to the next round. Have fun! Oh, and one more thing… you have twenty minutes to finish the round. I'll be up here counting down, and you don't want to see what happens if I reach zero."

Erika stares at the slides, admiring the workmanship and how fittingly horrifying the whole thing is. Three tube slides, all in various stages of completion, the one in the center little more than a small, round scream. A set of wooden steps lead to the flat wooden platform where vacationers would wait for their turn at the slides—and directly below the platform, an empty pool, the inside painted a pale shade of blue. There are clear outlines of the three trap doors on the underside of the platform.

"This is insane," Olivia says, her eyes wide. "We're not doing this."

"What's the other option, Liv?" Rowan snaps. "There's no way out."

"The phone," Britt says, her gaze focused on the bottom of the pool, no doubt pondering the meaning behind its shiny blue finish. Erika nearly died of secondhand embarrassment when Britt went on her rant about the pink walls in the lobby.

"Oh shit, yeah. It's connected to Wi-Fi. We can call for help." Rowan pulls the phone out of his back pocket and taps at the screen. "Damn it. There's no option to call or text."

"How is that possible?" Britt asks.

"I don't know. Parental controls?"

"What's the point of the phone if we can't do anything with it?"

Mallory's fingers dig into Erika's arm, and she presses up against her side, her shoulder hot with the beginnings of a sunburn. Even given the current circumstances, Erika savors the closeness. She's missed Mallory so much; it's a constant ache in the chest. Even after everything she did.

"I say we just wait the twenty minutes," Erika suggests. "Like, what's the worst she can do if we don't play? We're already locked in here."

"She could leave us in here to starve."

"We'd find a way out before then," Erika insists, though even she knows she doesn't sound the least bit convincing.

"We might as well play along," Rowan says. "I don't give a shit whether this is real or fake anymore, all I want is to get out of here."

Mallory presses in closer to Erika, and Erika fights to contain her smirk. "But whoever goes up on that platform might not come down again."

Rowan glances up at the slides, his eyes tracing a path from the bottom of the platform down to the pool. "Oh, they'll come down, all right. But whether it's down the stairs or smashed flat, only time will tell."

"That's not funny," Olivia murmurs, blinking back tears.

Mallory's fingers rake against her upper arm and Erika grabs her by the wrist, yanking her hand from the skin. Three lines, pink and angry, pop up where she was scratching interspersed by dots of blood, scabs that have been picked fresh in the process.

"You're not seriously doing that to yourself again, are you?" Erika grinds out, even though she noticed back in the parking lot. It's kind of hard to miss. The small pock marks in pink, and blue, and scabbed-over red that dot Mallory's arms.

Mallory has always been attractive in a non-conventional, alt-girl kind of way. She has the kind of features that look right at home slathered in dark shadow and black matte lipstick, and Erika has always envied her for that to a certain degree. The emo look? So not Erika's thing, but Mal, Mal can pull it off. Effortlessly. Which is why it's all the more infuriating that she feels the need to destroy herself. That's the thing about Mallory, she's never been able to appreciate what she has.

Erika's eyes narrow, and Mal looks at her guiltily before pulling her arm back. Instead of addressing the scabs, she folds her arms over her chest and scowls. "Don't you think we have more important things to worry about right now?"

"Hey, we just got a text," Rowan says, and Erika is grateful for his interruption. He holds up the phone in the red case—a fresh message bubble at the top of the screen.

"We can receive texts but can't send them?" Olivia asks and Rowan shrugs.

They crowd around the phone to find that the message is a transcription of the rules for the round.

Erika skims the paragraph and when no one else offers to

say something she steps up. "Okay, so we need one person to go up on the platform with the slides and one to stay down here to do the buttons."

"I'll do the buttons," Rowan offers.

"You only want to do that because it's the safest option," Britt glowers.

"The safest option would be not to play at all," Erika reminds them.

"Whatever. I called dibs on the buttons, so you guys should pull for who goes up on the platform."

"Who made you the defacto leader of the group?" Britt hisses.

Rowan shrugs, looking the oddest mix of smug and bored. "No one else was doing anything."

Erika watches with fascination as they volley insults back and forth with the grace and precision of professional athletes. She's not sure if it's the stress of what's already happened, or what's yet to come, but their voices go soft like cottage cheese, blending into the ambient noise of the water park. The distant creaks and echoes of beams, and boards, and dripping pipes sink through her head. Erika feels very far away for a moment, a fairytale-like stillness replacing her panic. She floats in the back of her mind until everything fades to static. The pop, hiss of a carbonated drink, a feeling like insects fizzling through her as she clings to her affirmations. *Everything I want, I already have. I am abundant. I am in control.*

She grits her teeth. Emotional spirals are so not cute.

I am in control!

The white noise inside her mind sputters out and the group's voices snap back at full volume.

Rowan and Britt are up in each other's faces, squaring off.

"Fine, but Olivia isn't doing shit."

"Oh, so you *and* your sister don't need to do anything? Yeah, seems like a fair compromise."

"I'm doing the buttons!" He gestures wildly as if to drive his point home. "And yeah, Liv is my sister, so I don't want her up there. If this thing goes to shit, you really want me to be responsible for killing my twin?"

He sighs, easing back slightly and pinching the bridge of his nose. "The buttons are a risk as much as the platform is. Maybe I volunteered because I know I'm the only one who won't be severely fucked in the head if things don't go the way we want them to."

The corner of Erika's mouth twitches and it's all she can do not to grin. So that's the angle he's playing. "I'm the only one who could live with the guilt of killing someone." That's how he's going to avoid the platform. It's smart and from what she knows about him, not entirely wrong. She waits for Britt to object, but she stands mutely, and just like that, it's settled. All at once too dramatic and not nearly dramatic enough for Erika's tastes.

Rowan takes three cigarettes out of his pocket and snaps one in half. He closes a fist around them so that they all appear to be the same height and shuffles them until there's no telling which is the short one. Olivia inches behind him, and he nods to the remaining women. "Leaving it up to chance is the fairest way to do it."

Erika volunteers to pull first, and even though her heart thunders against her ribs, she refuses to let the others see how nervous she is. She dips a hand into her pocket, fishing for the carnelian stone but finding the handle of the scalpel instead.

Her skin prickles. It's a bad sign.

She pulls her cigarette, wrapping her fist around it immediately, like she's trapping a fly. She does her best not to focus on the way it feels or mentally calculate how long it is, concentrating instead on Mallory as she pulls hers and does the same. Britt is the only one who doesn't conceal the cigarette, it's like she couldn't take the hint. Hers is full length, meaning it's down to Erika and Mallory. They uncurl their fingers at the same time.

Mallory winds up with the short one and she sways, the color draining from her face.

"I'll go up instead," Erika offers, maybe a little too quickly because Mal shoots her a look. But they've wasted enough time already, Peyton's invisible clock is counting down.

Mallory grabs her arm. "You can't. I'm the one that pulled—"

Erika shrugs her off. "Let me prove to you that I really am over everything that happened last year, okay? This is my way of making it up to you."

"Making it up to *me*?" A fat tear rolls down Mallory's cheek. "If I hadn't posted the pictures…"

The pictures. Of Erika and Kimber's fiancé Brandon. Their tangled limbs. Their arms like tentacles, like a kraken taking down a ship. The wet lock of their lips. The slight blur, the stink of beer practically wafting off the images. It's like some kind of fucked up stop motion where Brandon's hand slips up her shirt, and her hand sinks down into his jeans, and she can still taste his tongue as it presses deeper and deeper into her mouth.

Starbursts, and stale beer, and cigarettes.

Sweet, sour, bitter.

She wanted more, and more, and more. She wanted to drink him in, devour him. Lips, and legs, and the curve of his spine. More, more, more.

Erika wishes she could say it was the first time, or the last. But it's the only hook up that was immortalized, courtesy of Mallory's Instagram stories. She posted that shit online like they were a couple of high school kids, like they weren't twenty-fucking-six years old. Mallory tagged Kimber and Erika's company's account in the pictures and seeing how Kimber's fiancé was also Erika's manager—it did not go over well. Erika begged Mallory to take them down, but Mallory was relentless. Hell, she even had a highlight bubble for a hot minute, pinned to the top of her profile like a butterfly in a shadow box.

Twenty-four hours then it's gone forever, her ass. These things never die.

Remembering it all, Erika is momentarily overcome with the thought of knives. Big ones. Butcher knives, and bread knives, and cleaving knives. She dips a hand into her pocket, reaching for her carnelian stone but finding only the scalpel again, the steel cool against her fingertips. She's okay with that. Her fingers curl around the handle and she imagines tracing a red ribbon around Mallory's neck. What's that story they used to be obsessed with as kids? The girl whose head was held in place by a ribbon. She doubts a scalpel could do that much damage but if she managed to pry the bone saw from Britt then heads would most definitely roll. She frowns. She's better than this. Her grip falls away from the scalpel and she places a hand on Mallory's shoulder, her touch light.

"None of that matters anymore," she says, her voice dripping with so much sincerity that she nearly believes it herself. "Fresh start."

Mallory hesitates for a moment, but Erika knows her. She knows that she'll eventually relent. Aside from their falling out, there's never been an ounce of fight in Mallory. And sure enough she steps to the side, nodding.

Erika crosses to the waterslides. This is who she is. She's always been the one to take initiative. She was the one to order their drinks when she and Mallory went out, the one to make dinner reservations and book appointments because Mallory hated talking on the phone. She was the one to search for apartments, and choose the Pilates classes, and water the plants. It's always been her responsibility to get shit done.

And that's exactly what she'll do now.

She makes her way to the steep wooden steps that lead to

the platform at the mouth of the waterslides. She hates to admit it to herself, but she's nervous—sweating, acutely aware of her pulse. It's something about the high ceilings, the way that the water park is constructed. Even though it's only half built, the scent of chlorine permeates the air, a distinctly public pool scent that brings her back to childhood summers, when she would skin her knees trying to kneel at the bottom of the deep end.

The climb to the top of the platform is long and lonely. It gives her too much time to get lost inside her head when she should be repeating her affirmations and creating her perfect reality, one where everything goes exactly the way it should. But all she can picture is her skull hitting the bottom of the concrete pool and her brain unspooling. Red and pink over robin's egg blue.

"That's not going to happen," she mutters. "Get your head in the fucking game. It's going to be fine."

Her nerves aren't helped when she makes it to the top of the platform and in front of the tubed entrances to the slides are three squares, each with a big red button in the middle—exactly like Peyton described. It's suddenly so much more real and she swallows hard before approaching them. Three fat, black flies drift lazily through the air before settling on the railings which surround the platform. They're still in a semi-completed state and slabs of plywood are pressed up against the slats, so that her body must look as if it's cut in half from where the group stands. She glances over the railing at them, and they look so far away down below.

A giggle bubbles up from her throat and she stands there for a second, laughing softly, feeling six shades of crazy.

"Are you okay?" Mallory calls up to her. "Is it... Are they marked like she said they would be?"

"Yeah, but I was thinking... I should be able to divide my weight between two of the trapdoors at a time. So like, if they do fall out from underneath me, I can move to the side and it'll be fine. Honestly, I think this chick is only trying to scare you. It looks like all this was literally just thrown together." She's rambling. She knows she's rambling, overcompensating, trying to talk down her nerves. But it's normal to be nervous in a situation like this, it's completely normal. She fishes past the handle of the scalpel, finally finding the carnelian stone and giving it a squeeze. As long as she sticks to the plan, everything will work out the way that it's meant to.

Pulling her hand out of her pocket, the soft pad of her finger knocks the plastic cap on the scalpel loose and catches on the blade. She hisses at the sudden pain and lifts her finger in front of her face as a large bubble of blood wells up. A bad omen.

She wipes the blood on the thigh of her leggings and straddles two of the trap doors, flashing Mallory the thumbs up. "Okay, I'm standing on two of them right now. Even if the platforms do move, I won't fall."

She steps on one of the buttons, and it lights up bright red. Down below she can barely make out the top of the line of buttons Rowan stands in front of, now all lively and glowing.

"What next," he calls up and Erika rolls her eyes. He's the one with the phone, every instruction neatly written out in excruciating detail. Men are so fucking useless. But she makes sure to check herself before calling down, in her sweetest tone to read the instructions on the phone again.

"Okay," he says after scrutinizing it for a moment. "Which one do you think?"

"Try the one on the right," she suggests, and he presses the button immediately, slamming it with the heel of his palm. Her eyebrow twitches in annoyance. The least he could do is give her some kind of warning or countdown. That's men for you though, no foreplay, all about the main event.

At first nothing happens, and she stands numbly. Then

there's a high-pitched whine and the trapdoor snaps open a second after she pulls her foot away. For a moment she stumbles forward slightly, so afraid that she's going to swan dive through the trap door. It all feels so much more real now. She second guesses everything, but she's already in it, and she'll just have to be quick with the final button press—she'll have to be smart.

Mallory's friends gape at the freshly opened trap door as Mallory makes a run for the foot of the stairs. Erika steps away from the remaining trap doors and crosses to the far edge of the platform, looking down through the wooden slats at her friend.

"What are you doing?" Erika asks, even though she already knows. If there's one thing in this world she knows better than Mallory, it's Mallory's guilt.

"I can't let you do this by yourself. I can't leave you alone up there, especially since I'm the one who pulled the short—"

"Peyton said that there can only be one person up here. Do you really want to break the rules?"

"I don't care. You shouldn't have to do this alone, you weren't even supposed to be here to begin with."

Erika's mouth opens for a moment, but she snaps it shut. An uncomfortable heat spreads from her neck up to her forehead. Mallory would deserve it... to go up on the platform and risk spilling her brains across the tiles, risk cracking her skull like an egg. But Erika exorcises that line of thinking. Mallory doesn't belong on the platform. She needs to do this herself. "Look, there's only one more to go after this and we already triggered the trap door. Only one is supposed to actually open, remember? I'll be fine. It's really sweet that you're so concerned though."

"Of course, I'm concerned. What if she's lying, what if they're all rigged to open?"

"Then I'll do exactly what I did for the other button this time around—straddle both trap doors. Even if the next one springs open, I'll jump back before I get the chance to fall. Stay with the rest of the group, I'll be fine." Even though she's not sure anymore. She thought she had the whole thing mapped out, but it seemed so much easier before she got up on the platform. She scratches at her neck, her nails leaving angry lines across her pale flesh. She's all heat, and sweat, and itchiness. Still, she keeps a confident smile tacked in place until Mallory steps down from the stairs and sulks back across the floor to rejoin the others.

"Which one should I press next?" Rowan asks, but Erika isn't ready yet. The flies leave their perch on the railing and buzz around her, like vultures, circling for when she drops. She takes deep breaths and starts to wonder how she even got here, and if it was the right decision. She's second guessing everything, and she *never* second guesses things. She's always been confident in her choices.

Her affair with Brandon for example. She was certain it was the right thing to do.

She built it up inside her head until it was less about the romance and more about company secrets and corporate espionage. When really, the information she managed to suck from Brandon was only worth a few thousand dollars, and she hates to admit it to anyone, especially herself, but she resents the way he let her use him. She resents the way that Kimber forgave her so easily, how she's been glued to her side ever since. Always up for a morning run because women are safer in packs. Always free for a cocktail or a coffee. When they were getting their nails done earlier in the week—Kimber insisting on the same, rose gold stilettos that Erika chose, of course—all she could think about was how quick Kimber was to blame Brandon, to spout some bullshit about women sticking together and men being predatory.

As if female lions aren't the hunters of the pride.

As if female spiders don't eat their mates once they're done with them, and female mosquitoes aren't responsible for the most human deaths across all of human history.

As if Erika herself isn't an apex predator while Kimber is nothing more than a watered down, wannabe feminist version of her. Hair a few shades lighter, wrists a fraction of an inch thinner. Brandon definitely has a type.

"Make a decision," Rowan calls up to her. "I don't wanna be here any longer than I have to."

"Try the left one," she says over the lip of the tube slide.

"Are you sure?" Rowan asks.

"Positive. This will all be over soon."

The relief on Mallory's face. Holy shit, she could eat it with a spoon. All the tension is gone, the light back in her eyes—a light that was all but extinguished last year.

In this moment, Erika loves her. She really does. It's a love that goes deeper than romantic attraction, a love that could only be cultivated through their shared childhoods, the swapping of secrets, the late nights spent pouring their guts out to each other. She thinks that maybe this is all it really would have taken for the spark to reignite with Mallory—the thing that's been missing since their falling out last spring. After all this time, what they needed was the spike of adrenaline that comes from surviving something together. A new excitement rushes through as she thinks of all the ways she'll show her that she's finally completely, blissfully content. Everything is going to be okay. Erika loves her, and this is only the beginning.

But then Mal screams, her voice gravely and desperate. "Get back to the stairs now!"

"What?"

"Get back to the stairs, Erika, it isn't safe. The whole platform is rigged like a trapdoor, it isn't just the spots in front of the slides. Rowan, don't press the—"

It all happens in an instant. A gust of wind and Erika's bun whips loose. She draws in a sharp breath as her foot sinks and keeps on sinking. There's nowhere she can step back to safety as the entire platform swings out beneath her. Mallory's face contorts into a mask of pure terror, and it's the last thing Erika sees before her body dips down below the plywood barrier and Erika tries to scream, she tries to reach for Mallory, but she's already falling through the platform.

She's already gone.

5

MALLORY

There's a sickening crack as Erika hits the bottom of the empty pool. Her neck snaps at a ninety-degree angle, her body pitching back as her face grinds into the concrete.

A feeling like hot embers sears its way through Mallory. It's like there's a swarm of wasps inside her head. No sound, no motion, just white-hot pain. The world around her blurs, colors pulsing. The others are making noise, sharp, desperate noise, but all she can focus on is the bottom of the pool. She's trapped in the moment before Erika's face met the concrete, focused on the way her hair flayed out around her, the red-blonde flames of a candle. Mallory sees her, again and again. Dropping down through the platform—hanging suspended in the air. Blonde hair with glints of red.

She turns to the side and gags, spittle dripping down her chin. She floats for a long time in a sticky in between, terrified that she'll be trapped in limbo forever, until it all snaps back, like a rubber band. All the noise of the world outside her head shoots back in. It's too much—everything's too much.

The ambient sounds of the water park take on a sinister note, each drip from leaky pipes, every clang and groan of the half-built attractions amplified in the chaos providing a twisted soundtrack to terror unfolding.

A high-pitched wail from Olivia.

Britt, face buried in her hoodie, speaking in rapid succession, her voice more hurried and animated than Mallory has ever heard it before. Though she can't make out the individual words, she can feel the emotion behind the sounds, the desperation.

Only Rowan remains silent, and she looks at him, questioningly. She can't understand how he's not screaming, how if even Britt, the human statue, can express something in this moment, he can remain so calm, so untouched by it. He notices her staring and reaches for her, but she brushes him off.

Mallory runs to the edge of the pool and begins to descend the ladder. The others are reaching for her, screaming for her, but everything is fuzzy around the edges. Heat soaks her face, she's nauseous—broken, breaking, and someone—Olivia? Britt?—manages to grab her arm, but she pulls away.

In the back of her mind, she knows that there's no way anyone could have survived a fall like that, but there's a terrible anticipation as she crosses to where her best friend lays face down at the bottom of the pool.

Erika looks so much worse up close. As Mallory blinks through tears, trying to see if her chest will rise and fall, there's only stillness. A stillness that leaks into the air and makes it heavy. Erika's hair is spread out around her. It's littered with glints of rich, meaty colors that Mallory has never seen before but knows aren't meant to leave the depths of the human body.

There's a sound from the edge of the pool, and she turns to find Rowan walking toward her, his sister staring down at them over the edge of the pool, tears cutting lines through her makeup. Mallory frowns, wondering why he's bothering when he so obviously doesn't care.

"Mallory, don't," Rowan warns. He crouches next to her and reaches to pull her back, but she shakes her head.

"She can't breathe like that," Mallory moans. "I need to help her."

Heat pulses through her forehead and each slam of her heart against her ribs repeats *she's dead, she's dead, she's dead*. Still, Mallory refuses to believe it.

She flips Erika over, her best friend's hair falling like a veil over her face. She grips the sides of Erika's head, trying to ignore the lumps, the dents, the parts that so clearly shouldn't be there as she tilts Erika toward her.

Mallory's chest feels like it's going to burst, she's so hopeful, so deliriously happy. "It's going to be okay. I'm here now."

She brushes Erika's hair back and her face comes into view.

Mallory's body recoils. She opens her mouth, but no sound comes out. She can't think, she can't breathe. Sticky heat floods through her, but she's cold, she's so cold.

Erika doesn't have a face anymore. In its place there's red pulp, and fragments of white—of teeth and bone, Mallory realizes numbly, that stick out of her like pushpins. She's caved in, shredded, and red. Bright red.

The gaping hole of her face is only visible for a second. Rowan removes his leather jacket and throws it over the wreckage, but it does little to cover the awkward bend of her limbs, or the pool of blood oozing across the ground. Mallory collapses against him, burying her face in his shirt, and he lays a hand awkwardly across her back.

"I'm sorry," he says stiffly.

Mallory cries against him, her chest tight, her entire body aching until Rowan peels her away from him and helps her stand.

"It was supposed to be me. I was supposed to be the one up there."

"She's the one who decided to go instead."

"It's my fault," she wails. "I brought her here, I let her go up on that platform. I should have kept her down here with me, or I shouldn't have let her come here to begin with. We were fighting, did you know that?" She's aware of how she's rambling, and the words pour out between heavy breaths, they pour out of her like tears. "We hadn't spoken since last spring when I... I wrecked everything. And that's the reason why I came to Hyve-Fest alone last year... and then Jared... and now this." She pauses for a moment to breathe, like a diver coming up for air, trying desperately to slow the words that continue to flood forward. They become more and more tangled. "She texted me a few weeks ago, she wanted to fix things. And I thought... I thought if she came here, if she saw me with you guys, I thought... "

Mallory thought that it would somehow prove that she could be a good friend, that her momentary lapse in judgment was just that, and Erika would realize that they could make it work again. Erika may have insisted on coming with her to meet the members of the Discord, but it was only because Mallory set the bait for her as if she was laying a bear trap. She knew how protective Erika was of her, she knew that she would never let Mallory meet up with strangers from the internet alone. It was the only way Mallory could show Erika that what happened last Spring was nothing more than a blip, a temporary slip of her sanity.

Even though Erika insisted she was over it, Mallory could tell that she wasn't. Mallory clung to the foolish belief that they could fix things, they could get better. But now, there really is no fixing it. There's no fixing them, and there's no fixing Erika. She's gone.

"I don't understand half of what you just said," Rowan says, though there's no cruelty in his voice, only pity. "Come on, let's get you out of here."

"We can't leave her here."

"We don't know what else Peyton has in store for us. We can't drag a body along for the ride."

"I can't leave her," Mallory insists, and Rowan grabs her under the armpits, hoisting her up.

"There is no her anymore." While his tone is gentle, there's no comfort in it.

She allows him to guide her back to the ladder, out of the pool. She fights the urge to look back down at where the body lays.

Rowan brings Mallory as far from the pool as possible, so when she finally does look back, she can't see down to where Erika's body lays and she can almost pretend that she isn't really gone.

Britt's expression remains blank, but there's a spark of something—fear, excitement?— behind her eyes that unnerves Mallory.

Olivia is a wreck, her eyes red and puffy. "Peyton's going to kill us all. She's really gonna do it. She's really gonna kill us."

Rowan lights another cigarette and lazy trails of smoke drift up from between his fingers. The locked door at the far edge of the water park swings open as Rowan expels a particularly large cloud of smoke, but no one moves.

The intercom system clicks on again, the telltale static sending a jolt down Mallory's spine. "Hello again darlings, congratulations on completing the first round of our game. As you can see, you can now move further into the resort. I have tons of other fun games waiting for you, but don't take too long: the door won't stay open forever."

No mention of Erika. Mallory's cheeks flush at the audacity of it. Peyton kills her and then pays about as much attention to the act as she would if she killed a fly. Who knows if Peyton could even see what had happened in the water park and only assumed that her game was complete. Numbly, Mallory files this information away. Even in her grief, she realizes that she may need it if she has any hope of surviving what's to come.

"What are we waiting for?" Rowan rolls the cigarette between his fingers. "Let's get going."

"No way," Britt says, peeking over the sleeves of her hoodie. She inhales deeply and shakes her head. "Mallory's friend just got murdered."

Mallory twitches at the word murder. Some of the shock is beginning to fade, but Erika's brutalized face slips into her archive of traumatic memories, nestled alongside the silver flask, and Jared's bloody nose. There isn't enough therapy in the world to undo all the damage.

But thinking of Jared, she's convinced that Peyton isn't just some sadistic freak. Even if she was catfishing them, there are some aspects of her personality that she couldn't have faked. She's meticulous, calculating. If she used Jared as the bait to get them here, there has to be a reason for it.

She turns to the group. "Why Jared?"

"Huh?" Rowan asks.

"Why would Peyton use Jared to get us all here?"

"Because she's a psychopath." He exhales another cloud of smoke.

"No, because he factors into this somehow." Mallory pauses for a moment before continuing. "Peyton was super picky about who she let into the Discord. I suggested a few people from the Reddit group I was part of, people who knew way more than I did and were way closer to him than I was... and she shot down every one of them. Why us? What's our connection to Jared?"

"He was my friend," Britt says, finally letting her hands fall to her sides. "We weren't close or anything, but we would hang out and drink sometimes."

"I saw him last year at the festival." Mallory chooses her words carefully. "He got a bloody nose in a mosh pit, and I helped him away from the stage."

They both turn to Rowan, who is busy sucking his cigarette down to the filter.

"What?" he asks, his eyebrow twitching.

"What's your connection to Jared?"

He glances over at Olivia. "What do you want me to say? It's completely up to you."

"Why would it be up to me?" she says, looking down at her feet. "It's *your* relationship."

Rowan sighs and runs a hand over the top of his mohawk. "He was my ex, okay? My psycho ex that I'm writing the memoir about."

"You're gay?" Mallory asks, her heart sinking. She isn't surprised. He always used they/them pronouns for his ex, and she never bothered to clarify their gender. She had always hoped they were a girl because of how she and Rowan used to flirt, but it's not entirely unexpected.

Still, her insides twist. She thought he was into her, at least at some point. And while she knows sexuality is a spectrum and it can take a while to sort things out, this just goes to show how Rowan really is a stranger. She doesn't know him at all, even after all these years. It stings worse than it should.

"Are you bisexual?" She asks when he fails to respond.

"No... I mean, it's complicated."

"You like guys though?" She asks and he shrugs, which only works to confuse her more. "Jared is your ex?"

"Sure, whatever. Does any of this even matter? We need to get going before Peyton locks that door on us."

Olivia has sunk down to the floor, curled her knees up under her chin, looking more like a broken doll than a person.

"Come on, Liv," Rowan says, crouching down next to her. "We need to keep going."

She stares at him through tears. "I didn't make it this far to die like this."

There's something heavy, something implied between the

words that touches Mallory. A darkness she's been nursing for almost a year now slithers forward, and curls up behind her eye socket, coiled, ready to sink its fangs in. Olivia's faced death before, she realizes. She's stared it down and won, same as Mallory, but now—

Office chair.

Silver flask.

Blood splatter.

—it's catching up to them.

Now—

Star tattoo.

Silver flask.

Red. Red. Red.

—Mallory rakes her fingers along the backs of her arms, the motion as soothing as it is destructive.

There's a pang in her chest when she realizes Erika would be disappointed in her. Erika hates—*hated*, Mallory corrects wearily—when she would pick at her skin. She stopped completely after college, but last year's HyveFest reignited the sick spark and it's not like Erika was there to help her through it. Even though that was completely her fault... She wasn't exactly there for Erika when she needed her either. At least she can be there for Erika now though, there to mourn, there to remember. Vaguely, she wonders if Kimber will bother to be sad at all or if she'll just latch onto the next girl who crosses her path.

Rowan sighs deeply. "You're not going to die, Liv."

She stares vacantly ahead. "I'm already dead... We're all already dead." Then, in a voice that's barely above a murmur, "You we're right, this is too much for me. It's happening again. I'm slipping..."

Her voice is hoarse, and Mallory feels dirty listening in, like a voyeur watching someone get undressed in front of their window.

This is obviously a conversation Olivia and Rowan have had dozens of times before, and one that Mallory is hauntingly familiar with herself. It's happening again... The weight of those words, the hollowness of Olivia's voice. It reminds her of nights she spent seated on her bedroom floor, picking at the carpet, the walls, her arms, tears streaming down her cheeks for no damn reason. How sharp the cries from her phone sounded—pings from concerned friends. How she didn't have the energy to check the messages. Her phone was too heavy, arms too heavy, head too heavy. Everything too heavy.

Rowan straightens up, his mouth set in a tight line.

Mallory averts her gaze, ashamed to be caught eavesdropping, but Rowan clears his throat, and she glances back at him.

"This has gone too far," he says. He repeats it a little louder, so he catches Britt's attention too. She and Mallory huddle together while Rowan helps his sister to her feet. "We're all going to be okay. She only wanted to scare you guys."

"What do you mean?" Mallory asks slowly.

"Peyton. She pulled your friend off the platform before it fell. This whole thing is a practical joke. A sick joke, yeah. But a joke. She wanted to make you feel what Jared felt before he died. She was disgusted with you—with us—for being so into this... into his death, I mean. I think she was a friend of his or something. She told me that she wanted to fuck with your heads, and I agreed to go along with it, to make sure that we wound up in here because..."

"Because even though he was an abusive sociopath, he was still your boyfriend at one point," Britt finishes for him. He seems to consider it for a moment before nodding in agreement.

"No," Mallory says because it doesn't sit right with her. Peyton has a dark streak, sure, but why go this far for a prank? Why leave them real blades if it was all fake... why build all of this? "You saw Erika's face."

"Peyton is really good at special effects makeup. She told me it would look real."

"No," Mallory repeats. "It's Erika... her clothes, her nails, her hair. How could Peyton replicate that, how would she know what Erika was going to wear today? Think about it for just a minute, it doesn't make any sense. I'm telling you, Peyton really killed her."

"And I'm telling you that it's a prank," Rowan insists, then looks over at Olivia.

Olivia blinks rapidly as if she can't understand.

"It's all fake, Liv. I'm sorry, okay? I wouldn't have gone along with this if I knew you were going to freak out this badly."

A pit opens in Mallory's stomach. She doesn't believe for a minute that it's fake: she knows that Erika is gone, and she feels like she's never going to stop feeling sick. She can't stop thinking about Erika's smashed in face. Erika's twisted limbs. Images that strobe along with *office chair, silver flask, blood splatter* and not even the drag of nails along her skin is enough to chase them away this time. "Really? You didn't think that seeing someone's face get smashed in like a pumpkin was going to freak any of us out?"

"Well, it was supposed to freak you out, that's the point. But I didn't know Liv would have a full-on mental breakdown."

"Then you and Jared really were a match made in heaven because only a psychopath would be that clueless." There's more acid in her voice than Mallory intends, but she can't help it. She's boiling over. Pain, and fear, and anger fly like foam from her mouth and she imagines a dog with rabies would feel the same way. Confused and consumed with white-hot rage.

Britt suddenly books it to the edge of the pool and descends the ladder before anyone gets a chance to ask her what she's doing. There's a brief pause, then Mallory follows her to the pool's edge. The twins come up behind her and they look down to find Britt crouched next to Erika, two fingers pressed to her wrist. Mallory gags again and needs to twist away. Even with her face covered, the sight of Erika's twisted body is horrific.

"It's real," Britt says.

"You're a crime scene cleaner, not a coroner," Rowan hisses.

"You're a crime scene cleaner?" Mallory asks, goosebumps breaking out over the backs of her arms. "You never told me that."

"You never asked," Britt says in her signature monotone. "But yeah, I'm a crime scene cleaner. Sometimes I do hoarder houses too."

"But you're not a coroner," Rowan repeats.

"I know what a dead body feels like."

"How the hell would you know that?"

Mallory glances over the edge of the pool to find Britt taking another deep inhale of her sleeves before she stares up at Rowan, eyes burning into his. "I just do, okay? And this is real. If you don't believe it, why don't you get over here and stick your hand down its throat? Would that be enough to convince you, or should we slice it down the middle right here and see how real all the organs inside are? I bet they're still warm."

Mallory grimaces against the crass suggestion. She can't help but picture Erika's mouth unhinging like a snake as Rowan fists her mouth. It's enough to make her gag for a third time and she chokes against the sour burn rising in her throat.

Rowan seems to hesitate for a moment and Mallory is terrified that he'll take Britt up on her dare. Her body tenses, ready to defend Erika's corpse. Mallory looks at Rowan, pleading silently with him to please see this for what it is, to sense the danger as it thickens around them. Olivia steps up next to Mallory and weaves her fingers through hers, but she pulls away. It's the kind of intimacy that she has difficulty with when it comes to strangers and with Erika gone, she's more alone than ever. Her head aches from crying, and a tightness wraps around the front of her skull.

She looks to Rowan, but he won't meet her gaze. He's already stepping back from the pool, ushering them away from the wreckage that used to be Mallory's best friend.

"One more room," he says. "We continue through one more of Peyton's obstacles, then she'll let us out of here and you'll see that it's all a fucked-up prank."

Down next to Erika, Britt gropes around the bottom of the pool, her fingers knotting through thick clumps of blood. Even in the vast expanse of the indoor water park, the metallic tinge to the air is sickening. It brings Mallory back to the previous summer—how stale the air was inside the arcade, swirling with sawdust, the bulk of the gaming machines covered by heavy white sheets. She knows this smell. She knows this feeling. She only wishes that she didn't.

"What are you doing?" she calls down to Britt, who continues to sift through the gore, her forehead knotted in determination.

"Do you see the scalpel anywhere?" Britt asks, which causes a queasy flip in Mallory's stomach.

She can't bring herself to take her eyes off Erika. Britt has managed to flip her on her stomach, her strawberry blonde hair falling over her like a tarp, her arms and legs splayed like a starfish. Rowan's jacket lays off to the side, and Mallory's thankful that the red pulp of her face isn't visible, but it still brings tears to the corners of her eyes.

"Mallory, do you see the scalpel?" Britt asks again and Mallory shakes her head.

"Oh weird," Britt says, crossing the length of the pool, and Mallory watches her in confusion before her gaze finally settles on the glimmer of the blade, on the opposite end, wedged in the far corner. "I wouldn't have thought it would have fallen so far."

She picks it up and slips it into the front pocket of her hoodie.

"You went back in there so you could rob her body?" Mallory asks, disgusted.

Britt climbs back out of the pool, the sharp tip of the scalpel winking from where it peeks out of her pocket. "It's not like she needs it anymore, and something tells me we will."

The unspoken implication hangs between like a blade over a chopping block. Without Erika, Mallory is trapped inside the resort with a collection of strangers.

Rowan has a sister and a nephew. Britt is a crime scene cleaner. Mallory swallows back a lump in her throat. She really doesn't know them at all, and she sure as hell doesn't know what they're capable of.

6

ROWAN

Rowan's wife doesn't know that he blew off his bartending gig to come to the resort today. If she did, she'd be pissed. Not because he's missing out on making money—he makes more than enough freelancing, to the point where the bartending cash is gravy—but because he hasn't exactly been honest about the extent of his conversations with Peyton. And Kate, his wife, is known for being spiteful. Not that he minds. If anything, he respects it. They're both spiteful people; it's what brought them together to begin with.

Spite has been his constant companion for as long as he can remember.

It's what forced him to graduate college on time when his senior advisor told him that it would take another year *minimum* to meet his credit requirement. He finished with three more credits than he needed and even tacked on a minor in English Literature—all because of spite.

It's what kept him going when he first started freelancing, when his credit cards were maxed out and he was lucky if he could land one writing job a month, all while it seemed like every other writer he knew was bragging about their book deals and speaking gigs. Now he makes a steady six figures while they scramble for their next advance. All thanks to spite.

Spite is what made him the first homeowner in his family. It's what got him his dream car and what takes him and Kate on vacation to the Caribbean every year. Any time someone tells Rowan that he can't, he tells them to go fuck themselves.

He's always been rough around the edges and spiked in the center. The way he sees it, that's the best way to survive. Stab everyone else in the back before they get the chance to stab you.

Peyton is the only one who's ever seemed to agree with him. How the hell she found him is a mystery, but he's glad she did. He finally had someone he could talk to.

"No one understands, do they?" Peyton asked him after he came clean about the whole thing. Jared, and Instagram, and everything leading up to HyveFest last year. There were things about that night that he swore he'd never tell anyone, not even on his deathbed. But there's something about Peyton that's so disarming, and he knew that she wouldn't judge him. By the time he had finished, his throat dry and scratchy from the effort, there was a long bout of silence before she simply said, "Sounds like you did the right thing." And he knew he could tell her anything.

I'll be honest with you, she messaged him a few weeks later. *I didn't pick the Discord group at random. I've had my eye on everyone for a while. I think they had something to do with Jared's death and what you told me pretty much confirmed it. I have a plan to get back at them, but I need your help to make sure that they go where I need them to. Will you help me?*

He didn't even need to think before responding.

Obviously. And, after a moment of contemplation. *Including Liv, right?*

Obviously. She's a part of this as much as they are.

Spite had his lip curling. Spite had him readily agreeing to offer his sister up on a silver platter.

Make it good, he told Peyton. *Whatever you have planned, make sure it wrecks her.*

Harsh words, but in the moment, he meant them.

Not that he doesn't love Liv, of course he does, but it's more obligation than anything else. He's thought about it a hundred times over, and he doubts they'd be so much as acquaintances if they weren't related. Ever since he was little it's been his job to watch over Liv, make sure she's okay even though they're the same fucking age. She's volatile. He may be a raging volcano but she's a dormant one. And in his opinion, that's far more dangerous. She's like the behemoth beneath Yellowstone, poised to reshape continents when things blow. She bottles everything up, lets it thrash around inside her until she reaches her breaking point, and no one in her life can even tell until it's too late.

Except Rowan.

He's the only one who's ever been able to get an accurate read on his sister and gauge her moods. He feels her pain like a phantom limb.

So it's his job to be there. It's his job to watch for the warning signs, however scarce, however well concealed they may be.

He was there in elementary school when a group of girls stuck gum in her hair. He was there in middle school when one of the popular boys sent her a love note as a joke. He was there every time, bloodying his knuckles so that Liv wouldn't destroy herself. Now that they're adults, the stakes are higher, and Liv's lows are damn near rock bottom. It's constant stress. On him and his family.

He's always been a spiteful prick. But not toward Liv, never toward Liv. He's always been so understanding, and accommodating, and goddamn *good* to her. And for what? What's his reward for saving her, for *always* saving her? Razor blades, and inpatient programs, and always needing to be there to fix her world when it falls apart. Again and again in an endless cycle. It built up inside of him over the years until *he* felt like that monster of a volcano under Yellowstone, until *he* was ready to blow and destroy himself along with everything around him.

This was supposed to make him feel better.

This was supposed to make up for all the unreciprocated, twisted love he poured into his ungrateful sister.

But if Rowan had stopped to consider the razor blades, and the inpatient programs, and the pills... if he had accounted for the look in Liv's eyes and the heavy feeling in his own chest, a warped mirror of his sister's suffering...

Maybe, just maybe if he thought about it for even a fraction of a second instead of reacting, instead of letting the volcano beneath his skin win, he would have realized what a shitty idea it was to do this to her.

Seeing her panic snapped it back into place for him with frightening clarity. He was torturing his sister. And by hurting her, he hurt himself.

But he was in too deep now, and he'd be lying to himself if he didn't admit that he had a hell of a time planning the whole thing.

When Peyton first told him about her idea for the prank, he was sure it would be too obvious. Plus, there's no way some influencer could pull off something that required so much engineering. But Peyton assured him that it would go off without a hitch.

I'm gonna seal you guys in there, she told him one night when he was still on the fence, because it really did sound insane.

No fucking way you'll be able to do that.

It's easy. If I rig a gear system and have one of my friends help with construction. I can have barriers outfitted to drop with the push of a button. I'm smart, Rowan, don't underestimate me.

How are you even going to get in there? he asked. She sounded confident, throwing out facts and figures that he couldn't make heads or tails of. She made it seem like she knew her shit, but he still had his doubts. *Isn't the whole place crawling with security after what happened to Jared last year?*

Don't worry about security, Peyton responded immediately. *I've been building this thing for months now. I haven't had any issues.*

How??

I have my ways. ;)

Seems like a lot of effort for a prank.

Wouldn't it be worth it though?

It would.

At that moment, he didn't have many questions. Like how Peyton was going to make the body look real or what she would do if her door system failed to shut. Who was going to help her with the construction of all this shit, and what would she do if things went too far? If someone got hurt?

When they first entered the resort, he regretted not asking more questions. But clearly, it's working. Clearly, he was wrong to underestimate Peyton.

Even though he's told Liv the truth, fear continues to roll off her in waves, making him feel sick to his stomach. He doesn't believe in all that twin psychic connection bullshit, but he can't deny that there's always been some sort of tether between him and his sister. When she broke her arm in the second grade, he had phantom pains up his own for weeks. He sighs. It's so tiring trying to sift through her emotions and his, so exhausting to decide whose pain is who's—like a giant jigsaw puzzle that makes no goddamn sense.

He loves his sister, but as she leans against his shoulder while they navigate to the next section of Peyton's maze, all he can think about is the nausea that roils his stomach and whether it's actually a product of *her* discomfort.

But he's still there for her when she needs it, as fucked as it is. Lying about being in a relationship with Jared, for instance, was more for Liv's benefit than his. He could have covered up the fact that he's married in a million different ways, but he was willing to take one for the team and say he was with the bastard. If that's not devotion, he doesn't know what is. He'd do anything for his sister.

They pass through a narrow hall to a refreshment station dotted with half-finished bars and concession stands. The area is decorated in a jungle theme, fake plants in pots the size of small children crowding every corner of the room. Polka dots and stripes and triangle patterns in yellow and pink and cotton candy blue parade down the walls. This place would have been a trip if it opened. Expensive as hell, he's sure. Something he would have to save up to take Gabriel to, even with his recent career success.

The windows have been boarded up, the only light coming from neon standing lamps in the shapes of flamingos and palm trees—not exactly fitting with the jungle theme.

They approach the concession stands and another of Peyton's telltale neon signs sits in front of the bar area.

Pick one, it declares in flickering pink.

Across the unfinished, wooden surface of the bar sit three dark, plywood boxes, with velvet fabric flaps in the front. They're roughly large enough to fit a hand, like something a magician would whip out at a kid's birthday party. Rowan smirks. They look exactly the way Peyton told him they would. He stomps up to the boxes and turns to the group, the three of them clustered together like a colony of ants.

"We shouldn't go along with this," Liv says, trying to press up closer to Mallory, who inches back, clearly wanting nothing to do with her. "We should be looking for a way out."

"It's a prank!" Rowan screams, his frustration finally boiling over. "For fuck's sake." He takes a deep breath, pinching the bridge of his nose and willing himself to calm down. "This is all bullshit. I already told you that Peyton talked to me about it beforehand, and it was only meant to scare you guys."

Mallory stands off to the side looking like she's about to spill her guts. "But Erika... " she murmurs, her eyes puffy and red. At least she's stopped crying. He hates it when people cry.

"I know that looked real, but Peyton told me it would," he says with a shrug, doing his best to look nonchalant even though his insides feel coiled.

"Just like she told us that she was an influencer?" Mallory asks. "She already admitted to catfishing us. We have no idea what she actually looks like or if she's even named Peyton. What makes you think any of what she told you is real?"

He hates how Mallory keeps tearing holes in what little information he has about this chick.

"She does special effects makeup," he says through gritted teeth, pushing down the pinprick of doubt. He won't allow himself to soak up everyone else's energy. It's clotting up the air like glue and he breathes through his nose, settling his pulse. "She planned this to scare you guys because she's pissed about Jared, but it's all fake."

"What about Erika?" Mallory asks again. "You heard what it sounded like when her body hit the bottom of the pool, you can't pretend that you didn't hear it."

The doubt drills in again, and he pauses for a moment, running through a mental list of all the messages Peyton sent him. "Erika is probably waiting for us with Peyton over by the exit right now. Let's get through this and get out of here."

"Why tell us it's fake in the first place?"

"Because I couldn't take you bitching and moaning about it, going on and on about how we were all gonna die, okay?"

Because Liv was shattering again. That's what he calls the moments when his sister loses herself, when her eyes dull and she goes somewhere else, burrows back into the mess of gray matter inside her skull. She's always been prone to it—shattering—but it's gotten so much worse since everything with Jared. Not that he blames her, he'd be a piece of shit to blame her for that, but he would have handled it differently if it had been him.

He's never understood how they could only be separated by three minutes and be so different. The way he sees it, those three minutes are an ocean's length, they're everything.

Rowan doesn't understand, will never understand. He struggles to be patient in his own way, gritting his teeth and asking the right questions, saying the right words, but it gets so repetitive and there's no talking Liv out of it when she's in one of her moods. One thing fractures into another, a whole web of cracks until there's no telling where it started, and it takes all his effort to keep her together. No matter how hard he tries, he can't feel what she feels, only ripples of it—shades of discomfort—and it makes him so mad he could bash a wall in, or smash a window, or crash a car.

Kate hates how much time goes into it. All the late night calls. All the times Liv has shown up on their porch crying her eyes out or lacking emotion entirely. Those moments are the worst, when she's completely numb, when she's like a ghost.

His pulse quickens at the thought of Kate. She's probably home on the couch reading one of her romance books or watching some trashy reality TV show. He knows it isn't exactly cheating to be here without her, far from it considering the circumstances, but he still can't help but feel guilty. Especially given the way that Mallory keeps looking at him.

He hasn't told Mallory about Kate yet, and he's still hoping he won't need to. It's not like he's planning to ever see any of these people again after this. And he knows that he can't be held responsible for whatever the hell Mallory thinks is going on between them.

Which is nothing.

He's been in love with Kate since they were in high school, and at first it was because she was the only one to push back against him when it came to his bullshit. Liv was always pointing out that it's not a woman's job to fix a man and that Kate deserved more. She had an air of power about her, a hint of elegance, a gritty, take no shit attitude that he couldn't get enough of.

They were on and off for a while. Because of his temper. Because deep down he thinks she knows that she really does deserve better than him. But they finally put all that to bed three years ago and decided to stick together for good. And he would work on his temper, of course he would work on his temper. It would all be close to perfect if it wasn't for Liv.

"She's a nightmare," Kate has lamented to him more than once as they cleaned the kitchen after dinner, or lay in bed watching TV, or tried to enjoy the rare couple's weekend.

"She's my sister, my twin sister."

"What does that mean, Ro? That you're going to kill yourself trying to keep her from killing herself? She's a grown woman, and if she needs help, she can find it. It's not your responsibility to fix her."

He swallowed a laugh because that's exactly what Liv said about him and Kate—it's not her responsibility to fix him—and Rowan wondered if maybe it was the curse of their family to be so fucked up and in need of fixing, so absorbed in their own bullshit, that they can't recognize when someone else is pulling the same shit on them. His temper. Liv's sadness.

Rowan shakes his head, pulling himself from his thoughts and back into the present.

He moves to push his hand inside the box on the far side of the bar, but Olivia catches him by the wrist. He didn't even realize she had left the others to come up next to him. She's like wallpaper: she blends. She's so easy to lose track of.

He jerks his hand away.

"It's like a haunted house," he explains, as if to a child. "There are probably grapes and spaghetti and stuff inside. Nothing to freak out about."

"What if you're wrong?"

"I'm not." He shoves his hand inside the box and sure enough, his fingers squish into a bed of what are clearly peeled grapes, a smug sense of victory pangs through his chest. But just for effect, just to fuck with them all, he twists his face into a grimace and Liv raises her hands to her mouth. A little hiss escapes from her lips, something between a sigh and a scream. Mallory twists away and Britt stands by with her blank, Ted Bundy stare.

Satisfied with their reactions, he plucks a grape from the pile and pulls his hand out. Olivia frowns as soon as she sees it, and Britt looks unimpressed, but Mallory is still twisted around, shaking.

"Mallory," he says, a singsong lilt to his voice. "Look at me."

"I told you," She whimpers, digging her fingers into the flesh of her upper arm. "I told you that it was real, and you wouldn't listen."

"Mallory, look at me!"

She whips her head around to find him holding the grape up between his two fingers, and the look on her face is even more priceless than when he pushed her in front of the memorial.

He plops the grape into his mouth with a wink and bites down, savoring the juice. "See? It was a fucking *grape.* There's nothing to worry about."

Mallory scowls.

"That wasn't funny." She wraps an arm around Liv's shoulder and Rowan can't help but smirk at the look on her face—caught between bliss and fear, uncertain of what to do with the proximity. "Olivia looked like she was going to throw up, she was really worried about you. We all were."

The look of surprise on his sister's face is priceless. It's like she doesn't know how to handle having Mallory so close.

Britt stands off to the side, her expression steely. "You made your point, Rowan. Now let's forget about the boxes and leave."

"No can do." He positions his hand in front of the next box. Peyton told him that he would have to play along with the boxes, that the only way out of the exit at the far end of the concession area is the key that lays at the bottom of box number three. And it was very important that he went in order, from left to right. One, two, three.

What's the point? he had asked Peyton one night. Kate was pissed at him for texting at the dinner table, and he made the mistake of telling her that it was Liv, which only worked to solidify her anger.

"Tell her that we're eating," she said tartly, stabbing her knife into the slab of meat that sat squarely in the center of her plate.

"You have your phone out," he said, pointing his fork at where it lay on the table next to her. "You've been texting on and off the whole time, same as me. Why is it so different when I do it?"

"Because my attention is still on you," she shot back. "*I* don't have my nose pressed to the screen. *I'm* still trying to make conversation. *I* can multi-task."

He knew that she wanted to take the opportunity to bond, have a romantic dinner like they used to before real life sunk its claws into them, but he was so amped up about the possibility of the prank, of getting everything right, that it was impossible to concentrate on the meal.

Does there need to be a point? Peyton responded as Kate glared daggers at him. *It'll be fun to watch them squirm for a little bit longer, isn't that reason enough to play along for as long as possible?*

He had laughed at that. Out loud. Which pissed Kate off even more.

"I'm guessing it's not one of her infamous breakdowns then?" she asked with her eyebrow cocked and Rowan sighed, slipping the phone into his pocket. He did his best to concentrate on his steak, his wife, the half empty glass of wine in front of him. He worked hard for the rest of that dinner to be a good person, the person who Kate thought she married. But all he could think about was the prank and how he would really have to commit to get through it, to play it off correctly.

Except he fessed up to it being a prank before the big reveal and drawing it out now isn't funny, it's painful. Not that it was funny before. The sound Erika's "body" made when it hit the concrete is something he'll never be able to wash from his mind—even if it was fake. He looks out at the group, specifically his sister. Her eyes are bloodshot from crying, her mascara smeared down her cheeks. There's a pang in his chest and he chews at the inside of his cheek. He's not sure if this is what he wanted when he signed on to help Peyton, but he's too deep into it now. He smirks at the girls.

"The only way out is through," he says, hand poised against the lip of the flap. "A servant to servants."

They blink at him.

"What, none of you fuckers have ever read Robert Frost?"

"Is he the 'path less traveled' guy?" Britt asks with the slightest twitch of her lip.

"Exactly! *Two roads diverged in a wood, and I took the one less traveled by, and that has made all the difference.*" With that, he stuffs his hand into the second box and immediately recognizes that something is very wrong. The fit is too snug, too sharp, and he's caught at the wrist. At first, he chalks it up to nerves, to Mallory's constant questions and the pinprick of doubt that she planted... but as he tries to press deeper into the box, his stomach sinks.

He thinks about how realistic Erika's pulp of a face looked, the noise her body made when it hit the floor. Everything Mallory pointed out to him. The clothes, the nails, the hair. The sound it made; he can't get past that sound. He ran over a squirrel with his truck once, and the horrible crunch, the snapping of bone was so similar, and the fit is so snug and sharp around his wrist. He might actually be in trouble.

His fingers graze along the bottom of the box. At first, there's nothing. Then, his chest seizes as his fingers wrap around a small metal key. But Peyton said that the key would be in the third box, and for a frantic, nonsensical moment, without even thinking about it, he shoves his free hand into the third. Maybe Peyton just put them out in the wrong order. His stomach sinks as he realizes that the fit isn't the same—the tightness, the sharpness around his wrist in the second box is missing in the third. His fingers explore the bottom of the third box, and he finds a folded scrap of paper. He pulls it out immediately, his left hand still stuffed uselessly into the second box.

"Rowan?" Olivia asks, a slight tremble to her voice. "What's going on?"

He doesn't answer, he can barely think with all the sticky heat pooling in his forehead. He unfolds the piece of paper and finds the same red scrawl that was waiting on the note outside the loading docks. It's a single word—*Surprise!*—with a winky face scribbled beneath it.

It's another joke. Peyton is getting one over on him along with the others, she's pranking all of them. He tugs at his wrist again, and grimaces at the sharp pain. It's like a fucking blade. It certainly doesn't feel like a prank. He inches his free hand around the outside of the box. There's got to be a trapdoor, a spring, something that will free his hand, but the sides are smooth.

He attempts to rotate his hand but the metal digs in and he flinches against the sting. It's like the blade of a saw, jagged teeth clamping down on him. Each small, gentle movement he makes causes the blade to bite in deeper. His flesh catches on the metal again and again, wetness blooming around his wrist.

Blood. He's bleeding.

A trickle of sweat drips down the side of his face.

He twists toward the others, his eyes wide.

"Something's wrong," he says, letting the scrap of paper drift to the floor. Olivia stoops to pick it up, her brow furrowing as she reads Peyton's message.

"Come on," Mallory huffs. "We're not falling for that again."

"I'm not fucking around. I'm really stuck this time." His mouth feels like it's stuffed with cotton. His fingers continue to grope along the bottom of the box, and he finds the key again. It's stuck to the bottom of the box, and he tugs at it, feeling something give when he pulls it free. As he lifts it from the bottom of the box, the intercom system rattles to life and a stream of laughter pours out.

With the key pressed tightly in his palm, Rowan tries one more time to pull his wrist from the box, wincing as the blade opens him wider. The wetness surrounding the skin spreads and not being able to see the damage makes it worse somehow. He imagines all that salt and plasma and *him* leaking out in a stream. The more he shifts against the blade, the more he discovers about the device. And the more he discovers, the sicker he feels.

The blade is only circling the top of his wrist, fitting around it like half of a handcuff. The bottom is made of rough, unfinished wood and it splinters off into his flesh as he tugs against it. He's going to get a fucking infection if he somehow manages to escape this. He's fucked.

Peyton's laughter tapers off and there's a pause, a crackle of static before her voice marches in over the intercom again. "Have you guys ever heard of degloving?"

Rowan's blood turns to ice. He gives his hand another tentative tug, and he swears he hears a rip as the blade rips his flesh apart.

"My first introduction to degloving was a Stephen King novel," Peyton continues. "The one with the woman handcuffed to the bed. It was okay. I wasn't super into it. But it gave me an idea. Did you know that flaying, which is basically degloving but for the whole body, has been a form of torture since medieval times? I thought it would be a neat thing to incorporate into the game. By the way, Rowan, I didn't lie to you. Not completely. That key you're probably holding onto right now really is the way out of here. The only problem is you need to get it out of the box first, and there's only one way to do that."

Liv rushes to his side and he flinches as her hand comes down on his shoulder, a numbness spreading through his entire body. It's real. It's not a prank.

Which means that Erika is dead.

The blade surrounding his hand is real.

And there's only one way out.

Through.

7

MALLORY

When Mallory and Erika were kids there was a stretch of abandoned train tracks that ran through the woods behind their houses. Erika was obsessed with them. She would wander up and down the tracks for hours, loosening railroad spikes and collecting snail shells. Two girls were murdered back there in the eighties, which made Mallory uneasy, but for Erika it was the basis of their appeal.

"Are you sure we should be back here?" Mallory asked once when they were still in high school. She stood along the edge of the tracks, arms wrapped tightly around her middle. Maple trees loomed over either side of her, their leaves a bright, burning green against a flat gray sky.

Erika crouched in the center of the tracks, poking at a fat black spider with the sharp end of a stick until it flipped over onto its back, legs flailing.

"I really fucking hate spiders," she said wistfully as she continued to prod at it.

"Erika, please. This place is dangerous," Mallory said, doing her best not to sound whiny. The only thing Erika hated more than spiders was when Mallory whined.

But Erika was completely focused on her task, head cocked to the side, pink streaked hair falling in a curtain across her face.

"Erika?" Mallory tried again as the wind picked up its pace, the top of the trees flickering like lit matchsticks. "People were murdered back here."

"Yeah, forever ago. Plus, lightning doesn't strike the same place twice," she said, jabbing the stick deeper into the spider's abdomen and Mallory cringed against the squish as its insides tumbled out. "There's already been a double murder, so it's not like more people are going to die. It's the safest place we could possibly be."

Thinking back on it, Mallory supposes that Erika has always been superstitious in her own way. It wasn't always crystals and astrology, but she had a habit of clinging to ideas that most people would label irrational or bizarre.

Now, with Erika gone and Rowan's hand stuck in the box, Mallory retreats to the places in her mind that are familiar, safe. She's sixteen and the sun drips low over the train tracks as Erika balances on the rails. She's seventeen, wandering through the stacks of books at her local library while Erika laughs a little too loudly, earning them a stern look from the librarian. She's eighteen and holding Erika's hair back while she pukes freshman year after taking too many shots at their first house party. All the memories seem so much more precious now than they did before Erika's fall. She'd give anything to be there and not here, there and not here, there and not here.

"What the fuck are you waiting for?" Rowan yelps, pulling her out of the past. "Smash it open or something."

They had checked the red phone for instructions, but unlike the water park trap, there were only six words: *remove your hand from the box.*

Mallory watches as Olivia grips it around its edges, digging her nails into whatever crevices she can find, trying without success to pry it apart.

"We can't smash it open," Rowan's twin says. "It might force the blade in and we're trying to make it so you *don't* lose a hand." She leans in and lowers her voice, but Mallory can still make out the words as she whispers, "I told you not to test your luck."

Rowan glowers before muttering something back to Olivia that makes her eyes widen. She blinks quickly and two perfect tears trace trails down her cheeks. In her old-fashioned dress, her curls still perfectly in place, she could be an actress in a black and white movie.

Britt is the only one not visibly upset. Her expression is unnervingly blank as she moves behind the bar and squats down, rifling through the shelves. Olivia dips in closer to Rowan as the two share more whispered words, and Mallory goes around the bar to where Britt crouches. She knows she shouldn't feel slighted. She knows that Olivia is his sister, but there's a bone-deep ache when she sees him turning to someone else in his time of need. First Britt, now Olivia, anyone but her—why is it never her? Especially when they were supposed to be the closest of anyone in the group.

She deflates, retreats back into her mind—trying to get lost in her daydreams, finding nightmares instead. No comfort, only the dull pain of a knife in her side.

Mallory's brain clicks through images of Jared's hand and his black star tattoo. Only this time she pictures the skin peeled back like a blanket pulled from a bed, the red mattress of his muscles underneath, the tattoo puckering as the skin is stripped away. She wonders what's left of Jared now, whether he was eaten by wild dogs or if his bones were picked clean by flies. She wonders if whatever happened to him was terrible enough, whether it was everything he deserved and more.

She waits for Britt to acknowledge her, to pull her in on

whatever she's trying to accomplish, but she doesn't so much as look up.

"So, is there anything left in any of the bottles? I think we could all use a drink right now." The words get jammed up in Mallory's throat. They taste gummy and wrong, and it's all she can do not to dissolve back into her head, to the swirl of Jared being picked clean to the bone.

"My head hurts like a bitch," Britt says, continuing to sift through broken glass and half standing bottles. "That sludge Rowan gave us out by the memorial is fucking me up."

"Oh, is there anything I can do?"

Britt doesn't answer and Mallory realizes that she was talking to herself. She inches closer, peering back at where Rowan and Olivia are locked in heated conversation.

"Damn it, Liv!" The sharpness of Rowan's voice causes both Britt and Mallory to turn and find Olivia in the throes of a full meltdown, her limbs shaking, her eyes bloodshot. If she looked like the star of an old timey movie before, she's part of a low budget horror film now. Her mascara streaks down her face and she mutters something that causes Rowan to throw his free hand up in annoyance.

"Are they okay?" Mallory asks. "Do you think we should go over there or give them space? Britt, did you hear me?" She leans down next to her and claps her hands in front of her face.

Finally, Britt looks up from what she's doing, though her eyes remain focused on an area to the left of Mallory's head. "What?"

"Do you think we should go over to the twins or give them space?"

"I think Rowan is about to lose a hand unless we find something to help us open that box."

Mallory wrinkles her nose at Britt's bluntness, but she knows she shouldn't be surprised. In a way, she's thankful for it. The slideshow in her mind keeps clicking through images of

Jared and she digs her fingers into the flesh of her upper arm, refusing to allow herself slip back into the woods, the shelves, the simpler, safer places. Sun on the train tracks. Erika, still alive. She's afraid that if she lets herself linger in the memories for too long, she'll never find her way out again.

"Do you really think there's anything we can use back here?" Mallory asks, fingers still hooked into her arm. One of the scabs she's been trying desperately not to pick has flaked off and the wound is bleeding fresh. A bubble of red swells and then smears when she hides it beneath her palm.

Britt shrugs. "Doesn't hurt to look."

"How can you be so calm about this?"

Britt looks up at her, her expression blank. "It's not my hand in the box."

Mallory takes a step back, a pit forming in her stomach. She can't imagine not having empathy. Even now, just thinking about Rowan's hand in the box sends ripples of unease through her body. It takes her back to the moments before Erika hit the bottom of the pool, and she silently curses herself for not being lost to grief or as visibly upset as Olivia. The last funeral she went to, the last time someone she loved died was when she was still in high school.

She has no idea how to act in a situation like this. It's an ache chewing right through her, it's a gaping wound, and she never thought something as universal as grief could make her feel inadequate. What kind of a person doesn't know how to mourn? What kind of person's mourning looks so much like self-hatred that it takes all focus off the person who should be missed?

She's used to the self-aggrandizing loathing that comes with discontent in herself and her circumstances. She's used to staring out the window of her studio apartment and imagining burrowing into the grit between the bricks in the wall of the building next to hers. She's used to running circles around the labyrinth of her mind wondering if this is all there is and how much longer she'll need to do it—when everything in life is made up, and death is the only absolute, then who in their right mind can manage not fantasizing about driving off bridges? She's used to spiraling. That's the kind of grief she knows. That's her brand of selfishness, but nothing like this. Nothing like someone you love dying right in front of you and not knowing how to feel—or how to act, or what to say.

She pushes the thoughts to the back of her mind and resolves not to spiral, not now. She'll deal with it later—assuming she lives long enough.

Mallory supposes that the silver lining of there being more to this game is that if there are more traps, more trials waiting for them, not all of them will be deadly. Sure, this trap is bad, and it'll hurt if Rowan does need to pull his hand out, but it's survivable... assuming he doesn't die from shock or pass out from the pain. Or bleed out... She doesn't know the first thing about that kind of a wound... Could it actually be deadly if he doesn't get medical attention in time? She shudders.

Britt straightens up and shakes her head. "There's nothing usable here." She hops the bar while Mallory goes around the side and they both head back to Rowan and Olivia.

"Does degloving hurt?" Rowan asks, his shoulders slumped, and mouth drawn into a tight line. "Maybe I could yank it out quickly and it'll be okay?"

"How are you going to be okay without any skin on your hand?" Olivia's voice is barely above a whisper.

"Are there towels behind the bar?" he asks Britt, and she nods.

"There's a stack of washcloths."

"Okay." Rowan lets out a shaky breath, his eyes darting back and forth. "Okay, so you grab the towels, I'll pull my hand out, and we'll wrap it up as fast as possible and get the hell out of here to call an ambulance. We can even use alcohol from behind the bar to sterilize the wound!"

"The bottles were empty," Mallory says but Britt is already talking over her.

"Degloving shreds everything, including the nerves so it's excruciating. Bleeding out is a concern, but there's also a chance that you would go into shock. And if that happens, there's no way we would be able to get you out of here safely. You'd likely die."

Olivia digs her fingers into the corners of the box, grunting as she struggles with it. "Someone help me with this."

Mallory hesitates for a moment. The last thing she wants to do is inadvertently be responsible for Rowan losing a hand, but Olivia stares at her with wide, pleading eyes, and she eventually relents. She takes a place on the opposite side of Rowan, and claws at the box. The plywood splinters beneath her fingers, and she flinches as there's a sharp prick in the pad of her thumb.

"I really thought it was a prank, I swear." The words barely slip from Rowan's mouth, his voice thin.

"We'll figure it out," Mallory assures him, but he brushes her off, his face contorting into a grimace.

"I can't die here, I can't. I have Gabriel to think about. He's practically a baby still. I'm not going to let him go through that."

"Gabriel will be fine," Mallory says, her head spinning. "Everything will be fine." If she repeats it enough times, it'll be true. What did Erika always say about thoughts becoming things? We manifest our realities. A wave of queasy heat washes over her at the thought of Erika's face—smashed flat, so many shades of red. She pushes it back as she digs her fingers deeper into the sides of the box. One thing at a time. Mallory resolves to get out of this, and when she does, she'll rip apart Jared's memorial, replace his picture with Erika's and she'll visit every year on the anniversary of her death. She'll leave a box of chocolates and water the dirt with her tears. She'll be so damn pious about the grieving process.

Mallory's fingers ache. As she picks at the corner of the box, one of her nails breaks and fresh pain jolts up her arm. A bright weep of blood tails from the corner of her finger where the nail ripped too close to the skin. She draws back her hand and frowns. "We need to try something else, this isn't working."

"Well then make it fucking work!" Rowan cries before lifting the box and smashing it against the tile floor. Again, and again, and again. He howls as blood freckles the tile floor, glaringly red against the white. Tiny pinpricks and larger splashes. Blood soaks the wood around the opening to the box looking like sickly paint. Blood, blood, blood.

"Don't lose your head. We need to stay calm if we're going to get out of this." Mallory has seen this kind of behavior dozens of times when animals are cornered, frantic. Dogs at the shelter who would nip at the bars of their kennels, some going as far as breaking their teeth, breaking the bars, stabbing into their gums, their mouths. Their blood was always mixed with so much saliva that it appeared frothy and pink.

She wishes she knew how to calm the behavior in humans, but people have never been her strong suit. Not that animals are much easier...

"I'm not supposed to be here!" he cries, finally. "This isn't how it was supposed to go, and it isn't fair."

Olivia steps back from the box, seemingly too overwhelmed to continue fighting with it. But Mallory won't give up. She's already lost Erika, she's not going to let the rest of them drop like flies. "I know—we'll figure something out."

"No," he snaps. "You don't get it. I can't die." He reaches into his pocket and pulls out his pack of cigarettes. Britt stoops over and helps him take one from the carton. She lights it up and he brings it to his lips, inhaling deeply. "You know what I mean, Liv."

Mallory turns to Olivia who's swatting tears away from her eyes.

"Our father died in a car accident when we were three," she says, her bottom lip trembling. "We barely have any memories of him. He's like this ghost—this emptiness that's been there all our lives—but we don't remember him, only the gap where he was supposed to be."

Mallory shivers. It's word for word what Rowan sent her one night when he was having an especially rough time with his ex—when the domestic aggressions had escalated to the point where he was seriously concerned that things were going to come to blows.

"I know, Rowan told me." A sick part of her is relieved that despite their lack of chemistry in real life, certain intimate parts of him still belong to her. There's proof of their connection.

"Well, I don't want my son to go through the same thing," Rowan says before taking another puff of his cigarette.

Mallory is about to open her mouth, give a canned response like *he won't*, or *it won't come to that*, but after a moment, the words catch up with her. My son, not my nephew. She thinks back to the wallpaper on his phone and the way he's been talking about Gabriel, and numbness spreads through her chest. "What do you mean your son?"

"Rowan," Olivia warns.

"I can't keep doing this," he says. "I don't care how you feel about it, Liv, I can't keep lying."

"But you promised."

"Yeah, back before I knew I was gonna get fucking degloved." He gives up on the cigarette and tosses it to the ground. "I can't keep covering for you, especially since my life is on the line. How is Kate gonna feel if I go home in a body bag, huh?"

A pit opens in Mallory's stomach. Her mind is stuffed with all the things that Rowan has said over voice chat. All the things he confided in her over the years, all the friends he's mentioned. She's never heard the name Kate before and the way that he says it, the familiarity, the warmth, is almost too much to take.

"Who's Kate?" she asks, already dreading the answer.

"My wife," he says. "My wife of three years and the mother of my son, Gabriel."

Mallory's brow furrows. It's not like Rowan and her ever did anything that would constitute cheating, but there was an intimacy in their messages that went beyond a normal friendship. As far as she's concerned, they were too close for there to not be something more there, something between the messages—the feeling when his name ignited her screen was as close to love as she could get to someone whom she never met.

A shiver passes through her when she realizes... three years. He's been married for three years. Unless he was cheating on his wife, there's no way Jared could be his ex... and even if he was cheating, why stay with someone that abusive when you're already married? Unless that was a lie too and the ways he bled for her, the ways he cut himself open and exposed every bit of pain, and fear, and emptiness, was fake.

Her insides churn and she holds a hand to her stomach to keep from spilling her guts. Bile burns the back of her throat. What kind of person would lie about things like that? And for what? A little bit of light flirting over the internet?

She hardens her gaze and glares at him, the rage a slow simmer beneath her skin. "What the fuck is wrong with you?"

Completely unfazed, Rowan turns to his sister. "You need to come clean, Liv."

Olivia opens and closes her mouth several times, tears welling up behind her eyes. And there's a terrible sinking feeling in Mallory's gut.

"What is he talking about?" she asks and Olivia flinches against the words before turning to her brother.

"Please." Her voice cracks and a tear traces a perfect line through her already ruined makeup. "I can't."

Rowan stares daggers at her. "If you don't tell them, I will."

Olivia turns to Mallory and Britt, wringing her hands. "My brother isn't supposed to be here." She pauses to take a shaky breath and Mallory can already anticipate what's coming next —it's like watching Erika, airborne, and having no way to stop the impending splatter.

Olivia fiddles with the edge of her skirt. "I'm the one who's running Rowan's Instagram profile. I'm the one that you've been talking to in the Discord for these last few months."

"But I haven't been talking to Rowan for a few months," Mallory says slowly. "I've been talking to him off and on since middle school."

Since they met on AIM chat. Since a friend showed Mallory his MySpace profile and Mallory spent days listening to the HyveMind song on his profile on repeat scrolling through his selfies with his hair in his eyes and polish on his fingers and looking through his top friends, all while trying to figure out if if he would even waste his time talking to her. He did.

She still has printouts of their first messages stuffed into a shoebox in the back of her closet. And she still remembers the three weeks in eighth grade when they called each other girl-friend and boyfriend until the distance got to be too much.

Now, she looks at Olivia, really looks at her for the first time since she pushed her way through the tall grass in front of the resort. She considers all the times she's caught her staring, caught her looking queasy as she tried to gain her attention.

"Olivia?" Mallory asks.

She nods. "You've been talking to *me* online, off and on since middle school."

Mallory runs through all the nights she spent pining after

Rowan, all the secrets she spilled to him. All the times she would picture him curled around her like a protective shell.

It was Olivia.

She thinks of all the books she read. She spent damn near a month trying to memorize *Hamlet* because Rowan was obsessed. They watched the 1996 movie with Kenneth Branagh and Kate Winslet together over voice chat one night, and all she could think of the entire time was wrapping her arms around Rowan and kissing him deeply.

"I talked to him over voice chat..." Mallory says weakly. "We've been talking over voice chat since..."

"Since high school," Olivia finishes. "When I told you I couldn't meet in person, and you got so upset that we decided voice chat would be a good compromise. But not video because—"

"Because you didn't trust webcams, and you were insecure... but the voice... it was Rowan's voice, it sounded exactly like him."

"Voice changing app. We're twins so I guess it makes sense that it would sound like his voice."

The revelation hits Mallory right in the solar plexus. It's like the wind has been knocked out of her. "Rowan never dated Jared?"

Olivia shakes her head. "He's my ex-boyfriend... He's the one who... well, you know the story. All of that was true... even if the memoir bit was an exaggeration. Rowan's the writer, not me."

The time Rowan's ex tried to scratch their name into the back of his hand with a paper clip and called him crazy when he confronted them about it later that night, said that he did it to himself, that he was sick in the head.

The time Rowan showed up at their apartment only to hear someone else's laughter trickling out through the window and see another person on their couch. His ex wouldn't let Rowan hear the end of it for showing up unannounced and doubting them when they told him that nothing was going on.

The time Rowan's ex slapped him across the cheek so hard it left a welt.

All of it was true, but it was Olivia and Jared.

Mallory knows that she has a right to feel angry, hurt, lied to. But is a lie still a lie if it's laced with the truth? All the nights spent staying up into the early hours of the morning, sunrise bleeding across the sky like a heart poked until it burst. That was real, regardless of the person behind the screen.

She steps up next to Olivia and takes her hand. It's slick with sweat and shakes in her palm. Olivia stares at her, eyes wide, and Mallory is acutely aware of the rise and fall of her chest, the way her red lipstick has smeared down her chin making her mouth appear mangled, and Mallory tries without success to find the perfect words, the perfect way to let her know that she remembers the night they watched *Hamlet*. But she struggles for too long and Olivia pulls her hand away. Mallory feels its absence like an ache in her chest.

She wants to ask if any of it was real, but her mouth is dry, and she catches a hint of Erika's perfume, soft floral notes. And Jared's memory, heavy as a guillotine, slices the air between them.

Then there's a loud bang and an ear-piercing scream, the death cry of a frightened animal.

Mallory spins around to find Britt standing over Rowan, his hand clutched to his chest, the box scattered in pieces around them both like the aftermath of an explosion. Britt grips a length of metal pipe in her left hand.

8

MALLORY

"What did you do?" Olivia howls, rushing to her brother's side.

The blood is unlike anything Mallory has ever seen. Spraying from the tip of his finger, in cartoonish exaggeration. Bright red, like a notification bell. But his hand is intact, at least his hand is intact. Mostly.

Rowan cups his finger, but it does little to control the spray. The blood coats his hands like slick plastic gloves stretching down to his wrists, pooling on the floor beneath him.

Mallory is numb while Olivia struggles to slow the bleeding.

Britt stands off to the side with an emptiness in her eyes that sends a shiver up Mallory's spine.

"Why would you do that? He looks like he's going to bleed out."

"Neither of you were doing anything," Britt says, tossing the pipe aside.

Olivia whips her head around, her eyes frantic. "Someone help him!"

The shrill alarm of her voice is enough to snap Mallory out of it, and although still numb, although it feels as if she's on autopilot and her legs move without her, she manages to come up next to Rowan and along with Olivia. She struggles to stop the flow of blood. The tip of his finger lays like a sad chunk of hotdog next to them, the chipped polish on its nail making her feel sick. It was cleaved just beneath the knuckle.

Britt watches with detached fascination for a bit then crouches next to them. She pulls a lighter from her front pocket, flicks it open, and peels Olivia away from her brother.

Rowan stares up at her as she runs her thumb along the striker and a bright orange flame springs to life.

"What are you—" His question is interrupted by another horrific chorus of screams as Britt forces his bloody stump into the flame.

"I'm cauterizing the wound, so you don't die from blood loss," she says calmly.

A horrible smell like oil and roast pig fills the space between them. It sets off the slide show inside Mallory's head. Flashes of her and Erika at the neighborhood barbecue, and her dad carving a whole suckling pig, the slices of pork getting stuck in her teeth. Then, the images burn away—Polaroids with bubbling emulsion, chewed up by more images of Jared. The tattoo of a pig with wings, fat and faded down the side of his neck. The vein in the back of his hand. The way his fingers looked wrapped around a beer bottle.

She forces herself to leave the past and focus again on the scene in front of her.

To Mallory's surprise, Britt's attempt to cauterize the wound works. The charred flesh, although raw, is no longer spouting blood. Rowan attempts to ease up onto his knees, but his eyes roll back into his head, and he hits the ground with a sickening crack.

Olivia shrieks, her hands raised to her face in a perfect caricature of shock and horror.

Britt moves calmly to his side and shouts to Mallory that

they need to check if he's okay, but Mallory can barely hear her over the splintering sound of skull against tile repeated on a seemingly endless loop inside her mind.

It's so much like when Erika hit the bottom of the swimming pool that she's convinced he must be dead—if not from the shock, then surely the back of his skull must resemble a broken eggshell at this point. She fixes her gaze on where his head lays on the floor but there's no telltale leak of blood, no spray of spongy pink.

"Is he..."

"He's fine." Britt points to his ribcage, and Mallory stares intently at the rise and fall of his chest as the others argue over what to do next.

"We open the door and get moving," Britt says, prying the key from Rowan's fist.

"What about Rowan?"

"We take him with us."

"How? He's too heavy for us to carry."

"Then we'll drag him." Britt hoists him under the armpits but after a few moments of struggling, switches to his ankles.

Mallory watches, brow furrowed, as Britt pulls Rowan across the tile. He remains completely limp, and Mallory can't help but think of Jared's blood trail, the drag marks through dark crimson.

She shudders.

Britt isn't the least bit gentle as she pulls Rowan across the room and his head smashes against the corner of a snack stand as she turns them toward the exit. Olivia claws Rowan away from her.

"We'll wait until he wakes up," she says, smoothing his hair back.

"If he wakes up," Britt mutters, and Olivia practically shrieks.

"Maybe," Mallory says, reaching for Olivia, who continues

to sit vigil by Rowan's side, "Maybe, while we're waiting for him to wake up... we could talk?"

But Olivia's attention remains fixed on Rowan, and she doesn't so much as acknowledge Mallory.

Finally, he stirs to life and Olivia helps ease him into a sitting position.

"You're a freak, Britt," he says, staring at her with wide eyes. "But thanks. It's better than my whole hand, I guess."

She nods once before inching back against the far wall, giving Olivia and Mallory space to tend to Rowan. But neither of them know what to do, how best to help, and every time Mallory glances up, she locks eyes with Olivia, only for her to glance away immediately. Mallory's insides are tensed, and the air tastes bloody, tinged metallic. They sit with him in the pool of his blood until he catches his breath.

"Should we collect the finger?" Olivia asks, her voice shaking.

Mallory can't stop staring at her, counting the flecks of color in her eyes, tracing the contours of her face. She's stupefied, she can't bring herself to move. Between the stress of the game and the stress of Olivia's revelation, she can't concentrate on anything except the pounding of her heart against her ribs.

"We don't have any ice," Britt says matter of factly. "The tissue would die before we'd have any chance of getting it reattached. Plus, if things go badly in here, it'll be good to have some evidence for people to find. Better to leave it."

Her implication sends waves of dread through Mallory.

"How is it that he only lost a finger anyway?" she asks, but no one answers.

The overhead speakers crackle on and the group jolts. "Hey darlings, as much fun as it's been to watch you squirm, best get a move on, the door will only stay open for so long. And I'm not a very patient person. I worked very hard for a very long time to put this whole thing together, and I'll be super pissed if you all ruin it by not playing along."

Mallory stares at the doorway at the far end of the concession stands, the door sprung open on its hinges.

Her mouth goes dry.

They don't need the key to open the door after all. How did they not notice before now? The only thing that could have triggered it was Rowan pulling the key from the bottom of the box, but then what would the point of the hand trap be? Mallory's stomach churns when she realizes that freeing the key from the bottom of the box likely started a countdown and that the door would have been set to open regardless of whether or not Rowan pulled his hand from the box. It's almost too cruel to take.

"Do we really want to keep going with this?" Mallory asks. "Wouldn't it be better to stay here and see if we can find a way out of the room. It's not like she can do anything to us if we stop playing. We could survive back here until someone finds us."

"Could we though?" Britt asks. "There's nothing but empty bottles behind the bar, no food or water."

"HyveFest starts tomorrow. People are bound to trespass here. They'll find us."

"Only if they manage to make it into the water park," Rowan says. "Or are you forgetting the huge fucking sheet of metal that came down between the hallway and here? And another one when we left the water park. What drunk concert goer is going to spend time trying to get into something that's sealed airtight? Best case scenario, they make it into the lobby, and then what? It's not like anyone would be able to hear us."

"So we're already dead?" Mallory asks, exasperated. "There has to be something we can do."

"We can keep going." Rowan struggles to his feet, clutching his bandaged hand tightly against his chest. "I'm not letting Gabriel grow up without a father."

Mallory sighs and falls into line behind the others, neck craned toward the red blink of the security cameras as they follow a hallway lined with light green tiles. They move slowly, their shoulders hunched, the energy in the hall tense as Mallory stares at her feet, stepping lightly as if that would make any sort of difference if there were more of Peyton's trigger-traps. She shivers, imagining how Peyton must be watching them right now.

The walls are a pale cream color, unfinished in places, large dabs of drywall poking out from beneath the paint. They walk until they come to a split in the hallway, a pair of doors that are shut tightly. Rowan attempts to open one, then the other, but soon gives up with a grunt. His bloody hand leaves a smear of red on each knob.

There's a slab of wall between the two doorways the width of a small child, and another neon sign hangs fastened at eye level in swirling yellow text. *Antidote,* the sign declares. It blinks at them, each flicker bright and stinging.

Britt steps up to it and traces the swoops of cursive, her fingers shaking.

"Antidote... yellow antidote," she mutters, pulling her hand away abruptly as if the sign snapped its teeth at her.

"What the fuck is it supposed to mean?" Rowan asks.

"It's one of HyveMind's songs," Olivia says. "Off their second album."

"No, you're thinking of 'Our Antidote.'" Mallory steps up to the sign, cringing against the bright hum spitting from the neon. Beneath the sign there are three small outlines in the wall, so thin they're barely visible. She presses against them, but they won't budge, and she can't find a place to hook a nail in. She trembles as she turns to the others. "Peyton's setting up for another game."

"The antidote... Do you think she's going to pump something into the hallway?" Rowan asks.

"I wouldn't put it past her," Olivia says.

Mallory walks the length of the hallway from the now sealed door that they came in through to the split, making note of the security cameras (three of them), and the intercom system (a single speaker fastened above the neon sign). "There aren't any vents that I can see..."

If there were vents Mallory would have suggested plugging them up somehow, trying to disrupt the airflow, but there's nothing. The back of her neck prickles. If Peyton is planning to poison them, there's nothing she can do.

"Whatever it is, it's gonna be bad." Rowan reaches into his front pocket and pulls out a joint. "Do you still have my lighter, Britt?"

She nods, passing it over to him and he ignites the end of the joint.

"Is that smart?" Mallory asks. "Whatever she has in store for us is going to be brutal, shouldn't we... I don't know, stay alert?"

"I think the more relaxed we can be, the more likely we are to get through this."

Mallory considers it for a second, but all she can think about are the dogs in the shelter and how they snap at the bars of their cages, hopped up on adrenaline. Maybe Rowan really thinks that it will give them a fighting chance, but weed makes her so sleepy, she doubts it would help her in this situation at all. All she thinks it would do is put her under and then she'd be out for the count before the game even begins. She wishes desperately that Erika was still alive. She would know what to do; she would have some sort of plan or unique way of attacking this so that everything wouldn't feel completely hopeless.

The intercom crackles and Mallory flinches as Peyton's voice leaks back in over the speaker. "As you can probably guess, my darlings, you have a choice to make. Divide up into two teams. One goes left, and one goes right? Easy enough...

right? I'll make it even easier for you. Left leads to mini golf; right an escape room. I'm not sure if you have a preference for which game you play, but I promise this will be fun. And before that, a mini game! I'll be back on in a few to explain."

With that, the intercom falls silent, and Rowan passes the joint around. Mallory takes a puff, breathing in deeply and hoping that the hit is enough to take the edge off without dulling her senses. Though a morose part of her thinks it might be better if she fell asleep and didn't have to deal with what was coming. Dying in her sleep would be better than whatever waits in store for them, she's sure of it.

Olivia is the only one who refuses a hit even though Rowan insists that given the circumstances, he should have let her have the shot earlier.

Mallory breathes the secondhand smoke in deeply, and shutting her eyes, pretends that she's standing on the edge of the main stage at HyveFest, surrounded by college kids and elder emos. The weed leaves her lightheaded, and her whole body tingles as she thinks back to better times.

Unsurprisingly, Britt goes to finish off the joint, and Rowan needs to jab her in the ribs to get her to give it back. Britt seems married to her substances, and it makes Mallory ache to think that's how she used to be with cocktails, hard liquor, mixed drinks. She's not sure how she did it. Even Erika, who was known to chase her shots with even more shots, couldn't keep up in terms of sheer volume. Mallory wraps her arms around her middle. It's strange and a little sickening to think of Erika in the past tense.

"What do you think she meant by mini game?" Olivia asks but no one has an answer.

Rowan tosses what remains of the joint to the ground and winces.

"Are you okay?" Mallory asks.

He holds up his left hand, a watered-down shade of pink

seeping through the makeshift bandage. "I just lost a finger, so no, I'm not okay."

"Technically, you lost the *tip* of a finger," Britt says, and Rowan flips her off, grunting as his middle finger brushes up against the mess of the bandage.

"The weed took the edge off a little, but it still hurts like a bitch. Anyone have anything stronger?" Rowan looks around the circle. "Come on, I can't be the only one who brought stuff here."

Britt fishes around in the pocket of her hoodie before pulling out a small ziplock baggie full of white powder. She holds it out to Rowan.

He immediately throws his hands up in protest. "Jeez, I meant booze, like... vodka or something, not hard drugs. What the fuck is wrong with you?"

"You asked if anyone had something stronger, and I did."

"I have a kid, I can't get hooked on heroin."

"It's not heroin—it's coke."

"Like that's any better. I can't get hooked on coke, okay?"

"Well, maybe we'll die in here and you won't have to."

"What the actual fuck, Britt?"

"Wait," Mallory says slowly. "Didn't you bring whiskey or something with you?"

"We drank it all." He sighs. "Or I should say that Britt damn near guzzled the whole thing herself. She drank more than..." He trails off, his mouth set in a grim line.

"Rowan?" Olivia asks, grabbing at her brother's arm, but he shakes her off and stumbles back from the group. "Rowan what is it? You're scaring me."

"Peyton gave me the flask." The words are barely audible, and everyone is so quiet, listening so intently that the only sound is staggered breathing. The air is heavy with smoke and tinged with panic.

Mallory's heart sinks. "What do you mean Peyton gave you the flask? You know who's doing this to us?"

"No, I never saw her." Rowan sinks down against the far wall and stares blankly ahead. "She left it for me in the parking lot and texted me with instructions on where to find it. She said that she thought it would be a good way to loosen everyone up before the prank."

Mallory's stomach roils and the peace she had been feeling from the high dissipates. She knows where he's going with this but wants desperately to get off the ride, stay in the dark. Heat pools between her ears and she strains to hear Rowan over the sound of her heartbeat. The rush of blood in her ears, the itchy heat snaking its way up her neck. It's like snake coiling tighter and tighter around her body, squeezing until she's certain all her guts will spill through her mouth.

"It tasted weird," he says. "Didn't it? It didn't taste like regular booze."

They stare at the sign on the wall. The swirling yellow.

Antidote.

"Fuck." Rowan presses his thumbs into his eyes. He stamps his boot against the floor and punches the wall. "Fuck, fuck, fuck."

"She poisoned us already," Mallory says, hand pressed to her stomach. A wave of nausea runs through her and she's not sure if she's actually ill or it's all psychosomatic. She's not sure if it even matters. Feelings are real, even if the symptoms aren't.

Britt sways slightly, staring blankly at the neon sign. "I drank more than any of us... I drank so much..."

That's when the music starts: "Sulking Seething," Jared's favorite song.

9

BRITT

Britt has always blamed her inability to connect with others on the fact that her mother painted her childhood bedroom yellow. It was so bright it stung, and if she stared at it too long, her skin would start to itch. She'd get sent to her room a lot as a kid, and spent hours surrounded by the color, soaking in the yellow paint. She always likened it to lead poisoning, a prolonged exposure seeping in and rewriting her, ruining her. She'd always been sensitive to vivid colors, but the yellow was on another level. She couldn't understand why it hurt the way it did and was single-mindedly obsessed with figuring it out.

In the end, she discovered Scheele's green, and Vantablack, and Baker-Miller pink, but couldn't find the reason why yellow felt like insects.

The color still sets her on edge.

Britt doesn't believe in ghosts, but she believes in hauntings.

And yellow haunts her.

She can trace it all back, every unhappy memory, every uncomfortable feeling, to the yellow walls of her childhood bedroom.

Peyton is the only person Britt ever shared this with. She

told her everything. She rambled on and on about her color fixation and her excessive drinking, and how she doesn't know how to control herself when it comes to either.

Peyton was always peppering Britt with questions.

What is it about yellow though?

Is there anything you won't drink?

Are there any other colors that you absolutely hate? What about liquor? Do you consider the color of a cocktail before you drink it?

Britt didn't think it was strange at the time. She liked talking about herself and didn't get enough opportunities to do so outside of virtual chat rooms. In real life, she couldn't find the words half the time—it was so much easier online. And Peyton was always there to listen.

"This was designed to ruin me," Britt murmurs as she stares at the neon sign. *Antidote* flashes in acidic yellow while "Sulking Seething" continues to blast.

Britt knew something tasted off about the booze, but she'd drank a lot of sketchy shit and aside from the rogue, especially vicious hangover, it never bit her in the ass before. Plus, she had pre-gamed with a double shot of tequila and a White Claw before meeting the others outside the resort. Even when her guts started to bubble, and the nausea kicked her right in the solar plexus, she blamed mixing liquors, she blamed Rowan for not filling the flask with a proper whiskey, she blamed anything other than poison. Who the fuck would think to blame poison?

She's so lost in her head, spinning around in her thoughts, that it takes her a moment to realize that the same lines of "Sulking Seething" keep repeating over and over.

I'm sorry, but not as sorry as you're gonna be, when I seethe, I seethe, when I seethe, you bleed.

I'm sorry, but not as sorry as you're gonna be, when I seethe, I seethe, when I seethe, you bleed.

It's a ringtone, she realizes. The sound is closer than when Peyton comes over the speaker system and has a distinctly tinny edge to it. It fills the hall, and she waits for Rowan to answer the phone, but the music continues to play on loop.

"It's the red phone," she says, eyes still fixed on the flickering sign.

"Oh, shit." Rowan digs through his pocket and, shaking, pulls it out, hesitating for a moment before lifting it to his ear.

"If this is who I think it is, you have a lot of explaining to do." He pauses, his jaw clenched as a muffled voice comes in through the other end. "I lost a finger! Mallory's friend is dead." He gestures for everyone to come over. "It's Peyton... She wants me to put her on speaker."

"She's on the phone now?" Mallory asks, her eyes wide. "How is she even calling us? I thought it didn't work."

Olivia doesn't say anything at all, but a fresh pair of tears trace salty trails down her cheeks. Her makeup has smudged badly, sweat causing her foundation to sheen and cake so that it looks as if she's melting.

Rowan holds the phone out and presses the speaker button. Britt crouches along with the others though she wobbles in place. There are so many things she wants to say to Peyton, but they slip away, they drown in the neon sign's acidic sting until there's only yellow.

Yellow panic, yellow anger, yellow fear.

"Hello, darlings," Peyton begins in a sing-song lilt. "You don't know how happy I am that you made it this far. I'll be the first to admit that I haven't exactly planned this out as well as I hoped, and I've been super nervous this entire time. How far are they going to make it? Are they going to go where I need them to go? Will everything work the way it's supposed to? Don't get me wrong, this took a ton of planning, but there are so many factors outside of my control."

Britt does her best to place the voice. It must be someone she knows, but she doesn't know many people... let alone anyone who would be capable of this. The voice on the other end of the phone, although slightly muffled, sounds like the Peyton she got to know over voice chat. A stranger who became a friend, now an enemy.

"You killed my best friend," Mallory says, her voice hollow.

Peyton lets out a peel of blood-curdling laughter. "Oh, you sweet angel. It's cute that you actually believe that."

For a moment, Britt considers this confirmation that it somehow really is all a prank. Despite Rowan's run-in with the degloving machine and Erika's swan dive, none of it is real. Whatever Britt drank, whatever the flask was filled with, wasn't toxic after all. Just cheap liquor. This whole thing is a mind fuck. She lets the hope well up like a blood bubble in her chest, until Peyton speaks again, and it pops, leaving a gaping wound in its place.

"Babe, the two of you have been on the outs for almost a year now. Don't pretend you weren't crying to me almost every night about how Erika wouldn't return any of your texts. I did you a favor." Peyton's voice is still high-pitched and sickly sweet. "She wasn't your best friend. The closest thing you have to a best friend now would be Rowan... or should I say Olivia? It's so hard to keep up with all the lies you've been telling each other."

Olivia lets out a whimper and Mallory recoils.

"What's the point of this, Peyton?" Rowan asks, his voice coming out clipped.

"Well, the point of this phone call is to kill time until what I slipped into that whiskey kicks in. I'm honestly so terrible at timing these things out, I'm afraid it might still be a while yet. But you'll be able to tell when it finally starts to work its magic. I promise."

"What is the point of trapping us here?" Rowan flexes his bandaged hand. A dribble of pink leaks from his finger into the groove of his palm, staining the fabric. It's so light it could be watercolor paint. Britt watches the stain deepen as Rowan continues. "We get it, you're pissed about Jared or whatever, but none of this is going to bring him back."

"Do you think I'm stupid?" Peyton snaps. "I'm not trying to reanimate the dead here; I'm trying to have some fun."

Britt lets out a shaky breath. It's getting more and more difficult to concentrate on what Peyton is saying. Her brain seems to swell inside her skull, and she leans against the wall, sinking to the floor across from the yellow sign. *Antidote* flickers in time to the pounding in her head. All that horrible yellow. Pulsing.

"Are you okay?" *Antidote* is eclipsed by Mallory, who stares down at her with the most curious expression on her face. Britt can't quite place it. Everything warps in small flickers at first. The yellow of the sign eats away at the white of the wall behind it for one, two, three seconds before it's back to normal again. The paneling on the lower half of the wall droops down into the tiles before snapping back into place. Then Mallory's face leaks into the sign. Her eyes liquify and her nose dissolves, until she's nothing more than a floating set of teeth. A tongue. An upper lip ripped apart at the seam so that fat drops of red hang suspended in the air.

Britt moans.

She feels Peyton's voice more than she hears it, the words spiking along her back in a vicious staccato. She claws at her neck as Peyton continues. "It seems like it's safe to explain the rules now. This one is super simple, I promise. Kind of like an amuse bouche before the main course. I was hoping to turn this into its own round, but an associate of mine thought it wouldn't hit as hard as some of the other games."

Peyton is working with someone...

Britt struggles to commit this to memory, but she can't take her eyes off the pieces of Mallory, each individual tooth ripping from the gums, their roots coated in gore as they fall to the floor, sounding like loose change as they hit the tile.

"So obviously, you're playing for the antidote. Here's how it's gonna go. There are three compartments in the wall under the neon sign. I'll pop them open now, all at once."

On cue, the compartments open to reveal three squat bottles in a sickly shade of yellow. So much yellow. The color seems to swirl around Britt and all she can think of are the thick slabs of wallpaper in her childhood bedroom and how the glue might taste on her tongue. Except it wasn't wallpaper —it was paint. And pill bottles shouldn't be yellow, they should be orange.

Britt grips the sides of her head.

Warmth moves up the base of her neck, pooling in the back of her skull. Something shifts along the highways of her veins, and she whimpers as it inches through her, to the vulnerable depths of her body. It floods her. Consumes her.

Britt is no stranger to drugs, but this, like the yellow of her childhood bedroom, is an entirely different animal.

An overdose, she thinks numbly. *I'm dying.*

"One of the bottles contains the antidote to that nasty little cocktail that's working its way through your systems right now. You won't need much of it to stop the effects, but it's super important that you choose the correct one. And there's no cheating. Each bottle sits on a spring trap. Once you pick one up and remove it from its platform, the other doors will seal shut. And you can't take more than one at a time or I'll see, and I'll leave you sealed in the hallway. Understand?"

"Yes," Olivia says quietly. Mallory and Rowan both seem to be feeling the effects now, though not as strongly as Britt. She watches them stagger; their movements stilted as if they're marionettes. Mallory is in one piece again, but her teeth remain in a pile on the floor and Britt reaches straight through them, swatting the vision away.

Peyton continues talking but her voice fades in and out of focus. "Here's the fun part. The game part of it. Two truths and a lie, only this time it's two lies and a truth. About the night that

Jared died. Good luck! Given Britt's sorry state, I'd say you only have a few minutes. Better act fast."

Rowan shouts something into the receiver but the words bleed together, and Britt only catches the tail end of Peyton's latest monologue.

"Earlier, you asked me what the point of all this is, Rowan. Well, the point is, you're all going to die excruciating deaths. And I get to watch."

With that, the line goes dead.

Voices drift over Britt as if she's sitting at the bottom of a pool and she stares down at her palm. It's red and flaking from when she sifted through the organic wreckage that used to be Erika. She blinks three times, shifting her focus to the wall as it bends and waves at her. She raises her hand and waves back, the red on her palm leaving bloody ribbons suspended through the air.

There's a loud clap and she looks up to see Olivia crouching over her. Her lips move but the sound that comes out is muted. Britt tries her best to focus and the final bits trickle to her. "... not doing so well, but you're gonna have to try."

"Huh?" It takes all her effort not to let her head lull to the side. The red ribbons fizzle around the edges. They freckle out into specks of dust, of glitter, of nothing at all. Somewhere in the soft cheese of her mind, she recognizes that whatever Peyton dosed them with is some kind of psychedelic. She takes comfort in this. If it's shrooms, or acid, or some combination of both, it can't be deadly. Can it?

Depends on the dosage.

Depends on the substance.

It's an overdose, she reminds herself.

"Peyton opened the compartments and we're gonna need everyone for this," someone says, though Britt can't place the voice. The words fall across her cheek in little wriggling syllables. They're worms. They're young insects. She swats at them as the voice continues. "Please try your best to concentrate. I know you're not doing so well but you're gonna have to try."

Britt wobbles to her feet and staggers toward the open compartments.

Two lies and a truth.

She doesn't stay standing for long and, dizzy, falls back against the wall across from the compartments. "What do they say?"

"Mallory killed Jared, Olivia killed Jared, Britt killed Jared. It's two lies and a truth... Peyton thinks one of us killed him."

Britt's mind twists slowly through the memories of last year's HyveFest. She may have done a lot of things that night, but she didn't kill Jared. She knows that for sure.

"Wasn't me," she slurs. The others argue amongst themselves, but she stays focused on the compartments and the little yellow pill bottles. Behind them, in the depths of the cubbies she swears she can see a drip of strawberry blonde, the pink sponge of brain matter.

Erika.

Britt sensed that something was off with Mallory's friend the moment she saw her. She's not usually good at reading people, but something about Erika set her teeth on edge. She was surprised that Mallory was friends with her at all. Erika seemed too much like the people in high school that would make Britt feel insane for not being able to talk the way they did or be content with such small conversations. The weather, crushes, pets. She knows what to say in those situations, but it's like a script in her head that's exhausting to follow.

Something about Erika felt so familiar... she can't quite place it. She's never been good with faces or names. She hyper focuses on small details—a glint of jewelry, a smudge of dirt under a person's nails. But there was something about Erika...

Britt leans in closer to the cubbies, squinting until her vision doubles. Through the blur, she can almost make out—

she's sure of it now—the fountainlike cascade of Erika's hair, threading its way through the cracks in the backboard strand by strand.

"You guys?" Britt asks, as the hair continues to squeeze through the cracks. "Can you see that?"

"You don't look so good. You should rest."

"Do you see it though? The strawberry blonde—" She hiccups, running a finger along her chin. She pulls it away to find it stained yellow. No, not yellow. Red. She's bleeding.

Erika's strawberry-tinged hair continues to tumble from the cubby, curling like a nest around the pill bottles. More and more of it. Glossy and splattered with gore.

This is definitely a hallucinogen of some kind, and Britt's not having a fun trip. Not fun at all. Usually, she's so much better with these kinds of drugs, but given the stress of the situation, and her mindset before the high kicked in, she isn't exactly surprised that this is more nightmare than fantasy.

Britt keeps her hands shoved into the front pocket of her hoodie, one fist curled around the baggie of cocaine, the other resting on the handle of the scalpel. She's not sure why she pulled out the baggie earlier. In the back of her mind, she knew that Rowan wouldn't approve, and it would only paint her as a heathen in everyone's eyes.

Britt loves drugs and alcohol for the same reason she loves sleeping. When she's doing it, she doesn't need to think about anything else. It makes it easier to exist in a world that seems wired for someone else.

"Olivia."

For a moment Britt wonders if she's the one who said Olivia's name again but then realizes that it's Rowan calling for his sister. The words shatter against her side, and she presses a hand to her ribs.

I can't let myself leak out, she thinks, digging her fingers in deeper.

Rowan's mohawk is especially green right now, and the stain on his bandaged hand, especially pink. "Olivia, you're the only one who didn't drink, so you need to help us out here."

"I can't do anything unless I know which bottle to pull."

Erika's hair drips down over the lip of the cubby, a cascade of strawberry blonde with chunks of red and pink tangled through. Britt can even smell it—the metallic tinge, the acrid smell of death—it's so real.

Britt gags against it and squeezes her eyes shut. Her heart pounds in her ears, so much liquid pooling in the back of her head that when she twists it to the side, she fears that she'll drown inside herself.

She's done enough drugs to know that some substances can take up to an hour to kick in. And how long has it been now? What did Peyton dose her with? Maybe it isn't actually deadly —maybe it's just meant to make her feel like she's losing her mind. She's tripping. Hard. She knows that. But it's hard to remember all the reasons to stay calm when the thoughts turn to liquid, and the liquid keeps filling up behind her eyes.

She opens them to find Erika's hair slithering across the tiles, wrapping around the others' ankles as it advances toward her. She bats at it, but her fingers slip right through.

Britt doesn't belong here. She was only ever a friend to Jared.

She met him when she was eighteen and had just started at the community college. He was a year older, almost finished with his degree but more focused on his fledgling social media career. It was during one of her art electives, figure drawing. The model was taking a break from posing, and most of the other students were using it as an opportunity to chat or grab some water from out in the hall. But she was busy smoothing out the charcoal on her drawing pad and trying to turn her scribbles into something that could pass for art.

"Hey, you dated Seth, didn't you?" His voice was deep, and she was immediately taken with how confident he sounded.

"Yeah," she said, looking up from her drawing pad. "Back in high school."

She stared at him while he digested this information. He was attractive, in an unpolished, wannabe musician kind of way. He was tatted, but most of his tats were stick and pokes. He wore a leather jacket, but it was clearly second hand and worn until faded and soft. He looked both dangerous and inviting. It was a combination that made Britt feel right at home.

"Thought I recognized you," he said with a small shake of his head. "It would make sense that Seth sourced all his girlfriends from the high school. The guy was a creep."

"Was?" She asked, a knot forming in her stomach. "Did he die or something?" She hadn't looked him up since she broke up with him, but she was sure she would have heard something if he died.

Jared laughed. "No way, he moved out to California last year. I'm a friend of his younger brother's. Jared."

"His brother's name is Jared?" She felt stupid talking to him, like there was something between the words that she wasn't catching on to.

"No, I'm Jared," he said with a grin that showed off the dimple in his cheek. "His brother doesn't matter."

Britt knows there's a reason why she keeps drifting. There's something she's meant to remember. As everyone around her argues, she becomes more and more convinced that she has the answer to everything, the reason why they're trapped in this game.

Erika's hair crawls up to Britt's neck, sliding around it like a noose. She wonders how the others haven't noticed it. Surely, she can't be on this trip alone. If whatever Peyton dosed them with kicked in at the same time, shouldn't they be in this together?

Britt's used to being the only one to notice certain things, but as the hair tightens around her neck, soft, and real, and coated in a fine sheen of gore, she needs to remind herself that it's just a bad trip. Especially as she hiccups again, and three bright yellow dots splatter across the floor. She waits for the filter to drop and the drops to turn red, but it doesn't and even Erika's hair has taken on a more yellow tinge, as if sickly, which only works to emphasize the brain matter tangled through.

Someone grabs her by the shoulder—she thinks it's Rowan. The hand is strong and smells like nicotine, but the figure's face drips, mixing with Erika's sea of yellow hair. Britt leans in for the figure to hold her, to drain the liquid, to make everything all right but instead they shake her.

"Did you hear me, Britt?"

"Huh?" she looks up, and the face continues to drip in broad, honey-colored brush strokes.

"I know for a fact that Olivia didn't kill Jared, so was it you?"

Was it her? Memories and dreams, thoughts and feelings, knit together until it's a clot of blood in the center of her skull and she isn't sure anymore.

Rowan claps his hands in front of her face. "Britt! Fucking focus. We're running out of time. What happened last year? Why is this psycho bitch suggesting that you killed Jared?"

"I saw him the night he died," Britt sputters. "He was in a bad way, bleeding. But I was... I didn't..." She was too high to care. She remembers how the blood across his face glowed like star splatter, like sugared candies, and how hungry it made her.

She was with some guy—Mike or Mac—a wannabe drug dealer and they had smoked together. He was rail thin, with a scraggly beard which accentuated his narrow chin. She knew him vaguely through a former classmate and was painfully aware of how their expectations for the night differed.

She wanted to get high.

He wanted to get lucky.

Britt shut him down quickly once she realized what he was after, and even though he was respectful of her boundaries, he was still pissed about it. The night had taken on a sour tinge, and she was looking for any opportunity to bounce. Then Mike or Mac offered her more drugs, better drugs, and she was so tempted it hurt. The stuff they had smoked was good and made her brave. She did want more. She did want something stronger, and it wasn't like he would try anything. But his hand kept drifting to her arm, and she kept having to swat it away.

They were in front of the resort and had started a makeshift bonfire, but it was dwindling, the flames low and little more than glowing embers. Britt sat angled away from her companion, facing HyveFest's venue. She watched the lights from the amphitheater and felt the bass snake its way up through her legs. She wanted to catch HyveMind's set, but they weren't going to be on stage for at least another half hour and she was trying to figure out how to time things if she did decide to do harder drugs. She wanted them to hit at exactly the right time.

Then Jared showed up, looking like a mess.

There was blood down the side of his shirt, and freckled up his arms. He kept insisting that it wasn't his, as if that made it any better. Britt didn't think much of it in the moment. The blood seemed to sparkle, and it made her think of sugar, and the sugar made her hungry.

So, she left, the guy who wanted to sleep with her nipping at her heels. Mike or Mac thought he might get lucky after all, but instead he split a burger with her while they rolled another joint.

At Jared's insistence!

He told them that he wanted alone time with a friend.

A shadowy figure that stood a few paces back from him, partially eclipsed by the tall grass.

So, Peyton thinks one of them killed him... that other

person must have been Mallory or Olivia. And didn't Rowan say that Olivia has already pledged her innocence?

Mallory then. Except that's not quite right.

Jared walked through the grass, the moon high, and fat, and bright. A girl trailed after him, slow and hesitant. A thin silhouette. The shadowy figure in the grass stepped forward and—

It's yellow. Everything is yellow. Yellow blots out the memory. Yellow flecks across her vision as Erika's hair continues to snake around Britt's neck. It trails down her back, tracing the curve of her spine. Britt rolls her shoulders, trying to loosen its hold. Every time she gasps for breath another fat drip of yellow goo rolls down over her chin.

"Britt... you need... now..." Someone is speaking to her, but the words flash like strobe bulbs, and she's back outside the resort, and Jared moves across the pavement toward her.

The yellow figure waits by the grass, running her fingers across the tops of the blades. In the moment Britt didn't pay the figure any mind, but now, as they step forward... as they strain against the confines of Britt's memory all she can think about is high school, and that story about the woman trying to claw her way out of the wall. Required reading. A warning. Britt was never any good at school.

The hair noose tightens, and Britt squeezes her eyes shut again. It's over. She hasn't come to terms with it, but that's fine. She lets the hair smother her, let's the yellow blood pour from her mouth and when she closes her eyes, all she sees is yellow.

"It was me!"

Mallory.

It's Mallory.

"I killed Jared," she says. Her voice seems to reverberate off the inside of Britt's skull. Feedback from a guitar, an echo in a cave. Jared's name screamed back to her a dozen times in a dozen different ways, and it's Mallory who killed him.

But no, that's not right.

"He got a bloody nose in the mosh pit at the main stage. I tried to take him back to the medical tent, but he wanted to come here, to the resort instead."

The girl in the grass. Yellow gushing from her fingertips.

"I came here with him," Mallory continues. "And he told me that his family owned the place, so he could get us inside."

No, that's not right. It wasn't her.

"We went into the arcade, and that's when he started bragging about that girl that he was accused of assaulting the previous year, the one who was finally going to press charges. He kept saying that his dad was friends with a bunch of people in the court, and he wouldn't see a day of jail time and that he had gotten away with it… and I don't know what happened. I snapped."

Britt wants to scream. It's all wrong.

And then it all comes crashing in on her. The girl drenched in yellow, the one that Jared took inside the resort with him. She lets out a low moan when she realizes who it was.

"I snapped and I killed him," Mallory finishes, and Britt wants to correct her, but she slumps against the wall—Erika's noose tightening until she can't breathe.

It wasn't Mallory.

Fuzzy stars. A sour taste.

She's slipping.

Away.

Her mouth droops open as the hair tickles the back of her throat and she figures it's the end.

She's.

Sinking.

She's.

Sunken.

She's gone.

Then her eyes snap open, and her breath hitches, and she's

slammed back into herself. She startles awake, not to a noose of hair, but to the others, staring down at her intently.

Her mouth feels as if it's stuffed with cotton, and her head pounds, but she's alive. She's alive, and everything is in sharp focus.

"The antidote?" Britt asks, the words thick on her tongue.

Rowan stands over her, frowning. "Yeah, you should be okay in a few minutes."

No one looks happy about it, and no one bothers to explain.

Britt stands, dizzy at first but once the spots clear, she makes her way to the neon sign to find the compartments snapped shut, all but one, and an empty pill bottle on the floor. She stoops to pick it up.

Mallory killed Jared.

She recalls her final moments before she fell into darkness. What she realized, what she remembered.

Mallory killed Jared.

Except that's not true. Mallory isn't the one she saw with him that night.

It was Erika.

10

MALLORY

Mallory is a killer.

She knows what it's like to break a human being, to crack them open and watch them leak across a floor. She knows what it's like to watch a person flail like a fish on a line, struggle until their energy is depleted and they get that hopeless, empty look in their eyes. It's slow, vampiric. It's messy. Enough to haunt a person for the rest of their life... but Mallory isn't haunted by the act.

She doesn't regret killing. Her only regret is not being better equipped to handle the guilt.

Jared deserved it, but that doesn't quell the sick feeling in the pit of her stomach. No matter how many times she talks herself through what happened that night, she's haunted by the moment when she stomped Jared's skull in with the heel of her boot.

She only told the others a shade of the truth. It's true that she came here with Jared after he got a bloody nose in the mosh pit. It's true that he snuck them into the arcade and was bragging about the assault charge. But everything else...

Mallory swallows back a lump in her throat.

She keeps thinking of a shelter dog, Baxter, who had to be put down after biting a neighborhood kid. He was so sweet, a yellow lab with big brown eyes and a constantly wagging tail. She couldn't fathom him hurting anyone and cried for days when he was euthanized. She was convinced that he must have been provoked, it must have been self-defense, and that's what she tells herself about Jared—it was self-defense.

Can she really blame an animal for defending itself?

Can she really blame herself for fighting to survive?

The slideshow inside her head clicks through image after image and Mallory watches numbly.

The moon is fat and bright, and there's a splattering of stars through a hole in the ceiling the size of a grave.

Jared catches her by the wrist. "We're not done here."

And her foot. And his ribs. And his skull. And her rage.

Blood drips from his shattered nose.

Blood spreads beneath him in a cushion of red.

The images swirl as if on a carousel, each moment whirling into the next, again and again. Until there are stars, and ribs, and red. Snapshots of the moments before, during, after she brought her foot down and felt a crunch.

She killed Jared.

But she didn't dismember him.

She didn't drag the body away, leaving only a trail of blood and body parts behind.

He attacked her, and she defended herself, and then she fled.

The next morning, he was missing. The next morning, there were ribbons of red painted across the tile floors of the resort, but that had nothing to do with her.

She's not sure if that makes it better, or worse. That someone else was there that night lurking, waiting to clean up her mess.

The group stays rooted in place while Britt regains her

composure, if it can even be called that. Whatever Peyton dosed them with has clearly taken its toll. One of Britt's eyelids droops, a thick trail of red weeping down the side of her face. Mallory has never seen so much blood pour from inside a person without any visible wound. She can't take her eyes off Britt. There's red crusted over her chin, and little dots of it have dried to rust down the front of her sweatshirt. The entire time Mallory confessed to the twins, Britt was writhing on the floor, spitting blood and screaming, but now she's silent. She sways in place, a thin line of drool leaking from between her lips.

Both Mallory and Rowan experienced hallucinations thanks to the toxin, but Britt's lucky to be breathing, and Mallory knows that she should be glad that she didn't have it worse.

What she saw wasn't too different from the images that flicker through her head daily, though there was a nightmarish quality to them that transcended her own imaginings. Jared's tattoos melting into the wall, writhing there, spreading out like moss. Erika's teeth sprouting from the top of Jared's head, tangled through the dark mop of his hair. It was horrendous, but the longer she's trapped in the resort, the longer she's forced to play Peyton's games, the more she numbs to the experience. She's not the same as she was before, but whether she's growing or devolving, she can't tell. And she's even less sure of what will happen if she makes it out of the resort alive.

It seems like the group waits in the hallway for an eternity before the two doors open and they're prompted to split up, move on, go forward. But no one will even look at Mallory, not after what she admitted to, and Britt continues to sway, her eyelid drooping lower and lower.

"We shouldn't go right away," Mallory suggests, acutely aware of how Olivia turns to stare at her. Her eyes are wide, her forehead knotted, and Mallory can't stand the fear in her expression. She drags her nails along the backs of her arms and as her scabs bleed fresh; all she can think about is Hamlet. *"Doubt thou the stars are fire; Doubt that the sun doth move; Doubt truth to be a liar; But never doubt I love."* Right now, all she has is doubt, fear, pain. Right now, she'd give anything to be sixteen again, watching the Kenneth Branagh movie over voice chat instead of navigating this hellscape.

"Britt isn't in any condition for another one of Peyton's games," Mallory adds.

"I'm okay." Britt wipes her mouth on the back of her sleeve, the movement stilted. "My head just feels very... full."

"We need to keep going," Olivia says quietly. "I know Britt's not in good shape, but we can't stay here."

Rowan scoffs. "What's the point? Mallory is the one who killed Jared. She's the one Peyton's after." He turns to her, his eyes burning. "She has your confession. What does she need us for?"

There's a sharp edge to his voice and the hair on the back of Mallory's neck prickles. Rowan's good hand moves to his belt and rests on the handle of the steak knife. He taps it gently, one, two, three times and takes a step forward. "You're the reason that my son might grow up without a father."

He raises his bandaged hand and wiggles the stump where his fingertip used to be. The fact that he still has any mobility beneath the knuckle is a miracle. Mallory half expects the cauterized skin to tear and a bit of his bone to poke through. "This is your fault."

Mallory wags a finger right back at him. "You're the one who insisted this whole thing was a prank and stuck your hand in the damn box." It's the wrong thing to say, and as soon as it's out of her mouth, Rowan rushes forward and grabs her by the wrist.

He hisses in pain as he tightens his bandaged hand around her and the heat from the wound leaks through the gauze causing her to wince.

That's a sign of infection, isn't it? A wound being warm to the touch...

Rowan leans in close, the sour tinge of alcohol on his breath. Mallory's stomach roils. She's never been this close to him before, this man who she thought to be her friend since middle school, this man who she thought she was in love with a thousand times over, and now that she's finally close to him, all she wants is to get away.

He pulls the knife from his belt. "Maybe if we take care of you, she'll let the rest of us out."

"Take care of her? Ro, stop and listen to yourself." Olivia grabs his arm and tries to drag him away from Mallory, but he stands firm. Olivia scratches at him, and Mallory notices her nails kicking up flurries of skin, but Rowan shoos her as if she's a fly, and she stumbles back, a pained expression on her face.

"You're not a killer," Olivia pleads but Mallory knows from experience how quickly that can change.

Her pulse thrums, and Rowan's knuckles burn white as one hand grasps the handle of the blade and the other tightens around Mallory's wrist.

"I'm not going to see Gabriel again if things keep going like this and I can't do that to him. I can't do that to Kate. I know that Mallory's your friend or whatever, but I think it's safe to say that at this point, it's every man for himself. We don't deserve to be here, Liv, you know it. She's the one who killed Jared, she can play the rest of Peyton's fucked up little game."

He lifts the knife in front of Mallory's face, and she locks eyes with her reflection as it stares out from within the blade. Her hair is disheveled, her eyes are wild, and she thinks of Baxter. She thinks of the way his tail would hit the bars of his kennel when he wagged it, so excited, so happy, even up until the end. She never wants to be like that, oblivious... helpless.

Erika used to say she was naive. She used to hover around her when they went bar hopping, so concerned that the wrong guy would say the wrong thing and poor, innocent Mallory wouldn't know any better.

Her insides clench.

Mallory didn't know any better with Jared. She was so taken with the fact that he seemed interested in her. She felt like a teenager again. She felt like she was fifteen with no concept of the fact that when you're a girl there are a thousand and one ways to lose your life simply by existing in the same place as a man.

She promises herself that she'll be strong, she'll survive, she won't make the same mistakes again.

Then she jerks her wrist forward and bites down on Rowan's stub of a finger, hard.

He howls, releasing her wrist, and with the metallic sting of blood fresh on her lips, Mallory peels the knife from his good hand and points it back at him. "I don't want to fight you."

Her hand trembles beneath the weight of the blade. It's heavier than she expected it to be, the handle solid and thick.

Rowan grits his teeth. "Is that why you're pointing a knife at me?"

"You pointed it at me first. I'm only defending myself." Her voice cracks at the end of the sentence.

"Like you did with Jared?"

Mallory steels her expression and raises the knife higher. "Yes."

Rowan attempts to charge forward, but Olivia grabs his arm again.

"What, Liv?" he snaps, pulling his arm free. "You think she doesn't deserve to get her ass handed to her just because she sent you some flirty IMs in the eighth grade... when she thought you were me? Grow the fuck up. She's not your girlfriend, she's not even your *friend*. She earned every bit of this."

A vein bulges in his neck and Mallory watches it pulse, her breathing ragged. There's something so inherently violent about his body and how the soft parts strain against the casing of his skin. There's so much violence in the way his veins jerk and struggle. If anything, it proves her point. How can her reactions be anything other than self-defense when faced with the worst kind of monster? One that walks and talks like a human but at its core, is nothing but an animal with no respect for the female species and what she has been made to endure?

She steadies her hand, the knife glinting, and narrows her eyes.

Rowan scoffs at her. "Don't look so smug, you know I'm right."

Olivia places her hand gently on his arm. "You know what Jared was like. We're not here because of Mallory. We're here because of him."

Rowan opens his mouth to object, but Olivia cuts him off.

"Jared did this," she repeats, and Mallory's heart pounds against her ribs as Rowan locks eyes with his sister.

His expression softens, and it's as if a switch has been flipped. He pulls Olivia in for a hug, his eyes trained on Mallory the entire time he holds her, chin resting on her head. He pets Olivia's hair and Mallory can almost see how this glass shard of a man could be a father. There's something so protective about the way he grips his sister to his chest.

"We don't deserve this," he says and Olivia nods into the front of his shirt.

"None of us do." She pulls out of the hug and Rowan takes slow, intentional steps toward Mallory, waving off his sister as she moves to stop him again. He easily plucks the knife from Mallory's hand but makes no attempt to turn it back on her. She blinks up at him as he loops it back through his belt, and even though her pulse races and sweat drips in a cautious line down her forehead, Mallory allows her body to relax a bit.

"I shouldn't have done that." Rowan runs a hand along the back of his neck. "I let my anger get the best of me."

"You weren't angry. You were afraid," Mallory says quietly. She understands fear, and even though Rowan is a stranger, she thinks that she's beginning to understand him too. Even though it doesn't make her feel any better about his outburst. The air seems to crackle between them, a tense thrum of energy pulsing through the hallway.

Mallory stares at the open set of doors and for a moment, she considers bolting. Screw Peyton and her games, screw the rest of the group. She'll run, and she'll fight to survive on her own. Except her legs won't move, and the heaviness in the air presses down on her, rooting her in place.

Rowan sighs, moving his hand to what remains of his mohawk, most of it falling flat against the side of his face. "Well, I say we split up and get going. Liv, you go with Britt to the escape room, and I'll go with Mallory to mini golf."

Mallory bristles at the suggestion. "No way. I'm not going anywhere with you after what you just did to me."

Rowan continues to fuss with his ruined mohawk. "I didn't do shit to you, Mallory. I lost my temper for a second, but it's all good now. And Liv is right: we can't wait around in here forever. Who knows when Peyton plans on closing those doors?"

Mallory turns to Britt. "Are you sure you're okay to continue like this?"

Britt nods and hand trembling, pulls the scalpel from the pocket of her hoodie. Wordlessly, she offers it to Mallory. Thinking of Rowan's sudden outburst, she takes it without question, but the moment her fingers wrap around the handle, Britt latches onto her upper arm.

"I saw... that night," she rasps, sounding even worse than she looks. She clears her throat with a terrible, wet gargle, and tries again. "I saw your friend that night. Erika. I saw Erika with Jared. She was here with him."

Mallory's blood goes cold.

The hallway seems to crush in against her, fleshy and alive.

Heat spikes to her forehead, and each time she blinks the walls pulse. She sways and for a moment, worried that whatever Peyton dosed her with hasn't drained completely. But no, this panic is familiar. All consuming.

She sucks in air and wills her pulse to steady as her mind works through what Britt has told her. Britt, who for all she knows still has life threatening levels of poison coursing through her veins. Britt, who is more stranger to her than friend. Britt, who doesn't know the first thing about Erika.

Erika was never as embedded in the emo music scene as Mallory. She didn't attend HyveFest last year, and she definitely didn't know Jared. Not beyond what Mallory would tell her, anyway. She would roll her eyes every time Mallory brought up his Instagram page or mentioned how she caught a glimpse of him at a concert or festival. To Erika, idol worship was pathetic, especially when it came to influencers.

Mallory shakes her head. It's impossible.

"Blonde hair," Britt insists. "Blue crop top. Gold necklace."

Mallory's skin prickles. Erika always wore silver, and never anything gaudy enough to be noticed from a distance. She was obsessed with thin silver chains and wristlets – so small that they seemed to disappear against her skin.

But Kimber...

Kimber lived for gaudy jewelry and designer brands, anything to get her noticed. Her signature piece, a large heart locket, was a brassy gold. Even as she adjusted her appearance to look more like Erika – even as she replaced her chunky gold bracelets with silver chains, the heart locket stayed.

"It wasn't Erika," Mallory says, her head spinning. "It was Kimber."

"Who the hell is Kimber?" Rowan is already standing at the mouth of one of the doors, his arms folded over his chest.

"She and Erika look alike... she must have been the one with Jared that night." Except that makes even less sense. A headache blooms behind Mallory's eyes as she struggles to understand how Kimber fits into all of this. As far as she's concerned, Kimber knows even less about Jared than Erika did. She isn't into the emo music scene, and prior to Erika and her hanging out, she was barely on Instagram—Jared's social media platform of choice. Kimber is unhinged enough to do something like this, even if she doesn't necessarily have the skill, but how does Jared factor into it?

"What does that mean, exactly?" Rowan asks.

"I'm not sure exactly," Mallory says, turning toward Britt. "But whatever it is, it can't be good."

Britt is busy blotting at her chin with the sleeve of her hoodie. She seems to have regained some of her awareness but watching her sends a jab of discomfort through Mallory.

Her mind is still reeling as Rowan walks up to Britt, reaches into the large front pocket of her hoodie and pulls out the bone saw. Britt either doesn't notice or doesn't care, and Rowan crosses the hallway again, motioning for Olivia to join him by the door.

The twins stay locked in heated conversation for an unbearably long time. Though they keep their voices low, parts of their argument drift back to Mallory, snippets of words and short phrases. She can't piece them together and part of her expects them to take off through one of the doors without so much as a word to her or Britt. Then, Olivia turns and crosses back to where Mallory stands. She grips the bone saw tightly in her fist, her knuckles burning white around the handle.

Mallory's pulse quickens and she silently curses herself for being so excited despite the situation they're in. Olivia is walking toward her, that's all that matters. Maybe they'll finally get a chance to talk.

Sweat gathers across Mallory's forehead as Olivia comes to a stop in front of her. She's not sure what to say, or how to say it, and she lets out a relieved sigh when Olivia opens her mouth first.

"I made Rowan promise not to freak out on you again," Olivia says, worrying the hem of her dress.

"Oh." Mallory's stomach sinks.

"He swears that he wasn't really going to hurt you, that he got carried away. He understands that you'll need to work together for whatever game Peyton is going to make us play next, and he won't risk your chances by making things more difficult."

Olivia leans in. She smells like powdered sugar and vanilla. There are so many things that Mallory wants to say but her throat is dry, and pressure inside her head keeps building. She can't stop thinking about Kimber, and Jared, and that night—what it all means. Even though it wasn't really a rejection, Olivia's earlier dismissal pushes Mallory further into the raging inferno inside her mind and she hates herself for it. She hates herself for everything.

"For what it's worth, I don't think you killed Jared," Olivia whispers.

There's something else, something she cuts herself off from saying and Mallory almost goes after her, but then Rowan's hand comes down on her shoulder and all she can do is watch as Olivia is swallowed by the hallway past the doorway. As she disappears, Mallory feels something akin to a blister on the back of her ankle, a sharp sting through her whole damn body.

"So," Rowan says, slapping a hand down on her shoulder. "Tell me about this Kimber chick."

11

OLIVIA

Olivia has always preferred desserts with bleeding centers: chocolate, cherry, caramel. She loves the surprise of biting into a cupcake or cookie with something extra hidden inside. She understands what it's like to look one way on the outside and be completely different deep down.

On the outside, she's vanilla ice cream. She's plain Greek yogurt. Bland and basic, nothing worth noticing.

No deeper thoughts, no deeper feelings.

She's the quiet one, the shy one, the *nice* one. As if the only thing someone needs to do to be considered nice is to keep their mouth shut, smile and nod.

Inside, she's a bubbling vat of sensitivity and nerves stripped raw. She breaks every social interaction down to its base ingredients, sensing every minute shift in a person's body language. Every eye roll, every jaw twitch, every tilt of the head digs into her like the dull blade of a knife.

She feels everything; she feels too much.

When she bakes, it's the only time she numbs. There's a predictability to baking that's missing from the world outside her kitchen, and she spends hours every weekend stooped over her oven, testing batch after batch of bloody-centered desserts. Following recipes, focused on everything other than the way that people's disappointment, and sadness, and rage, soak into her like she's a sponge cake.

At least now that Rowan and Kate got their own place, she doesn't need to worry about what Rowan thinks of her baking.

No more Rowan looming over her, judging. No more Rowan telling her that it's a waste of money, a waste of food, to bake so much when there's no way she could possibly eat it all. No more Rowan making her feel guilty for taking up so much room in the freezer, and the fridge, and the cabinets.

She always takes up too much space.

"It's not worth it," he would tell her repeatedly. "I don't understand why you bother. You make like fifteen dollars an hour, get a less expensive hobby for fuck's sake. Or at least dial it back a little."

Her heart twists as she thinks of her twin.

As far as he's concerned, she's a burden not a sister. Resentment oozes from him every time they're in the same room, clotting the air, making it impossible for her to breathe without feeling like she'll choke. She doubts it will ever get better.

Especially now that the truth is out about the social media pages.

She expected him to blow up when she came to him in tears, laptop clutched to her chest. Peyton had just told the group what she found, and they were planning to meet in person. Olivia knew she should make up an excuse, some reason why she couldn't show her face... but Mallory... she wanted to meet her. She *had* to meet her, even if the thought of coming clean about the profile was enough to knock the wind out of her.

Rowan sat on her ratty couch, picking at a loose thread on one of the cushions and nursing a beer. It's like he always needed to be a little bit drunk or high to stand being around her. She felt his hate like a knife to the jugular.

As she explained, tears streaking her cheeks, salt stinging her tongue, she kept waiting for him to get angry, but instead he pinched the bridge of his nose. Instead, he shook his head and the disappointment, the judgment, she saw in his eyes was enough to bleed her dry.

"I know that Rowan gave you the bone saw," Britt says pulling her from her thoughts.

They walk down a narrow hall, a series of bright fluorescent lights humming overhead. No windows, just chalky white walls that scuff with the slightest brush against them. Black marks scar the paint, evidence that prior to Jared's disappearance, a construction crew had been through, lugging lumber and materials to different parts of the resort. Signs of life should make the space seem less ominous, but there's a chill to the air reminiscent of a haunted house, a feeling of presence in the otherwise empty structure.

Olivia shudders.

"The bone saw," Britt repeats, her voice an unnerving monotone. She's regained most of her strength, and her sentences aren't as slurred as they were earlier, but she still wobbles on her feet. "I know he gave it to you. I was out of it, but not that out of it."

"I-I can give it back to you." Olivia stuffed the handle of the saw into her boot so that the flat side of the blade presses against her lower leg. As she walks, it pushes up slightly, feeling as if it might knock loose at any moment.

"Don't bother. I'll take it back if I need it."

Olivia's skin prickles. "Rowan only wanted to—"

"Rowan should be more concerned about himself. He paired off with Jared's killer after all."

Except Olivia doubts that's what really happened. As far as she's concerned, Mallory isn't capable of murder. She's gentle to a fault, and that gentleness is what initially sparked Olivia's attraction. She remembers the sick feeling that rolled off Mallory when she confessed to running the account, and heat rushes to her cheeks. Confusion, betrayal. They may have a chance of surviving this nightmare, but their friendship certainly doesn't.

It's one thing to lie about your identity when you're a kid and don't know any better, and another to continue into your twenties. She sank so deep into the lie that she couldn't stand the hurt of owning up to it... or what she would lose by coming clean.

With Rowan's profile as her shield, Olivia discovered a boldness in herself that she'd only dreamt of embodying in the real world. As Rowan, she wrote poetry, she bared her heart, and she spoke her mind.

She was herself, amplified.

As Rowan, she had Mallory.

And things with Mallory felt right—they felt so much like baking.

Olivia liked talking to Mallory, and she knew the recipe by heart. She could anticipate the variables; she knew exactly what to say and how to say it. And everything with Mallory flowed so naturally that after a while Olivia didn't need to even follow a recipe anymore. Their conversations were organic; they were cane sugar and freshly tapped maple syrup. They were everything. The only fiction between them was Rowan's name and photos. Everything else was so real, and so precious... She couldn't lose that.

Which is why she didn't hesitate to agree when Rowan offered to pretend to be her for the meet up. She supposes a part of her had wished that Mallory would see through it and recognize that it was Olivia, not Rowan, that she'd been talking to all those years. Olivia kept waiting for Mallory to see *her*. Instead, she was just as invisible as ever.

It was a disaster even before Peyton's game started, and things just kept spiraling from there.

Erika's murder.

Rowan's severed finger.

Everything is—as her twin would put it—completely fucked.

Still, of all the secrets that have come to light in the heat of Peyton's games, Mallory's murder confession isn't one of them. There's no way she killed him. There's no way Jared is dead.

He *has* to be Peyton.

No one would go through all this trouble to avenge his death. Hell, the Discord group only agreed to meet at the resort to make sure he actually did die.

And in Olivia's experience, no one loves Jared more than Jared. It must be him. Only he would be enough of a psychopath to put something like this in motion.

He's not dead, no way. Jared is like a cockroach; he infests and endures. It would be damn near impossible to kill him. She should know, she's thought about it more times than she can count... and even tried it once herself.

She rubs at her wrist, nursing away a phantom pain. Pink irritation blossoms beneath her touch.

Olivia feels nothing toward Jared anymore. Nothing close to love anyway. A lingering sense of fear? Yes. A complicated, poisoned, sort of nostalgia? Sure. But she hasn't forgotten a moment of their time together, and she wants nothing more than to pay him back in turn.

She's tried before, all the pain she bottles up, everything he put her through was enough to bring it out. She'd never felt violent before him; she'd always been so accommodating. She was a lot louder as a child, but people found her morose and hard to be around. So she stopped talking, she sat and smiled and nodded. And suddenly she had friends. Because other people liked control too, and the easier Olivia was to control and the more she got along with everyone else. Ignored, or revered. It didn't matter. Until Jared. That's when Olivia's silence, the thing that protected her for so long, became her downfall. Because Jared exploited it. She spoke in whispers, silent tears. She wasn't the type to scream for help, and he loved that. But that's the thing about Jared: he's a manipulator, but not a particularly clever one.

Jared isn't smart enough to dream up something like this without help. He's never been especially meticulous or good at planning; he's too impulsive. She curses under her breath. None of this makes sense.

A lot like Rowan's insistence that she pair off with Britt. She glances over at her partner, the blood crusted over her chin, the glazed look in her eyes, and a pang of something between pity and fear shoots through her.

Rowan assured her, with his forehead pressed to hers—all sweat and blood and symmetry—that she was strong, that she could handle herself.

"Liv," he said, hands clasp firmly on the sides of her face just like he would do when they were children, tethering her to him, not letting her sink into the swirling mess inside her head. "You've survived so much already, and you'll survive this too. Look at Britt, she's a mess. If things get bad, you can take her down easily."

"I-I can't." Tears pricked the corners of her eyes. "I can't kill someone, I would never even consider killing someone... I can't."

His eyes softened for a minute, not anger, that familiar disappointment, the kind that seared her gut. "We both know that's a lie, Liv."

All the feeling left her as he slipped the handle of the bone saw into her palm and didn't let up pressure until she grabbed hold of it.

"Rowan, I..."

"You can do this."

"What if we need to work together?" she asked. "What if—"

"Trust me, you'll be safe pairing off with her."

Olivia hadn't quite believed him then but didn't want to argue. Now, she thinks that maybe he was right, or maybe it won't even be an issue and Britt will drop dead before the game even starts.

Britt drags a finger through the blood that crusts her chin, and Olivia watches wearily as bits flake off, a sick trail of breadcrumbs marking where they're going and where they've been. She keeps mumbling to herself, as if she's still stuck halfway inside a dream.

Olivia hugs her arms to her chest. The smell of smoke and cedar invades the space around her, the same scent as Jared's cologne.

"You're worse than I am," Britt says, and an icepick of dread pierces through her. She can't be in worse shape than Britt, that's impossible. She didn't even drink from the flask.

"What do you mean?" she squeaks.

"You haven't said more than ten words to me since we paired off. I thought I was socially awkward, but you're on another level."

"I just... I know you're still recovering from the last round. I didn't think you'd be up for talking." Olivia is hit by another wave of Jared's cologne, but she pushes all thoughts of him down deep. Her last memory of him—the way his lip curled when he saw her, like a predator showing off its fangs—she stuffs it away until it all but fades. The feeling lingers though, a knot in her gut that refuses to unwind, a sheen of sweat across her skin. Things never fade completely; they always stick to her like flypaper. She collects bad feelings the way some people collect ex-boyfriends.

"I'm doing much better," Britt insists, even as one of her eyelids hangs in a curtain of loose skin halfway across her eye.

She hiccups and a fresh trail of spittle joins the crust on her chin, but at least there isn't any blood, and the further they walk, the more she seems to perk up.

Olivia watches her with a mix of fascination and horror as her body jerks. Once, twice. Her movements snap back to normal over the course of several steps and it reminds her of the final scene in *The Usual Suspects* when Keyser Soze goes from a limp walk to a confident gait.

Olivia's pulse pounds in her ears. What if Britt was faking the whole time, and now that they're alone... Olivia is acutely aware of how the bone saw presses against her skin. She runs through the steps it would take to grab the saw, turn on Britt, slit her throat. Would she have enough time to wield the blade before Britt's fingers wove through her hair or clamped around her neck? Would she have the nerve to fight back at all?

"Fuck," Britt says suddenly, and Olivia jumps. "It's like I just woke up out of dead sleep. Holy shit." Her hand trembles as she lifts it to her face and runs it across her eyelid as they stop near the end of the hall. She leans back against the wall, looking like a deflated puppet.

The fluorescent bulbs sputter, a panicked zap, zap, zap as Britt folds in on herself.

But there's something in her stance, a tension in her legs that looks out of place next to her crumpled upper half. It's like she's braced to lunge, and Olivia's fingers trace the handle of the bone saw worrying again if she has what it takes to survive.

Britt watches her. Britt watches so closely. Through drooping, blood-crusted eyes.

"Are you okay?" Olivia asks, her voice so incredibly small, drowned out by the rush of blood through her ears, but only a low, throaty gurgle escapes Britt's mouth in response.

Something isn't right. The air in the hall has shifted, and the hair on Olivia's arms stands on end. Every nerve in her body screams out electric bright, begging for her to retreat back the way they came, but she can't seem to will her legs to move. "Britt, are you okay?"

A second too late, she notices how Britt's feet slide across the tile floor. A second too late she notices her push off the wall. And Olivia doesn't get a chance to turn and run before Britt cracks her skull into hers, knocking her to the ground.

A soft grunt as she hits the tile. A loud yelp as Britt comes down on top of her.

They roll, Britt latching onto her, and Olivia kicking wildly.

The bone saw knocks free from her boot and clatters against the floor. Olivia gropes for it blindly, but Britt continues to pull at her, they continue to roll. They roll so much that Olivia is dizzied by the force of it, and as they ricochet off the walls, as they claw, and tug, and scream, she knows that even if they were to stop, the hall would keep on spinning.

Jared's scent wraps around her like a blanket, and they're a blur of limbs, and sharp angles and in her confusion, Olivia isn't sure where the smell of his cologne is coming from or why. Maybe it's a sign that she's going to die. Maybe it's a sign that she'll knock her head against the tile the wrong way, or Britt will rip out her jugular, and her psycho ex-boyfriend will be there waiting to ferry her to hell.

"So you were just pretending to be messed up this whole time?" Olivia wails as her back smacks against the wall, adding another black scuff to the chalky white.

Britt pauses, pulling back slightly, and Olivia's chest heaves as she tries to catch her breath. She jabs a finger toward the loose skin around her eye. "Does this look pretend to you?"

Up close, the eye is so much worse than from a distance, the skin puckering, pockets of curtainlike flesh clotted with blood and pus.

Olivia is still staring as Britt pushes against her shoulders, knocking her to her back.

Her head hits the tile with a dull thump, and she shrieks. A wicked sense of vertigo drowns her as the fluorescent bulbs buzz overhead.

She's so dazed she hardly notices as Britt straddles her, only rousing slightly as Britt leans in—Jared's scent bursting from her like the fallout from a mushroom cloud.

"Why does it smell like Jared in here?" Olivia chokes out, head still spinning, aching, *hurting*. She hurts all over. She fears it'll never stop. She squeezes her eyes shut, but the dark inside her mind thrashes like the sea.

"Shhhh," Britt murmurs, and Olivia stiffens as she feels the pads of her thumbs grazing her eyes. "I'm sorry I can't make this quicker for you."

Britt presses down slightly, and Olivia yelps, the pressure causing orange lights to spark beneath her eyelids.

Soon I won't see colors anymore, she thinks, her heart rabbiting against her ribs. *Soon I won't have eyes, they'll be jelly.*

But then the pressure against her eyelids is gone, and the weight on her chest shifts, and after a few cautious breaths, Olivia cracks her eyes open.

Britt still hovers above her but has eased off considerably. From where she lies, the other woman's face is silhouetted against the bright fluorescents, the light haloing around her bleached hair. Her expression is unreadable.

She lifts to her feet, swaying slightly as Olivia's chest heaves. She wants desperately to sit up, to run back down the hall, to do anything at all, but she's frozen in place, blood pounding in her ears.

In her peripheral vision, Olivia watches Britt sink down against the wall before extending her leg and nudging her with the toe of her boot. Olivia stays perfectly still despite the kick.

"I really thought I could do it," Britt slurs, the words thick and liquidy. "I thought it would be easy. I'm sorry. I'll try again in a minute, okay?"

"N-no, not okay." Finally, Olivia eases into a sitting position and turns to face Britt, whose eyelid looks dangerously like melted wax, her open eye glassy and bloodshot.

The air clumps inside Olivia's throat. The bone saw lies to the left of where she sits, and she hooks her fingers around the handle, pulling it closer.

"I don't want to kill you," Britt says, her voice flat, gaze focused on something to the left of Olivia's head.

"So then why…"

"That's the game." Britt laughs darkly. "I'll never make it through the next round like this. It's you or me. I don't want it to be me."

She takes a moment to cough, pink-tinged phlegm flying from her mouth. "Besides, you'd be better off dying now. You're too nice for all this bullshit."

The word nice reverberates through Olivia's head, a serrated wire behind her eyes. Cutting, and cutting, and cutting. Until there's nothing left. Until Olivia is in chunks, until she doesn't even know who she is anymore.

"I'm not as nice as you think," Olivia murmurs, lifting the saw, the blade winking under the fluorescents. Britt's good eye flashes at the sight of the blade, and Olivia tenses as Britt lunges toward her again.

Only this time, Olivia is ready. She kicks out, catching Britt in her ribs, a soft grunt escaping her lips as she hunches over.

Olivia doesn't even think—there's no way she can think, not with the blood rushing in her ears, and her heart knocking so hard inside her chest that she fears it'll leave a bruise. She takes a deep breath, Jared's scent burning her nostrils, and dives against Britt.

She hesitates for only a moment before hooking an arm around Britt's throat, and raising the saw, pressing it against her flesh. Britt feels so soft, so fragile. Olivia's pulse roars in her ears. She's so fragile, and all it would take is a little bit of pressure and—

"Oh no, no, no," Peyton's voice slices into the hall and Olivia freezes. "Not yet, my darlings. Believe me, as much as I'm enjoying the show, you'll want to save the bloodshed for when you get to the next round of our little game. In fact, you'll need a little bit of blood to get into the escape room. Which was *supposed* to be a surprise, but who knew the two of you would be so *eager*. Now Olivia, be a dear and march Britt the rest of the way down the hall and wait for further instructions."

Peyton.

The game.

Blood.

It's enough to snap Olivia back to reality, and suddenly she's painfully aware of the vein in Britt's neck and how it pulses under the saw's blade. Suddenly, she bites back a scream as she realizes how close she just came to slitting her friend's throat.

"I-I'm sorry," she mumbles, lowering the saw. "That wasn't me. I didn't mean to."

Britt runs a hand along her neck, divots from the blade still visible in her pale flesh. "I did the same thing to you."

The game is starting to get to them both, Olivia realizes helplessly. She's not safe from Britt. Britt's not safe from her. Tears prick the corners of her eyes, even though she promised herself she wouldn't cry anymore. But the tears come anyway, hot and salty. They blur her vision, but she blinks them back, refusing to let them fall. Rowan thought she was strong enough to do this. She isn't going to prove him wrong.

Thick ribbons of tension permeate the air, and Olivia eases up off the floor, helping Britt up with her. Her head spins. What does Peyton mean they're going to need blood to get into the escape room?

"Are you okay to walk?" she asks Britt.

Britt glances from Olivia's face to where she jabs the end of the bone saw into her ribs. Even though her hand shakes, she stands firm.

"It doesn't seem like I have much a of a choice," Britt murmurs and Olivia half pulls, half herds her along, careful to keep the bone saw angled between them just in case. But Britt seems to deteriorate again, scraping another crust of blood from her chin and grimacing as the flakes float down to the tile floor. She gulps back a hiccup, moving like an automaton as Olivia nudges her along.

Smoke and cedar crowds Olivia's nostrils and she takes a second to remind herself that Jared isn't here. Something nags at the back of her head every time the scent invades her space, but she can't think straight—not with the threat of blood looming, and the bone saw clenched in her fist. Not when walking next to Britt feels like walking next to a ghost.

They reach the end of the hall, and there's a slight turn before the space opens to reveal a square, tiled entryway and a cream-colored door. Fear jackknifes up Olivia's spine at the site of the escape room's entrance.

The sign is only half painted onto the board fastened above the door, but it's clearly fifties themed. It's mint green, with the words *Escape Room* scrawled across it, the text flanked by two cartoons of smiling girls in poodle skirts.

It's fifties themed.

Olivia's mouth goes dry.

She's always envied fifties housewives to a certain, shameful degree. Her mom instilled in her from a young age that there was a right and a wrong way to embrace her femininity, and the way Olivia's worship of domesticity disturbs her mom to no end. But Olivia can't help it. She loves the idea of it. Of them. Housewives.

Their thin wrists, expertly tailored skirts, and high heels. The sharpness of their nails, and the way they'd hum while doing chores or cooking dinner. It's not that she would want to be that way—not really. She tried with Jared, who was thrilled to find that she fit so nicely, so meekly into the mold, and that ended in disaster. It's more that it seems so much simpler to know exactly what's expected of you, to not have to think, or feel, just to fold laundry.

She knows the reality is so much messier, but she can't help but wonder if she was completely different, if she might have been happier in that role. Baking... not desserts with bleeding centers, not dozens of batches of cupcakes because none of them turn out quite right, but because it's all she could do. All the burden of choice taken out of it. The thought of this alone makes her feel weak and ashamed. Her grip tightens around the bone saw.

"There's no way in," Britt says, snapping Olivia out of her thoughts.

Olivia frowns. She was so focused on the sign that she failed to notice the padlock clamping the door shut. She jiggles the knob and pulls on the lock, but the door is sealed shut.

Only when she lowers her head in defeat does she find a red arrow scrawled onto the tile. Not paint, lipstick. Before she even realizes she's doing it, she raises a hand to her mouth, the pads of her fingers grazing over her bottom lip. It's her exact shade of lipstick.

How would Peyton know? Did Rowan tell her?

Or...

Olivia sucks in a breath.

Jared is the one doing this. Jared really is Peyton.

"Olivia?" Britt asks, and Olivia stiffens.

She can't afford to space out like that. Britt might not be poised to attack again anytime soon, but the threat is still there. It lingers like the scent of Jared's cologne.

Before the thought of him can pull her back into the fractured recesses of her mind, Olivia clamps her hand around Britt's wrist, and they follow the arrow into another thin, chalky-colored hallway. It only takes a few steps for them to reach what appears to be a dead end, and Olivia's brow furrows.

It's the same, easily scuffed color as the hallway, only this one is pristine, hauntingly clean. There's a small panel carved into it and Olivia jumps when it springs open to reveal a small cubby with plastic beaker on what looks like a food scale.

"Okay, Olivia," Peyton says, her voice slicing in over the speaker system. "Now, you can make her bleed."

12

OLIVIA

Olivia doesn't even realize that she's let go of the bone saw until it clatters against the tiles. Faintly, she's aware of how Peyton continues to speak, grinding out instructions, joking about how for someone who seemed so bloodthirsty just a few minutes earlier, Olivia's looking awfully pale right now.

"All you need to do is make her bleed *a little bit*. I still need both of you for the next round so definitely don't slit her throat or anything, but you have to fill that beaker a certain amount, and trigger a certain weight on the scale if you want to—"

Somewhere in the middle of Peyton's tangent, the solution hits Olivia with blinding clarity and it's all she can do not to burst out laughing. It's so absurd. There's no way. It's too easy, and yet...

Nausea creeps up her throat when she realizes—

It's Jared.

It's really Jared.

Only he'd design a trap this fucking stupid.

She pushes the sick feeling down and squares her shoulders. She can do this.

"No," Olivia says firmly, bending to pick the bone saw back

up. She tucks it back into her boot and straightens to find Britt leaning against the wall, staring at her questioningly.

A pause as static crackles in over the speaker system.

"What the fuck do you mean 'no'?" Peyton hisses. "You don't have a choice."

"And you're not as clever as you think you are." Olivia plucks the beaker from the scale and tosses it behind her.

"If you don't participate, you'll be trapped in that hallway and starve. Is that what you want?"

"We're not going to be trapped in here, and there isn't going to be any blood either. I use something like this when I bake to measure out ingredients, I know how it works." Olivia lays her palm against the scale, applying tentative amounts of pressure. After fiddling around with it for a few moments, there's a loud click and pride wells up inside her chest. It's a burst of adrenaline, and she can't help but grin. Rowan would be so proud of her right now, and a smug little piece of her wishes she could rub it in his face.

"See Ro," she'd tell him. "My baking is good for something after all!"

Her smile falters, however, when the panel in the wall swings open to reveal a dark, crawlspace-like passageway. "Oh, no."

Peyton's laughter pierces through the speaker system. "Oh, yes, darling. We're just getting started. And you're going to have to go through my specially designed... I guess you could call it a tunnel, to get into the escape room."

Endless, deadly possibilities ricochet through Olivia's head. A dark space filled with sharp blades, or noxious gas, or... her attention scrapes over to Britt, who hovers just behind her, eyes glazed.

The tunnel, as Peyton called it, would be the perfect place for Britt to attack her again. No cameras, no way for Peyton to watch, it's a golden opportunity for Britt to ruin the game before it even begins. She stands rigidly as Britt shuffles over to the makeshift doorway.

Britt doesn't even hesitate before dipping inside, and the darkness gobbles her completely.

"Let's get this over with." Britt's voice leaks out from the swirling black, and Olivia can't help the low moan that escapes her lips.

The fluorescent bulbs hum overhead, and she's stricken by the contrast between the artificially lit hall and the organic swirl of shadows beyond the doorway. It's wrong. It's so wrong. Olivia feels unsafe in a way that would only be logical in a dark alley or on a walk home alone. Then again, Olivia has always been paranoid about that kind of thing—gripping car keys between her fingers when she would leave her waitressing shifts late, calling Rowan when she felt especially dodgy.

She takes a few deep, evenly spaced breaths and focuses on the feeling of the saw against her calf. If things do go to shit inside the tunnel, if Britt tries to hurt her again, she'll be ready. She'll fight back. She'll fight to... She gulps back a gob of spit, and it feels like glue in her throat... She'll fight to the death if she must.

"Olivia?" Britt calls, pulling her out of her thoughts. "Are you coming?"

"How do we know it's not a trap?" she asks.

"This whole thing is a trap."

Olivia sucks air in between her teeth and follows Britt into the doorway. After the initial entrance, it opens up slightly, and Olivia can stand to her full height, but the passageway is narrow, claustrophobic. The air inside tastes sour and smells like a mix of perspiration and detergent, remnants of whoever dug it out to begin with. Even though it's close to pitch black, the light from the entrance reaches through the length of it for a while, and she can see Britt's outline waiting just before there's a twist in the passage, like a kink in a spine.

Olivia hurries to catch up with Britt and another wave of Jared's cologne hits her. She's left lightheaded, struggling to stay upright in the narrow space. She wishes that Rowan were there to calm her down—knock some sense into her, as he would put it. He's harsh with her, she knows that, and she still feels like a little kid around him even though they're the same age. She doubts he'll ever see her as fully grown or self-sufficient, but sometimes that's exactly what she needs, someone who's straightforward with her, even if it hurts her feelings. That's what she thought she was finding in Jared when they first got together. He had the same gruff, no-nonsense attitude toward her long list of personal quirks, and it wasn't until much later that she realized that he and Rowan were nothing alike.

Rowan's tough guy approach is rooted in love.

Jared got off on the control.

Her mood darkens and she pauses for a moment, bracing against the wall of the passageway, which is remarkably smooth, almost stone-like.

A shuffle in the darkness as Britt undoubtedly notices how far behind she's fallen. Olivia's surprised she's chugging along as quickly as she is given her condition.

A wave of unease pierces through her.

Unless Britt's not as bad off as she seems. Unless she's just been waiting for an opportunity to strike again.

"Are you okay back there?"

Olivia's throat feels like it's stuffed with cotton, and she struggles to get the words out. "Fine, just thinking."

"I'm not going to try to hurt you again," Britt says. "You don't have to worry."

"What makes you think I'm worried?"

"Out in the hall, you kept looking at me like I was contagious. And now your voice is shaking. It sounds like you're crying."

Olivia raises a hand to her cheek and frowns when it comes

away damp. She is crying. She hadn't even noticed, but the tears trace salty tears down her face and her stomach tightens. She thought she was so much stronger than this. It's so easy for her to fall apart.

"How was someone like you with someone like Jared? It makes no fucking sense," Britt mutters, her voice soft through the dark.

"You were friends with him," she shoots back like an accusation, but Britt continues to shuffle through the darkness. When Britt first said she was Jared's friend, Olivia was sick with fear that she'd figure out she was his ex-girlfriend. But the fear didn't last long.

Jared had a thing against sharing their relationship with his friends. His excuse at the time was that he didn't like how weird it made things. The guys in the group would give him hell for settling down and not being open to his usual debauchery, and the girls would get jealous that they couldn't hook up with him anymore.

"Are you still hooking up with them now?" She had asked, terrified that he was keeping their exclusivity a secret so that he could cheat.

"What the fuck is wrong with you?" He spat, the conversation dissolving into one of their many arguments. He never confirmed either way.

Britt turns suddenly, making her way back down the passage, and stopping so close to Olivia that she nearly slams into her forehead. "How long did you and Jared date anyway?"

"What? Why?" she chokes.

"He never mentioned you."

"He never mentioned you either." She doesn't bother to add that Jared refused to tell her anything about his friend group. Anytime he went out without her it was always "hanging out with the guys," or "with a couple of buddies of mine and the girls they're seeing." Now, she regrets not learning more about his life outside of Instagram, outside of the public image that he so carefully cultivated for his brand.

The smell of smoke and cedar soaks the space between them, and it's like Jared is pressed up against Olivia. She nearly gags. It's as if he's saying, *"Back off, she's mine."*

Her heartbeat pounds in her ears as Britt leans in closer, the smell of smoke and cedar closing in with her.

Jared.

Why does *she* smell like Jared?

Her head aches, pain left over from their earlier fight.

Olivia searches Britt's face, really studies it. People look different in the dark and Britt is no exception. Olivia doesn't recognize her. All her features are morphed together, like wet clay. All her colors are muted.

The smell of smoke and cedar continues to crowd Olivia's senses, and it's like Jared is standing right beside her. She's so panicked by the thought that her breath hitches.

Britt is the only one here, she reminds herself.

Britt is the only one here.

Full body chills.

Violent tremors in both her hands.

It takes everything she has not to spill her guts, and she forces herself to stay standing and maintain eye contact with Britt. "Why are you wearing Jared's sweatshirt?"

"What?"

"Your sweatshirt, it's his, isn't it? It smells exactly like him. This whole time, I kept smelling him and I thought I was losing my mind, but I wasn't. You're wearing his sweatshirt."

Britt sucks air in between her teeth and nods her head slightly, the movement blurred in the dark.

"Did he give that to you?" Olivia asks, her voice strained. "He never gave me any of his clothes, and I was his girlfriend."

"You were a punching bag," Britt shoots back, her voice flat.

The comment shouldn't hurt. Olivia knows that Britt is

right. In the beginning she thought that Jared was attracted to her because she was nice. He told her as much, that he was used to girls who wore leather and weren't shy about sex, but Olivia was different. He said that he liked how she got shy around him, like a schoolgirl with a crush. She was so *nice*.

"It's nice, you're nice. Such a nice girl," he would say and kiss her on the forehead.

She knows the real reason is because she's weak. She's the kind of girl who hangs onto every word, tears into every scrap of affection. She hates herself for it, but even after everything that Jared put her through, she doesn't think she's changed. She still clings to the smallest compliments, still lives for the most fleeting attention. If anything, it's even worse now, like he's knocked all sense of autonomy out of her, and she needs constant validation as she tries to unravel if there was any truth in the complex web of insults he peppered her with daily.

She's weak. She's always been weak. She sinks deeper and deeper into her negative thoughts and it's like she's drowning in them. And even though it's the last thing that should matter right now, Britt wearing Jared's sweatshirt hurts. It hurts so badly.

"So what, you dated him after me?" she asks, shame branding her like a hot iron as her voice cracks. Why does she care? Why does it *hurt*?

Britt isn't the kind of girl that Jared would normally go for. She can't imagine someone like Britt putting up with any of his antics and part of her panics when she wonders if maybe that's something she could have done when they were together. Maybe things could have been different. Maybe she just needed to be stronger, for once in her life, be stronger.

Britt shakes her head again and inches forward, her arms stretched out as if she might embrace Olivia, grab her, squish in the sides of her head. The energy inside the passage shifts, and she can feel the danger radiating off Britt in waves. She considers using the bone saw but the thought of spilling blood causes bile to scotch the back of her throat. So instead, Olivia pushes past Britt, continuing down the passage.

Britt follows closely at her heels.

Olivia pauses near the end of the passage, suddenly unsure, overwhelmed. Even though she's desperate to escape there's no telling what waits for her in the next room. She has no idea if everything is about to get a whole lot worse. Her hesitation gives Britt the chance to lean in close, her fingers grazing the blade sticking out of her boot. Olivia presses up against the cool wall of the passage, the cold burning into her back. She tenses for another struggle.

Instead, Britt hovers close to her face, her hot breath fanning over the bridge of Olivia's nose.

"Did you sleep with him?" Olivia asks, because it's been eating at her and she's not going to be able to let it go until she knows.

Britt cocks her head to the side and there's a beat of silence before she answers. "Technically, yes."

"While I was with him?"

"I didn't know you were with him."

Olivia wishes it didn't feel like a slap in the face.

"Did you kill him?" she asks.

"Mallory killed Jared," Britt says, but there's something in her voice that's so cold, so detached. And she lets her fingers fall away from the blade. "I was telling the truth before; I don't want to kill you."

She pats Olivia on the shoulder and Olivia wants so badly to believe her, but she can't stop shaking, can't stop waiting for Britt to change her mind again and lunge for the blade.

Olivia inches back, and her spine presses up against a wall, the plaster cool through the fabric of her shirt. There's a mechanical click as it shifts from behind her. She tumbles into a brightly lit room.

As promised by the sign, the escape room is modeled after a fifties style diner. Complete with fake milkshakes on the counter, swirling white with bright maraschino cherries on top. The dining counter is mint green, and the floor is tiled in black and white. It even smells like what Olivia imagines an old-timey malt shop would smell like. The air seems sweet to the point where it makes her teeth ache. It's like a room is encased in a cloud of powdered sugar.

A light trickle of music floats in as if through a jukebox. Olivia recognizes the tune immediately. It's an instrumental rendition of "Sulking Seething," Jared's favorite HyveMind song. Olivia cringes. It's like the song is stalking them, a sick thread through this twisted game, a constant reminder that Jared is the reason why they're all there. The melody has been slowed down, the whine of the instruments is high-pitched and fuzzy around the edges. As it loops repeatedly, Olivia's chilled to her core.

Jared used to play "Sulking Seething" on repeat anytime he was in an especially sour mood. He kept the volume so loud that their framed photos would shake against the walls, and they received more than a few noise complaints from neighbors in their apartment complex.

"Listen to the lyrics, babe," he would tell her—a hard edge to his voice. "Really listen to them."

She still can't hear certain words without her stomach flipping.

Britt slips from the passageway into the escape room and Olivia watches as she makes a beeline for a giant screen that sits fastened against the far wall. She stands up on her tiptoes, but her fingers barely graze the bottom of the screen. Behind Olivia, a sheet of metal seals off the passageway, and she is painfully aware of how there are no windows, and the only doors—two massive things on either side of the room—don't have knobs.

"Sulking Seething" loops again, and she hugs her arms to her chest. "What are you doing?"

Britt glances over her shoulder. "This is the first screen we've seen in here. It's all been an intercom system up until this point." She hops in place before giving up with an exasperated sigh. "I thought it might mean something."

Olivia scans the room. It's not like Peyton to leave no instructions, and sure enough, there are two red X's carved into a set of tiles under the screen to the left of where Britt is standing.

She points at them. "I think we're supposed to stand there."

Olivia makes her way over to the X opposite Britt, but since giving up on the screen, her partner's entire focus is set on the dining counter. She pulls at the loose skin around her eye, her head cocked to the side.

"That shade is called Cool Mint," Britt says. "Or maybe it's Faint Clover. They're practically identical. It's different from hospital green... originally named spinach green, which they used to paint asylums in the fifties. They used spinach green because it complimented blood red—that's why scrubs are that strange shade of turquoise."

Olivia steps up next to Britt, placing a hand lightly on her shoulder. "We should get started. Whatever this is... I want to get it over with as quickly as possible."

The last three bars of "Sulking Seething" pierce through the room, and Jared's cologne rolls off Britt in waves.

Olivia recoils. "You need to tell me why you're wearing Jared's sweatshirt. By the smell of it, it hasn't been washed in over a year. That or you've been spritzing it with his cologne." Olivia isn't sure which possibility is worse.

"He was my friend," Britt says simply. "He was my friend, and this is all I have left of him."

Olivia's pulse pounds in her ears as "Sulking Seething" starts over again. "Was he... nice to you?"

"He wasn't nice to anyone."

They fall into an uncomfortable silence, and while Olivia steps into place on her red X, and the tile clicks down, nothing happens. Britt crouches next to her tile and runs a finger along the red X before straightening back up and turning to Olivia.

"If this were my trap, I would paint it better," Britt says, resting the tip of her shoe against the tile, but not pressing down yet. "I wouldn't start with Baker-Miller pink, that's for sure. That's a grand finale color, that's a color you lock someone in a room with and let them stew in for hours. It's no way to start off the tasting menu of pain."

"Tasting menu of pain is sort of poetic." Olivia's pulse continues to hammer against her insides, and she wants to slam the other tile down, to get this over with. "But you're right... something is off about this."

Because Jared is the one behind it. Because Jared doesn't have the skill to actually pull something like this off.

"It's just not put together cohesively," Britt says, her voice cold, analytical. "The way things are wired is impressive. The buttons and the metal dividers between hallways and rooms seem complex, but at its core, the set-up is very simple. I don't think whoever built this is a genius; they just did their research. And the actual traps are kind of lame, right? She referenced *Saw* when she first came on the intercom system, you'd think she would be more creative than this."

Olivia swallows back a lump in her throat. "Do you... want her to be more creative?"

"Not at all. If anything, it's better for us if the traps are predictable." Britt continues to toe at the red X but doesn't apply any pressure, and Olivia hyper fixates on how scuffed and dirty they are. She points up at the black screen. "Like, this is probably going to be timed. So, are you ready?"

Olivia gives a small nod as Britt stretches the length of her foot out over the tile and stomps down. The tile dips into the floor with a click, and the screen on the wall lights up green.

At first that's all that happens, and Olivia doesn't think that anything else is going to come of it. The screen is the extent of the horror. It's too mundane, too manageable.

Then, the music grinds to a halt.

A plexiglass barrier slices down like a guillotine between them, and startled, Olivia jumps. Her first instinct is to throw herself at the divider but before she gets a chance to do so, Peyton's voice trickles into the room.

"Hello, darlings. Are you ready to play?"

The entrance to the miniature golf course is christened with another one of Peyton's red arrows. Paint slices up the center of the door to a large skull and crossbones sign fastened above the entryway. Two pirate carvings poke out of the skull's eye sockets. They're jolly caricatures with plump cheeks and wide grins, but their eyes have been scraped away, and their swords, which cross at the bridge of where the skull's nose would be, drip with the same red pigment as the arrow.

The back of Mallory's neck prickles.

"Well, that's not ominous at all," Rowan says, pausing for a moment. "That was a joke, you're supposed to laugh."

She folds her arms over her chest. "You nearly gutted me a few minutes ago, sorry if I don't feel like laughing."

"I had a momentary lapse in judgment."

Her eyes linger on where the knife hangs curled through his belt. "What happens the next time your judgment lapses?"

"You better be ready." Rowan rests a hand on the handle and Mallory's body tenses.

She's listened to enough true crime podcasts to know that this is the moment when he pulls out the knife and goes right for her throat. She imagines the blade sinking into the soft center of her neck and her insides clench. Knowing that he's a stranger, and a strange man no less, makes it so much worse. She hasn't been alone with a man since what happened with Jared and she's not sure if she knows how to navigate this kind of interaction. She's not sure if there's a way for women to exist in the world without men wanting to stomp the life out of them. It's so odd to her that this is the way it is with humans when in the animal kingdom it's quite the opposite. Whales and elephants are matriarchal groups, praying mantises and tarantulas eat their mates after they're done with them, lionesses are the hunters of the pride, but somehow, it's the female dog that gets called a bitch, and human girls get their throats slit.

"That was a joke too," Rowan says flatly, pulling his hand back. "Damn it, Mallory. I'm trying to lighten the mood."

"And how exactly does one 'lighten the mood' while trapped in a situation like this?"

"Well, apparently shitty jokes aren't the way to go." He sighs. "Look, I know you didn't want to get stuck with me, but we might as well make the best of this."

"There is no making the best of this," she mutters, stepping off to the side and putting as much distance between herself and Rowan as possible. If Erika were still alive, she'd give Mallory an earful for agreeing to go off with him, but all that's left of Erika is the pulpy mess where her face used to be. Every time Mallory blinks, it strobes inside her head.

Erika's eye, milky and dislodged, staring up from a smear of red. Erika's jawbone, a sharp glint of white against the fleshy carnage that used to be Mallory's best friend.

Every time she closes her eyes, she sees Erika, and Jared... and Kimber too, perfectly intact but sinister all the same.

Mallory digs her fingers into the flesh of her upper arm.

There's a chance that Britt is wrong about seeing Kimber

with Jared, but a tug in Mallory's gut says that she's not. Kimber must have known Jared somehow. She must be involved in all of this. This horror. This chaos. Mallory clings to the idea of Kimber being a suspect not because it's logical or likely, but because it would make Erika's death mean something. Deep down, she knows that there's no meaning in chaos. Deep down, she knows that terrible things happen to good people just like good dogs get abused, and abandoned, and put to sleep. But she's not sure if she can stomach it anymore. She's surprised that she doesn't collapse under the weight of how unfair it all is.

"Mallory," Rowan says. "I know you wanted to be paired up with Liv but—"

"I wanted to be paired with someone who didn't just try to kill me," she snaps, secretly grateful that he pulled her back from the carnival of terror inside her head. "Besides, I don't think Olivia wants anything to do with me since I murdered her boyfriend."

"Ex-boyfriend. And I'm pretty sure that offing Jared won you points as far as Liv is concerned." Rowan reaches out and grabs onto the door's handle but turns back to Mallory before he opens it. "Actually, I do have a question."

"What?" she snaps.

"Why aren't you pissed at Liv for pretending to be me? She's basically been catfishing you since middle school."

"I never said that I'm not pissed..." Mallory isn't sure that she has the emotional bandwidth to process everything with Olivia right now. Instead, she clings to the good memories, the nights spent eating takeout over voice chat while they streamed movies together. Mallory's already lost one of her oldest friends to Peyton's game, she's not ready to give Olivia up too—even if she isn't who she claimed to be. "We have bigger things to worry about right now."

"Well, you clearly care what she thinks about the whole Jared thing."

Mallory cares what *everyone* thinks, but she doesn't bother to correct him. "I care that she thinks I'm a murderer."

"You are a murderer. Unless the definition has changed."

"It was self-defense," she screams, the words scraping through her throat, but Rowan barely reacts.

"Whatever helps you sleep at night." With that, he pulls the door handle, and they step into a pirate-themed reception area. A slow ooze of carnival music plays over the intercom system and Mallory frowns. It seems out of place given the pirate theme.

The lobby is narrow and cluttered, more like a hallway leading through to the main golf course. Two cardboard cutouts stand on either side of the entrance—the same dueling pirates from the sign, and there's a bisected ship set up near the entrance to the course. It's a heinous shade of electric blue, and Mallory wonders what Britt would have to say about the color choice. It clashes with the rest of the room, which is painted in a dizzying array of neon green and red. Only the tile floor, a pristine, glitter-flecked white, provides some relief... or would if it weren't for the red arrows.

"Follow the yellow brick road," Rowan says flatly, and they allow the arrows to guide them back to the course which consists of a series of miniature putting greens built into a wide, reception hall-like maze. It's only half completed. Each hole seems to be set in its proper place, but there are giant plastic sharks, and swords, and skulls laying on their sides throughout the course—each one cocooned in layers of plastic and bubble wrap.

The walls are painted black, and neon signs glow in orange, and purple, and red. Ships, and swords, and flags.

They step deeper into the room. There's a familiar click and gears grind as a sheet of steel comes down, sealing them inside.

The room stirs to life. The air conditioning cranks on first, and there's a deep rattle as it sputters cold air into the space. Goosebumps break out along the backs of Mallory's arms. A secondary set of lights click on igniting blacklight paint that's splattered across the walls. More nautical designs, and among the skulls and sails, a splatter of text, *Hello darlings. XOXO P.*

The blacklights not only ignite the text, they also cause the whites of Rowan's eyes to burn blue. The scrap of bandage around his hand glows dully, and the stain from his ruined finger appears darker, deeper, messier. He looks so much more threatening under the blacklights.

Mallory's skin crawls.

Something's been nagging at her since the group divided up into pairs.

"I'm surprised that you didn't want to go with Olivia when we split up," she says carefully, a prick of fear in her gut. She has a feeling she knows the reason.

"Hate to break it to you, Mallory, but I made sure not to pair off with Liv in case this is a two walk in, only one walks out kind of scenario. I've seen enough movies to know that this is usually how situations like this go down."

Mallory's heart pounds against her ribs, but she does her best to keep her voice level. "And you think that Olivia would be able to hold her own against Britt?"

"Have you seen Britt?" Rowan laughs, showing off a flash of teeth—shockingly blue in the glow of the blacklights. "I'm pretty confident she can."

Mallory runs her fingers over the scalpel in her pocket, knowing that it won't do much against Rowan's knife or his brute strength. She can't ignore the muscles corded through his arms or the solid expanse of his chest beneath his tank top. Even without weapons, she'd be screwed if she had to go up against him one on one.

"Olivia has the bone saw, doesn't she?" Her fingers tighten

around the handle, her gaze fixed on the whites of his eyes, the stinging blue.

"Yes, she does."

"You think that will be enough? Britt is tough."

"So is Liv," he says resting his hand against the knife. "It runs in our family."

Waves of heat flash up into Mallory's forehead. She grapples with the handle of the scalpel, acutely aware of how her palms are slick with sweat. "And you would really kill me if it came to that?"

Rowan scoffs, showing off another flash of his phosphorescent teeth. "What, like you wouldn't kill me if push came to shove?"

"I don't know if I could. You're a person."

"So was Jared."

Mallory draws in a sharp breath, her body tensing. She pulls the scalpel from her pocket and grips it tightly against her side. If Rowan wants a round two of their fight, he's going to get it. She won't hold back; she'll struggle to her last breath if she needs to. But she also knows that it would be smarter to hold off until after Peyton announces the next round. If Rowan is right, and they're forced against each other, fighting now would be one thing. But if there's a chance that they need to work together to make it through this, and she doesn't want to kill their chances before the round even starts.

"That's different. Jared was a *terrible* person," she tells him, easing her grip on the scalpel.

"So that means you chop him up and throw what's left of him around like he's chum?" Rowan sucks air in between his teeth. "That's the thing I don't get, Mallory. You don't seem like a cold-blooded killer in the least, but what you did to him...You scattered him in little pieces all throughout this damn place. That's some heavy shit. At least help me understand what happened to get things to that point."

Even though Mallory had nothing to do with the dismemberment, she bites her tongue. She doubts that Rowan would believe her if she told him the truth, and even thinking about spilling the whole thing leaves a bitter taste in the back of her mouth. She narrows her eyes and crosses her arms. "I haven't told anyone the full story of what happened that night, what makes you think I'd tell a total stranger?"

"Don't be a bitch."

Mallory grits her teeth. "Don't be a dick."

"In case you haven't noticed, being a dick is kind of my whole thing."

"How the fuck is someone like you married? Did your wife lose a bet?"

His jaw twitches, and his hand dives for the knife, but then his eyes flash and he pauses, a cruel smile tugging at the corner of his mouth. "How the fuck didn't you realize that Liv was catfishing you? Were you so desperate for attention that you chose to ignore the red flags, or are you just stupid?"

Mallory has to restrain herself from lunging at him. Rowan shouldn't underestimate a cornered animal. It's freeing, the rage surging through her. Erika always used to tell her that she never stood up for herself, and it's true. She's been forcing down the hurt and pain, forcing down the anger and retreating into the back of her head. Daydreams and nightmares to distract from the pain. But not anymore. Not now. She needs to keep things as civil as possible with Rowan, at least until the round starts and they know what they're up against, but that doesn't mean she can't stand her ground.

"Maybe you didn't kill Jared after all," he goads. "I doubt you have the skills to get away with murder."

"Why do you care about Jared at all?" she asks. "He abused your sister."

He lets out a tight laugh. "It's so much more complicated than that."

Mallory frowns. She keeps glancing at Peyton's glowing message, waiting for the intercom system to crackle on and the other shoe to drop. But there's only silence. Only her, and Rowan, and their blades. "Olivia told me everything."

"She talked to you online for a few hours a day, off and on since she was twelve, I've known her my entire life. And her relationship with Jared..." He takes a deep breath. "There's a lot you don't know about her."

Mallory shakes her head. "I know her better than I know myself."

"You thought she was me."

"All she did was use your name. She's told me all kinds of things, Rowan. I don't want to piss you off any more than I already have, but I feel like there were some things that maybe she didn't feel comfortable confiding in you about."

He drags his teeth along his lower lip as if he can't quite figure out how to respond. Then, with a small shake of his head, he says, "If she told you so much, then she must have told you about all the times she's called me late at night having a mental breakdown over some menial thing, like her job or the state of her apartment, or how she hasn't done enough with her life yet. Has she told you how my wife hates her guts because she's so needy and emotional, and that we've had discussions about whether we're going to allow her around our son on her own when he's older because Kate doesn't want her messing with his head? Oh wait, you didn't even know I existed. You don't know shit about my sister's life."

Mallory's face stings as if he's slapped her. Rowan's dig about not knowing Olivia was a twin pales in comparison to the idea of her being so wildly unstable that she can't be trusted around her nephew. It doesn't make any sense. The person he just described doesn't sound anything like the Olivia that she's gotten to know over the years. True, Olivia is sensitive. True, she feels things deeply, but she's nothing like this hurricane of a person that Rowan's making her out to be.

"Has Liv told you about how many times she's had to move in with me?" Rowan continues. "Sleeping on my couch, in the spare room, on the fucking floor, because things got too overwhelming for her and she forgot to pay her rent, or she lost her shitty retail job, or whatever piece of shit boyfriend she was with at the time got a little too handsy with her?"

"Yes, actually, I do," Mallory says glaring. "She might not have told me about you, but I know she's had to move in with family a few times. I *know* her, Rowan."

He cocks an eyebrow. "Then I guess you also know about her suicide attempts."

Mallory's chest tightens as if someone's squeezing her heart in their fist. Olivia has talked to her about her depression, but never mentioned anything about trying to end her life. "She tried to kill herself?"

Rowan scoffs, offering a look that's somewhere between smug and pitying. "You don't know her, Mallory. You know the version of her that she chose to show you, the version of her that she created for you. So please, tell me again how I'm the one in the wrong here, and how I'm the piece of shit for wanting to get back at her."

Mallory's brow furrows. "Don't get me wrong, I think you're a piece of shit. But I never said you're a piece of shit because of—"

Rowan cuts her off. "For just once in my life, I wanted to to fuck with her. I came here to help Peyton with what I thought was a prank—that's my bad—but I also came here for Liv. Like, yeah, I brought her here, but only because I knew I could keep her safe through whatever we came up against. It's my job to make sure that she's okay. It's my job to look out for her. There's no way you could possibly understand. She's everything to me—she's part of me—but she also suffocates me.

And I'm sick of dealing with it. You would be too if you were me."

Mallory blinks slowly as Rowan's chest heaves, his breath coming in short bursts. This isn't what they were talking about at all. He's going off the rails, he's projecting and as alarmed as Mallory is by the information he's spilling, by the thought of Olivia in inpatient programs and mental health facilities, she knows that understanding what sets Rowan off is a strength.

The initial shock wears off and Mallory takes a moment to consider everything he's told her. True, Olivia wasn't exactly chomping at the bit to show her what a hot mess she is, but neither was Mallory. When Mallory had to move back in with her parents two years after graduation because of money problems, she lied and said it was to help with her dad's illness. When Mallory got fired from her call center job because she went off script, she claimed to have left of her own accord for another opportunity.

She lied. She lied a thousand times over.

But she was also messy and raw in front of Olivia in other ways. And Olivia was honest with her where it counted too. With the books that she loves, and the things that make her cry, the moments that give her the strength to get up in the morning. That has to count for something. Lies, however large, can somehow add up to the truth if told with the right intentions.

"Do you really think it's fair to talk all that shit about your sister?" she asks, breaking the long silence. "You make it sound like she's some master manipulator, but everyone is only showing the version of themselves that they choose to show the other person. The internet has nothing to do with it."

Rowan scoffs. "Don't try to get deep with me."

"I'm not getting deep; I'm stating a fact. You can't shit all over your sister for not wanting to air every piece of dirty laundry she has."

"Yeah, but she was lying to you for years."

"Why do you care? Just because you can't stand Olivia, doesn't mean that everyone else needs to hate her too."

"I love my sister." Rowan pushes Mallory up against the wall, his face inches from hers. She lets out a gasp as her spine hits the plaster. Even though he pins her in place, his grip is loose, his bad hand barely digging into her shoulder. She keeps her gaze focused on the pink stain oozing from his stub of a finger. Her grip tightens on the handle of the scalpel. He may be physically stronger, but now she knows how to set him off emotionally, and he's injured.

He glares down at her, his eyes narrowing when he notices the scabs that dot the backs of her arms. "Looks like you're just as self-destructive as she is. Guess it's a match made in heaven after all."

Heat floods Mallory's cheeks. "I'm not self-destructive."

He cocks an eyebrow. "But you self-harm? Make it make fucking sense."

Her pulse pounds in her ears and she can feel the heat from her cheeks rocket up into her forehead. "I pick at scabs; I don't fucking hurt myself! It's not the same thing!"

"Like how killing Jared wasn't murder?"

She kicks at him, creating space between them and raises the blade. But Rowan catches her by the wrist with his good hand and squeezes, hard.

The scalpel clatters to the floor and her pulse races as he stares down at her. She refuses to flinch but inside she feels like a cornered animal. He knocks her back against the wall again.

"Why the fuck would you pull the scalpel on me?"

"Why aren't you retaliating?" she asks, eying where the knife glints against his thigh.

"Because we might need each other for the next game, dumb ass."

"I thought you said you were almost certain it would be a 'two walk in, one walks out scenario.'"

"Yeah, *almost* certain, as in not one hundred percent. We might still need each other. You slit my throat, you could be screwed."

"I could be screwed, but at least I wouldn't have to put up with your shitty attitude anymore."

"How about we just drop it, okay?" he says. "I don't want to hurt you unless I absolutely have to."

"Then why act like such an asshole?"

Rowan steels his expression. "I'm the only one here with a family. I have a wife and kid at home. They need me. Who do you have waiting on you, Mallory? What do you have to live for?"

He pulls his hands away, though he stays inches from her face, his breath hot across the bridge of her nose.

She stares at him, images strobing through her head of the neon lights of the arcade and Jared's crushed skull.

Up close, Rowan seems to soften around the edges. His eyes are wide and dark, same as Olivia's, and even as he threatens her, Mallory can't feel any weight behind it.

Up close, Jared seemed so much sharper. If she were the same as last year, she would cower, she would sink deep into herself. If Rowan were the same as Jared, she might back down as well, all too aware of how unevenly matched they were.

But she isn't, and he isn't. And she does have something to live for, a reason to keep fighting through this.

"Myself," she says, taking a step forward so that her nose is pressed up against his—her eyes narrowed. "I have myself to live for."

"That is a fucking corny answer, Mallory. But, whatever. You want to hype yourself up with self-love bullshit, be my guest. I doubt it'll do you much good when this round of mini-golf from hell actually starts." Rowan backs off, turning his attention to the wall, and the manic scrawl of Peyton's welcome message. "What do you think Peyton is gonna have us do this time anyway? It can't be as easy as a game of putt-putt."

Once Mallory stoops to pick up the scalpel, her body shakes violently. It's as if all the stress is catching up with her, but she steadies her hand and scans the room for a hint of what they're supposed to do. While the course does continue around a corner, there aren't any arrows marking it as where they need to go. So much time passes that Mallory begins to wonder if there's truly another game at all or if this was all a ploy to split up the group.

"What if this is all there is?" Mallory says, her mouth dry, her knuckles cramping around the scalpel's handle.

Rowan looks up from where he's crouched next to a plastic shark. He's been slitting open the bubble wrap that encases each of the figures. "What do you mean?"

"What if she was trying to get us away from the oth— "

The intercom crackles on, interrupting Mallory jumps, her pulse spiking.

"Hello darlings," Peyton's voice drips into the room. "Sorry I kept you waiting, there was some... drama with the other team."

"If you hurt my sister, I'll kill you," Rowan growls.

"Don't you worry about pretty little, Liv. She's fine. For now."

Rowan's shoulders relax slightly but he's still tense, and Mallory can't help the tension ricocheting up her own spine at the thought of Olivia facing something sinister on her way to the escape room.

"Now," Peyton continues. "Don't you just love mini golf? I used to go all the time when I was little. This round of the game is going to be fun, I promise. Neither of you need to die, and if you play along, no one will. This is merely a stop over until you get to the next round. If you move along through the course to the tenth hole, you'll find your instructions."

The static dies down and is replaced with the same nause-ating carnival music that played in the reception area. As the music loops and they advance through the neon tinted hall, Mallory can't help but think of Erika's face, smashed face, the bright bleed of her insides... how they would look illuminated in the lights. Or would they darken, black ink against neon glow...

The hall isn't lit like the rest of the course and the only light comes from the glow of the blacklight paint.

Even in the dark, Mallory's expression must be visible because Rowan pauses, placing a hand on her arm. "Are you okay?"

Mallory bites back her initial impulse to snap at him. Why should he care how she's feeling when they're likely walking into a situation where they will have to kill each other? Peyton may have promised that no one needs to die, but after what happened with the waterslide platform, her promises don't mean a thing.

"Just thinking about Erika." She fights back tears and tightens her grip on the scalpel, channeling all her pain into the handle.

Rowan draws in a sharp breath. "I would never have pushed that button if I had any idea of what would happen next."

"I know." Even though she also knows that if things had been different, if she had been up on that platform as fate intended, if it were Erika in the hall with him right now, he would be prepared to kill her to survive. It's all a matter of circumstance. The thought numbs her.

They exit through to the back half of the course and it's a more complete version of the front half. Each plastic statue is unwrapped and standing upright. There are ships, and crus-taceans, and a skull and crossbones. The black lights are more aggressive in this space, so much more of the course glowing and Mallory is filled with fresh terror as they approach the tenth hole. Beyond it, there's a screen fastened to the wall, massive, like a scoreboard. Black for now. Everything seems condensed in this area, each hole clustered together... Maybe Peyton built it especially for this round of the game. It doesn't look like a normal mini golf layout.

Two golf clubs lay on the ground in front of hole number ten, and next to them, a large metal box.

Rowan runs a hand over his mohawk. "Well, let's see what we're up against."

Mallory flips the lid open and there's a piece of paper.

Pick a color is written in bold letters.

With shaking hands, Mallory moves the paper to the side and finds two golf balls nestled inside—one purple, one blue.

The intercom crackles on.

14

ROWAN

"All right, darlings," Peyton says, her voice grating through the intercom. "I'll give you some time to decide which color you want to play with, then we'll get started."

Rowan scoffs. She's trying to make them believe that this game won't be deadly, but he has her figured out. Peyton may have been able to pull one over on him before, but he's learned his lesson. He presses his thumb into the stub where the tip of his finger used to be, savoring the acidic sting. It reminds him that he's smarter now. He's made his mistakes, and he's learned from them.

He knows that to survive this round he'll need to kill Mallory. The only question is whether he'll actually be able to do it. He's not worried about stabbing her if it came to the knife, and he has her beat on brute strength and could easily gain the upper hand. But if he needs to beat her at mini golf to kill her? That might be a problem.

The last time Rowan went mini golfing was right before Gabriel was born. Kate was so pregnant that she looked like she was about to go into labor at any minute, but she insisted on having one last night out before the baby came. The course they went to was outdoors, none of this day glow bullshit, and there were a ton of other families putting around. So, it was a different vibe.

No shit, it was a different vibe. They weren't playing for their fucking lives. He grits his teeth.

At the time, he hated the loud din of the crowd, the screeches of children and hurried whispers of teens.

But here, with only the hum of the air conditioner and Mallory's nervous breathing, he misses the noise. The two golf balls lay like offerings in a nest of red velvet, and when Mallory lifts the box to him, he hesitates. Flashes of heat pulse into his forehead as he thinks of the degloving trap, and the desperate moments before he lost the bulk of his finger.

"What if it triggers something?" His voice is thick, the words sticking inside his throat. The stub of his finger burns beneath its wrappings, and he trembles. He actually *trembles*. It makes him sick to his stomach to imagine how weak he must look right now. Mallory is probably lapping his terror up like it's a damn ice cream cone.

How the fuck is someone like you married? Did your wife lose a bet?

Her words hurt worse than he cares to admit. They cored him like an apple. She's lucky she didn't make a snide remark about Gabriel, or he would have lost his shit and slit her throat right then and there, Peyton's games be damned.

"Well, are you gonna tell me to suck it up, or what?" he snaps, curling his remaining fingers into his palm. "Where's your witty insult, Mallory?"

He stares her down, and she stares back for a few moments, confusion flickering across her eyes.

"It's okay," she says finally, her hand resting lightly on his shoulder. "I can do it if you want."

Her voice drips with sincerity and he recoils, prying her fingers off him. "No, I'll do it."

He dips his hand in and grabs the purple ball before he can psych himself out of it.

"Olivia's favorite color," Mallory says, and he turns to find the smallest hint of a smile tugging at her lips.

"Yeah." He can't help but smile too because choosing purple was completely unintentional. As much as Liv pisses him off, he can't go a fucking moment without being reminded of her. Seeing the purple takes him back to when they were kids and Liv's favorite Teletubby was Tinky Winky because he was purple—which was so stupid because no one's favorite Teletubby is Tinky Winky. He was the worst one, but because he was purple, she was obsessed. It's the stupid things like that, completely useless memories, that occupy the most important places in his heart.

It's that kind of stuff that makes him want to try his best for Gabriel. Even though his friends say that he won't remember anything from these early years, Rowan knows in the back of his head that what he does now could make or break his relationship with his son later. In twenty years, Gabriel could be thinking back on a random tuna sandwich or a trip to a park and be reminded of how great his dad is. He could remember certain characters from *Bluey* or *PAW Patrol* and suddenly a dumb little moment in time could become meaningful. Become everything.

"You really care about Olivia, don't you?" Mallory asks, and Rowan scowls at her.

"Does it really seem like I don't?"

"It's hard to tell." She picks up the blue ball and places the box back on the floor. "You went off on a rant about her like five minutes ago, and the entire time we've been in here—"

"These are kind of extreme circumstances." He curls his lip. Mallory has some nerve. Olivia is his *twin*. She's the one constant in his life. Hell, he went out of his way to make sure that she got paired up with Britt, the walking corpse, for this round. All to ensure her survival. Of course, he fucking cares about her.

Mallory tosses the ball from one hand to the other. "Well, it's moments like these that bring out the truths in relationships. It's why couples who compete on game shows together, especially high stress ones like *The Amazing Race,* always seem to fall apart, need a bunch of therapy afterwards."

"There's no way you just compared this to *The Amazing Race.* Besides, you should be more concerned about how I'm probably gonna wind up slitting your throat at the end of this round." He doesn't mean for it to come out as vicious as it does, but it works to shut Mallory up.

The color drains from her face and she tightens her grip around the golf ball. She's been putting on a strong front, but Rowan can tell that she'll be easy enough to overpower when it comes down to it.

Even though there's this nagging fear in the back of his mind that he won't be able to kill her. It's not that he would hesitate—he'll do anything to see his son again. It's more that she won't go down without a fight, and he's not up for a struggle right now. He keeps thinking of how Mallory bit him during their earlier confrontation. His stub of a finger doesn't really hurt anymore, but it's a weakness and she knows it.

The intercom continues to crackle overhead, and they stand waiting with their golf balls curled in their fists. Then the big screen TV mounted on the far wall flashes to life, the picture exploding in vibrant color. It bathes the room in a cold glow— taking the sting out of the neon elements of the room.

"Liv!" Rowan cries. His sister stares out through the screen, her eyes wide, a fine sheen of sweat plastering her hair to her forehead. His pulse hammers in his ears. The escape room looms behind her in a horrible mint color, a human-sized dollhouse of a fifties style diner. It takes him a moment to notice what looks like a divider down the center of the screen, Britt standing on the opposite side of the barrier. Both women look like animals in cages and panic ripples under his skin.

Rowan was so focused on what would give Liv the best chance of survival in a one-on-one scenario that he hadn't even considered that it could be up to luck or dealer's choice.

"Why is she showing us this?" Mallory asks and he turns to find her brow furrowed. "You don't think she's going to kill them both, right? Peyton wouldn't kill them both and make us watch... would she?"

She would, he almost says. She definitely would.

The panic continues to simmer, building toward a boil. He should have never left his sister's side.

"Hello darlings," Peyton's voice smashes in through the speaker and hits him like a blow to the chest. "By now you're probably wondering why I'm showing you the other team of two. But before we get to that, here's your game. Starting at hole number ten, you're going to play mini golf. All the way to hole eighteen. You're playing for speed, not points. Whoever finishes the course first, wins. Easy enough, right?"

"Too easy," Rowan mutters, his grip tightening around the golf ball, dreading the inevitable twist that will take the game from innocent to deadly.

"Well, here's where it gets fun," Peyton continues, a sharp edge to her voice. "I wasn't lying earlier when I said that you have nothing to worry about. No one on your team needs to die. As you can see on the screen, the other team of two are locked up in the escape room separated by a pane of plexiglass. Each side of the room is assigned a color."

No.

"One side blue, and the other purple."

Oh no.

"So you're not playing for your lives, darlings. You're playing for your friends. Because here's the catch. They don't know which side is which, and neither do you. So whoever wins, saves whomever was assigned the color associated with their golf ball. The other one dies. It's a game of chance. Fun, huh? And don't you even try to end it in a stalemate."

At the top of the screen, a countdown clock appears, frozen at twenty minutes.

"If you don't finish the game before the clock counts down, then they both die."

Just as aggressively as her voice cut into the room, it cuts out and they're plunged into silence.

Rowan wants to be sick, he wants to spill his guts, puke so hard that his insides turn out. He wants to cry. But instead, he screams. A long, guttural sound that rips his throat up, but he doesn't care, he continues to scream through the pain.

Next to him, Mallory drops her golf ball, raising her hand to her mouth, her eyes wide.

He sees her in his peripheral vision but can't tear his eyes away from Liv.

He made a horrible mistake.

15

BRITT

Britt feels like a bruised apple. She may not be dead, and she may not be tripping anymore, but whatever Peyton slipped into that flask has done a number on her, and no amount of time is going to help her bounce back, not completely.

She thought she was done for out in the hall, the way spots danced in front of her eyes as she fought with Olivia. Every time she blinked the spots multiplied like stars splatted behind her eyelids. Lemon, citron, champagne exploding like fireworks inside her head. Yellow, all yellow, as she clawed at her friend.

In that moment, she would have done it. She would have murdered one of the only people who have ever been genuinely nice to her. The thought sits like a stone in the back of her head.

Luckily, Olivia fought her.

Britt's neck aches where Olivia pressed the blade and she's still not entirely convinced that she's not bleeding all over a floor somewhere, and this isn't some extended pre-death hallucination.

She stumbles forward.

Her vision blurs as she tastes blood like a bad penny in the back of her mouth.

The world is still fuzzy around the edges and voices sound like they are coming in through a filter. In a way, it's not too different from the way she usually feels: separate from the rest of the world, like there's this invisible barrier she can't cross.

She's just glad the room isn't yellow. No, this horror seems catered toward Olivia and her fifties style attire and shrinking housewife demeanor. But something about the situation *feels* yellow. It settles like a film across her eyes and all she can see are the walls of her childhood bedroom, and the spots behind her eyes, afterimages she'll always associate with murder.

It makes sense that Rowan would pawn her off on Olivia and she wouldn't get much of a say in where she wound up for this round of Peyton's game. She was always picked last for team sports back when she was in school. Part of her likes to believe that the others didn't really consider what she would want in all this because of the antidote round and her question-able state, but the cynical part of her says it wouldn't have mattered. She could be healthy, and sober, and totally put together, and they still wouldn't consider her. She's always been excluded.

Once, when she was thirteen, Britt stood alone at the back of her middle school gym, fingers hooked into the padded wall behind her. The room was stuffy, and even though the back doors were propped open, there was no air flow. She squirmed, head bowed slightly, staring at her shoes. It was suffocating; the collar of her shirt like a noose. She hated gym. Hated how her clothes felt too tight and wrong against her skin. Hated being picked last for dodgeball. Always picked last.

The kids on her team stood a few feet away, tossing the ball around and chatting before the game started. Their voices drifted back to her, broken up by the smack of the ball.

"I can't believe we got stuck with her."

"It's not like she's gonna play anyway. She'll be the first one out."

"Yeah, but I don't wanna have to stand near her. What if she's contagious?"

A chorus of giggles.

"Shhh, what if she hears you?"

"She's *slow*. Even if she heard us, it's not like she'd get what we're saying."

Britt slaps a hand against the plexiglass, pushing the memory away. Not that reality is any better. The plexiglass is sturdy, and while she's tempted to suggest that Olivia try to carve her way through it with the bone saw, she knows that it won't make a difference. They're trapped.

She stares around her half of the escape room, frowning at the color choice. This sort of green is meant to calm, not provoke.

The first thing Britt looks at when she's at a house cleaning up a violent crime is what color the bedroom is painted. She has an excel spreadsheet documenting them, and shades of red are the most common offenders, but some patterns of wallpaper bring out the worst in people as well.

There's a certain comfort in color theory. Violent colors make violent people. It gives a whole new meaning to the term red flag.

But this...

After all of Peyton's questions, she didn't learn a thing from Britt, did she?

Mint fucking green. It's deplorable.

The screen at the front of the room sparks to life and Britt furrows her brow. Mallory and Rowan stand looking up numbly, surrounded by blacklight mini golf set pieces. The effect is jarring. The expressions on their faces, the blood splattered like dark ink across their clothes contrasted by the whimsical colors and designs, it's almost too much to take.

Olivia taps on the plexiglass and Britt turns to find her eyes wide.

"I think they can see us," she says, a manic edge to her voice before she turns back to the screen. "Rowan, can you hear me?"

Sure enough, Rowan's lips move, but Britt can't hear a thing—and she's certain it's not the lingering effects of whatever Peyton drugged her with. They're muted on purpose.

"Can you make out what he's saying?" Britt asks Olivia. There's a feeling like spider's legs along the back of her neck. It should be a good thing that their friends can see them, but she worries that perhaps this is part of the game and that maybe it's like charades or telephone, games that she's always struggled with. She can never get the messages right. This whole thing makes her feel like she's eleven years old again in the worst way.

"I'm not sure," Olivia squints at the screen for a moment. "I can't read lips. But he looks like he's wound up. Something must have happened."

"Or they know something that we don't," Britt says, the feeling of spiders seeming to multiply, the scratch of their legs dipping beneath her collar bones.

They're left like this for a few terrible moments, trying without success to work out some way of communicating with the others, until finally, the intercom system rumbles to life, and they both crane their necks to the ceiling.

"Okay darlings," Peyton announces through the speaker. "Here's the deal. This game is, for the most part, completely out of your hands. Your friends on the screen are completely in control of your fate."

Britt's mouth goes dry. She's already gone through one round where she had no control; she can't do it again. She kicks the plexiglass barrier. She buries her face in the sleeves of Jared's sweatshirt, breathing in the scent of his cologne.

Normally, it would be enough to calm her down, but there's still a nervous swirl in her gut.

Olivia's reaction to the sweatshirt is exactly why she lied about it back when the group was together. Well, not exactly. She didn't know Olivia was Jared's ex. But because it made it seem like she was obsessed with him or something. And they'd look at her like she was a freak.

Jared may have been an asshole, but he was unbothered by all the things that sent her spinning. Really unbothered. He never needed to try to control his environment or the people around him. He managed it seamlessly, with ease. She could fake being unfeeling, but he didn't have to. And life certainly did seem easier for him, though that was due in part to the fact that he was an attractive man in a world that caters to, and rewards, attractive men simply for existing.

Britt wonders how much simpler her life might have been if she had been a man.

She wonders how much simpler her life might have been if she had been anyone other than herself.

"You can't see it," Peyton continues. "But each side of the escape room is assigned a color. One blue, one purple. I'm sorry to say that only one of you will survive this round. And who that is, is completely dependent on who wins at mini golf."

At least there isn't more yellow in this round, Britt thinks dully, sickness continuing to swirl through her gut.

She buries her face in her sleeves again, but it still doesn't quell the nausea. What's the point of sitting in the escape room, waiting to be slaughtered or spared? Part of her is grateful that the color remains a mystery to both teams. She knows that Mallory and Rowan would both save Olivia if given the chance. Maybe it's a good thing that it's left up to what's essentially a roll of the dice. Russian roulette with miniature golf clubs.

"However," Peyton continues. "You will be given a chance to save yourselves. I can't let a perfectly good escape room go to waste. It's one of my favorite activities after all. A key is hidden on each side of the room and will unlock the door corresponding to your side. If you're able to find the key before the twenty minutes are up, you can let yourself out and avoid getting killed. The key will also have the color associated with your side on it. So in theory, you'd be able to spare your teammate or—in the event that you can't make it to your door in time and there's someone on the other end of that screen who wants to save you—ensure that your teammate is the one who meets their untimely demise. Fair warning though... if you want the key, you're gonna have to bleed for it. Twenty minutes on the clock. Make me proud, darlings."

There's a timer above the video feed of Rowan and Mallory. A harsh buzzer sounds, and twenty minutes starts ticking down. In sharp, bloody red.

Not enough time. The clock ticks loudly, an analog click with each slipping second.

Britt takes a moment to look around and analyze her surroundings.

Something nags at the base of her skull, something she can't quite reach. Something knocked loose by her brush with death, the poison still swirling in the hollow of her skull. Like the girl she saw with Jared at HyveFest last year...

Erika, but not Erika.

Before she can figure out what's bugging her, there's another knock on the plexiglass and she hurries to the divider as Olivia's voice comes through, muted.

"Britt," she says, hurriedly. "I know that things are tense between us right now. And I know that you're still hurting from whatever Peyton dosed you with, but we should work together on the clues so that we can both find our keys at the same time. We can make sure that we both survive the round."

"I tried to kill you earlier," she says flatly.

There's a shimmer of fear in Olivia's eyes, there only for a second, before she shutters her expression. "And I almost slit your throat. That makes us even, don't you think?"

"You don't like that I'm wearing Jared's sweatshirt."

"Britt..." Olivia stares at her intently, but all Britt can think about is yellow, and the Discord, and how she's always picked last: excluded, unwanted.

Embarrassment heats her blood when she thinks of how excited she was when Peyton invited her to join the Discord. She was thrilled to be chosen. The specifics of the group didn't matter. Truthfully, as much as Jared's absence hurt, the last thing she wanted to do was dwell on it. But over voice chat, with these strangers, she felt something close to belonging.

Usually, Britt needs at least one drink to feel anything close to functional in a social setting, and when she first joined the Discord, she'd down half a bottle of tequila anytime they got on voice chat. But as time wore on, she cut back. It was almost easy to talk to them. Britt wasn't used to easy.

"You're basically my only friends," she admitted one night, knees drawn up to her chin, empty Tequila bottle on the floor beside her desk. "You're the only ones I can talk to, I mean really talk to, not just party."

She regretted it as soon as the words left her mouth. Especially when her confession was met with awkward silence. As the conversation continued on, a familiar ache bloomed in her chest. She was alone. Always on the outskirts. Always last pick.

"Britt, please!" Olivia's knuckles against the plexiglass pull her back to the dilemma at hand and she frowns as she takes stock of the young woman in front of her.

It's self-preservation, she realizes. Olivia only wants to work together because she thinks it could save her. It has nothing to do with Britt. Hell, given the fact that she still has the bone saw, she'd probably just slit her throat once they made it through anyway.

She can't help but think ahead to later in the game. When

the group inevitably turns on her. She curses silently when she replays the events out in the hall. The way Olivia's body had felt so frail beneath hers. The way her thumbs sunk into Olivia's eyes and all it would have taken was a push to reduce them to raspberry jelly. She should have done it. She should have killed her and gotten it over with. Even if the thought makes her sick to her stomach.

Because eventually, Peyton is going to pit them against each other.

And Mallory, and Rowan, and Olivia will gladly sacrifice her to save each other. She's the odd man out, same as she always is.

How does she say that to Olivia in a way that she would understand? It feels like a game of telephone, all the meaning getting lost in the whispers. How does she tell her friend that she's as good as dead unless they separate now. That's what she resolves to do, make it through whatever fresh hell Peyton has cooked up for them and then book it away from the rest of the group. She'll take her chances on her own. It's how she's always been. And right now, it's her best chance of survival.

"We're not working together. We don't have enough time," she says simply. "And they're probably different clues. Different hiding places."

"Then at least let's both promise not to screw each other over, okay? If I find my key before you, if I can't make it to my door, let's leave it up to chance, okay?"

A sharp pain rings out in Britt's chest. She buries her nose in her sleeves—Jared's sleeves—and drinks in the smell of his cologne. It reminds her to be removed, to be calculating enough to survive. It's what he would do.

"No," she says, an added harshness in her voice. "If I find my key, I'm saving myself and I'll leave the rest up to chance."

Olivia's mouth drops open, and she looks so hurt that for a moment, Britt almost regrets what she's done. Even more than actually attempting to kill Olivia earlier. But she knows that it's the smartest way to play it. Olivia will let her emotions get the better of her. She'll lose sight of the game and Britt will have a chance of beating her.

Sure enough, Olivia continues to plead on the other side of the plexiglass, but Britt is already busy hunting for her key. And in the back of her mind, all she can think about is gym class and her childhood bedroom, painted in that sickly shade of yellow.

16

MALLORY

Mallory has never been any good at mini golf, and her palms are slick with sweat as she lines her club up with the ball on hole number ten. The tension between her and Rowan still crackles like a live wire, but it's fizzling with each passing moment. He's the only ally she has right now.

"Any luck?" she asks Rowan.

He's been trying to communicate with Olivia, formulate some sort of game plan on how to approach this round.

"I'm shit at reading lips," he says. "But based on what I could make out, she has no idea what color she's been assigned. I think Peyton is having them look for something or try to solve the escape room while we're playing. Maybe that's how she'll figure out what color she's been assigned? Or it's a get out of jail free card, so there's a chance that it's not completely up to us. But like I said, I'm shit at reading lips."

"You got more from lip reading than I would." The whole thing chills Mallory to her core. She would prefer having to take Rowan on herself. She would prefer fighting to the death over holding any responsibility for what happens to Olivia.

Not to mention Britt.

Waves of discomfort rock through her. She has such strong loyalty to Olivia, and if she had a choice, she would pick her hands down. But Britt is her friend too.

Peyton was right to bring us together, Britt had messaged a few weeks before they were set to meet in person. *You all get it in a way other people don't. You're my only real friends.*

It's not the first time Britt admitted it. There had been a night over voice chat when she had slurred out the same thing after downing what the group could only guess was at least half a bottle's worth of tequila. Mallory had been caught completely off guard and just sat there blinking. From the silence, it was clear the others didn't know how to respond either. Because Britt didn't really talk to them. She quipped back and forth, and had a dry, no-nonsense brand of humor... but she never really opened up. The group didn't really *know* her.

And they had no idea what to do with her confession.

Mallory had stared at the words in silence feeling pangs deep in her stomach. Guilt? She couldn't name the feeling; she only knew that it made her nauseous.

The message brought the same nausea and might as well have read "I fucking love you." In Britt-speak, that's basically what it meant, and even though they were friends, Mallory didn't consider them close. Not like her and Olivia with their shared history, or her and Peyton with their trauma-dump sessions. Britt was on the fringes of the group, and as much as Mallory wanted to return the sentiment, it felt too much like a lie.

Her guts swirled. She changed the subject, avoided the way her insides bubbled at the thought of getting to a new, more emotionally intimate level with Britt.

Sometimes I feel weird obsessing over the death of someone I didn't even know, she said.

People do weird shit every day. Wanna go on voice?

Mallory got the impression that Britt was lonely. That tugged at a part of her because she was lonely too.

There was a faint pop and hiss as Britt opened a can.

"You're drinking?" Mallory asked. "It's like noon."

Britt's voice was already slurred, slight emotion ringing out behind the monotone. "Five o'clock somewhere and all that."

They sat in silence for a few minutes and Mallory fidgeted in her seat. "So... Do you want to talk about something... or?"

"We don't have to," Britt said. "It's enough to just know you're here with me... well, not *here*, but you get it. You're the only person who gets it, Mallory, I can tell."

"Gets what?"

"Why we're doing this. Jared was a piece of shit, but he wasn't a villain, and no matter what happened to him in his final moments, he wasn't a victim either. He was just... Jared. He was fucking Jared and he's what keeps me up at night. Because this whole thing makes me sick to my stomach, Mallory. And you're the only one who gets it. How fucking complicated it is."

Another wave of guilt rushes over her as she's tugged back to the present. She's one of Britt's only friends. Britt doesn't have anyone else and now she's in a position where she'll likely be forced to sacrifice her in favor of Olivia.

"There's nothing," Rowan says, tugging Mallory out of her thoughts. She raises her head to find him staring down at the red phone. Mallory had completely forgotten about the phone, and her stomach does a nervous flip.

"Still no signal?"

He shakes his head. "No texts from Peyton. No instructions. It's like she forgot she even gave it to us. The phone has been bothering me for a while, actually."

"What about it?"

"Parts of this fucked up game seem so meticulously planned, so precise. Which is classic Peyton. But other parts are so disorganized, so chaotic. I don't know. It's like she can't make up her mind or keeps getting distracted or something. It's weird."

Mallory nods, understanding what he means. "Yeah, it's weird."

"Anyway, it's lucky that the video isn't on a delay or something," Rowan says, his voice shaking. "Not to try to put us in a worse situation, but you'd think someone who follows the *Saw* movies like they're her bible would do something to make this even more unbeatable. Peyton makes for a shitty Jigsaw."

"That's Amanda though, not Jigsaw." Mallory stoops to collect her golf ball and they move on to the next hole. "Amanda is the one who builds unbeatable traps. The whole point of Jigsaw's traps is that they *are* beatable. He wants people to survive them and learn their lesson."

It's Rowan's turn, but he stands in place stoically, golf ball clenched in one fist, club in the other. He keeps casting glances at the television screen, watching Olivia as she rushes around the escape room, opening cabinets, turning over chairs. Mallory nudges him with the handle of her club, and he jumps—dropping the ball. It lands on the putting green with a muted thud.

"What?" he hisses.

"It's your turn."

He takes a deep breath and, after another quick glance at the screen, lines his club up with the ball. "How do you know so much about the *Saw* movies? Liv said you steer clear from gory shit, that you're a psychological horror kind of girl."

"Erika really liked them." Her name sends an ache through Mallory's body. A familiar guilt prickles the back of her neck. It should have been her on the platform. It should have been her face, pulped and red, and spread across the bottom of the swimming pool. She hooks a nail into one of the scabs on her upper arm. It's not worth it to dwell, she'll have plenty of time to drown in self pity when they make it out of here... if they make it out of here.

Rowan hits his ball and curses when it goes in the hole on the first try. "The thing that really sucks about this is that I don't know if that just helped Liv or hurt her."

"I know what you mean." Mallory hits hers into the hole, unsure if she should be upset at being in second place or relieved.

The red numbers click down as they move on to the next hole.

Ten minutes left.

Mallory looks up at the screen, but instead of Olivia, she focuses on Britt, who works her way through her half of the escape room clinically. While Olivia rips apart her half, Britt dissects hers with surgical precision, not so much as sparing a glance at the screen.

"It must be hard for Britt," Mallory tells Rowan as he lines his club up with the purple ball. "She's got to know that we're both rooting for Olivia."

"She's kind of out there, so maybe she can't tell."

"Olivia's your sister and was technically my first boyfriend... She can tell."

Rowan sinks another hole in one and grunts as he bends to collect his ball. "This whole thing is fucked. Like what's the end game here? We all kill each other? If she knows that you killed Jared, and that's what this is all about, then why keep the rest of us around?"

It's a good question. Something makes Mallory feel like this whole game is a slow march to the scene of the crime. The low lighting, the blacklights inside the golf course take her back to last year's HyveFest. As her club connects with the ball, the hollow clank knocks her back to the arcade. It stank of mildew and something else, a kind of heightened, animalistic fear. She'll never forget the way Jared looked in the glow of the machines, and the veins that stood out against his hands, his arms. The way the lighting twisted the saturation in his tattoos —the illustrations, lions, lyrics, and leering skulls.

The sound it made when her foot connected with his head.

Except...

"I didn't dismember him," she says suddenly. "I killed him, but the blood trails, and everything that came after... it wasn't me. I left his body where it was, and I ran."

Rowan's brow furrows. He opens and closes his mouth a few times before settling on what to say. "Maybe it was Liv."

Mallory's pulse pounds in her ears. She doesn't remember seeing Olivia that night, but she didn't know who she was back then, and she was too focused on Jared. But still...

"She attacked him that night," Rowan tells her. "He didn't get a bloody nose in some mosh pit, he got a bloody nose when my sister punched him right in his damn face."

Mallory shakes her head. "That's not what she told us during the poison round, she said that they argued over text, that's all."

"No," Rowan insists. "They fought, like *really* fought. She didn't tell me until after he was reported missing. She was really shaken up about it." His eyes widen. "And there was blood all over her dress. She said it was from when she punched him, but... Not that I think she's capable of dismembering someone, but if anyone was gonna push her to it, it would be Jared."

A wave of nausea washes over Mallory and she sways slightly before propping herself up against the wall.

"Britt ran in the same group as he did, and she saw him with Erika's friend, right?" Rowan asks.

"Kimber."

"Yeah, her. So you're not the only one who came here with him that night. There was that Kimber chick, maybe Liv... What if you didn't kill him, you only think that you did?"

"No," Mallory says, heat rushing to her forehead. "We were here alone. He got a bloody nose and I tried to help him to the medical tent, but he insisted on coming here... and then..."

She takes deep, even breaths as her mind clicks through images of Jared from that night. The deep cut in his side *(got it in the mosh pit, it's nothing)*, the way his phone kept buzzing *(my bitch of an ex probably)*, the way his eyes were so glassy, so strung out *(I'm a little buzzed, that's all)*. And then *(what's wrong)* and then *(you fucking bitch)* and then RED, RED, RED.

Six minutes left.

Mallory presses her cheek up against the wall, letting the cool plaster blot out the memories. She rakes a hand across her upper arm, tugging at the edges of the scabs there and cringing when she thinks of what Rowan said earlier about self-harm and her destructive tendencies. She never thought of it that way before, but now...

He comes up next to her, placing a hand on her shoulder, and she's surprised by the lightness of his touch. "There's something we're missing. I don't think any of us know the whole story of what happened that night. Maybe that's what Peyton wants us to figure out. She's Jigsaw, not Amanda, right?"

Mallory is caught off guard but knows that he's not wrong. If Peyton is playing the role of Jigsaw, there needs to be a larger purpose to the game. Everyone is here for a reason.

Rowan was brought here to make sure they got inside the resort and started to play.

Mallory was brought here because she killed Jared or thinks she did at least.

It's all connected.

But the clock continues to count down and they don't have time to pick apart every little thing that happened last year. They step up to the final hole and Rowan lowers his ball onto the putting green—purple, Olivia's favorite color.

Five minutes left.

Five minutes to save one friend and kill the other. Five minutes to complete the game or both Olivia and Britt will die.

It's too much pressure, and as Mallory lines her ball up next to Rowan's, her mind churns through everything that happened last year. The sound it made when she stomped Jared's skull into the tile. The bright color that burst out of him. Red against white. Only now the details are fuzzy, now she can't remember if he was still breathing when she ran, or if they were truly alone, or what she'll do if it turns out that she didn't really kill him that night after all.

Four minutes left.

17

OLIVIA

Ever since Olivia can remember, Rowan has been looking out for her. He's overprotective to the point that it's smothering, but in a way, she thrives on it. There's a safety in it that makes her world go soft around the edges. In the twin bubble there's no such thing as individual pain, everything is shared. In the twin bubble, she's never alone.

Olivia isn't sure why she's surprised when Britt decides against working together. It's not even that she wanted to partner up with Britt, especially after everything that happened out in the hall, but now that she's completely on her own she feels exposed, vulnerable.

Now all she has are fifty-fifty odds.

A one in two shot of dying a horrible death.

She rushes around her side of the escape room, every inch of her shaking as she tears it apart, searching for the key. Her way out. Her lifeline. This kind of panic is achingly familiar: it's the same type of hopelessness she felt while she was dating Jared.

There are things about the relationship that Olivia will never forget.

Like the way his hands felt when they gripped her fingers, her forearm, her wrists.

All the things he used to scream at her, a laundry list of grievances. Too stupid. Too slow. Too much of all the wrong things.

When his fist hit the wall, it sounded like a snare drum. When he threw a plate, depending on where it landed, the sound was as sharp as the pieces it shattered into. There was a melody to the madness, discordant, deranged. Terrible music that set the rhythm for the relationship.

Hearing a door slam sends a wave of dread through Olivia, even now. Hearing certain songs makes her reminisce until she's back there with him, and she is loved, and she is cherished, and she is bruised, and she wants nothing more than to bury a fork in the soft skin of his neck.

How could she love someone so much and hate them at the same time? How could she love someone so much and still imagine all the ways she could take them apart? Piece by piece, like pulling the stuffing out of a toy.

His name cuts into her.

Jared.

Jared Joseph Jones.

His name made Olivia laugh so hard in the beginning. It was their inside joke that it was on par with Donnie Darko and made him sound like he was some kind of knockoff superhero.

She used to love the way he would lean in and whisper, "If I'm Donnie, you're Gretchen."

When really, she was Frank the rabbit.

And he was the one who put a hole in her head.

Olivia spent half a year living with him and by the end it felt like a prison sentence. But not in the beginning. In the beginning, he was the man of her dreams.

The man who would pick flowers for her from the side of the road and trace a line of kisses along her jaw. The man with moods that came and went in a pattern she could never nail down no matter how hard she tried. She always considered herself finely attuned to mood shifts, but with Jared, it was never enough.

She's not sure if there are words to describe the Jared that she knew.

The Jared who buried his face in her shoulder during the scary parts of movies. The Jared who threw her phone against the wall, shattering the screen, when he saw that she liked another guy's picture on Instagram.

The Jared who found a bird with a lame wing on the side of the road and was so concerned, so gentle when he scooped it up into a shoebox and brought it home with him. He caressed its head and spent over an hour on the phone with the vet, taking detailed notes on how to care for it while waiting for animal control to pick it up. Olivia's heart nearly burst watching all the love he poured into such a fragile thing.

The Jared who sent her mom flowers for Mother's Day and mowed his grandfather's lawn without fail every Saturday morning.

The Jared who always kissed her on the forehead when they'd meet up for dinner.

The Jared whose fingers gripped like a vice.

The Jared who split her lip. More than once.

She looks up at the screen, watching Mallory and Rowan work their way through the miniature golf course. She tries to concentrate on turning out drawers and throwing open cabinets, but so much nervous energy pulses through her that she's practically frozen. Out of the corner of her eye, she sees Britt move methodically through her side of the escape room. She's oddly composed, and except for a slight wobble every few moments, Olivia would never guess that she was still feeling the effects of whatever toxin Peyton dosed them with earlier.

Olivia's insides curdle. There's a very good chance that Britt will find her key and make it out. And Olivia is convinced at this point that if that happens, she'll be left to die.

Unless Mallory and Rowan happen to save her.

Fifty-fifty odds.

Olivia scans the room for a way to escape, but there aren't any windows. The passageway that they entered through has been sealed off by one of Peyton's metal panels and the exit on her side of the room is sealed tight. There isn't even a knob, only a keyhole.

But if Olivia learned anything from her relationship with Jared, it's that there's always a way out.

Her eyes continue to scan the room, searching.

There's always a way out.

Still, the clock counts down and panic burns the highways of her veins, and she can't stop thinking about how if she'd only had the good sense not to bother with Jared to begin with, she wouldn't be in this position.

He was older than her and more streetwise, things that she was immediately attracted to. The age gap was barely three years, but those years felt like an ocean as time went on, as the waters rose and the salt eroded her down. She should have known when he laced his fingers through hers, when he squeezed a little too hard and pulled her in a little too close, that it wasn't going to end well.

He's the one who taught her that thoughts can become blood, and gore, and grime.

Love can feel like a punch, a bruise, a darkening sky.

Rowan liked Jared right away, maybe because they were so similar. Both of them rough around the edges, dark in a way that intrigued more than disturbed. Both of them harboring a type of not-so-secret resentment toward Olivia, one that she enjoyed in her own sick way. Because it meant that they cared.

When Rowan met Jared, Rowan had only recently moved out of the apartment, and Olivia spent hours making sure that everything in the main living area was perfect for when Jared arrived. She fussed over the glass fishbowl filled with key chains, and dangly earrings, and hairclips. The silver-plated teacup with a string of daisies painted up the side, the gray ottoman full of her sweaters, and oversized t-shirts, and fuzzy socks. The stacks of books along the sides of the couch.

Olivia wanted Jared to see this, to see *her* the first time that he came to visit. On top of meeting her brother, her twin, her blood, it was also going to be his first impression of the place where she lived, so she was very deliberate in the staging of things. She kept twisting the knickknacks on the end tables this way and that until they were positioned to her exact liking.

Rowan scoffed while he watched her. "You're wasting your time. You do know that guys don't notice that kind of shit, right?"

"He will," she said, so certain that he would. "He's the kind of guy who notices everything."

"Everything?" Rowan asked, and the way he stared had her pulling her sleeves down past her wrists. The scabs were at the point of flaking, soft pink already taking the place of angry red, and Olivia's cheeks heated. He always found a way to throw her instability back at her.

"I wouldn't be able to be with someone who did that to themselves," Rowan continued. "Whoever this guy is, he gets points off for putting up with it."

"I haven't done anything in weeks." Two weeks to the day. "And Jared has been super supportive about it, unlike you." Jared ignores it entirely.

Rowan's eyebrows shot up to his hairline. "Oh, I haven't been supportive? Try to tell me that again the next time you end up on my porch at two in the morning, or the next time you call me in the middle of date night, and I need to rush home to you. I drop everything for you, constantly. And I'm not supportive?"

"Are you trying to make me feel bad?" she asked, tears pricking the corners of her eyes.

"If it keeps you from butchering yourself, then yeah. I hope you feel like shit."

They settled into uncomfortable silence, and Olivia's eyes raked over the staged living room. "Jared will notice," she says quietly. "He'll notice."

Except when he finally showed up, fifteen minutes late, he didn't give the living room so much as a glance.

He gravitated toward the kitchen and the beers in the fridge, and the room that used to belong to Rowan and Kate, now a storage room—packed to the brim with HyveMind merch.

"Trust me, you don't wanna go in there. It's a wreck," Rowan said. "My wife and I are still in the process of moving everything over to the new house."

"You didn't tell me your brother was into HyveMind," he said approvingly.

Olivia shrugged. "He's related to me, isn't he?"

"Babe, you are a casual listener at best." He popped the cap off his beer and took a swig, while Rowan led him into the dining area.

They got along instantly.

It should have made her happy, but she had a sinking feeling in her gut and picked at the freshly healed skin on her arm more and more as the night wore on. Rowan didn't interrogate Jared like he did her previous boyfriends. There was none of the scrutiny or eye narrowing that she had come to expect. Instead, it was like he was meeting a celebrity and he kept glancing at Olivia throughout the night, shooting her a look that seemed to say, *how the hell did you manage this?*

She wasn't sure, she really wasn't.

Olivia bites down hard on her lower lip, the metallic squirt of blood enough to bring her back into the present nightmare.

She lifts an arm in front of her face and twists it so that the thin white lines shine like plastic under the fluorescents. They're faint, barely noticeable thanks to Mederma gel and the time she's given herself to heal. She hasn't had the itch in almost a year. But the stress of this game, it makes her want to draw blood in the worst way. She's almost tempted to hook a nail into the soft flesh of her wrist, right above a vein that looks so purple, so bruised. She wants to pop it like a berry. Let the juices flow free.

But she doesn't.

She can't.

She keeps casting nervous glances at Britt who—despite not finding her key yet—seems so much farther along than she is. She sinks back into her head as the clock counts down to ten, nine, eight minutes.

The scars on her arms branch out like spider webs, patterns of history across her skin. She follows them back, back, back.

The night Jared met Rowan, it was like Olivia didn't even exist. She'd leave the room and return to find them speaking in low voices, huddled together like vultures over a fresh kill.

She sat on the couch, sandwiched between them. They kept casting glances at each other over her head, and she kept pulling her sleeves down past her wrists, hiding, hiding, hiding.

Later, in the kitchen, after Jared left, Rowan grabbed another beer from the fridge while Olivia stood off to the side, fiddling with the hem of her shirt.

Rowan shut the fridge door so hard that she jumped at the sound. "Your boyfriends are usually such tools, but I think I might actually like this guy."

"Yeah, me too—I also like him, I mean."

He rolled his eyes. "I'd hope so since you're the one dating him." He leaned back against the counter. "Maybe we could all go out sometime. I'm sure Kate would just about die, she's been following him on Instagram since college. Damn, Liv. You did good with this one."

He's not who you think he is, she thought desperately. And deep down she realized that she didn't want Rowan to like Jared at all.

She wanted him to... she swallowed back the nausea scorching her throat. She wasn't sure what she wanted Rowan to do exactly. She couldn't articulate it. But in the pit of her stomach, and in the center of her chest, she ached.

"Thanks," she forced out. "And yeah, it would be nice to go out as a group."

The rest of the night, she was silent, thoughts splintering apart inside her head. *Maybe then you'd see the way he hooks his fingers into my shoulders, maybe then you'd see how he yanks my beer from my hand—because he doesn't like me drinking. He doesn't like me wearing tank tops or shorts that go above my mid-thigh. He doesn't like when I make plans without him, even with my family. Even with you, Rowan.*

But she was convinced that Jared loved her.

And in a twisted way, maybe he thought he did too.

The taste of blood on her lips drags her back to the task at hand. Back to where her scabs have flaked and faded to scars so fine that she can almost pretend that she's okay. Back to the escape room and the timer ticking down to her destruction.

She crawls up on the counter and runs her fingers along the underside, but there isn't anything taped to the bottom. She's running out of places to look, and the clock keeps counting down, and she can't get out of her damn head.

Then, she notices a panel all the way behind the counter and against the back wall. It's the same as the cubby from the poison round and the entrance to the escape room. It blends almost seamlessly into the wall so that it's difficult to see at first. Or maybe that's the tears blurring her vision. She swats at them, and yes, there's definitely a panel along the back wall.

The small, plastic tube sticking out of the top is what gives it away. At first, it's easy to miss. It's thin and straw-like and completely clear. She tilts her head left, and right, and left again, the tube flickering, ghosting in the light.

Like my scars, she thinks dully. *So faint you can pretend it's not there.*

Even though every inch of her scarred skin yells HISTORY, and every former cut begs her to REMEMBER, and knowing what she knows about the entry to this room—

Okay, Olivia. Now you can make her bleed.

—there's a sour taste in the back of her mouth. Her scars sting. The itch is back under her skin.

She attempts to grip the panel around the edges and pry it open, but it doesn't work.

The clock keeps counting down, and it's so difficult to stay in the present when all the memories keep flooding in.

All the moments that make it difficult to breathe.

She'd been living with Jared for a little over four months when they were sitting curled up on the couch one night, bathed in the blue glow of the television.

"I love you," she told him, snuggling in close so that she could feel his heartbeat. He felt so human, so normal. Soft. She wondered what he was like as a child, if there was a point when he would play in the dirt and collect worms and draw pictures for his mother.

In that moment, she could almost imagine that kid and who he might have grown up to be if he made different choices, if he still had the potential to be someone new, someone softer. She reminded herself that he was sweet with his mother, and that was supposed to be important. The way that men treat their mothers was supposed to be important, and he was so gentle with her, so loving.

So how come he wasn't gentle with her?

"I know you do, babe." He grinned down at Olivia, the hint

of a dimple in his left cheek. "And I hope you know that I really am sorry."

For what, she wanted to ask. The list was too long, and her memory too fuzzy. Did it even matter when this moment was so perfect, and she could picture him at five, and ten, and fifteen?

"I know," she said, because it was the right thing to say, the perfect thing to say. The perfect way to avoid an argument.

There had been more of those since they moved in together, but even with everything, she tried to convince herself that she liked living with Jared.

He smoked too much weed. His eyes were always glassy, bloodshot, burnt out around the edges—but she convinced herself that this was a good thing. He was more mellowed out when high. More fun to be around. He was goofy, and sarcastic, and fell asleep easily, without demanding sex first.

She loved it when he screamed in his sleep. She loved it when his brow furrowed and he kicked his legs out against the comforter, because it made him seem vulnerable.

It reminded her that he had fears, and he had a heart, and that there were things that frightened him.

It helped her when he would yell at her for drinking too much, and she would vomit for what felt like hours after the binge, like she was purging him from her body.

It helped when she would sit in the bathtub for half a day, scrubbing until her skin was red, until her arms ached, until she couldn't feel him anymore.

The daydreams are what got to her, the way her mind would wander after they'd gone to bed—Jared snoring next to her all splayed out, a foot kicked from beneath the covers, an arm across his eyes.

How easy it would be to slit his throat.

He was such a deep sleeper, he wouldn't notice a thing, not even as he bled out.

It was always knives, never a pillow, never pills. Always

something sharp. Because it was only after he'd fallen asleep that Olivia would replay the moments in her head, focusing on the way his hands gripped her wrists, and how she barely left the house anymore, and how he would stare over her shoulder whenever she texted.

Quiet rage when she thought of all the things he did to her. Strange excitement, a flutter deep in her gut when she thought of all the things she could do to him.

It would be easy to slit his throat.

So easy.

And then there was last year. HyveFest.

Blood on her palms, still sticky when she woke up in the wee hours of the morning. Blood on the bottoms of her shoes. Tacky, like melted candy.

The memories stir under her skin threatening to rip her apart at the seams. Feelings, sounds. A squish beneath her feet, warmth between her fingers.

Blood.

The clear straw, so much like her scars.

Olivia runs a hand along the flat edge of the bone saw and pulls it from its place inside her boot. The funnel leading into the area behind the panel. It's sick, but it's the only way. Peyton told them exactly what they'd need to do to survive.

She needs to pay in blood.

She has no idea how much, but she hopes that a trickle will do it. On closer inspection of the funnel, it doesn't disappear completely inside the panel. Instead, it leads to what appears to be a strip of paper... some kind of reader? Olivia can only hope that once it's saturated, it'll trigger the locking mechanism for the panel.

Olivia kisses the blade against the tip of her finger and draws in a shaky breath. Once she breaks the skin, she holds her hand over the funnel and watches anxiously as the paper at the bottom saturates. But nothing happens.

The intercom system clicks on and Peyton's voice drifts into her half of the escape room. "Oh, no, no, no. You didn't think it would be that easy, did you? I'm the only one who can open that panel, and I expect you to bleed for it."

"I am bleeding," Olivia screams, holding her hand up over her head, unsure if Peyton can even hear her. Blood slips down the length of her finger and she cringes. "I'm bleeding, so please..."

"I want you to bleed more." There's a pause, and then a sharp giggle. "Actually, I want you to open up your arm and gush rivers over that thin little straw, Olivia. I want you to paint the wall red. I want you dizzy from blood loss. And then maybe I'll open the panel and you can get your key."

"You said that we would be able to open the panels ourselves."

"Surprise, I lied. Besides, you cheated early. You didn't bleed earlier when I told you to, so I'm expecting you to bleed now."

Olivia fights back the lump in her throat before answering. "How do I know you'll open it at all?"

"You don't. So you better bleed unless you want to leave your survival up to fate."

The intercom clicks off and Olivia trembles, the room feeling as if it's pressing in on her. She can't do this. She twists her arm so the thin white lines on her arms shimmer. She can't hurt herself like that, not again. But the itch is there.

The itch is there, and there are only five minutes left on the clock.

There are only five minutes left, and she can't rely on Rowan to save her like he always does.

In here, all she has is herself.

She squeezes her eyes shut and pictures Jared.

The dimple in his left cheek, the dark curl of his hair, the muddy brown of his eyes.

His fingers in her upper arm, his hand around her throat

while they had sex. The star tattoo on his hand and how she'd stare at it, wiggle out of her body, and wait until he was done before she crashed back down into herself. The whole time painfully aware of the ink and how it snaked along the vein in his hand. Such a weird thing to focus on, even now, when he's been gone for a year. That damn tattoo.

She won't reopen her scars, she won't retrace her history, not like that. But she can do this. She can be strong.

Olivia digs the toothed blade into the back of her arm and drags it along the length of her skin. The pain sears all the way up into the base of her skull, but she doesn't let it slow her down. She pulls the blade away and as red bubbles out over the wound, presses her arm against the tube, but it doesn't gush the way she expects it to.

Peyton remains silent and she knows, she knows it isn't enough.

Olivia pinches at the edges of the cut, willing it to bleed more, willing it to paint the tube, the panel, every damn thing in sight so that Peyton will cut her some slack.

The entire time, in the back of her head she's wondering how she got to this point.

What if she never said yes when Jared asked her out? What if she left at the first sign of trouble instead of focusing on the few moments of peace in between the turmoil?

No, she can't blame herself. Not anymore.

Jared did this.

He made her rage boil over. Every time he raised his voice, every time he dug his fingers in. Every bruise, every cut set the temperature higher, pushing her anger to its boiling point, pushing her to do what she had to in order to survive.

She presses the bone saw against her arm again. One final slash of the blade, one final squirt of blood.

But she's not cutting into herself anymore. She's carving into Jared.

Just like she did the night that he died.

Finally, her blood drenches the wall and Peyton's voice is gleeful as she comes back in over the speaker. "That's what I'm fucking talking about, Olivia. Look at all that blood. And look at this, I'm actually keeping my promise. Enjoy your key."

The panel clicks open, and she pulls out the key, blood still weeping down her arm.

Olivia stands numbly for a moment, fresh tears clouding her vision. It's really him, isn't it? Jared really is Peyton. Only he would take such sadistic pleasure in watching her carve herself to pieces.

But she can't get lost in the past, and she can't waste time speculating. She flicks the tears from her eyes and focuses.

It's blue, the key is blue.

But there are only thirty seconds left on the clock. Twenty-nine, twenty-eight, and the door is too far. She's frozen in place.

Britt pounds on the plexiglass divider. She begs Olivia to save her.

But Olivia doesn't trust her. All she can think of is how Britt tackled her out in the hall, and how Britt is wearing Jared's sweatshirt, and how there's still so much game left to play.

She spins toward the screen and waves at it, heart pounding in her ears, blood freckling the front of her dress. She could save Britt, and she knows she should. But Britt slept with Jared, and Olivia is the one who bled for this. Olivia is the one who suffered, and just once in her life, she thinks she deserves to be selfish… no, she believes that that game relies on it. Peyton built the game this way so that someone would die. If they both make it out alive, she'd only be delaying the inevitable. It's better to get it out of the way now… isn't it? And the door is so far away, there's no telling if she'd make it in time.

Finally, Rowan looks up.

Twenty-four, twenty-three.

And Olivia screams desperately.

"Blue!" she yells. "Blue, blue, blue!"

Hoping, praying that he figures it out.

Fifteen, fourteen.

"Blue! Blue, Rowan. My color is blue!"

Three, two.

Finally, her brother hits the ball into the hole. The clock stops. Olivia breathes again while Britt lets out a wail on the other side of the plexiglass, a sound that would be more at home in the throat of a wounded animal.

There's a terrible grinding of gears and the door on the far end of her half of the escape room swings open and Olivia takes one final look across the plexiglass at Britt.

Britt, who up until now has been so calm, so calculated, so borderline pathological.

Britt, who's eyeliner is smeared down her cheeks in a macabre display of pain.

"You killed me," she screams, slamming on the plexiglass. It bends beneath her palms. "You killed me."

18

MALLORY

Mallory watches the grainy television screen as Olivia bolts out of the escape room door and she lets out an audible sigh. Her heart continues to pound, and her legs feel like jelly, but for the first time today, she feels like they've finally gotten lucky. It was down to the wire, but they saved her. They won. Although guilt sours the victory when she thinks of Britt, Mallory forces herself to stay focused on Olivia. She's not sure how she'd be able to move forward if she were to linger on the friend they sacrificed.

Rowan lets out a yelp and claps his hands together before crouching down low to the ground and running a hand over the remains of his mohawk, tears springing to his eyes.

"She made it," he says, his voice breathy and exhausted. "She fucking made it."

The mini golf course, which felt so ominous before, so cold and calculating, loses all of its sting and the bright neon colors look cheap, watered down in the aftermath of the game.

Mallory's relief is short lived, because no sooner has Olivia escaped, then a terrible siren blares through the miniature golf course. She clamps her hands down over her ears and scans the room for where the next sheet of metal is bound to fall or which wall is going to snap open to reveal a series of gatling guns pointed straight at her chest. But to her confusion, everything in the room appears still—no flashing lights to accompany the sirens—and Rowan comes up behind her, tapping her on the shoulder and motioning for her to drop her hands.

When she does, wincing against the sound, he leans in close and says, "Peyton turned the sound on the TV, the sirens are coming from the escape room, look."

She turns to the screen and sure enough, red lights flash in time to the horrible blare of the siren.

On the television screen, Britt lifts one of the stools next to the dining bar and throws it across the escape room at the plexiglass barrier. It makes a sound like a bass drum, but the barrier holds. Britt then pounds against the barrier with her fists, the sound muffled in the blare of the siren.

She twists to face Mallory and Rowan, her face contorted, showing something other than apathy for the first time since they found themselves stuck inside the resort.

"You're a murderer!" Britt screams, her voice piercing, and Mallory cringes against the raw emotion behind the words.

The siren continues to blare.

Rowan grabs her arm. "Come on, let's go meet up with Liv."

"I need to watch," she insists, shaking off his hand.

He shakes his head as he makes his way out into the hallway. "You really love to torture yourself, don't you?"

Maybe she does, maybe it's because she feels she needs to take responsibility for the whole mess. Maybe she's punishing herself for what happened to Erika. Maybe she needs to feel the pain to remind herself of why she continues to fight to stay alive. Because if she lets herself become numb to it, what's the point of fighting? What's the point of living if you can't feel anything?

So she watches. She watches as the siren continues its

hideous scream, and Britt sinks down against the wall, and goes still.

Only when the feed cuts out does she leave.

Mallory learned her lesson with Jared. She learned to watch until the end.

Once she steps out into the hallway, there's another terrible clanking of gears and a sheet of metal falls behind her, effectively cutting off the miniature golf course from the rest of the resort. She takes a moment to crouch down next to the doorway and inspect the metal, following it up to where the door meets the ceiling. Who does she know who could engineer such a thing?

She can't stop thinking about what Rowan told her: how she may not have killed Jared after all, and there's more to that night than what happened between them in the arcade.

Olivia was there that night.

And Britt saw Kimber.

A chill runs through her. It's so mind-numbingly obvious. Kimber's dad owns Erika's old company, which is a manufacturing distributor, so that's how she could have gotten the supplies. If she reconciled with Brandon, then he could easily have been the one to help her get the place booby-trapped. Except Brandon is a tool, and the most hands on he is when he's taking off a bra.

Mallory tries to work through it in her head for a few minutes before giving up and turning away from the door. This hall is dark. Dark tiles and dark walls, both in an inky shade of blue. Even the lights overhead seem dulled, a blue hue to their glow. She wanders the length of the hallway, which is unnervingly long and so silent she could hear a pin drop. She wonders if she's ever going to catch up with Rowan or if she's in this alone now. But then, she rounds a corner and voices drift back to her.

Rowan and Olivia.

She's struck by how close the golf course and escape room were to each other, even though the hallways they set off down when they split up seemed to go in different directions. It makes sense, she supposes. The attractions on this side of the resort are set up in a loop. She's just glad Olivia is so close and they're not going to stay separated.

She finds the twins embracing, Olivia trembling in her brother's arms. If it were earlier in the whole ordeal, she would hang back and give them a private moment, but she's tired, and confused, and just wants to get this over with. So she approaches the twins and hovers next to them while Rowan smooths back Olivia's hair.

"I killed Britt," Olivia murmurs. "I could have saved her, but I panicked. She attacked me before we got to the escape room, and I didn't know if I could make it out the door in time, and I panicked."

"You didn't kill anyone," Rowan assures her. "That psycho bitch is the one doing all of this, it isn't any of our faults."

Well, depending on motive, that might not be true, Mallory thinks cynically, but she steps up next to the twins and places a hand on Olivia's shoulder anyway. "We're just glad you're okay."

Olivia's arm drips blood onto the tile floor, and her face has lost a lot of its color. Rowan rips a strip of fabric from the bottom of his shirt and wraps it around the wound, but blood quickly stains the fabric a bright red. Rowan moves to tear another strip from his shirt, but Olivia stops him.

"It's good enough," she says, pulling her arm tight against her chest.

The intercom crackles on again and Peyton's voice comes in, more abrasive than ever.

"That was fucking brutal," she says with a laugh. "I had no idea you had it in you."

At the Peyton's urging the three of them continue down the hallway, still unsure of their destination. Mallory runs through her mental catalog of the pictures she found online, the makeshift maps she created, and tries to figure out where this march is leading them.

Not to the hotel rooms, they're separate from the main building and still in a skeletal state of construction. Not to the laser tag maze, that's still far enough away to practically be on the other side of the building.

Her breath catches in her throat.

The arcade.

The double doors are painted an inky black. There's a neon sign above them with the message *Let's Play* lit up in neon yellow.

Mallory takes a deep breath as they reach the doors. She remembers parts of the arcade from last year, but the memories are fragmented.

The way the floor warped beneath her feet.

The smell of mold mixed with burnt popcorn and weed.

Most of all, she remembers the way Jared looked inside here. He seemed so much shorter than he actually was, dwarfed in comparison to the massive neon signs, his tattoos snaking up his arms like the graffiti on the walls. There's still graffiti across the doors, massive smears of red and royal blue.

But when her hands hit the doors, they won't open. She shoulders them, smashes her fists against them, but they won't budge.

Rowan grabs her by the wrist, pulling her back roughly.

"They're bolted shut," he says, drawing her attention to the seam between the doors and the line of metal slipping up the gap.

"Sealed shut is more like it." Mallory fights back the lump in her throat.

"It's the same as the escape room," Olivia says. "The door wasn't sealed, but it was padlocked shut. Britt and I had to enter through a hole in the wall."

The arcade... Mallory has been dreading this moment since stepping inside the main entrance of the resort. As they crowd around the entrance, all she can think about is Jared. Jared in the amphitheater, jumping the divider between the pit and the seats, red streaming down his face. She closes her eyes and she's back there, with Jared reaching for her over the seats. The rabble behind him, the sea of crowd surfers, and sweat, and so many bodies continuing to swell like it's nothing. Like they don't know what kismet feels like.

His blood spewing in a bright stream, almost fake looking. All sticky syrup and maraschino cherries. His face, beneath all that red, contorted up into a half smile, half grimace that didn't quite reach his bloodshot eyes. So unlike the pictures she had seen of him smoking with friends, or the far away glances she had caught of him over the years, always surrounded by a group of people who look more like accessories—accents to highlight how set apart he is.

Her fingers twitch as if she's directing the memory. And she knows when she opens her eyes, she'll be back in the resort, back outside of the arcade. But not yet. She stays in the moment a heartbeat longer. Her mind scrolling through all the things she should have done, instead of reaching for Jared. Instead of guiding him toward the back of the amphitheater.

She should have flinched away when he cupped a hand over his nose, and the red seeped through his fingers, freckling the ground beneath him.

"I don't know where to go," he said to her. "I've never been clocked in the face like this before."

Her hand found his, and he wove his fingers through hers, and that was the beginning of the end. And neither of them knew it. Those were the last precious moments before destruction. Before eternal ruin.

A hand comes down on her shoulder. Heavy. Warm.

She opens her eyes expecting to see Jared—a ghost ready to

deal out her punishment, but instead it's Rowan, his expression grave. "Let's get this over with."

The group moves around from the doors to the side wall, and sure enough there's a hole. Covering the length of the hole is a red velvet curtain, and above it, there's an arrow pointing down to a wide, red button, like something that would be found on an arcade game. Without a second thought, Mallory slams her palm down and the button ignites.

"Why the fuck would you do that without checking to see what we're dealing with first?" Rowan hisses and Olivia pulls him back by the arm.

Music pours in over the intercom: a slow, queasy carnivalesc rendition of "Sulking Seething." The velvet curtain lifts and the hole in the wall lights up orange, and yellow, and red, and the three of them peer inside to find that the passageway empties into what looks like a claw machine game, except it's huge, big enough to fit all three of them. It's filled with stuffed toys, but the skins seem floppy, the faces of the bears and rabbits deflated. Only the bellies are bloated, the jagged outlines of wicked things straining against the fabric. Above the sea of misshapen creatures, where there would normally be a claw, there's a long, sharp knife.

Mallory can see the arcade through the glass walls of the claw machine. It's neon bright, weeping. Patterns of electric pink splattered across the walls, echoing blood splatter.

There's a sign next to the opening. *Step right up,* written in red.

Finally, the intercom system clicks on.

"You're going to need to be really strong to make it through this one," Peyton teases. "I had a lot of fun designing it, and I can't wait to see if it works the way I intended. It's simple enough. It's a one player game, meaning one of you needs to enter that lovely contraption there. If you want to make it to the next round, find the key hidden in the claw machine. The key will not only release you from the machine, but it'll allow the others into the arcade. So if you don't make it out, if you don't find the key, everyone dies. Oh, I just love claw machine games."

The claw machine... the human claw machine.

Mallory takes a deep breath and steps forward.

19

MALLORY

Mallory never liked circuses, theme parks, or arcades. There were too many people silhouetted against too many bright lights. Too many noises and small spaces bloated with crowds. Erika loved it all, especially theme parks, and especially roller coasters. She used to drag Mallory to Six Flags every year at the beginning of summer. Mostly, Mallory would sit alone on benches or at tables guarding their drinks, squinting against the sun and dripping with sweat.

"You won't go on even one ride with me?" Erika asked one summer when they were teenagers. It was back when Erika still dyed her hair and wore mostly black. She was dressed in an oversized band t-shirt, her left hand clamped around a blue raspberry slushie.

"I don't like all the drops," Mallory told her. "They make me feel sick."

"That's my favorite part though!"

Mallory raised a hand instinctively to her stomach. She always assumed that she was the only one who felt that way on roller coasters, that there was some kind of flaw in her anatomy, so she stared at Erika, dumbfounded.

"You feel the... the weird flip in your gut when you're on roller coasters too?" she asked.

"Yeah," Erika said, taking a huge gulp of her slushie. "Everyone does. It's why I love them so much. That feeling, like you're gonna lose your stomach through your nose, it's so awesome."

It's the first time Mallory realized that people could have different reactions to the same experience, that pain isn't universally pain. Some people crave the discomfort, some people live for the thrill of it.

Staring at the claw machine, her stomach feels the same way it used to when Erika would force her on roller coasters. Flipped upside down, forced up into her throat, and she gags against the nausea, she wills herself not to spill her guts all over her shoes. Peyton, or whoever is behind the profile, had to craft all of this over time, meticulously. The amount of love baked into such a horror show sickens her.

Mallory shakes her arms out, hoping to dispel some of the uneasy feeling, but it only seems to make it worse. She'll never be ready to brave the inside of the contraption, so she digs her fingers into the flesh of her arms, centers herself, and makes a move to go inside the opening when Olivia reaches out and pulls her back.

"Don't," Olivia pleads. "I have a bad feeling about it."

Mallory's chest aches. They still haven't gotten a chance to talk since Olivia revealed that she's the one behind the Rowan profile. Her heart pounds when she thinks of how Olivia just barely made it out of the escape room.

But not Britt.

Her gut twists. *We killed Britt.*

The blood from Olivia's arm soaks the front of Mallory's shirt, and she glances between the twins, both painted in layers of red.

"I'll be okay," she murmurs, doing her best to keep her voice steady.

"I have to agree with Liv," Rowan adds. "It makes me think of what you were saying about Amanda's traps in the *Saw* franchise earlier, how they're not designed to give the players a chance to win... they're just built for death. This thing is gonna wreck whoever steps inside it."

Mallory's stomach churns again. She knows that everything they're saying is valid, but she also knows that there is no stopping the game, not if they want to make it out of the resort alive.

"What if we don't do it?" Olivia asks. "Seriously, at this point we're in the best position we've been. There are multiple hallways leading to who knows where. We could find some way out of this without having to go through another one of her traps. What's the worst she can do if we don't play along?"

Mallory doesn't want to think about it because something tells her that Peyton's worst is horrific. Gingerly, she peels Olivia's hands away and shakes her head.

"Who knows how many of those big metal dividers she has on standby to trap us somewhere and starve us to death? It's impossible." Mallory stares into Rowan's eyes. "The only way out is through."

He opens his mouth to say something but glances over at his sister and stops abruptly. Instead, he places a hand on Mallory's shoulder.

"We've already come this far," she says, fully expecting to have to fight him off. "Peyton's not going to let us off the hook until we're finished with her games."

"I know," he says instead, giving her a reassuring squeeze. "But you need to promise me that you're not going to get killed in there, and that we're all walking out of here together."

Her brow furrows. "Why aren't you acting like a dick?"

His eyes shimmer, and if she didn't know any better, she'd think he might actually be on the verge of tears. "You mean a lot to my sister, and it would fucking gut her if you died. Plus, you had my back during mini golf. It was stressful as fuck, and I don't... I feel like we..." He blinks rapidly and sucks in a breath before continuing. "I feel like you're not so bad, I guess. Now, promise you won't get yourself killed."

She can't help but grin. So the glass shard of a man has a heart after all.

"I promise," she says as he pulls his hand back and rolls her shoulders before crossing the threshold.

She steps inside the machine, having to duck to avoid the massive, hanging mechanism where the claw would usually be fastened—and the large knife that hangs in its place. The thing looks like it's rigged to swing like a metronome and Mallory shivers at the thought of it.

Broken glass crunches beneath her boots and she cringes looking down at the sea of stuffed animals and the glints of glass that poke through the fabric: a million little mirrors of death. Somewhere, buried in the mess, is the key out of the box and into the arcade.

There's a mechanical click as a pane of glass slides down between the entrance and the box and Olivia cries out, her voice muffled. Mallory looks back at the twins just in time to see a waterfall of red pour down over Rowan, coating him completely. The liquid splashes against the floor and freckles up Olivia's left side as she jumps back.

"Motherfucker!" Rowan yells, as Peyton chimes in over the speaker system.

"Pig's blood," she says between bouts of laughter. "I'm positively tickled that you got the brunt of it. First my *Gerald's Game* degloving machine and now my *Carrie*-inspired—"

"But, why?" Rowan sputters, cutting her off.

"Because it's fun."

Sound inside the claw machine is muffled, and Mallory

strains to listen as Olivia rushes to Rowan's side, but he holds his hand out, warning her to stay back.

"You don't wanna get this stuff on you, Liv. It's sticky as hell." Rowan's eyes meet Mallory's and she's struck by how shockingly white they are against all the red.

She also thinks about what Rowan told her during the mini golf round. Peyton keeps seeming to seesaw between being meticulous and spontaneous, chillingly mature and downright childish. None of it makes any sense.

"You okay in there, Mallory?" Rowan's voice brings her back to reality.

Just as she's about to call back that everything is alright, just when she gets her bearings, there's a hideous crackle and music explodes into the machine: "Sulking Seething"—a song which, if she makes it out of here alive, she vows to never listen to ever again. The top corners of the box light up like firecrackers with multicolored, strobing lights.

Slowly, the machine groans to life and begins to rotate. Mallory's heart jumps to her throat as it halts and starts, the mechanics of the thing obviously not operating smoothly. It's like a rusty can opener of a contraption, jolting as it spins. The sudden motion unsteadies Mallory, and she falls forward, her knees planting firmly in the glass, her hands stretched out to brace against the wall of the box.

"Fuck." The music blares louder and she pushes to her feet again, her knees shredded and bloodied. They sting. Everything stings.

As the box completes its first rotation, a painstakingly slow task with all the sputtering of the gears, she looks back to see Rowan pounding against the panel separating them from the arcade. His fists leave smears of red down the panel and Olivia balks next to him.

"It's okay," Mallory says, even though she knows they can't

hear her—and to be honest, she doesn't believe it herself. "I'll be okay."

She begins the slow, painstaking process of combing through the matted stuffed animal skins, and the glass that juts out from the fabric. She starts at the edges of the machine and attempts to work inward but there's so much jostling that any sort of methodology is a lost cause. She winces as her fingers prick on broken glass, the stuffed animals decapitated and deflated, their jagged entrails catching on her skin. But there's no time to be delicate. She digs in deeper. She bleeds more. The pain radiates through her hands, and she grits her teeth.

Then, the music picks up pace and the box picks up speed, rotating faster as the knife on the hanging mechanism groans to life. It creaks heavily as it begins to slice through the space.

"No," she whispers, dread pooling in the back of her head. "No, no, no."

The massive blade swings back and forth and she huddles against the edges of the box, trying her best to avoid it. But the rotations pick up speed and she's tossed back and forth, narrowly missing the sharpened edge.

She continues to dig into the glass and sagging stuffed animals along the bottom of the case, trying without success to locate the key. The music seems to increase in volume due to her with each rotation of the box. It's all she can hear through the panic and frustration. Her insides clench and she lowers her eyes to avoid hurling as the room blends around her. Her weak ass stomach was not designed to withstand this kind of shit. It's so much worse than a roller coaster, so much worse than one of those carnival rides that spins, and spins, and spins.

The massive blade grazes her shoulder, and she screeches.

The pain is bright, acidic. She dips down low, glass poking holes through her shirt, through her jeans, through everything. It crunches into the side of her cheek and smashes into her arms and she feels like a human pushpin. But even as she's getting torn to pieces, she avoids another possibly devastating blow by the skin of her teeth. She squeezes her eyes shut for a fraction of a second to slow the spinning, and all she can see is Jared's hand as she attempts to guide him back to the medical tent, the blood on his face beginning to congeal.

As she struggles inside the claw machine, she's pulled back to that night last year, sitting in the grass on the hill above the resort, the blades dewy and cold against her bare legs.

With Jared.

They sat in silence for a few moments, the sounds of the band carrying over on the light breeze. A cymbal crashed. Drumbeats pounded like hail, and the crowd roared from within all the noise.

Now, there's the crunch beneath her feet, the shredding of her jeans, sharpness everywhere until she feels raw all over, and she still can't find the key to her survival. She begins to doubt that there's even a key at all, and maybe Peyton just designed the claw machine to shred her alive. Just like the pig's blood she dropped over Rowan. No reason except to make her suffer.

As she huddles along the edges of the box and fights back vomit, all she can think of is how the band continued to play while she sat with Jared. She watched the rise and fall of his chest, imagining what it would be like to nestle her head against him, close enough to nibble the skin stretched over his heart.

It was sick. She knew all about him, she knew all about the assault charges, and she still wanted to be one of his chosen few. She still wanted him, not because of him specifically but because she wanted to know what it felt like to be chosen, even if it was by a psychopath. At that point, Erika had already broken ties with her over the photo she posted. She was alone. Erika wasn't whispering in her ear about how she should be careful, Erika wasn't lecturing her, holding her back... or protecting her. She could do what she wanted. And what she wanted was Jared.

The metronome-like blade slashes back across the glass box and she presses her body into the bottom, wincing as it grazes her back. There's a slashing sound as her shirt rips, and horrible, wet pain as she bleeds.

The world around her blurs into a trail of neon, and she smashes herself flat against the broken shards at the bottom of the machine, swallowing her nausea, fighting through the pain. She considers that maybe it would be easier to stand and end it, let the giant blade find a home in the side of her skull.

Except Rowan and Olivia are counting on her. If she doesn't survive this then they'll never make it to the end of the game, they'll likely rot in the hallway. The rational part of her likes to imagine that they'd find a way out, but everything inside her heart is telling her that their lives are her responsibility, and this is the game with the most at stake. It's not only her life, but theirs that are hanging in the balance as well.

She listens to the woosh of the metronome blade, she strains to hear it against the blaring music, and that's when she realizes that she can time it. This is a beatable trap after all.

She grits her teeth and takes a breath.

But even as she finds her new strength, she's pulled back. Back into the tall grass outside of the resort, trailing behind Jared.

She trailed after him as the band's music faded, the noise dampened by the dark.

Fireflies blinked like hazard lights over the grass, and the sounds of clashing symbols were replaced by chirps—frogs or crickets—somewhere in the woods behind the field. It was so quiet, so still. All bugs and burning.

"There it is," Jared said, pointing. Mallory followed his finger to the soft glow of what appeared to be a bonfire, the faint outline of a building just behind it. "My dad's the one building it, so I can get us inside. It should be open sometime in the next few months, really the only thing that needs to be completed are the hotel rooms."

She remembers being so impressed, and the thought paired with the constant spinning finally empties her stomach. The sour tang of vomit assaults her nostrils and nearly forces her to be sick again, but she takes deep breaths in through her mouth and steadies herself.

Mallory would give anything to go back to that moment, to make different decisions, to see the resort for the first time and feel not impressed, but afraid. In her memories, the building looms. She remembers it looking so still. Flames licked at the sky, the empty slab of the unused parking lot stretching almost to the horizon.

They were alone.

And then there was Jared, his outline lit up against the dark sea of the sky.

Jared, before the beginning of the end.

Mallory grits her teeth and dives back into the mess of stuffed animal skins. Her fingers graze against something metal at the bottom of the case, and her heart rabbits against her ribs. The key. There's really a key in the box after all. But right when she thinks that she'll finally grab it, she slips as the box pitches forward, slowing its rotation.

She curses under her breath as she regains her bearings. Until finally, her bloodied fingers manage to grab hold of the key, but her hands shake, and she struggles. She struggles so damn much. Until she finally manages to pull it free from where it's tethered to the floor.

The box squeals to a halt, the blade inches from her neck and when the front panel opens, she spills out onto the floor of the arcade, the silver key clenched in her bloody fist.

She flops over on her back—wincing as sharp pain travels the length of her spine. She doesn't want to know how bad the damage is. For now, all she can do is wait for the world to stop spinning. The ceiling above her looks like that of an open warehouse, only everything down to the exposed beams are painted black and speckled with white paint in a poor attempt to mirror the night sky.

Without the music from the box, the sounds of the arcade wash over her—the hum of the machinery and white noise trickling in over speakers. It's so different from the night Jared died, when he had to fiddle with the controls for what felt like hours before the neon lights finally sprung to life. That moment feels so far away now, and suddenly, she's very concerned that she might in fact be dying.

Mallory stays sprawled out on the floor, painfully aware of the pool of blood spreading beneath her, warm and oddly soothing. The twins pound their fists against the plastic divider, undoubtedly mistaking her for a corpse. She certainly feels like one. She doesn't have the strength to lift her head just yet. Every part of her feels as if it's bruised or bleeding.

Carefully, she picks the stray pieces of glass from her palms, surprised to find that the damage, at least to that area of her body, is minimal.

Inside the box, she pictured her hands shredded, but now she looks down to find minor cuts drenched in more sweat than blood. The final test comes when she sits up, slowly at first and runs a hand along her back. While it is cut, there's a distinct sting as the pad of her finger traces the tear from her tailbone to her mid-back, it isn't as deep as she would have assumed while caught in the chaos of the box trap.

Finally, she turns to where the twins stand at the plexiglass barrier and flashes them a tentative thumbs up. Olivia looks like she's about to pass out from relief and Mallory can't help but smile to herself as she eases gingerly to her feet.

She limps over to the panel and unlocks it for Rowan and Olivia.

Olivia barrels in first and throws her arms around Mallory who winces against her embrace. Olivia shivers as her shredded arm presses into Mallory's side and attempts to pull away once she realizes the extent of the damage to Mallory's back.

"It looks worse than it actually is," Mallory says, holding onto her. "I'm fine. I'll be fine."

She made it through.

"How the hell did Peyton build that thing?" Rowan asks, eying the claw machine and the bloody handprints Mallory left on its walls like a finger painting out of a horror movie.

In the aftermath of the game, bathed in flashing blue and pink lights, the claw trap looks more like an art installation than something that almost killed her. Olivia is still holding onto her, even though she's loosened her grip significantly.

Mallory twists away, drinking in the terrible ambiance of the arcade. "At least it's over now."

A red exit sign glows at the far end of the room. The three of them wait for a moment next to the claw trap, anticipating Peyton's instructions for the next round, but instead, the only noise is the hum of the machines.

Olivia cocks her head toward the exit sign, which continues to stare at them in an ominous, gloating red. "Do you think that maybe that's all there is to it now? All we need to do is walk out?"

Mallory shakes her head. "She wouldn't make it that easy."

Not since she made it through the claw machine in relatively decent shape. If she's learned anything at this point, it's that Peyton is out for blood and if she can't find it one way, in one trap, she always has something else waiting to draw it for her. It's on brand with this kind of device since whoever made it through would need an especially long time to recover from whatever horrors they faced. It would be easy to surprise the survivor with one last obstacle to overcome.

It reminds Mallory of the haunted house she and Erika

used to go to in high school. Every time there was a big scare, there would be a moment of quiet immediately afterward. The attendees would start to feel okay again, and then something would pop out again—a way to spike the adrenaline one last time.

"Well, we can't just wait for her to throw another curveball at us," Rowan says. "We might as well try to make it out at least. Worst case scenario, it'll prompt her to say something and start the next round."

"Do you think you can survive another round?" Olivia asks, fingers continuing to dance across Mallory's shredded back. With everything going on, the feeling of Olivia's hands against hers helps her feel level. Almost safe. She wishes she could bottle the feeling. She wishes she could stay in this moment and block out everything else.

"Are you sure *you* can?" Mallory asks, tracing the red that bleeds through Olivia's makeshift bandage. Rowan's looking worse for wear himself, with his mohawk all but deflated against the side of his face, and the pig's blood covering him almost completely in a blanket of red. Mallory doesn't even want to consider what she looks like right now.

Rowan holds up his ruined hand and flexes the stub where his finger used to be. "I think we're all in shitty shape, and this thing is probably infected, but it's not like we have any say in what Peyton decides to throw at us next."

Mallory pulls away from Olivia as Rowan steps up next to them.

"We need to keep going," he says.

Olivia reaches for Mallory again, but she shies away. Now isn't the time, not with Peyton's game still looming over them. If Mallory knows anything, it's that relationships are fragile and messy. She cringes at the thought of a mess. She cringes at the thought of how things fall apart and how everything that was once new will eventually decay.

"Rowan's right," Mallory says.

"I don't know if I can." Olivia's voice breaks. Rowan lays his hand across his sister's shoulder, and she leans into him. She raises the hand she pressed to Mallory's back. Her palm is streaked with red. She stares at it, sheer horror in her expression. "Mallory, I'm worried for you. I'm worried for all of us."

"I'll be okay once we make it out of here," Mallory insists, though she doesn't quite believe it.

Olivia curls her bloodied hand into a fist, it's like she's pocketing a piece of Mallory and Mallory watches intently. It makes her feel so unbalanced to know that she's falling for someone while their lives are in danger, while there's a very strong possibility that they're not going to make it out of this alive.

"The only way out is through," Rowan says, and the group limps toward the exit sign. Mallory keeps her eyes on Olivia and her bloodied palm—thinking about the way their lives are intertwining. Thinking about, if they were to kiss, would Olivia bite her lower lip, would she bite Olivia's—would she draw blood? Can there be beauty in drawing blood? Non-violent, pure love.

The exit sign is only a few feet away and Mallory reaches out, weaves her fingers through Olivia's. They're almost home free. She keeps waiting for the blare of a siren or the crackle of the intercom system, but there's nothing. Heavy silence, only the sound of their labored breathing, of their feet against the tile floor, of them well on their way to being able to piece together some semblance of a life after this.

Then, there's a crunch, another set of feet, another set of lungs, and Mallory looks over her shoulder, and Olivia's hand goes slack as she pulls away, and just as everything was almost built up again, it crumbles.

A figure lumbers out from behind the crane game, their features muddled in the soft neon light, and it isn't until they inch closer that Mallory realizes who it is.

Britt.

There's blood dripping down her chin, and a blade gripped between her fingers.

She inches closer still and more of her face comes into focus, cast in yellow, and green, and violent pink. Vicious brush strokes of color paint patterns across her cheeks. As she gets closer, Mallory realizes that they're scabs of blood, fresh liquid still gushing from the open wound of her mouth. That's all it is at this point, a gaping wound where a mouth used to be—split open several ways so that her lips are parted like grotesque petals.

Britt spits and a fresh trail of blood slips from between her lips. She grips the bone saw in her fist—the weapon Olivia abandoned back in the escape room.

"Britt," Mallory says, the word escaping in a gasp of breath because there's something so hostile about the way she grips the saw.

"You look surprised," she slurs, clearly in bad shape. It's a wonder she's standing at all. She hunches over slightly, reaches for the machines around her to prop her up again.

"But I..." Olivia freezes in place. And it all clicks into place for Mallory. This is not a happy reunion; this is a threat. This is danger. This is the prelude to a river of red.

"You thought you killed me," Britt spits. "Well, you didn't, and now..." She twists the blade between her fingers. "I'm gonna show you how it's done."

20

BRITT, 30 MINUTES EARLIER

Britt opens her eyes expecting the afterlife, whatever the fuck that entails. She's never given it much thought before and would often scoff at the way that people got so hung up over the whole concept. Do this, not that. One wrong move and it's fire, or ice, or nothing at all. One wrong move and you come back as an ant, or a flea, or a fucking amoeba.

Growing up, her mother was the luke-warm kind of religious that only really mattered during major holidays and her dad was more invested in self-help books masquerading as philosophy than any set religion. Britt watched them both from the sidelines, never really understanding how someone could be with someone whose ideas didn't line up with their own. Watching her dad filled her with a special kind of dread and she swore to herself that she would never be middle aged and still searching—at that point she would already know what she believed.

Now, she opens her eyes to a cloud. A deep purple cloud. The same, unnamable shade as the bar back in the concession area. She reaches out to touch it, as if sifting it through her fingers will help her find the words, the history behind it.

Instead, the color shifts beneath her touch to a brown cloud of pigment that she recognizes immediately. Mummy brown. Originally made in the sixteenth century from the ground up remains of mummies—a cursed color.

She's definitely dead.

Britt leans her head back and waits for darkness, or light, or anything at all, but instead she becomes painfully aware of her body—the aches and pains.

There's a pounding in the base of her skull. The cloud—a heavy thing in front of her vision—clears to show that she's still firmly hooked into reality, and she's hit by something between confusion and disappointment.

Of course, her death wouldn't be that easy.

She coughs once and a glob of pink-tinged phlegm drips down her fingers and they shake as she struggles to wipe it onto her knee. She feels as if she's been run over, all her organs squished flat inside her fragile body. It takes her two tries before she's able to stand properly.

The door to her half of the escape room is open now, but she doesn't hurry out. Instead, she inches, slowly, painfully to the diner counter and ducks beneath it, leaning up against the underside and pulling a stool up against her, so she's sandwiched in the space.

Ever since she was a kid, tight spaces have helped her to feel safe, and some of her earliest memories are of the plush carpet on the floor of her parent's closet. She used to sit there among her mother's extensive shoe collection and squeeze her eyes shut until the dark behind her eyes was lit up by stars. It was quiet there, controlled, and she would run her fingers over the sharp heels, the suede fabric, the rhinestones.

Her mother would find her and flick on the light with a huff. She would pull Britt out by the arm and launch into a lengthy monologue asking what was wrong with her. Why couldn't she just be normal?

Britt doesn't understand what normal is or who her mother is to judge. In her opinion, it isn't normal to clean up crime scenes, or hoarder houses—to be exposed to so much sadness on a regular basis.

Britt didn't really understand her mother or her business until she started working alongside her and realized that constant exposure to that kind of messiness breeds apathy. She figures that it seeped into her mother's bones and Britt inherited it at birth. It's her birthright to feel nothing at all. In Britt's case, her natural apathy makes her freakishly good at cleaning sad places.

She leans her head back against the wood paneling, savoring the dark. An icepick headache drills its way through her forehead. So much effort goes into keeping her mask in place, pushing down all her despair and confusion, and even alone she won't allow it to slip. Just in case Peyton has cameras set up. She'd sooner die than let her see the weakness in her eyes. She thinks back on her slip, her single crack. She was so sure that Olivia had killed her, that she wailed in anguish. She cringes. Never again. No more. Done.

Waves of emotion shiver through her and she clips each one at the root.

She coughs again. More pink tinged phlegm.

She should have killed Olivia out in the hall.

Not long now before she'll be dead herself. Not long until she finally greets that lurking dark.

It's always been a matter of time. Britt can't kid herself, she always figured she would die young. Though, when she thought about it, she always imagined it would be alcohol poisoning that would take her out. Or maybe she would buy a bad batch of some designer drug. Or maybe she would be in the wrong place at the wrong time.

Now, it seems so sad. She fought her way against the current for twenty-seven years only for things to end like this.

Britt never really understood pain until she started cleaning up crime scenes. All that blood—the whispered remarks that buzzed around the dinner table like swarming flies, so loud, so deafening. All the traumas.

Britt understands at surface level what trauma is. She understands that if somehow she lives through this, she'll have trauma. Or should, anyway. She can already feel it pooling in the back of her head, being eaten away by the same fuzziness that invades her body whenever anything feels too heavy. Or should feel. It's confusing. She doesn't have the words for it— the numbness that isn't numbness. The idea that her body and what lives inside it are connected by broken wires.

Jared used to be the only one she felt somewhat normal around. He was in all likelihood a psychopath, she understands that. Like, there's no fucking other explanation for some of the shit he did. Logically, it makes sense. He had all the telltale signs. He was charming in a chilling sort of way, and she wouldn't be the least bit surprised if she ever found out that he tortured small animals as a kid. She wonders if he recognized some of that in her, if her apparent apathy might have been hiding something darker, if that's why he was so candid with her. Or maybe he knew that she would understand it.

In return, she'd indulge him.

Britt used to sleep over his apartment all the time, and they'd lay facing each other until they were so tired that their eyes burned and heads throbbed. Until the sunrise bled citrus across the sky and only when she was sure he was asleep, would she roll over and allow herself to drift off.

They never had sex. She's never had an interest in the act in general, but especially not with him, knowing how fucked up he was. He never initiated anything either, and part of her always wondered if it was out of respect or repulsion. Either way, she couldn't complain.

But when they laid together, she would tell him all about

the crime scenes she'd cleaned up—walk him through in sickening detail. He was always interested in them over the hoarder houses, which she was grateful for. Hoarder houses are sad in a way that goes beyond the trauma of a violent crime. It's a long, drawn-out wail rather than a scream of pain. The whole house would ache.

With crime scenes, there was a smell, a feeling—more sharp than sad—and Jared always wanted to know everything. The difference between blood splatter and brain matter, what kind of stain a corpse would leave on a carpet or a wooden floor.

He'd grin, showing off the smile that made so many girls melt, the dimple puckering his left cheek. "And how did they die?"

Britt never really knew. That's not part of the job. When she first started accompanying her mother and training for her shifts, she thought the way people died would play a bigger role in her day to day. But instead, it's just about the cleaning products—how to get out blood stains without ruining the floors. How to pay attention to detail so that no stray splash of blood is left behind. She learned a lot about cleaning solutions and which mops and sponges are the best quality. Her mother was proud of her for the first time in her life, it seemed, because this was an environment in which Britt thrived. When cleaning, she could focus on the task, she didn't have to worry about communicating with anyone or trying to fake sympathy or read social cues. She could put in her earphones, turn on her music, and clean.

She used to google some of the sites they went to and learn as much as she could about the deaths, but in the end, she realized it didn't matter. Plus, it took away from the therapeutic nature of the job. She didn't like putting a face to a name, or a weapon to a crime. But when Jared would ask, she would embellish or lie and watch his eyes glimmer as he ate it up.

It was the one time she was able to flex her creativity, close her eyes and make something out of nothing. Sometimes she would draw off actual true crime cases, and if he ever noticed that she was feeding him bullshit, he didn't let on to it.

"Thanks for not thinking I'm a freak for knowing so much about this stuff," she said one night as they lay in bed, facing each other. His fingers traced lazy patterns up and down her arm.

There was always a cold sort of intimacy between them. Jared never tried to take it beyond a brush against the arm, but Britt appreciated how he would attempt to feel closer to her, break down the wall that she inadvertently put up in her day-to-day life.

He grinned. "Thanks for telling me all about the messed-up shit you see. And not thinking I'm a freak," he added with a smile as he passed her a joint.

She took a deep puff. "Oh, you're definitely a freak. I just don't care about how messed up you are." She was pretty sure at that point that he was using the descriptions she was feeding him to nurture some sort of sick fantasy, but it's not like she was responsible for anything he did or didn't do. And she liked the way she could call him out on how fucking unhinged he was.

She let the smoke roll into the back of her mouth and savored the little buzz that hummed through her veins.

Jared laughed deeply as she passed what remained of the joint back to him. He took a final puff before grinding it out on the bedside table.

"Have you ever touched a dead body?" he asked.

"You know they're already gone by the time I get there, right? I'm just there to clean up the mess."

"Well, have you ever seen a dead body?"

"You mean in real life and not just in a picture?"

He nodded and she shook her head. "I never want to, that kind of stuff scares me."

"Nothing scares you, Britt," Jared said, propping himself up on his elbows, the sheet slipping to expose the tattoos trailing down the right side of his body. "You don't feel shit."

"Yeah, that's what scares me." She took a deep breath. "Sometimes when I'm working with my mother, she'll refuse to go into a certain room, or have to go out in the backyard for air. Not because of the mess or the smell, but because of the feeling. Like, when someone dies in that kind of way, leaving that much carnage behind, something lingers. Some bad feeling, some oppression. But when I go to clean up a scene, I don't feel anything. It's just empty. What do you think it's like to be able to feel what my mother feels all the time and still come into work the next day and pretend that none of that shit ever happened?"

"So you don't want it to affect your job?" he continued tracing slow lines down her arm, and for a moment, she expected him to make a move.

Instead, he reached over her for the cigarettes sitting on her bedside table and pulled one from the pack, placing it between his lips.

"Not really," she said. "It's a temporary thing until I can get something of my own. I don't want to be working for my mother forever, makes it feel like charity and not a job. My dad won't let me hear the end of it, keeps saying that the only reason I have a job at all is because of Mother—and he's not wrong, I guess. I just want to be able to rub it in his face that I was able to get something without either of them handing it to me."

"I'm taking over my dad's company. There's nothing wrong with it. It's better to have a safety net. Better to inherit something. Would my first choice be taking over some fucking construction company? Hell no. But it's free, and it's there, and you need to think about what life is gonna be like years down the line."

"That's different... and I feel like if I ever were to see a dead body, I wouldn't freak out like I'm supposed to. I would just stand there: I wouldn't feel anything."

"I don't know why you would want to."

"People give me weird looks when I don't react a certain way to things, I think it would be easier..."

"Screw other people." His hand moved from her arm to her cheek, and she flinched as he traced the line of her jaw. "You just have a different way of seeing things. It's not that your way is wrong, it's different. Not everyone's gonna get it, I sure as hell don't, you're completely fucked up. I just don't give a shit." He smiled again, showing off the dimple in his left cheek again. She had never been so thankful for a person in her entire life. It was the last night they had together like that, two weeks before last year's HyveFest, and she almost wishes that something happened. Even if she doesn't give a shit about his dick, at least there would be some sort of memory to hold onto past the almosts, past his lazy grin as he fell asleep with a cigarette still smoking in his mouth.

Britt misses that smile. That dimple. That night.

The way that she felt almost, not quite okay about everything.

Now, she's inching toward equilibrium, she's swimming in a sea of mint and tile, and fake milkshakes and even though she should be dead, she slowly finds her way back to almost okay.

Her breathing steadies and she pushes herself up off the ground.

The intercom crackles on as she straightens up and she's convinced that this is it, Peyton is going to finish her off for good this time, and it's all going to be over. But at least she'll see Jared. Maybe. If there is an afterlife and if they both end up in the same place.

"Hey Britt," Peyton says, a brightness in her voice that makes her wince. "Kind of a raw deal you wound up with, huh?

I saw how Olivia just left you to die, and that was ice cold, even for me. I know how you'd probably hesitate to trust me at this point, but I would never pull that kind of shit with you."

"Can you hear me?" Britt asks. Her voice comes out raw, and the inside of her throat feels shredded. She clears it and tries again the words coming out clearer. "Can you hear me?"

A pause.

"Yes," Peyton confirms. "I can hear you."

"Then why don't you just finish me off already? I don't have it in me to play any more games. I'm done." Britt eases onto the stool at the counter and cradles her head in her arms. It's suddenly so heavy. And the headache feels more like a helmet, and she would sell her soul to be able to smoke one final joint. With Jared. Make up some story about how some guy died, and wonder what he does with that information and if she's as fucked up as he is.

"Oh, you've got it all wrong, darling," Peyton says, the voice leaking over the speaker honey-sweet.

"Really?" Britt closes her eyes and she's back there. That night. In bed with Jared, the lazy trails of smoke tracing the contours of their bodies. The softness of his sheets, the way the room smelled like weed, and him, and him, and him. She buries her face into the sleeve of her hoodie and inhales deeply. His cologne steadies her pulse and maybe it's fucked up, and maybe it's not love, but it's something close. Being understood. Even if it's by a monster.

"Yes," Peyton says. "I was going to go ahead and off you. To be honest, I don't really care if you end up dying at the end of this, but I had the most amazing idea as I flooded the room with gas and I just couldn't allow you to tap out quite yet."

"What idea would that be?" Britt asks, feeling like the bugs she would pull the wings off as a kid. She never understood why they would continue to thrash around as she dismembered them, she didn't understand how something so close to an inevitable death could have so much fight left. Only now she does. Now she's the one fighting, and she's not finished yet, no matter how badly she wants to be.

"Well," Peyton begins, drawing out the syllables. "It's like I said before, I think what Olivia did to you is messed up. This whole thing is about righting wrongs and all that. I don't appreciate anyone playing dirty unless it's me. So, I have a proposition for you."

"Which is?" Britt says, raising her head ever so slightly so that her nose is still pressed into the fabric of her sleeve, though the smell of Jared's cologne does little to calm her.

Peyton chuckles. "How would you like to get some payback?"

Britt twitches. She never cared much about leveling the playing field—she never really connected to phrases like an eye for an eye, all of that crap seemed so out of reach. Even with everything that happened with Jared, she never understood when people, the women in his life especially, would get all up in arms about something he may have done weeks, or months, or years ago. Bad things happen and you move on.

Even with the taste of trauma burning the back of her throat, she's not sure how anyone could let something define them for the rest of their lives...

"Britt?" Peyton teases. "I see an awful lot of sitting around, but I don't hear an answer."

Britt hates to admit it, but turning on Olivia, helping Peyton with whatever sick finale she's working up to would be easy. She meant to kill Olivia out in the hallway after all, even if it was to spite Peyton rather than assist her. She doesn't like the idea of helping Peyton, but she can't help but think about middle school, and team sports, and how no one in the Discord so much as said a word when she poured her heart out to them.

They already turned on her. They already abandoned her. She's alone, left out, just like she's always been. Why shouldn't she try to get one over on them? These strangers who she loved and tricked herself into thinking she was close to?

Still, three against one? She doesn't like those odds.

And she's acutely aware of every ache and pain in her damaged body.

"Just let me out of here," she says, and Peyton huffs over the speaker system, clearly displeased with her answer.

A few moments of silence then the system clicks back on again.

"Counter proposal," Peyton begins. "You play one more round of my games and if you win, I'll let you walk out of here —no strings attached."

"I already told you, I'm done with games," Britt says, holding up the sleeve of Jared's hoodie to her mouth, but with the dark fabric it's impossible to decipher if there's still pink in her spit. She rolls up the sleeve and spits into her palm instead. Clear. "What happens if I don't play?"

"Then I leave you in there to rot."

"I'll find a way out."

Peyton laughs. "Good luck with that."

"Let's say I do play... what happens if I lose?" Britt asks after another moment of consideration.

"We'll discuss it if it comes to that. What I need you to do is go behind the counter of the diner set up, there's a locked trunk underneath, pull it out into the center of the escape room, lock facing the camera."

Britt hesitates for a moment, still woozy with whatever toxin Peyton filled the room with after she lost to Olivia. But then she goes over to the counter and sure enough there's a massive trunk beneath the counter, like something that would be found on the Titanic or in an old timey movie where rich people tout around luggage. She's surprised she didn't notice it before. It takes her several tries to pull it from where it's wedged up underneath the counter—but it's surprisingly light and she's able to pull it to the center of the room easily.

"Why is this in here?" Britt asks, staring up at one of the cameras fastened in the corner of the ceiling. "Did you always know that you were going to do this?"

Peyton laughs again. "No, no, not at all. It's a backup plan. There were a lot of moving parts to this game, so this was the backup plan. It's not as flashy as what you just went through, I assure you."

Britt crouches down next to the trunk.

"It's not locked, you can just flip the latch."

Britt takes one final deep inhale of Jared's sleeve and opens the trunk. Inside there are three smaller boxes that look similar to the ones from when Rowan lost his finger. Britt recoils. Her eyes flit around the escape room, trying to see if there are any ways to break open the boxes. "No fucking way, we already played this game."

"Look closer," Peyton instructs. "Or better yet, take the boxes out of the trunk and line them up. They're not the same as the ones from Rowan's round, not at all."

Tentatively, Britt lifts the box directly in front of her from the trunk and sure enough it's different. For one thing, it has a lid, and there's no place to stick her hand through. Also, there's a telltale swish as she lifts each one, as if the boxes are full of liquid. Britt takes the others out and lines them up on the floor, sitting cross legged in front of them.

"Now open them up. I think you'll be very excited to see what's inside. Just don't go sticking your hand in or anything... you'll regret it."

Britt lifts the lid off the first box and holds back an audible gasp. She quickly rips the lid off the other two, finding the same thing inside and Peyton's sharp laughter pierces in over the intercom.

"Do you understand how perfect this is now?" Peyton asks,

her words coming out in a manic stream, syllables bleeding into one another. "How can I not believe in fate when you're the one left here with this game, this game that was inspired by you! I built games for everyone, and I'll admit that I had an idea of how I wanted things to play out, I'll admit that I've been feeling a bit off because so many of these games haven't lined up the way I'd hoped. I mean, I've been really kicking myself over here. Why couldn't I have assigned players to each game? But how to do that... I mean, the whole thing is a logistical nightmare as it is but this... this is perfect. You and your colors. It's simply perfect! Like, I don't even have to explain what's inside."

Britt fights back the lump in her throat because the inside of each box is painted Vantablack—a color that absorbs all light. It makes it look like the boxes are holes in the floor rather than three dimensional objects. Despite hearing liquid when she lifted them from the trunk, she can't see anything—just velvety darkness. Darkness so deep that it looks as if she could crawl inside, contort her body to squeeze through the hole and fall, and fall, and fall.

"So what's the game?" she asks, focused on the boxes.

"Easy. Inside one of those boxes is a copy of the key out of the escape room. If you find it, you can unlock the door and walk out of here without a care."

"And in the other ones?"

Peyton's laugh comes in over the speaker again, sharper than before. "In the others, well..."

"How many tries do I get?" Britt asks.

"Two...if you can stomach it." More laughter. "Oh, did I forget to mention? You're not allowed to use your hands. It's like bobbing for apples."

"Is it... water in the boxes?" Britt's main concern isn't even what other things might be lurking in the liquid beyond the key. She figures that if there's anything sharp or dangerous, she'd be able to figure it out pretty quickly, but the idea of submerging her face in a mystery liquid puts her on edge. Especially after what happened after she drank from the flask.

Peyton doesn't answer.

Britt sits back on her heels and buries her face in Jared's sleeves, breathing in his cologne. "I changed my mind, I'm not playing."

"How about this," Peyton says. "I'll give you…mmmm…ten minutes to decide."

The television fastened to the wall comes to life and a red countdown clock comes up on the screen. Britt takes in another shaky breath of Jared's sweatshirt. She's going to die here; she's really going to die.

She pulls each box closer to her, trying to sense the shifting weight, the clock behind her counting down the minutes and seconds until impact. The worst part of it though, is that she's alone in this. Even with everyone ganging up on her in the last round, at least she had others going through the same thing with her earlier in the game. She could pretend that they were a team. Instead, they've probably already forgotten all about her. Instead, they're probably relieved that they're rid of her.

"I can't believe we got stuck with her."

"It's not like she's gonna play anyway, she'll be the first one out."

It's middle school gym, and it's getting picked last for dodgeball, and it's the thick layers of yellow that haunted her throughout her childhood.

It's Jared being the only one who ever seemed to truly tolerate her. *Tolerate*, not even like, and especially not love.

It's bottles of tequila and confessions without reciprocation. The Discord group's heavy silence when she told them they were her only friends.

Britt grits her teeth. She should have killed Olivia out in the hall.

She chooses the box to the left of her and dips her face in.

The liquid is cold and probably water—hopefully water, so that's good. She doesn't dip her face in very deep at first. It's like when she was in high school, and her mother pressured her into trying out for the swim team. She hated everything about indoor swimming pools—the smell of the chlorine, the way sounds would echo, and everything seemed dim around the edges. She hated the pool most of all. The temperature of the water was never quite right. She would dip her toes in and cringe because it was always too cold. The smell of chlorine would follow her home and the smell would bring back echoes of the noise inside the pool room, and the feelings that came with it.

She pulls her face back quickly, droplets of water splashing across the floor and over the sides of the box.

The clock counts down. She braces herself to dive back in.

This time, she doesn't hesitate. With her eyes shut tight, she lowers her face into the box and parts her lips. Whatever is lurking in the water can't be so bad, she reasons. If there's the option to try again, it can't be so bad.

Her teeth sink into something soft and rubbery. She pulls her head back and immediately spits it to the ground. It's a pig's foot like the ones in the stock room when they first came in. She shudders, taking a few seconds to gather herself before sticking her face back into the next tub of Vantablack. As soon as her lips part, there's a terrible sting.

She rips her face from the box and if she thought the pain was bad under the water, it's a hundred times worse when her lips hit the air. She lets out a sound that reminds her of a dying animal. She raises a hand instinctively to her lips and crosses to the mirrored wall panels behind the counter, blood already spilling through her fingers.

Shaking, she removes her fingers to assess the damage and finds a huge gash down the center of her mouth. It's split almost comically wide, and she immediately dives behind the bar, searching for a rag, a towel, anything. But when she comes up short, she peels off Jared's sweatshirt, and presses the sleeve to her tattered lips.

"You only have three minutes left," Peyton says with the cool detachment of a predator.

To Britt's horror, whatever she wrapped her lips around in the box knicked the tip of her tongue too. Her entire mouth tastes like metal. She can't stick her face back into the water, she can't risk another injury like this. She's not ready to die yet.

"Is payback still an option," she slurs through the bleeding.

There's a terrifyingly long silence and then the clock stops counting down.

"Kick over the boxes and grab the key," Peyton tells her. "Let's talk."

21

OLIVIA

Sticky heat pools in the back of Olivia's head. Her stomach clenches and bile burns its way up her esophagus. She should have known better than to leave Britt behind in the escape room; she should have known it would come back to haunt her. Any time she ever makes a decision purely in her own self-interest, she always winds up paying for it in the end. It always sours somehow. Her relationship with Jared, for example, her choice to be with him despite everything she had heard.

She was warned dozens of times, by dozens of girls: Stay away from that one. Be careful. Steer clear. But she continued to stalk his Instagram stories and hang around the places where she knew he'd be. She became a regular at his favorite café, and she went to all the bars she knew he loved, just to catch a glimpse of him. Sure, there were stories. Sure, there were young women who claimed that he had a habit of getting violent, but there was never any evidence.

He seemed to be sweet, and cute, and kind. Olivia was smitten, and she deserved something good in her life, something that made her feel beautiful.

Except it soured.

Except Jared turned out to be a monster, and the night that he died, Olivia sunk a knife between his ribs. Not terribly deep, not enough to kill him, but enough to teach him a lesson.

"What the fuck," he hissed as he staggered back.

"What's the matter, it was only the tip," she said, a ghost of a smile playing across her lips. It really was only the tip of the blade, barely enough to even constitute a stabbing, but it felt good, better than she imagined it would.

The power of it, the control when she stuck the blade in and yanked it back out again. The squish of his flesh, the strangled grunt as he fell to his knees. She couldn't get enough. It was like music.

Her favorite part was how surprised he sounded. She pulled him in for a hug before she dug the knife in and he had no idea it was coming. The fucker actually thought she'd be willing to hug him after everything he did to her.

She left him alone, kneeling on the ground and the next day, he was gone. Vanished.

For a long time, she was terrified that she had something to do with his disappearance. She confided in Rowan about the fight—shifting around some details to make it sound less incriminating. A punch to the face instead of a stabbing. She worried about it for weeks on end, and when she heard the rumors of what happened, she was almost disappointed that it wasn't her. Something always goes wrong when she stands up for herself, when she focuses on self-preservation.

Now, Britt staggers forward with blood crusted down her chin. Her eyes are glassy in the glow of the neon as if she's on something, like a junkie on a mission.

Tears sting the corners of Olivia's eyes. The exit was so close.

Rowan moves instinctively to shield her but Britt grins, showing off a row of reddened teeth.

"No, no, no," she says, waving the blade like a pendulum. "You don't get to stand in for her."

"Stand in for what?" Rowan asks, and Britt giggles, more and more red dripping from her mouth.

The intercom system crackles on, and Peyton wastes no time getting the point. "I thought it would be fun if we got a little one on one action. Britt deserves a chance to get even, don't you think?"

"No fucking way!" Rowan cries, but Peyton doesn't give him a chance.

"If you don't play along then I'll seal you inside," she says. "Maybe I have some fun devices hiding in the ceiling. Maybe I have a thousand ways to make you bleed. Or maybe you'll just starve."

"No fucking way," Rowan says.

Peyton lets out a chilling peal of laughter. "I thought you said that Olivia could hold her own against Britt. And that was when Britt wasn't half-poisoned, half-roasted from the inside. Surely, Olivia can hold her own now."

Olivia steps forward, her legs shaking. Rowan's already done so much for her, and this is her fault. She looks at Britt and her heart breaks for what she's been through. She understands how difficult it must be for Britt. She hasn't been quite right since the round with poison, and Olivia can hardly blame her for being angry that she abandoned her.

She wishes there was a way that she can explain how this is what she was trying to avoid—a situation where they survive one round just to have to turn on each other later.

Britt is hurting more than any of them, not only because of her physical wounds but undoubtedly because of what she had to go through, and how she had to go through it alone... because Olivia was the one to leave her in that position. Olivia was the one who left her to the slaughter—this woman who she considered a friend.

The energy in the air is tense, charged, and it makes Olivia's stomach roil, but when Rowan tries once again to push her behind him, she shakes her head.

"It'll be okay," Olivia says, the words tasting foreign. It feels so strange to be in a position to comfort her brother for once instead of the other way around.

She's not going to self-destruct. She's going to do this on her own—without Rowan or Mallory. Mallory, who she spent so many years pouring her heart out to, leaning on, soaking through with her trauma.

Olivia has never stood on her own before in her life. She's always had others to help her.

It's the role that she craved for as long as she can remember after all. The supporter, the background character. But now she's the main event and she's shaking as Britt advances and the two of them stand on opposite ends of an air hockey board that sits in the center of the arcade.

Cold streams of air puff up through the table and for a moment, Olivia feels like she's back in the unfinished basement of her childhood home. Her dad bought a whole assortment of game tables for when the basement would eventually be converted into a rec room. But they never went through with the renovation. Her mom didn't have the heart to do it after their dad died, so the tables were left untouched along with the rest of their dad's stuff.

Olivia and Rowan used to sneak downstairs and tear the plastic covers from the game boards and play in the precious hour before their mom would get home from work. And for a little while they could pretend that the basement was finished and their dad was on the sidelines, waiting to play against whichever one of them won.

She told Jared about this one night, about how certain things still make her feel like her dad will be there, waiting.

"No offense, babe, but didn't he die when you were like

six?" he said. "What makes you think you'd even like being around him? You didn't even really know him."

The words made her feel so broken, like she lost her dad all over again. And that's why she doesn't let Rowan interfere. Because he has Gabriel back home. Because he has unfinished house projects. Because seven years from now she doesn't want her teenage nephew sneaking through his dead father's things while his mother is at work.

Britt moves around the table and slashes the bone saw through the air.

Luckily, she really is in bad shape and nearly topples over as her blow fails to land. The edge of her chin catches the air hockey table, and a part of Olivia likes to imagine that it's her dad looking out for her. He's not going to let her die here. She's not going to let herself die here.

Britt raises the saw again and Olivia braces herself.

The way Britt's silhouette hovers above her—so dark against the neon pink, is so much like the way Jared used to stand above her. He'd raise his hand and she would flinch, anticipating what came next so that when the blow finally landed, it hurt in a way that she liked to imagine was softened by the expectation. The actual act was never as bad as what went on in her head.

Olivia does what she never did with Jared. She raises her hand. She catches the blow as it falls and grips the blade between her palms. Sharp, and bright, and stinging. It's almost enough to make her release her grip, but instead she thinks of the gash in Mallory's back, she thinks of the blood still on her hand and how no matter what happens, she has a part of Mallory with her now, really with her.

She owes it to Mallory—no, she owes it to herself—to survive this. She digs her fingers in and pulls. So that the bone saw comes free from Britt's hand and Britt face plants against the floor. She twists the blade around so that she's holding onto the handle, her hands stinging, feeling as if it cut through the marrow and left her shredded, but she doesn't even care.

Olivia only brings the blade down once, a single stab to the top left shoulder. A punctuation mark. She thinks vaguely about how Britt doesn't deserve this, how none of them deserve this, and when she opens her mouth to scream, no sound comes out. Instead, she tastes tears, a saltiness that takes her back to her father's funeral. A taste that takes her back to her dorm room, and Jared's kitchen floor, and Jared's queen-sized bed, and Jared's living room. She hunches over Britt for a moment, and watches her chest rise and fall, not sure if she should feel relief or fear. She knows that the neon lights are flashing, and she knows that they're in the arcade and Jared is dead, and Jared is dead, Jared is dead.

But it doesn't stop her from hurting.

"Olivia." Someone wraps their arms around her and for a moment she thinks that it's Rowan, but she turns to find Mallory. Her brown eyes are wide and dark, and Olivia wants nothing more than to drown in them.

"Your hands," Mallory says. "Are you okay?"

She nods once because she's numb to it, and Britt's chest continues to rise and fall, and she knows she should feel grateful that she hasn't killed her. She knows that she can be redeemed, and everything she's been through is just a prologue to the present moment.

She reaches out and wraps her arms around Mallory, leaving bloody handprints down the back of her shirt.

She's about to apologize when Mallory dips her face down lower and their lips meet and for a moment she can't feel the sting anymore, she can't feel the fear, for a moment it's only them—bathed in the pink light, lost in the kiss.

And she feels something she never felt when she kissed Jared, even in the beginning, even before things got bad.

She feels loved.

22

MALLORY

Mallory's first kiss was with Erika her freshman year of college. She had never kissed anyone before and was horribly embarrassed by it. Everyone she knew, including Erika, had already done everything you can do with a person, and she felt like she was behind the curve.

"I'm worse than a virgin," she complained to Erika one night in their dorm. She lay curled up in a fetal position while Erika sat on her bed, painting her nails a light shade of robin's egg blue.

"There's nothing wrong with being a virgin," Erika said, not looking up from her nails.

"Says the girl who lost her virginity at fourteen."

"It was fifteen, and I had been in a relationship for almost a year. I was in love with him."

Mallory sighed and checked her phone for the hundredth time only to find no messages. About two weeks before Rowan had messaged her saying that he didn't want to lead her on anymore and they should lay off the flirting.

Lead me on?? She had messaged back, heart in her throat. *You don't actually like me??*

Of course, I like you. You're one of my best friends, but it's never going to move beyond that, so it doesn't feel right to continue messaging like we have been.

Mallory felt like she was going to be sick. She couldn't understand why every time she suggested they meet in person, he deflected. He was always too busy at work or at school. She was convinced that it was his way of avoiding a real commitment. Erika was convinced it was his way of proving that he was a catfish.

Mallory knew that she didn't have a right to feel so gutted, especially since they'd never actually spoken face to face, but she couldn't help the way his messages tore into her.

I don't want to lose you, Mallory, he insisted. *You need to understand that this is the best thing for us going forward.*

They went back and forth for hours. He refused to get on voice chat with her and fresh off that rejection, she couldn't stand the thought of having to wait to find a similar connection before her first kiss.

"I don't want to wait for love," she muttered.

"Love makes it better though," Erika insisted, despite being notorious for using guys and avoiding emotional connections at every opportunity. The longest she kept a guy around those days was a few weeks, then it was on to the next, an endless supply lined up and all too willing to get their hearts broken by Erika.

Mallory was so jealous it hurt. She wished she could be the type of girl who attracted that kind of attention. Even if some of Erika's suitors were a little too obsessed.

A few months back, one of her exes tried getting into their dorm after Erika dumped him. He managed to pry the door open only for Erika to nearly claw his eyes out with her stiletto nails.

"You psycho," he spat at her, blood dripping down his face,

as they waited for campus security to come grab him. "You could have blinded me."

She grinned as she wiped her hands on the back of her jeans. "Try to break into our room again, and I will."

Mallory knew that she meant it, and the way she said it, the guy did too.

They never had a problem with him after that. That's how Erika was: dangerous, deadly. You didn't fuck with her. While her choice of warfare with women was soft, and lemon-scented, and strategic, she was all blood, and meat, and grit when it came to the men in her life.

Suddenly, Erika screwed the cap back onto her nail polish and crossed the narrow space between their beds. Startled by how close she was, Mallory scrambled into a sitting position.

"What?" she asked and Erika grinned.

"I just had the most incredible idea." Erika reached out and gripped the sides of Mallory's face, leaning so close that Mallory could count the freckles on her cheeks. She smelled like citrus fruit, her strawberry blonde hair gleamed.

"Do you love me?" Erika asked, pushing her nose up against Mallory's. Mallory was so taken aback and pulled away so hard that she hit the back of her head against the cinderblock wall next to her bed.

"Did I do something to make you think that I'm in love with you?" she asked, a fine sheen of sweat breaking out across her forehead.

She'd known that she was bisexual since she was eleven and first saw Alyssa Milano in *Charmed* but had never thought of Erika as anything more than a friend. Mallory's cheeks burned as Erika laughed, her eyes glimmering.

"I said 'love,' not 'in love.' Of course, you're not in love with me." Erika looked down and cursed when she saw that she smudged her nails, but quickly regained her composure. "I'm not in love with you either. I don't think I've ever been in love with anyone in my whole life."

"You just said that you loved the guy you lost your virginity too."

"Yeah, but not like... *love* love. Either way, that's not the point. The point is that you love me, right? Like, if anything were to happen to me, you'd speak at my funeral... or if I ever got married, you'd be my maid of honor? If anyone ever hurt me, you'd hurt them back on my behalf? You love me, don't you?"

Mallory blinked slowly, her pulse moving back into manageable territory, the heat draining from her cheeks. "Yeah, obviously."

"And I love you too," Erika said, leaning back in. This time Mallory let her take hold of the sides of her face and trace a finger down to her lips. Her heart beat hard inside her chest. "So let me be your first kiss."

Mallory did, of course. And she did feel better afterwards, like she had crossed some imaginary milestone that officially gave her the right to be a college student. They never talked about it again. But sometimes when Erika would drag her out to a bar and if they had a few too many shots, Erika would say "remember that one time" without specifying. Mallory would automatically know which time she was referring to, and her pulse would race, and the room would spin, and she would wait for Erika to kiss her again. But she never did.

After a while, she thought that Erika constantly reminded her of it in subtle, non-obvious ways because it gave her power over her, a level of control that she craved.

Mallory thinks of that now as she pulls away from Olivia.

Her first kiss was Erika, but it's the only time anything even remotely romantic happened between them and Erika made the whole thing feel so transactional afterwards, like she had done Mallory a favor, like she should be compensated for her efforts. Mallory has never had a truly romantic kiss with another woman, and she's not sure if this can even count given the circumstances.

Still, she doesn't regret it. For a moment they weren't locked in some deadly game, for a moment there was something to think about other than dying.

Mallory keeps her hand wrapped around the small of Olivia's back.

"Is this okay?" she asks because she still can't believe that it is, and that there's a place for something like this amid so much chaos.

Olivia looks over her shoulder, down at where Britt lays sprawled on the floor, and she tilts her head.

"It was the adrenaline, I guess... " she murmurs as if she's trying to piece the series of events together in her mind.

"But is this okay?" Mallory asks, when what she really wants to ask is... what is this? Does this have a place in our lives once we make it out of here alive, or is it just the adrenaline? She's heard of crazier things happening, and she really does like Olivia, and she's imagined them together for most of her adult life, even if she thought it was Rowan up until now.

Olivia doesn't confirm or deny, she merely steps forward, Mallory's hand in hers and for now, in this place of high tension and metallic tinged air, it's all she needs.

They make their way back to Rowan together.

His expression is unreadable, and Mallory worries for a moment that he won't approve but instead he steps forward and gives Olivia a kiss on the forehead, pulling her into a deep hug.

"I'm so glad you're okay," he says. "Don't you ever scare me like that again."

He looks up at Mallory and nods once. "I like you a lot better than her ex."

"Same though," she says with a ghost of a smile.

But their relief is short-lived because Peyton is back on the intercom, and there are more instructions, and Mallory isn't sure if she can survive another round of carnage. Mallory pulls away from the siblings as Rowan wraps Olivia's hands in scraps of shirt, and she braces herself for whatever comes next.

"Well, that was anticlimactic, wasn't it?" Peyton says, her voice terse. "I would have expected more from Britt... but I guess nothing in life really goes the way you plan, and the only way to move forward is to move on. But damn... that was so boring."

"Since when is this about entertainment?" Mallory asks, fishing for any scrap of information she can get.

A bang rings out over the intercom and Mallory imagines Peyton slamming her fist down on a desk or a table, the hand she imagines is of course, Kimber's. And she wonders if Brandon is looming behind her in whatever strange room she's squirreled herself away in.

"It's always been about entertainment," Peyton says, and it's in that moment that Mallory realizes that she really is making it up as she goes. Which seems so strange because the blueprint of the game, the traps have been meticulously laid out, and clearly tested. It's as if all of Peyton's energy went into the traps, the idea of the pain she could cause and none of the logistics of it.

"I thought this was about Jared," Mallory says, and then, thinking about her Kimber theory and feeling brave, adds, "Or Brandon."

"Who the fuck is Brandon," Rowan says but Olivia shushes him.

Mallory waits for Peyton's response but there's only lazy static coming in over the intercom. Then, after an eternity of silence, filled only by the buzz of the machines and the occasional wet gurgle from Britt, Peyton comes back in over the speaker.

"I don't know who you're talking about, and I'm getting impatient and worse, bored. Lay the weapons out in the bowling lane. We're going to play another round," Peyton instructs, her voice clipped. She's clearly not happy with the way things ended up with Olivia and Britt.

"Now!" She screams when they don't immediately move to obey.

They make their way to the bowling lane, but Olivia catches Mallory by the arm. "Who's Brandon?"

"It's just a theory I have," Mallory says, her cheeks burning. "I'm probably wrong."

But she can't stop thinking about how much she told Peyton about Erika and what happened with Brandon.

Peyton would always ask for more information, like she was pressing lightly on a bruise.

Isn't Kimber mad at her?

Yeah, you shouldn't have posted the picture, but your friend shouldn't have stolen Kimber's boyfriend.

Is there a chance that I'll get to meet Erika when I'm in town for the meet up?

I would really love to meet Erika!

It's like she wanted Mallory to bring Erika with her, and it occurs to her that maybe Erika was the intended victim this entire time, and everyone else is just collateral damage. It would explain why Peyton is so upset with the way things are progressing despite the increasingly intricate nature of the traps. She's already killed the person she set out to, the rest is just a long, drawn-out death rattle.

But Kimber being the one behind the Peyton profile doesn't exactly make sense either because no one knows what happened between Mallory and Jared last year, and Jared has to factor into it somehow. Thinking about it causes a headache to bloom in the center of her forehead.

"I still think it might be Jared," Olivia admits, lowering her eyes. "That there is no Peyton and it's been him the whole time."

"And he's really been alive in here for almost a year?"

"Well, not in here, but alive, and he brought us back to punish us for what happened that night."

They're almost to the bowling lane, but a terrible choking sound comes from where Britt lays sprawled out on the floor. Olivia shoves the bone saw into Rowan's arms and rushes back to her to find her body pitching against the floor.

"She's choking on blood," Olivia says, working to flip her onto her side.

"Leave her alone," Rowan calls. "For fuck's sake, Liv."

"I can't," Olivia says, crouching next to Britt and the row of pinball machines. Finally on her side, Britt appears to be breathing normally, but Mallory can't quite make it out from where she stands next to the bowling lane.

"Be careful," Rowan warns. He moves to a row of cubbies next to the lane and pulls a bowling shoe from them before tossing it to his sister.

It falls at her feet. "What do you want me to do with this?"

"Use the laces to tie her up, that way she can't attack you if she gets up again."

"She's dying, she's not going to do anything!" Olivia eases Britt up into a sitting position, but she shakes violently, a fresh stream of blood sputtering over the front of her sweatshirt. Olivia drops her and waits a moment before tugging the laces from the bowling shoes and wrapping them around Britt's wrists.

"Happy now?" she asks, glaring at Rowan.

He doesn't answer. Instead, he motions for Mallory to join him in laying out the weapons in the bowling lane. Mallory turns to join Olivia by the pinball machines instead, but Rowan shakes his head. "I don't know if you're dating or what, but Peyton wants us over here. Now is not the time to let emotions get in the way of our chances of surviving this."

Mallory crosses her arms. "Says the person who's made every decision here based on the way he feels about Olivia."

"She's my sister."

"And if we make it out of here alive, she'll be my girlfriend." Mallory's face burns while she says it and for the first time since kissing Olivia, she realizes how complicated she's just made everything. Britt is pretty much down for the count. The three of them are all that's left. If Peyton demands more blood, she'll have to choose between her almost lover or her almost brother-in-law. In no situation does this end well, and a pang of fear rings through Mallory's chest.

"About that Mallory," Peyton says. "I'm honestly a little hurt. I always thought I was the one you had a big old crush on. I mean, you used to be in my DMs at all hours of the night pouring your heart out to me. It's honestly pretty sucky to know that you were leading me on like that."

"Why, are you interested?" Mallory asks dryly. "Let us out now and I might agree to give you a chance."

"Look at that, you have a sense of humor after all. No, no, no. We're going to have fun in this arcade. Unfortunately, I don't have anything set up beyond that initial game, but I was thinking you could play a game regardless."

"Is this because you're bored or because I mentioned Brandon?"

"I don't know who that is," Peyton hisses.

"Seriously," Rowan says. "Who the fuck is Brandon?"

"A guy that Erika got to cheat on his girlfriend with her. The longer we're in here, the more I'm wondering if maybe it has something to do with it. Peyton practically begged me to bring Erika here."

"So then why bring Jared into it? Why bring the rest of us into it?"

Mallory looks from the row of blades to where Britt lays on her side next to the pinball machines. "I don't know."

"Enough!" Peyton screams. "I don't really think it matters who I am or why you're here. You came here to bleed and that's the only thing that matters, making you fucking bleed. So here's how it's going to play out. One of you needs to die. I'm giving you six minutes to kill someone."

Mallory freezes. It's not that the command is unexpected, it's the heaviness to it, the finality. Up until this long, they'd lucked out in that Erika is the only dead one—even Britt still clings to life despite her injuries, but this, how do they cheat this? How do they outsmart this? How do they win?

"You think that I'm some useless, unorganized piece of shit?" Peyton asks, her voice reaching a fever pitch. "You think that I haven't dreamt about this for months and know exactly what I want? I don't want any of you surviving this, do you hear me? I'm the top dog! I've always been the top dog!"

Mallory's blood freezes. She's heard the phrase before...

No, she's read it.

It's something Jared used to caption his Instagram posts with, the selfies he would take with his posse of friends.

Mallory cranes her head, slowly, painfully to the ceiling, cringing against the headache.

"Jared?" She asks.

But Peyton—or whoever hides behind the alias—doesn't confirm or deny, instead she clicks on the intercom one last time. Music pulses into the room. It's not the same creepy, slowed down version of "Sulking Seething" as when Mallory was stuck inside the claw machine. It's ambient concert noise. The far-off thrash of instruments. The bass is cranked all the way up so that Mallory feels the vibrations through the floor, and the walls of the arcade seem to pulse. It's the same as Hyve-Fest last year. She shudders.

"Six minutes," Peyton says over the thrum of music. "And

Mallory, you need to be the one to decide. Oh, and whoever you kill, I want you to crack through their ribs and tear out their heart."

Bile scorches the back of Mallory's throat.

"It's up to you Mallory. Time starts now!"

On cue, one of the screens fastened to the wall above Olivia's head clicks on and a series of red numbers starts their slow march toward zero.

Someone needs to die.

The choice is easy enough, but the decision weighs heavy.

If Mallory were in Britt's position, she could easily end up the same way, trying to kill any or all of them. She can't exactly blame her for playing along with Peyton—not after the rest of them abandoned her. She thinks of Erika and what she would do if she knew there was a chance of saving her. She thinks of Olivia and the possible future waiting for them outside the walls of the arcade.

The red phone pings, and Rowan pulls it out of his pocket with a grimace. "Oh, she picks now to go back to texting us instructions."

"What do we do?" Mallory asks, hating how watered down her voice sounds.

"It's up to you," Rowan grits out from between clenched teeth.

Mallory stares at him blankly from across the lane, pulse pounding in her ears.

"It's up to you," he repeats, holding up the cell phone. Its plastic case is the same red as a rare steak, a fresh cut, a crime scene.

"I know," Mallory hisses, her heart rate spiking at the sight of the phone. "Give me time to think."

"We don't have time."

Mallory curls her arms around her middle as Rowan slips the phone back into his pocket and bends to pick up the knife, tossing it between his hands, testing the weight. "I can't get over how heavy this thing is. The handle is so solid."

"Not the bone saw? Wouldn't that make things quicker?"

He shakes his head. "The knife is the only option."

"But don't we need to—"

"I know what we need to do! And I'll use the knife. I'll make it work—but *you* need to make the decision."

"Five minutes left," Olivia calls from where she crouches next to Britt.

"Has the bleeding stopped?" Mallory asks, not sure if she wants to know the answer.

Olivia shakes her head, her face flashing yellow, orange, red in the glow of the pinball machines. "You need to make a decision. Now."

"How are we supposed to do this in six minutes?"

"Four," Olivia says after a quick glance at the screen fastened to the wall above her head. It counts down the minutes and seconds in bright, bleeding color. "We're running out of time."

"Fine, I'll decide for you." Rowan grips the knife and turns to cross the arcade, but Mallory rushes forward, grabbing him by the arm.

"It needs to be me," she says, her insides curdling.

"Then decide. We already know what needs to be done, but just say it."

Bile scorches the back of her throat, and she clamps a hand down over her mouth.

"Britt." The word is barely more than a whisper but Rowan takes off across the arcade and crouches next to where their friend lays.

Mallory crosses to the row of pinball machines too, but she sinks down next to Olivia and pulls her close. "We both killed her..."

Even with the bone saw, it takes a lot of work to get inside

Britt's ribcage and Mallory forces herself to watch as Rowan struggles.

Olivia buries her face in Mallory's chest, fingers gripping the fabric of her shirt. She watches and she tries to feel horrified, but all she can do is observe the way that Britt's body seems to droop as Rowan finally pulls away. She deflates against the floor.

She's not a person anymore, Mallory thinks dully, her headache pulsing down her neck.

Rowan, who was already completely drenched in blood, is slick with fresh coats of red. He shakes as he stands, dropping the saw and a chunk of flesh that splats against the tile.

Mallory dry heaves, but nothing comes up. She has nothing left.

None of them deserve this. Mallory knows it for a fact. But all they can do is push forward.

"We're close to the end," she tells Olivia, even though she's not sure if they actually are. "We're going to survive this."

"What if she makes us kill someone else?" Olivia asks, pulling away and straightening up. "I can't choose between you and Rowan. It's impossible. And I wouldn't be able to live with myself if he killed you, or you were forced to pick me over him."

It's the same fear that's been gnawing at Mallory since she pulled Olivia in for that kiss. If she's forced to choose between the twins, the choice will be easy, but the aftermath will be the death of her.

23

ROWAN

Murder is unforgivable. There's no coming back from it, no matter what the reason. Although Rowan does his best to steel his expression, although he tries to be strong and insist that it's okay, he knows that it's not. It's not even the fact that he killed Britt, he butchered her. The sound that her ribs made as he cracked into them is something he's never going to get out of his ears. The way her insides felt as he reached in, hot, and soft, and horrible. He'll never live it down.

Maybe he'll make it home to Gabriel because he did this, but he will never be able to look him in the eye again.

Having a son is unlike anything Rowan could have ever imagined. Even though the pregnancy was planned, he was still terrified when Kate announced that she was expecting. With fertility issues on both sides of their family, he never expected it to happen so easily. Hell, he and Liv had only managed to be conceived through IVF, one of them being a bonus baby to parents who had been struggling for close to a decade to have even one child.

Then, seeing the first sonogram for his future son, all the ways that he fell short seemed so much more intimidating.

284

What if his child hated him? What if they grew up all fucked in the head because of Rowan's hairpin temper? What if he cursed too much and the kid's first word was "fuck"?

But he knew when Gabriel was finally earth-side that everything would be okay. Because he would do his best.

He snuck out to the backyard to smoke—so that the house never smelled like shit, and there was never any threat of the health risks associated with secondhand smoke. He took Gabriel to daycare every morning, even though he got weird looks—like, who is this young punk-ass looking motherfucker with a baby? He didn't even care. He was being a better man for his son. He was doing everything for his son.

Even this.

Murder.

I did what I had to do. I did it for him, Rowan repeats to himself, but somehow that only makes it worse. Somehow that makes it that much more unforgivable.

But with his action, they're able to make it through the arcade's exit and into a skinny hallway. Wherever it leads, Peyton insists, will be the site of her final game.

He chews the inside of his lip while he wonders what she could have in store for them.

Once they're in the hallway, the telltale grinding of gears rings out and Rowan doesn't need to look behind him to know that another metal barrier has dropped, sealing them into this next section of Peyton's game.

The only way out is through.

The narrow hallway is painted a deep shade of purple that borders on black, though chunks of white plaster are visible where the paint chips away. Rowan wonders what Britt would have to say about the color and its implications for the rest of the game.

Nothing, he reminds himself, bitterly. *You killed Britt. She wouldn't say a goddamn thing.*

Mallory and Liv lean on each other, and he shudders when he realizes that there's a very strong chance that he'll have to kill his sister's girlfriend in the next round.

He's always been skeptical about Liv's interest in girls. It seemed more like a phase at first, a cool thing to do for her to fit in with her online friends, lesbians and non-binary folks she met through Tumblr. In her late teens, Olivia practically lived on the site, reblogging posts about how men are pigs and eventually women would be the ones to take over. It was aggressive, but Rowan thought that his soft-spoken sister deserved some way to vent her frustrations.

He didn't understand the whole bisexual thing though. Still doesn't. In his mind there's either gay or straight, and nothing in between. But seeing the way that Olivia looks at Mallory, seriously considering for the first time the lengths she went to continue talking to her, posing as a guy, as him, for years— Rowan realizes that even if he can't understand it, it's real. And he's genuinely happy that Mallory seems so protective of his sister. It certainly takes some of the weight off his shoulders.

Still, the dark, cynical part of his brain reminds him to be cautious. They still have a final round to get through and there's still more blood to spill.

They finally make it to the end of the hall, where there's a large, black door. It's splattered with paint in various day-glow colors. A neon sign above the doorway declares that what waits for them inside is a fucking laser tag maze.

Rowan doesn't like that at all. Laser tag is usually dim lit, it's hard to see what you're doing, and he immediately flashes back to the mystery boxes from the second round. Instinctively, he clutches his hand with the bloodied scrap of fabric to his chest, expecting that more sharp objects lay in wait for them inside.

"All right, darlings, here's the deal," Peyton begins. "This will be your final test. It's the laser tag arena, obviously. But what makes this one so cool is that the part actually built it like a maze. The way the game is supposed to work—the original layout—was two opposing sides that met in the middle for some good old fashioned laser tag action. But I tweaked it a bit. Now it leads only through to the exit. It's pitch black in there; I removed a lot of the glow in the dark paint so it's difficult to navigate. You're only going to have a set amount of time, but all you have to do is solve the maze and you're home free."

"You mean if we manage to make it out of this one last place, we get to leave?" Mallory asks. Rowan cringes at how hopeful she sounds. She should know better by now; she should know that Peyton isn't just going to let them do anything.

"Honest to god," Peyton insists. "If you make it through this last round, you walk out of here. I'll be done with you. You're starting to bore me anyway."

He doesn't believe it for a second. Peyton literally said that she wanted them all to die only a few minutes earlier. She wouldn't put them through everything she had just to discard them at the last second. She definitely wouldn't give up on the game now, not when they're all so close to breaking.

Mallory is in especially rough shape. He figured Liv would be down for the count after the damage to her hands, but it's Mallory that needs to pause every few minutes to catch her breath. The cut on her back continues to weep trails of blood down her spine, and even though it's not particularly deep, it is inflamed and in all likelihood, infected.

He's not sure if she's going to make it, and he doesn't have the heart to point it out to Liv. Even though he knows they'll get through this faster if they leave her behind and navigate through the maze on their own. He gets what it's like to love someone, and he'd be hard pressed to decide to leave Kate if she were the one here. If Kate were bleeding and limping as bad as Mallory, he would stand by her side up until the end. But he still has his son to think about, and whatever Peyton has in store, he can almost guarantee that it's not going to be as easy as a maze.

Surprisingly, he doesn't have to suggest it; Mallory is the one to bring it up. Gently, she pulls back from Liv and leans against the wall next to the door.

"I'm not in any shape to do this," she says.

"You can make it," Liv insists but Mallory shakes her head.

"I think I was in shock before, my body was almost numb to it, but it's like everything that happened inside the claw machine is catching up to me. I'm only going to slow you guys down if we all go in there at once."

"I'm not leaving you behind," Liv says through tears, but Rowan feels like a weight has been lifted off him. This would save him from having to make the decision for Liv, from having to kill her girlfriend in front of her... from having to kill another person at all. Even though there's no telling what waits for them inside the maze, Rowan knows that it's not going to be good, and he never wants to be put in a position where he needs to hurt another person, yet alone actually take their life ever again. He would sooner die himself before sacrificing more of whatever innocence he has left.

"You wouldn't be leaving me behind." Mallory winces. "I'll go in after you, I just need a minute to get myself together. You guys go in first and I'll follow."

"I think that's a great idea," Rowan says before Liv gets a chance to protest. "Plus, think of it this way, if Peyton tries to send anything in after us, Mallory would be able to warn us."

"Warn us?" Olivia asks. "She could be killed before she gets the chance."

Mallory rests her hand on Olivia's wrist. "You know that Rowan's right. It's not smart to have all three of us go into the maze at the same time. Either something is going to come from outside or inside, and we have no way of telling so it's best to cover all our bases."

After some coaxing, Liv lets Rowan guide her into the laser tag maze.

"Keep your eyes out," he says. "I doubt this is going to be as easy as solving a maze. I don't trust that bitch one bit."

It's cool and dark inside the laser tag arena, and there's a constant drone above their heads signaling some kind of fan or air conditioning system similar to the one inside the miniature golf course. Rowan reaches his hand out to feel along the walls and warns Olivia to keep her hands at her sides just in case. But all he finds is rough plywood. He moves his good hand back and forth between either side of the walls but nothing changes. It strikes him that there isn't a screen in here displaying the time and he worries for a moment that Peyton will try to cheat them out of winning. Maybe that's the angle here. She's going to keep time in her own fucked up way and claim that the clock counts down faster than it actually does.

"You still there, Mallory?" Liv calls back.

"Sure am," she says. "Don't worry about me, I'm right behind you."

Rowan can tell that she's trying to be as positive as possible but there's so much pain in her voice, he's not sure if she has it in her to keep up with them. He listens though, for the shuffle of her feet, for any indication that she's stopped moving, for any indication that Peyton has a final trap ready to be sprung at any moment, killing them before they have a chance to escape.

They continue to navigate the maze and he keeps his eyes focused straight ahead. Then a tile sinks under Rowan's foot, and a laser pops out of the wall in front of them. It's cartoonish, shockingly green, and he almost reaches out to touch it, but Olivia pulls his hand back.

She unwraps the bandage from one of her palms and throws it across the line of green. Rowan's eyes widen as the fabric pops and fizzles. "It's an actual fucking laser."

The scrap, now split in two, drifts to the ground and Rowan steps over it as he ducks beneath the beam.

"Be careful. We've got actual fucking lasers in here," he calls back to Mallory.

"Of course, we do," she calls back and though her voice is strained, he's happy to hear that she's still alert.

He grabs Olivia's hand and helps guide her under the beam, scanning the floor in front of them for more traps.

"I'm sorry," he says as they move. "I should never have gone along with the whole prank thing. I wanted to hurt you. Not like this, but I wanted to hurt you. I let my emotions get the better of me. I should have known the whole thing was off from the start. This is all my fault."

Liv pauses for a moment and looks up at him, tears tugging at the corners of her eyes. He coaxes her to keep moving and she reluctantly continues through the maze.

"It's not your fault," she says quietly. "I know that this isn't what you wanted."

Rowan isn't quite sure. It's not what he wants now, but when they first entered the resort, he was consumed with a need to make his sister suffer. He knew that she was already suffering—already drowning inside herself—but he was so tired of how she would lean on him, constantly, relentlessly. He wanted to be cruel.

"I've always been such a dick to you, Liv. But I love you more than anything, you know that, right?" His foot hits another button, and a beam cuts across the maze in front of them—a sour shade of orange this time. Olivia tightens her grip on his hand as they duck beneath it.

"Not more than Gabriel," she says. "Not more than Kate."

"Yes, more than them." He hates himself for admitting it, but it's true. "You're the only one who's known me my whole life, Liv. You've stuck by me through everything. You understand me, because we feel the same shit, we just express it differently."

She lets out a small laugh at this and for a moment, Rowan feels like a complete idiot, until she speaks again, and he realizes that she wasn't making fun of him—she was agreeing. "I've always felt like we're two halves of the same whole and just got split in the womb... like if you put us together, we'd make a complete person. We balance each other out, don't you think?"

He smiles. "Yeah, we do."

"I've always been jealous of you," she says. "Everything seemed so much easier for you. You're so strong."

"You're strong in your own way, Liv. Don't underestimate yourself."

They trigger and easily dodge a third laser. It's mind-numbingly predictable. Rowan thanks his lucky stars that this is the one trap that it seems Peyton slacked on constructing properly. At this rate, they'll be able to trip and avoid all the lasers, Mallory will easily be able to step over or duck beneath them, and they'll all be out of the resort before they know it.

"Don't you think this is too easy?" Olivia asks.

He shakes his head. "I think that with everything we've been through, we're finally catching a break. Peyton may be smart as hell, but with the scope of this thing, she was bound to fuck up at least one of her gizmos. We're lucky that this one is it."

Olivia shakes her head. "It doesn't feel right. You can feel it too, can't you? There's a heaviness in the air here... like something bad is about to happen."

"Everything feels heavy because we've been through a lot tonight, Liv. We're exhausted, we're bleeding. Once we get out, we'll feel better. You still back there, Mallory?"

"I am. You guys still doing okay?"

"Sure are," he calls back. "Seems we caught a lucky break and Peyton's death machine is faulty."

While he does believe that they deserve the win, he can't deny that he feels the heaviness, the oppression that Liv mentioned. It's been thick in the air since they entered the laser tag arena, and every time he breathes it's like he can feel it gumming up his lungs. But he doesn't want to worry his sister. He's probably just off kilter because of what he had to do back in the arcade...

He has no idea how he's going to explain all this to the police. It's going to be damn near impossible for him to face Kate. And Gabriel... His chest seizes up and he's afraid for a moment that he's going to completely lose it. But he needs to be strong for Olivia, at least until they make it out of here.

Another tile sinks beneath his foot and he and Liv pause as another laser zips across the length of the maze. It falls in the exact same spot as the other lasers, a little bit above eye level.

"Things are going to be different when we get out of here," he tells Oliva as they duck beneath the beam. "I'm not gonna be a dick anymore, I swear."

"That's like saying you're not going to be you anymore."

"I'm serious, Liv... and I want to plan a dinner... so that Kate and Gabriel can meet Mallory."

Olivia pauses for a moment, and Rowan has to tug on her hand to get her to keep walking. "You're really okay with it... with us?"

He nods, keeping his gaze focused straight ahead, because he's gonna cry if he looks down at her, and he refuses to cry. "Maybe I'm a shitty judge of character... I liked Jared when I met him, after all. But I think she could be good for you. I'm sorry by the way, for not taking everything that happened between you and Jared as seriously as I should have."

She squeezes his hand. "You didn't know everything that was going on. I should have told you."

He squeezes her hand back, careful to avoid the slice in her palm. "I should have paid more attention."

They make it to the end of the maze and Rowan thinks for a moment that everything is going to be okay. The laser tag arena bottlenecks into the back of a warehouse-like room with high, vaulted ceilings and a concrete floor. A few steps beyond the finish line, there's a door. A ribbon of light cuts across the bottom of the doorframe. Deliciously bright. Even though it's the middle of the night and there shouldn't be any light at all... but Rowan doesn't allow himself to question it. The exit is right there. They're going to make it.

Liv slips her hand from his and pushes ahead. She's about to cross the threshold when he sees it, a split second before it flicks across the length of the maze. There's a final laser.

No buttons.

No warning.

Just a thin, white beam.

He realizes what's happening a few moments too late. This was the point of it all along. The earlier beams weren't meant to hurt them, they were meant to be predictable. To lull them into a false sense of security. Rowan should have seen it sooner. He should have trusted his gut feeling, trusted Olivia. He should have known that Peyton would get one over on him yet again.

But now it's too late and the laser is clicking on and he's stepping forward, pulling Liv out of the way.

His son will up without a father.

His wife will grow old without a husband.

But his sister will live.

As the heat slices across his throat, as the darkness steals his vision and his thoughts explode into nothing, he smiles, he smiles and releases his final thought into the universe before he rushes to join it.

His sister will live.

Because of him, his sister will live.

24

OLIVIA

It happens quickly. A firm tug as Rowan pulls her out of the way. A twist on the ground as Olivia looks up and finds a red line across her brother's throat, like a piece of string. At first that's what she thinks it is, a piece of dental floss, so thin that it's barely there.

"Rowan?" she asks, his name getting bunched up in her throat. He hangs in suspended animation, frozen above her with the thin red line circling his neck. It's another second before she notices the laser. And another before the thin red line expands, and weeps. The light leaves Rowan's eyes, and his head leaves his shoulders, and she starts to scream.

Olivia scrambles out from under him, still crawling desperately across the concrete as there's a sickening double plop. A head. A body. Not Rowan. Only pieces.

Her brother is gone.

Mallory calls for her. Olivia can hear her feet against the concrete floor as she runs through the maze. She wants to warn her, but instead she continues to stumble forward, her breath coming in sharp gasps. She makes it to the end of the maze, to the short passage that leads to the exit, and sinks down to her knees, waiting for Mallory.

She doesn't dare turn around, but she feels the presence of Rowan's body as it lays across the floor behind her. The pieces of her brother...

She hears the sharp intake of breath as Mallory discovers what's left of him, and listens as she gags, working through her own complicated set of emotions.

Rowan is gone.

Gabriel will grow up like they did after all, without a father. A numbness spreads from the center of her chest though her limbs, making them heavy. All of this pain was for nothing. All of this pain will bleed through to the next generation.

Mallory steps up next to her, her hand slick with sweat as it rests across her shoulder.

"It was a trap," Olivia says numbly. "Peyton made the maze easy on purpose so that one of us would trip the final laser."

Mallory crouches, grunting with the effort, her free hand pressed against her wounded back. She's deathly pale, with beads of perspiration across her face. Olivia can tell that she's in a lot of pain.

"Gabriel's dad is dead," she says hollowly.

"But his aunt is still alive."

Olivia knows that she's right and allows Mallory to help her to her feet. Her palms are bleeding again, the blood soaking through her remaining scrap of t-shirt so that it looks as if the fabric had been dyed red this whole time.

There's so much damage.

They limp toward the exit, a thin band of light reaching beneath the darkened door frame.

"Is it morning already?" Mallory asks, and Olivia figures it must be. At least some of the pain they feel must be from lack of sleep, a complete blowout of the senses. There's a sense of satisfaction in the knowledge that this horror story has two final girls.

Each step is torture. But Mallory is right, they've made it. And they have more work to do once they're free from this place. They'll need to help the police track down Peyton, and to navigate funeral arrangements for her brother, and to answer the questions that everyone will undoubtedly have. But one thing at a time, small victories. They may be the only ones left, but they're alive.

And the door is only a few steps away.

But before they get a chance to pull it open, before they get a chance to even approach the door, it swings open, and they're temporarily blinded by the harsh glow of a construction spotlight.

They pause like animals caught in the glare of an oncoming truck.

Of course, Peyton wouldn't make it that easy. Every villain needs their grand reveal.

The clapping is the first thing they hear. A silhouetted figure clapping slowly as they grind to a halt in front of the door. The sound is sharp. It's salt in their wounds.

"Well done, ladies." The voice is deep and masculine. It doesn't belong to Peyton at all. Olivia reels in this revelation for a moment before the figure steps forward and Jared is standing in front of them.

Jared.

Her mouth goes dry, and she sways, relying on Mallory to keep her upright.

It's really him.

Her first instinct is to flee, even if it means rushing back to where her brother's body lays butchered across the floor of the maze and Mallory twists with her, the both of them preparing to run for their lives. But then there's the familiar, terrible grinding of gears and a metal sheet comes down trapping them at the end of the maze. The narrow bottleneck leading to only one thing.

Jared.

He leers at them, the dimple in his left cheek standing out against his perfect, shark-like smile. "Well fucking done."

25

———

MALLORY

It's Jared.

Jared with his hair grown out so that it almost reaches his shoulders. Jared in the same dark skinny jeans and loose-fitting tank top that he wore to HyveFest last year, showing off his tattoos and sinewy muscles.

Jared, missing his left ear. A fact that he flaunts by pulling his hair back for a moment and wiggling his eyebrows.

All this time, Mallory thought that it was a few toes.

The piece of him that the cops found was an ear, and not even a full ear either. The fucker didn't have it in him to sacrifice an entire body part. He pulled a Vincent van Gogh, but a cheap, WalMart knock-off version.

"I couldn't have planned this any better," he says. "My two favorite ladies being the ones who made it to the end." He raises his left hand, which is wrapped around the handle of a knife, and swipes the blade through the air. "It was too freaking easy to pretend to be that Valley girl. I couldn't believe how easy it was to buy followers, or use the voice changing app, or get you idiots to trust me. Easy, easy, easy. Almost took the fun out of it."

"You were Peyton the whole time... " Olivia says hollowly. "You killed my brother."

"You killed your brother," Jared taunts. He takes a step forward, and the girls shrink back as if on instinct. The smell of his cologne weeps into the space between them, and the pain in Mallory's back spikes. She winces against it.

"What's the matter, Mal? You look like you've seen a ghost." He laughs, the sound deep and hearty, and terrible. "Hey, that's what Billy says in *Scream*, isn't it? I dunno, I'm more of a *Saw* guy myself."

"I killed you," Mallory murmurs.

"Think," he yells, tapping the smooth end of the blade against his forehead. "Really think about that night."

Mallory's head aches, a fuzzy heat soaking through her body. Back in the arcade, last year. When they were drinking in the tiny booth next to the bowling lanes. Jared was stretched out in an old office chair and kept tugging at her arm, trying to get her to sit on his lap. She barely touched the flask he gave her, but the room still spun, and Jared spun along with it. He kept reaching for her and she kept dodging. Like they were on a carousel, bobbing past each other. Again and again.

"We were drunk," she says. "You got me drunk."

"What else?" he asks, fingering the tip of the blade.

He swirled around her, his face even more swollen than when she first helped him from the mosh pit, the dried blood caked beneath his nostrils. And his eyes. Wrong somehow, his pupils too wide—the black swallowing his irises.

"We should get you back to the medical tent," she suggested, begged, pleaded with him. "I think you have a concussion or something."

"We're not going anywhere," he said, finally catching hold of her. He pulled her against him, his breath heavy and sour as he rasped in her ear. "You can't leave yet; we haven't even gotten started."

"You tried to assault me," Mallory says, her pulse hammering in her ears. Olivia reaches out and grabs her hand. Blood squishes between their palms, and Mallory shuts her eyes for a moment. Her back keeps stinging, burning, the fuzzy heat keeps creeping along the surface of her skin, but it feels good to finally talk about it. How Jared attacked her during HyveFest. She was ashamed for the longest time. Ashamed that she put herself in a position to be taken advantage of, ashamed that she ignored every red flag until it was almost too late. She was horrified at what she had done to survive, but now she's almost free of it. In a way, facing him down gives her a sense of power. Her last memories of him, every sound, every image, is replaced by what stands in front of her. Not a monster, not even a man.

Only a person.

And a sorry excuse for one, at that.

"What else?" he barks.

He held her tight, but she took a deep breath and punched him directly in the face, his already broken nose cracking again as her knuckles made contact.

She scrambled away from him, but the room continued to spin, and she pinballed off the walls, frantically trying to make it to the door. And then she tumbled out into the arcade again, and the holes in the ceiling, the back exit propped open. Almost safe.

A glassy sky stared down at her. The moon was fat and bright, a splattering of stars dotting its halo. A slight breeze came in through the exit and she felt safe.

But then Jared grabbed her ankle and yanked her back.

"You can't go yet," he slurred, his voice heavy. "We're not done."

She pulled her arm back and slammed her knuckles into his face again. And again, and again. Until he fell to his knees.

Once he was on the ground, she started kicking and she didn't stop until he face-planted against the concrete.

Using the tip of her boot, she rolled him over on his back.

Blood trickled out of his left nostril and pooled in the dip above his upper lip. She gave him a single kick, a soft thud as her boot connected with his head.

Only when she was sure that he wasn't going to get up again did she leave him there to die.

"And then I killed you," she says, but he clicks his tongue, waving the knife back and forth like a shaking head.

"No, no, no. We *danced* a little, and you knocked me down, but you didn't kill me."

I killed a version of him that night though, she thinks dully as the wound on her back screams. She killed the version that made her afraid.

"Why target me that night?" she asks.

"Why?" he mocks. "You really think you were so special that there had to be a reason that it was you. Hate to break it to you, sweetheart, but you're not special. You were there. And I was horny."

He shuts the door behind him and steps in closer, the smell of smoke and cedar invading the space between them. "And now, we're gonna have some fun, just the three of us. Olivia, babe," he grins, showing off a row of shockingly white teeth, "you know how much I always wanted a threesome."

Olivia squeezes Mallory's hand once, twice, three times before springing herself on Jared. She rips into him with her fingernails, she sinks her teeth into the soft flesh of his neck, and Mallory watches as he scrambles to raise the knife.

"You ruined my life," Olivia hisses as she tears into him. She sticks a finger in his eye, and he howls. "You killed my brother."

Shakily, he raises the knife and Mallory rushes forward. He only gets one blow in, a single stab to the top of Olivia's shoulder which causes her to screech, before Mallory manages to pull the blade from his hands.

He falls to his knees, the same way that he did at HyveFest, only instead of kicking him, Mallory sets her target for his eye. It's already half shut and inflamed from where Olivia dug her nail in, and Mallory knocks him onto his back. She straddles him, pressing all her weight down against his chest. She hovers the blade above his eye socket.

"Wait," he says, and she savors the terror in his voice. "Don't you want to know how I did it? Don't you want to know how I—"

Mallory doesn't give him a chance to finish. She plunges the knife in. There's hardly any resistance as the blade buries into the soft tissue. And only then, only when he falls back, limp against the concrete, the knife standing up in his eye like a flag. Only then does she stomp his skull, the same way that she did last year.

This time there's a squish, a crunch, and even though she doesn't look back until she's stepped out of the mess and approached the door, she knows he's gone for good.

Mallory helps Olivia to her feet and together they step into the cool light of early morning. Spots dance in front of Mallory's eyes. Her body feels like a piece of taffy that's been stretched too thin, and the tips of her fingers and toes are numb.

Olivia isn't in any better shape. The wound in her shoulder is deep and blood soaks the front of her dress. Her head keeps lulling to the side, and Mallory helps her stand upright. They may be out of the resort, but they still have to make it back to the main road... and Mallory isn't sure if either of them have the strength.

How fucked up would it be for them to die now? After getting so close...

It's happened before. Victims who are attacked ten minutes from home. People who die within hours of rescue.

"I don't understand," Olivia murmurs, her eyelids drooping. "Jared's not that smart, Mallory. He's not smart enough for all this."

No, from what she knows of Jared, he definitely wasn't, but it's amazing what money can buy you, what time can buy you. In all likelihood, he hired out people to create his traps, contracting shady connections off the dark web or recruiting his own fucked up band of friends.

He was clearly smart enough to know that they would all fall for the Peyton profile, and smart enough to know that they would agree to meet in person, and come back here, and insert themselves into the game.

They dip around the edge of the resort, their path lit by a series of shockingly bright construction lights, as Oliva goes limp in Mallory's arms and she curses.

"We're so close," she says. "Don't give up now."

But Olivia falls unconscious, the shallow rise and fall of her chest the only indication that she's still breathing. A small blessing in this fucked up mess, and Mallory leans her against the outer wall of the resort. They should be close enough to where they left their phones, if she can just get around the building...

"Mallory?"

Her skin prickles at the sound of her name. The voice is soft and feminine. She looks up to find Erika standing in front of her. Erika in her pink lululemon workout set and for a second, Mallory is convinced that she's passed away and her dead best friend is here to ferry her off to the afterlife.

But instead of embracing Mallory, instead of them melting into the light together, Erika frowns. "I guess this means that Jared didn't make it, huh?"

PEYTON

The first thing Erika had to ask herself was how does this girl behave? How does she take her coffee? French press? Cream? Sugar? Is she a Starbucks girl or does she have a home coffee bar? A Nespresso machine or a Keurig? Or maybe she's more of a tea girl—green tea with oat milk and honey, something clean and aesthetically pleasing. Something that screams "I'm a good girl, just look at me. I'm so fucking good."

Her name came to Erika immediately—Peyton. Erika had dated a guy named Peyton three months into her first job after college. He was a finance bro, completely forgettable and utterly disposable, but his name was something special. She was obsessed with it, frustrated that such a powerful, sharp name was wasted on such a doughy, useless man. All the best names, she thought, were wasted on men or stemmed from male surnames, and she decided that Peyton would be her way of reclaiming that energy for the female of the species.

Peyton is the kind of girl she would have been friends with in high school. She's the kind of girl who would have plush carpet in her bedroom, and only drink rosé, and always have her nails glossed with acrylic polish and sharpened into stiletto tips. She's the kind of girl who would be smart, and sexy, and totally what Joss Whedon was going for when he created Buffy. A bubblegum princess with fangs.

Peyton doesn't have to worry about her career.

Or her love life.

Or how it might feel to kill her best friend.

Peyton doesn't have to worry about bills or what she's gonna look like in twenty years if she keeps binging on Flaming Hot Cheetos. She doesn't have an apartment, she doesn't need a car, she's completely free to focus on the most important thing in life—getting what's hers.

She's the ultimate version of Erika. And she was so easy to build.

People always underestimated Erika in school, just because she was sugar coated and bubblegum sweet. Mal sure as hell didn't pay attention to what kind of electives she picked up or the gears turning behind her eyes. All the hours Erika spent in her bedroom building things and taking them apart again.

That's her favorite thing to do—take things apart. She loves dissecting the way that things work. She loves the way that wires and gears look strewn around her bedroom, like the guts of some mechanical animal. She's never considered herself a huntress, but in a way, she embodies the spirit of someone who fights for what she deserves. She connects with that. Because she imagines it like she's pulling an animal carcass apart, ripping it open, making it bleed. She loves making machines bleed.

But no one ever noticed, and she didn't advertise her fascinations.

No one ever suspected that there was more to her than the perfectly manicured, expertly perfumed, living barbie doll.

People can be more than one thing; that's what closed minded people—people like Mallory—don't understand. Erika can be colorful and personable, and she can be smart. She can build a torture chamber with nothing except a credit card and her own two hands. Well, along with Jared doing the heavy lifting. There were parts of it she would never be able to pull off on her own; she just didn't have the brute strength for it. Which is a fact that she begrudgingly had to accept after her first attempt at placing the metal doors in the lobby ended with the sheet of metal damn near crushing her hand. She was in a cast for almost four weeks and had to make up a story for Mallory, that she broke it while attempting a particularly ridiculous pose during a hot yoga class. She hated that she couldn't brag about the work she was doing.

Jared was a last resort, but thankfully, he was more than happy to go along for the ride. He did the heavy lifting, put the doors and things in place and tightened the screws, and she fine-tuned the gears of it all. In a way, they were the perfect team, and she grew to appreciate him more and more over the time that they worked together on this little project. Not that she didn't appreciate him before—it's just when a man submits to her, works under her, it gets her going in a way that nothing else can.

The first time Erika met Jared, he tried to take her home with him. He wasn't even subtle about it—there was no seduction. He just assumed that she'd jump at the chance to get in bed with him. Like *he* was doing *her* a favor. Not that she blames him; he was hardly the first man to notice her and definitely not the first to try to get in her pants.

She let him take her as far as the doorway to her apartment before kicking his ass to the curb. She slapped him so hard that her hand left a mark across his cheek.

"No one's ever hit me like that before," he said, his eyes wide.

He didn't think it was crazy of her; he found it endearing. Same as how she found his own depravities captivating.

They were drawn to each other because of their mutual

predisposition toward violence. She wasn't an idiot; she knew he beat his girlfriends and all kinds of other horrible shit. He left a long line of traumatized women in his wake, and she never expected him to be civil toward her. She never wanted him to be.

They were a powder keg, an atomic bomb when they were together.

And he had money. He was so fucking rich, the kind of fuck you rich she had always dreamed of. He was dumb too. So narcissistic, so used to manipulating people that he had no way of gauging whether he was being manipulated himself.

"Listen Erika," Jared said about a month before last year's HyveFest, when they were here at the resort of all places, sitting on the roof, their feet dangling over the edge. They had been drinking beers in silence for a few minutes and Erika tilted her head at the sound of his voice.

"What's up?"

"I can't keep sneaking around with you." He drained his beer and dropped it off the edge of the roof, grinning as it hit the pavement and shattered.

"I didn't know we were sneaking around," she said, sipping at her own bottle.

He glanced off to the side and lit up a joint, taking a deep puff and exhaling the smoke before continuing. "Well, whatever this is, I can't do it anymore. I've been seeing someone for a while now. I have a girlfriend."

"So?"

"We're exclusive."

"Bullshit."

"You're seeing other people, why shouldn't I? Only difference is that my girl doesn't want to share me. She moved in a few months ago and I think she can tell that something is up, she's acting super bitchy. So I think it's best we call it quits."

"You misunderstand," she said, trying to catch his eyes

through the smoke. "We aren't together, I don't care who you sleep with, it's none of my business. I just don't think that monogamy is gonna work for you."

"Like I'm going to take advice from you," he said with a roll of his eyes. "There's no way sleeping with your boss is gonna end well."

Of course, she had told him all about her thing with Brandon and the money she was making off the deal. She was so used to manipulating men, made a sport of it even, that she didn't feel like she would lose any leverage with Jared if she told him. Even if she fudged a few details. In fact, with a man like him, admitting to the affair would be likely to get him further on the hook since he would see her as slightly unavailable, uninterested, something worth chasing.

What she didn't have the guts to tell him was that the whole thing had already imploded. The previous week, Mallory posted a picture of Brandon and her making out at a corporate event and tagged her company in it. She was on vacation, but there was an email waiting in her inbox about scheduling a time for a review with HR. It was the beginning of the end.

"I don't care what you think," she said flippantly.

Erika had been making tons of cash, and Kimber was none the wiser, and everything was going great until she brought Mallory along to the party. She only did it to show off, because the way Mal gets when she's jealous is so fucking yummy and she thought it would be the perfect way to keep the power imbalance in their relationship going, but of course Mal had to go and screw it all up. Of course, Mal had to get all holier than thou and bitchy when Erika blew her off to hook up with Brandon. Now she was in big trouble and was still trying to figure out how she was going to play it off when she went back into the office on Monday.

"That's what I love about you, you really don't give a shit,"

Jared said, and she smirked. He was on the hook all right, he was putty in her hands.

"Don't tell me that you love me, Jared," she laughed. "It isn't true. And besides, what would your girlfriend think?"

He let out a deep sigh, a cloud of sour smoke escaping from his perfect lips. "I'll miss this. But listen, if you ever need something, you know you can count on me."

"Wait... you're breaking up with me, and my consolation prize is a favor?"

"We're not breaking up," he said, hitting the joint again. "We aren't together."

She shoved him hard in the shoulder.

"Seriously though, if you ever need anything, I'm on it. No questions asked."

Erika had the idea right then. Even though she wouldn't admit it to herself at the time, she had been considering it practically since the moment Mal posted the photo. She knew exactly how to get her ex-best friend back, and Jared would be the one to help her do it. At that year's HyveFest.

"What if it's not exactly legal?" she asked, taking the joint as he passed it over. "What if I asked you to hurt someone?"

Of course, she had no way of knowing that her plan for revenge would go so horribly wrong and lead to this. Her game. Her masterpiece.

She hadn't expected Mallory to survive this long.

When she designed the traps, she knew that there was a bit of chance involved. That's what made the whole thing so exciting. Every other aspect of her life was carefully curated. Her outfits, her meals, her shopping trips all cleanly laid out on a color coded, excel spreadsheet. Most serial killers are Geminis, a fact that she dug up during one of her late-night scroll sessions on a laptop that was now smashed to a pulp, its plastic pieces sunken somewhere along the ocean floor. She's a Gemini Rising. Virgo Sun. Sagittarius Moon. Sagittarius accounts for a good percentage of serial killers too. No one ever looks at the big three through, only the sun sign. And she's a safe, stuffy, predictable Virgo.

She credits her sun sign with more than just the basis for an alibi. It's the reason she was able to plan everything out in such perfect detail. It's the reason she was able to ensure that her plan was foolproof from every angle. She took everything into consideration, but still, there was that element of surprise. Blame her Sagittarius Moon, but the idea of a little bit of chaos thrilled her.

The only death that was painstakingly planned out was her own since that's what would set the whole game into motion, but beyond that, it really was a tossup of how long Mal would last. She kept going back and forth on it. Originally, she had looped Rowan in to keep her alive, but quickly realized that it wouldn't work since his sister was the one with the crush, not him. And really, what did it matter when Mallory died? It's not like Erika was planning on monologuing to whoever wound up being the final girl anyway—even though she has a speech prepared just in case.

Part of her is excited to see Mallory, worse for wear, the final girl. But a part of her does ache to know that Jared is really dead this time. Pinning all of this on him will be much more difficult. Still, that's why she built in contingencies. That's why there's a backup plan to the backup plan.

Erika is on Mallory before she has time to think.

The look on her face as Erika looms over her with a knife in her hand is everything.

"I watched you die." Mal struggles as Erika pins her down, the knife inches from her face.

"You watched Kimber's corpse face plant into concrete." She scoffs. "Did you even check for a pulse? She'd been cold for hours at that point, I was really concerned that you were gonna notice that, to be honest."

Mallory blinks up at Erika, once, twice, three times. Her wide eyes remind Erika of the horses she used to ride back when her mother tried to get her started in the equestrian arts. What little girl wouldn't want to ride a pony? Erika, that's who. The horses smelled like shit and cried at night, and always looked so dumb. Their eyes were wide and dark, without a single thought behind them.

Mallory looks just like one of those horses.

"What?" she asks, and Erika launches into her script, words she practiced over and over again, revised a thousand times over to get right. But in the heat of the moment, she adlibs, and she isn't even mad about it. She's all about the chaos.

"We look so much alike, me and Kimber. I knew that if I dressed us up the same and was able to obscure her face somehow, you wouldn't know the difference. She bought us the matching workout sets, a kind of olive branch after what happened with Brandon, so suggesting that we wear them while out for a run wasn't hard at all. The hardest part of the whole thing was convincing her to come running out here... oh, and making sure we got matching manicures beforehand. Just in case. Can't be too careful with the small details. I even gave her a necklace that's a close match for my own, but I guess you weren't looking too closely through all the blood."

"But...I watched you..."

"You watched me what? Climb to the top of the waterslides? What did you really see beyond that, Mal? Honestly. I'm disappointed in you, you should know me better than to think I would *ever* volunteer for something like that if my actual life was on the line."

Mallory blinks up at her and Erika holds the knife flush against her throat before continuing.

"Of course, I needed to loop someone in, to make sure that I everyone went inside the resort. I figured out the Rowan thing pretty much right away. Actually, I have you to thank for that.

Did you know that we bartend at the same place? Or, I'm sorry, *bartended*. Rowan's not exactly gonna be showing up to work after this. But yeah, we bartended at the same place. Different shifts, but it didn't take me long to recognize him, and to figure out that he wasn't the one you were talking to online."

She lets this sink in, savoring the horror that spreads across Mallory's face. "Anyway, Rowan did exactly what he was supposed to, we were exactly where we were supposed to be, and Kimber's face was already mincemeat at that point, so it was just a matter of making sure everything else fell into place."

Erika takes a moment to catch her breath. Her pulse races. Holy shit, is this thrilling. She always hates when the killer monologues in horror movies, and prior to this moment, she figured she did more than enough talking during the actual game. Jared did a good enough job voicing Peyton during the first round, mostly thanks to the script she insisted he read from, but the rest of it fell to her. She's fucking exhausted. But there's a tickle of excitement in the back of her throat, and her pulse radiates up her neck, she can feel it everywhere. Humming. She thinks of the hair dye Mallory and her used to use back in high school, manic panic. That's what this is, manic fucking panic. And she's living for it.

She takes a moment to brush a strand of Mallory's hair back from her forehead with the tip of the blade before she continues. "The only thing that I'm really upset with is that you didn't bother looking through the red phone. I loaded it with pictures of Jared and Kimber... well, Jared with me dressed as Kimber, but still. Did you know that Kimber's friend is the girl who was going to finally take Jared to court? It would have been the perfect motive, don't you think? Kimber wanted revenge because you stole her friend's chance at justice from her."

Mallory opens her mouth to answer but Erika presses the blade against her lips. "Or Kimber helped Jared fake his death so he could escape the assault charge and they did this together. I couldn't figure out which story I liked better. It's not like Kimber would be alive to deny either of them. All I had to do was bash her face to a pulp and make sure her body dropped when Rowan pulled the lever on the first trap. The rest was up to chance, but I really am glad that you made it out so I can do this myself. Jared was supposed to take care of it, but you know men, can't rely on them for anything."

Erika positions the sharp end of her knife over Mallory's pupil.

"You killed Kimber?" she asks, her voice strained.

Erika shifts position and runs the blade down the side of Mal's face, savoring every attempt she makes to squirm out from under her. "Yeah, I think I've made that pretty fucking clear at this point."

"But she was your friend," is all that Mal manages to choke out.

"So were you," she says with a shrug. "You were my best friend until you posted that picture and ruined my life."

"I didn't mean to—"

"But here's the thing about friends, darling Mal, they're replaceable. And I'm gonna be a hot fucking commodity once all this is over with, there's gonna be a line out the door. Do you know how many interviews I'm gonna be giving and how much fan mail I'm gonna get? The world fucking loves final girls."

Erika brings the knife down into Mal's shoulder and she cries out as Erika stands and digs her heel into the wound, savoring the squish of Mallory's flesh beneath her foot.

This is how it was always meant to end, with Erika on top.

MALLORY

Mallory winces as Erika grinds her heel into her shoulder. She tries without success to bat her away, but none of her punches land, and Erika howls with laughter.

"Come on, Mal," she teases. "You've never had a single ounce of fight in you, there's no way you're going to do anything to me."

Mallory grits her teeth. The gravel cuts into her wounded back, and sharp pricks of pain travel the length of her arm, but Erika's wrong. She has no idea what Mallory is capable of.

The Mallory that Erika came here with was practically incapable of violence. She was so torn up with guilt over what she thought she did to Jared, that she let it consume her. The Mallory that Erika came here with would have laid back, belly exposed and waited for the blood to cloud her vision. She would have made a list of excuses as to why she couldn't fight back, why she couldn't even try.

But Mallory isn't that girl anymore. For the first time in her life, she feels confident in who she is and what she's capable of. And there's no shame there, no guilt, only the will to survive.

She summons all her strength and kicks Erika hard in the ribs, causing her to stumble back and drop the knife.

Erika laughs like it's the funniest thing in the world. "Well, would you look at that, someone finally grew a spine."

"There's one thing that you failed to explain in your shitty little villain monologue," she says, using her boot to pin Erika in place. "What does Jared have to do with any of this?"

She collapses into another fit of giggles, and Mallory has to jab her to get her to stop. "That's the funny part, Mal. This game wouldn't have even been a thing if you didn't attack Jared that night."

Mallory releases some of the pressure. "What?"

A sickly sort of calm slides across Erika's face, the same look that cult members get in their eyes before a sacrifice, totally blissed out—completely at peace. "He was supposed to take pictures of the two of you together, humiliate you like you humiliated me, and that would have been the end of it. Instead, I had to find him practically drowning in a pool of his own blood and it was all I could do to convince him not to go to the cops and to help me out instead."

"You had Jared attack me that night?" Mallory doesn't even think, she dives down against her former best friend. Pain splinters up her side as she hits the gravel. Her head pounds, her chest aches, but she pushes herself to her knees and positions herself above Erika, tears springing to her eyes.

"You've been my best friend since the fourth grade," she howls as she claws at Erika's face, slashing into her cheek. "You were my fucking soulmate."

She keeps the knife pointed at Erika as she stops to catch her breath, her chest heaving.

"I never meant for it to go this far, Mal," Erika says. "You know that I love you more than anything, and what you did, it really hurt me. I wasn't thinking straight. You know how I get, I was totally blinded by all that stupid bullshit. But I love you, and we can still make this right."

Mallory lowers the knife slightly. "How the hell do you think we can do that?"

A glint in Erika's eye that says she thinks she's getting one over on Mallory and that this will all be over soon. She reaches for her, but Mallory stabs the air again and Erika eases back.

"It's easy," Erika says, hands raised. "You know me, I always have a back up plan for the back up plan. I was setting Kimber and Jared up to take the fall for this the whole time. Seriously, I have evidence and everything. I was going to be the final girl, but we can both be, Mallory. We can do it together. Imagine all the opportunities we'll have. Talk shows and book deals. You can quit your job at the animal shelter—we could go on tour together. Just the two of us. Doesn't that sound amazing? Doesn't that sound like so much fun?"

"It does," Mallory says. She can picture it—the ways her life could be changed for the better, how something good could come out of all this tragedy. "But I'm not like you, I don't think I can just cash a check and forget about all of this."

"Then I'll help you, Mal. We won't have to go at this alone, we'll have each other."

Out of the corner of her eye, she notices Olivia stirring and a weight feels like it's been lifted. She's still alive. They're still going to be able to get out of this together.

She turns to Erika.

"You're right, I'm not alone." And with that, she stabs the knife directly into the side of Erika's face.

She screams, a high-pitched wail.

Mallory pulls her arm back and sinks it in again, and again. Face, chest, stomach. Every soft scrap of skin that she can find. Over and over until Erika is practically pulp, until the mess of her coats the bottom of Mallory's combat boots and the front of her shirt, and the apples of her cheeks. Until she's sure Erika is dead.

EPILOGUE: MALLORY

The TV drones on. Morning talk shows and local news. Mallory wonders how long it'll take before her face shows up on the screen and what picture they'll choose this time.

She imagines them—the newscasters, the boardroom attendees, whoever the hell picks these things—combing her Instagram but finding only her black and white, wide-eyed selfies, all high angles, and pouts.

For Erika, she's sure they'll use the cheerleading picture from their senior year of college. The one where she's smiling widely, showing off too many teeth. Or maybe the headshot from her LinkedIn profile, the one where she's turned slightly to the side, her hair pulled back into a bun, with a perfect white grin and expertly pressed suit.

Mallory frowns, wondering if this is all they are. A collection of pictures. Of traumas.

The smell of a bonfire—warm smoke, drifts in with the light breeze. Summer heat is still clinging to the afternoons even though August is melting steadily into September.

Mallory keeps the windows cracked, and leans back in her chair, wiggling her body from side to side. She's been working on her book all day, doing her best to pull on the edges of her memoir proposal, stretch them into something usable.

It started with a few articles shortly after Olivia and her were rescued. A few hundred hits, a few hundred dollars. She got the idea from Erika to write about what happened to her, but she didn't do it for the money, it's her way of honoring Rowan who always wanted to get a book published. The least she could do, make sure that even if they weren't his words, his name would still be in print.

She never expected anything from it.

But when one of the articles went viral, suddenly she had a request in her inbox from a publisher—then it was a two-month whirlwind of proposals, and sample pages, and querying literary agents with the subject line "OFFER OF PUBLICATION IN HAND," words that felt like something out of a fever dream to type out.

Now, Mallory is six weeks out from her first deadline and surviving on a steady intake of Redbull and frozen burritos. Her publisher thinks it could be a bestseller, but she's just happy that something will spring to life from all the death.

Her phone pings from the side table and she cringes. She keeps forgetting to put it on silent. Even though she knows what it is—not Peyton posting in the Discord, not another message from her former best friend. Mallory deleted all the apps: TikTok, Snapchat, Instagram. She thought she would miss them more than she does.

She still has nightmares, but writing about it helps. Her therapist says that she's processing things the best she can—pouring it out onto the page, turning herself into a character and the nightmare into plot points. She hasn't picked at her skin in months and the scabs on her arms have long since flaked, the scars more white now than purple.

They tore down the old resort. Mallory and Olivia packed a

picnic and got as close as they could, ate sandwiches and drank lavender lemonade as they watched it crumble.

Mallory moved in with Olivia three weeks after everything happened, once they were both on the mend and released from the hospital. She broke her lease and just left. Now they share a small apartment in South Boston, with a tiny garden around the back where she plants lavender, and basil, and bleeding hearts. Olivia is especially fond of it, using the herbs in her baking. The apartment always smells like cake or fresh bread.

Olivia comes back inside from the garden, her hair pulled back into a messy bun, a tired smile on her face and dirt beneath her fingernails.

"How's Kate?" Mallory asks, because Olivia disappeared into the backyard after returning from her weekly visit with Gabriel.

"Still tense around me, but it's getting better."

"And Gabe?"

"Better... but he misses his dad."

"We all do," Mallory says as Olivia sinks down next to her on the couch, leaning in to read over Mallory's shoulder like she always does.

"I hate how her picture is next to Rowan's at the memorial," Olivia says. "And I hate how you have to lie about her in your book."

Mallory rests a hand on her arm. She doesn't have to ask who she's talking about; she already knows that it's Erika.

In the aftermath of what happened, they agreed to peg the whole thing on Jared. Erika did what she did in part for revenge, in part for infamy, so it seemed fitting that she be remembered as another helpless, female victim rather than the mastermind behind the game. She may still have some fame, but there's some degree of satisfaction in knowing that she'd hate what it's for.

There's a sense of justice in it, even if it doesn't blot out everything that happened.

Olivia cries out in her sleep, and Mallory's dreams are as red as they come. Most nights they start off on opposite ends of the bed only to wake up curled against each other, like animals huddling for warmth, bracing against a storm.

It's still hard, but it gets better every day.

Mallory's started a side project, something she works on when she's not chasing her deadline. Something she can't wait to dig into once her memoir is finished. Something for her and for Olivia, and no one else.

It's a story about two young women that help heal one another, about the garden in their backyard and how they grow tomatoes the size of fists. About cooking dinner with the windows open, and the way wind tastes different in the Spring.

Mallory writes and writes, some of it real, some fantasy.

Until parts of it blend, and suddenly there's a sentence about the freckle on Olivia's pinky finger, and the way her eyes crinkle when she laughs, about how every time it rains, they stand out on the porch and watch the lightning try to reach the trees.

Mallory writes about them, and how our story is far from over. It extends far beyond the tragedy of a locked arcade in the dead of summer. About how they screamed and bled. About how they cried and felt the ending of their days. About how her best friend tried to kill her, using a boy, and a blade, and a carefully laid trap. But through it all, Mallory is still here.

She survived.

ACKNOWLEDGMENTS

This book was an experience to write, and I owe thanks to countless critique partners and friends for keeping me sane during the process. I appreciate every one of you more than you will ever know.

In particular, thank you to Finch for being the best editor ever, and helping transform my nightmare/goblin child into something readable. You're a rockstar.

And Melissa Guida-Richards, this story wouldn't exist without your unwavering enthusiasm and constant support.

ABOUT THE AUTHOR

Danielle Renino writes horror and speculative fiction. When she's not writing she can be found exploring abandoned buildings, eating her way around Boston, or checking for monsters under her bed. Find her online at daniellerenino.com or @daniellerenino on Instagram and TikTok.